PRAISE FOR THE NOVELS OF CHARLIE DONLEA

THE SUICIDE HOUSE

"Gripping . . . the book's real strength is the idiosyncratic Rory, who suffers from OCD and is on the autism spectrum, a deeply developed character readers can't help rooting for. Hopefully, she'll be back soon." —*Publishers Weekly*

"Charlie Donlea is a superb psychological suspense writer . . . the book has a fast-paced plot and main characters unlike any typically found in this genre." —*Seattle Book Review*

SOME CHOOSE DARKNESS

"In Donlea's skillful hands, this story of obsession, murder, and the search for truth is both a compassionate character study and a compelling thriller." —*Kirkus Reviews*

"Part 1970s serial-killer thriller and part contemporary Chicago crime novel, this deceptively quick read has something for everyone." —*Booklist*

"Suspense builds, clues mount and dangers lurks seemingly everywhere as the story nimbly toggles between then and now in Donlea's twisty-turny mystery." —*Bookpage*

DON'T BELIEVE IT

"You can't blame Charlie Donlea if the ending of his novel makes your jaw drop. The title alone is fair warning that his characters are no more to be trusted than our initial impressions of them." —*The New York Times Book Review*

THE GIRL WHO WAS TAKEN

"A fast-moving page-turner. . . . Donlea skillfully maximizes suspense by juggling narrators and time all the way to the shocking final twists." —*Publishers Weekly*

SUMMIT LAKE

"Donlea keeps readers guessing throughout. The whodunit plot is clever and compelling . . . for fans of nonstop mysteries with a twist." —*Library Journal*

Books by Charlie Donlea

SUMMIT LAKE

THE GIRL WHO WAS TAKEN

DON'T BELIEVE IT

SOME CHOOSE DARKNESS

THE SUICIDE HOUSE

TWENTY YEARS LATER

Published by Kensington Publishing Corp.

THE
SUICIDE
HOUSE

CHARLIE
DONLEA

PINNACLE BOOKS
Kensington Publishing Corp.
www.kensingtonbooks.com

PINNACLE BOOKS are published by

Kensington Publishing Corp.
119 West 40th Street
New York, NY 10018

Copyright © 2020 Charlie Donlea

PINNACLE BOOKS and the Pinnacle logo are Reg. U.S. Pat. & TM Off.

ISBN-13: 978-0-7860-4642-3
ISBN-10: 0-7860-4642-2

First Kensington hardcover printing: August 2020
First Pinnacle paperback printing: June 2021

10 9 8 7 6 5 4 3 2 1

Printed in the United States of America

Electronic edition:

ISBN-13: 978-1-4967-2719-0 (e-book)
ISBN-10: 1-4967-2719-3 (e-book)

To Fred and Sue
Parents, Sanibelers, friends

Discovery consists of seeing what everybody else has seen and thinking what nobody else has thought.

—Albert Szent-Györgyi

Session 1
Journal Entry: THE TRACKS

I killed my brother with a penny. Simple, benign, and perfectly believable.

It happened at the tracks. Because, as life would teach me in the years to come, a speeding train was many things. Majestic, when it blurred past too quickly for the eyes to register anything but streaks of color. Powerful, when it rumbled underfoot like an impending earthquake. Deafening, when it roared along the rails like a thunderstorm dropped from the heavens. A speeding train was all these things, and more. A speeding train was deadly.

The gravel leading up to the tracks was loosely packed, and our feet slipped as we climbed. It was evening, close to six o'clock, the usual time the train rolled through town. The bottoms of the clouds blushed with a dying crimson as the sun settled under the horizon. Dusk was the best time to visit the tracks. In broad daylight, the conductor might spot us and call the police to report two kids playing dangerously close to the tracks. Of course, I made sure that scenario had already happened. It was essential to my plan. Had I killed my brother the very first time I brought him here, my anonymity in this tragedy would *have been paper thin. I needed ammunition for when the police came to question me. I needed to create an irrefutable history about our time at the tracks. We'd been here before. We'd been seen. We'd been caught. Our parents had been informed, and we had been punished. A pattern had been developed. But this time, I would tell them, things had gone wrong. We were kids. We were stupid. The narrative was flawless, and I would later learn that it needed to be. The detective who would look into my brother's death was an onerous force. Immediately suspicious of my story, he was never truly satisfied with my explanation of events. To this day, I am certain he is not. But my version of that day, and the history I had created, was watertight. Despite his efforts, the detective found no holes.*

Once we made it to the top of the embankment and stood next to the tracks, I fished two pennies from my pocket and handed one to my brother. They were shiny and unblemished but would soon be thin and smooth after we placed them on the rails for the roaring train to flatten them. Dropping pennies onto the tracks was an exciting event for my brother, who had never heard of such a thing before I introduced him to the concept. Dozens of other flattened pennies filled a bowl in my bedroom. I needed them. When the police came to ask their questions, the collection of pennies would serve as proof that we'd done this before.

Far out in the evening, I heard the whistle. The faint sound seemed to catch in the clouds above us, echoing in the bloodshot cotton balls. The evening was darker now as the sun melted away, grainy and opalescent. Just the right mixture of dusk for us to see what we were doing but not enough to betray our presence. I crouched down and placed my penny on the tracks. My brother did the same. We waited. The first few times we'd come here, we placed our pennies on the rails and ran back down the embankment to hide in the shadows. But soon we discovered that in the evening no one noticed us. With each venture back to the tracks, we stopped running when the train approached. In fact, we crept closer. What was it about being so close to danger that filled us with adrenaline? My brother had no idea. I was quite certain. With each successive trip, he became easier to manipulate. For a moment, it felt unfair—as if I had stepped into the role of bully, a role my brother had mastered. But I reminded myself not to confuse efficiency with simplicity. This felt easy only because of my diligence. It felt easy only because I had made it that way.

The train's headlights came into view as it approached— first the top light, and soon after the two ditch lights. I crept closer to the rails. He was next to me, to my right. I had to look past him to see the train's approach. He was aware of me, I could tell, because when I crept closer to the tracks he matched my movements. He didn't want to miss out. He didn't want to allow me more bragging rights or a greater surge of adrenaline. He couldn't allow me to have anything that he could claim as his own. It was how he was. It was how all bullies were.

The train was nearly upon us.

"Your penny," I said.

"What?" my brother asked.

"Your penny. It's not in the right spot."

He looked down, leaning slightly over the tracks. The roaring train barreled toward us. I took a step back and pushed him. It was over in an instant. He was there one second and gone the next. The train roared past, filling my ears with thunder and turning my vision into a blur of rusted colors. The train produced a current of air that pulled me a step or two to my left and sucked me forward, willing me to join my brother. I braced my feet in the gravel to resist the tug.

When the last car passed, the invisible grip released me. I staggered backward. My vision returned, and quiet filled my ears. When I looked down at the tracks, the only thing left of my brother was his right shoe, strangely standing upright as if he'd slipped it off his foot and laid it on the rails.

I was careful to leave the shoe untouched. I picked up my penny, though. It was flat and thin and wide. I dropped it in my pocket and headed home to add it to my collection. And to tell my parents the terrible news.

I closed the leather-bound journal. A long tassel hung from the bottom, keeping my place for the next time I read from it during a session. The room was dead quiet.

"Are you shocked?" I finally asked.

The woman across from me shook her head. Her demeanor had not changed during my confession. "Not at all."

"Good. I come here for therapy, not judgment." I lifted the journal. "I'd like to tell you about the others."

I waited. The woman stared at me.

"There are more. I didn't stop after my brother."

I paused again. The woman continued to stare at me.

"Would you mind if I told you about the others?"

She shook her head again. "Not at all."

I nodded my head. "Excellent. Then I will."

A fingernail moon floated in the midnight sky, its tarnished sheen intermittently visible through the foliage. The moon's erratic presence penetrated the interlocking tree branches with a pale glaze that painted the forest floor in the lacquered finish of a black-and-white film. Visibility came from the candle he carried, the flame of which died every time he picked up his pace and tried to jog through the woods. He tried to slow himself, to be careful and deliberate, but walking was not an option. He needed to hurry. He needed to be the first to arrive. He needed to beat the others.

He cupped his hand in front of the candle to protect the flame, which allowed him a few uninterrupted minutes to scan the forest. He walked for a few yards until he came to a row of suspicious-looking trees. As he stood perfectly still and scanned the tree trunks, looking for the key he so desperately needed, the candle's flame expired. There was no wind. The flame simply died, leaving a plume of smoke that filled his nostrils with the scent of burnt wax. The sudden and unexplained eclipse of the candle meant the Man in the Mirror was close. By rule—

rules no one ever broke—he had ten seconds to relight the candle.

Fumbling with the matches—the rules allowed only matches, no lighters—he struck a matchstick across the phosphorus strip on the side of the box. Nothing. His hands shook as he swiped again. The match broke in half and fell to the dark forest floor. He reached into the matchbox, spilling several others in the process.

"Dammit," he whispered.

He couldn't afford to waste matches. He'd need them again if he made it back to the house and into the safe room. But right now he was alone in the dark woods with an unlit candle and in great danger, if he believed the rumors and folklore. The tremors that gripped his body suggested he did. He steadied his hand just long enough to make a smooth sweep against the phosphorus, which caused the match to light in a sizzling blaze. The eruption gave off a cloud of sulfur-tinged smoke before calming to a controlled flame. He touched the match to the candle's wick, happy for the light it provided. He calmed his breathing and watched the shadowed forest around him. He listened and waited, and when he was sure he had beaten the clock, he returned his attention to the row of trees before him. Slowly, he made his way forward, carefully shielding the flame as he went—a lighted candle was the only way to keep the Man in the Mirror away.

He made it to the huge black oak tree and saw a wooden box at its base. He fell to his knees and opened the lid. A key rested inside. His heart pounded with powerful contractions that rushed blood through the bulging vessels in his neck. He took a deep, calming breath, and then blew out the candle—rules stated that guidance candles could stay lighted only until a key was found. He took off through the woods. In the distance, a train whis-tle blew into the night, fueling his adrenaline. The race was on. He crashed through the forest, twisting an ankle and unsuccessfully shielding his face from the branches that whipped his cheeks. As he continued through the woods, the rumble of the train shook the ground beneath him as it roared past. The vibration brought more urgency to his steps.

When he reached the edge of the forest, the train was charging along the tracks to his left in a metallic blur that erratically caught the reflection of the moon. He broke free from the dark foliage and took off toward the house, his grunting and panting overtaken by the roar of the train. He made it to the door and pushed inside.

"Congratulations," a voice said to him as soon as he was through the door. "You're the first one."

"Sweet," he said, out of breath.

"Did you find the key?"

He held it up. "Yeah."

"Follow me."

They crept through the black hallways of the house until they came to the door of the safe room. He inserted the key into the doorknob and twisted. The lock surren-dered, and the door swung open. They entered and then closed the door behind them. The room was pitch black, much worse than what the forest had offered.

"Hurry."

He fell to the floor and, on his hands and knees, felt along the hardwood until his fingers came to the row of candles that sat in front of a tall standing mirror. He reached into his pocket and pulled out the book of matches. There were three remaining. He struck a matchstick along the edge of the box, and the tip ignited. He lit one of the candles and stood to face the mirror, which was covered by a heavy tarp.

He took a deep breath and nodded to the one who had met him at the door. Together they pulled the tarp from the mirror. His reflection was shadowed by candlelight, but he noticed the horizontal lacerations that cut across his cheeks and the blood that streamed down from them. He looked eerie and battle worn, but he'd made it. The rumbling evaporated as the last train car passed the house and continued off to the east. Silence filled the room.

Looking in the mirror, he took one last breath. Then, together, they whispered:

"The man in the mirror. The man in the mirror. The man in the mirror."

A moment passed, during which neither blinked or breathed. Then something flashed behind them. A blur in the mirror between their reflections. Then a face materialized from the darkness and came into focus, a pair of eyes bright with ricochets from the candle's flame. Before either could turn, or scream, or fight, the candle's flame went out.

The detective steered his car past the yellow crime scene tape already securing the perimeter and pulled into the chaos of red and blue lights. Squad cars, ambulances, and fire trucks were parked at odd angles in front of the brick pillars that marked the entrance to Westmont Preparatory High School, a private boarding school.

What a goddamn mess.

His commanding officer had been short on details other than that a couple of kids had been killed out in the woods at the edge of campus. The situation was ripe for overreaction. Hence the presence of the town's entire police and fire departments. And, from the look of it, half the hospital staff. Doctors in scrubs and nurses in white coats glowed as they walked in front of the ambulance headlights. Officers talked to students and faculty as they poured through the front gates and into the circus of flashing lights. He noticed a Channel 6 news van parked outside the crime scene tape. Despite the bewitching hour, he was sure more were on the way.

Detective Henry Ott climbed from his car while the officer in charge brought him up to speed.

"The first nine-one-one call came in at twelve twenty-five. Several others followed, all describing some sort of mess out in the woods."

"Where?" Ott asked.

"At an abandoned house on the edge of campus."

"Abandoned?"

"From what we've learned so far," the officer said, "it used to be a boarding house for faculty but has been empty for several years since a Canadian National rail line went up that sent daily freight trains past that part of campus. It was too loud, so new faculty housing was built on the main campus. The school had plans to develop the land into a football field and track-and-field course. But for now, the house just sits abandoned in the woods. We talked to a few students. Sounds like it was a favorite hangout for late-night parties."

Detective Ott walked toward the gates of Westmont Prep, and then through the entrance. A golf cart sat parked in front of the school's main building; four giant pillars rose up to support the large triangular gable that glowed under the spotlights. The school's logo was engraved across the surface of the stone.

"*Veniam solum, relinquatis et*," Detective Ott said, his head craned back as he looked up at the building. "Arrive alone, leave together."

"What's that mean?"

Detective Ott looked back at the officer. "I don't really give a shit. Where are we headed?"

"Climb in," the officer said, pointing at the golf cart. "The house is on the outskirts of campus, about a twenty-minute walk through the woods. This'll be faster."

The detective clambered into the golf cart, and a few minutes later he was bouncing through the woods on a narrow dirt path. The trunks of tall birch trees were a blur in his peripheral vision, the light from the moon was gone, and as they drove deeper into the woods, only the golf cart's headlights offered any glimpse of where they were headed.

"Jesus Christ," Detective Ott said after a few minutes. "Is this still part of campus?"

"Yes, sir. The old house was built a ways from the main campus to give faculty privacy."

Up ahead, the detective saw activity at the end of the narrow path. Spotlights had been set up to brighten the area, and as they approached the end of the dark canopy of forest, it felt like exiting the mouth of a giant prehistoric creature.

The officer slowed the cart before they reached the exit. "Sir, one more thing before we get to the scene."

The detective looked over. "What is it?"

The officer swallowed. "It's quite graphic. Worse than anything I've ever seen."

Woken in the middle of the night, and stuck somewhere between the buzz he'd fallen asleep with and the hangover that waited, Detective Ott was short on patience and had no flair for the dramatic. He pointed to the edge of the woods. "Let's go."

The officer drove from the shadows of the path and into the bright halogen spotlights. The crowd here was smaller, less hectic and more organized. The responding officers had enough sense to keep the horde of police, paramedics, and firefighters to a minimum out here at the crime scene to reduce the chance of contaminating the area.

The officer stopped the cart just outside the gates of the house.

"Holy Christ," Detective Ott muttered as he stood from the golf cart. All eyes were on him as the first responders watched his reaction and waited for his instruction.

In front of him was a large colonial house that looked to come from a century long past. It was cast in the shadowy glow of the spotlights, which highlighted the ivy that crept up the exterior. A wrought iron gate squared off the perimeter of the house, and tall oak trees stretched up into the night. The first body Detective Ott saw was that of a male student who had been impaled by one of the shafts of the wrought iron gate. Not by accident. Not as though he were trying to scale the gate and had inadvertently fallen onto the tine in the process. No, this was intentional. Almost artful. The young man had been placed there. Lifted carefully, then dropped to allow the spear of the gate to rise up into his chin and through his face until it poked through the top of his skull.

Detective Ott pulled a small flashlight from his pocket and headed toward the house. That's when he noticed the girl sitting on the ground off to the side. She was covered in blood with arms wrapped around her knees and rocking back and forth in a detached state of shock.

"This wasn't a couple of kids screwing around. This was a goddamn slaughter."

PART I

August 2020

CHAPTER 1

The third episode of the podcast had dropped earlier in the day and in just five hours had been downloaded nearly three hundred thousand times. In the days to come, millions more would listen to this installment of *The Suicide House*. Many of those listeners would then flood the Internet and social media to discuss their theories and conclusions about the discoveries made during the episode. The chatter would generate more interest, and new listeners would download earlier episodes. Soon, Mack Carter would have the biggest hit in pop culture.

This inevitable fact pissed Ryder Hillier off in ways that were indescribable. *She* had done the research, *she* had sounded the alarms, and *she* was the one who had been looking into the Westmont Prep Killings for the past year, recording her findings, and posting them on her true-crime blog. Her YouTube channel had 250,000 subscribers and millions of views. But now, all of her hard work was being overshadowed by Mack Carter's podcast.

She had seen right away that the Westmont Prep story had legs, that the official version of events was too simple and too convenient, and that the facts presented by law enforcement were selective at best, and straight-up misleading at worst. Ryder knew that with the right backing and some smart investigative reporting, the story could draw a huge audience. She had pitched her idea to studios the previous year, after the case made national headlines and was open and shut before any real answers were given. But Ryder Hillier was just a lowly journalist, not a bona fide star like Mack Carter. She didn't have the All-American face or the strong vocal cords, and therefore none of the studios had paid any attention to her pitch. She was a thirty-five-year-old journalist unknown outside the state of Indiana. But she was sure her articles about the case, which had run as a feature in the *Indianapolis Star* and were referenced by several other outlets, as well as the popularity of her YouTube channel, had *something* to do with the sudden interest in Westmont Prep. Mack Carter didn't shift from prime-time television to a Podunk town in Indiana by chance. Someone, somewhere, had been paying attention to her findings, and they saw opportunity and dollar signs. They commissioned Mack Carter—the current host of *Events*, a nightly newsmagazine show—to run a superficial investigation and to produce a podcast around his findings. His name would draw attention, and the podcast would draw millions of listeners on the promise that the great Mack Carter, with his proven investigative skills and hard-charging attitude, would find answers to the Westmont Prep Killings, which had been too cleanly closed. But in the end, he wouldn't prove a goddamn thing other than that, with the proper sponsorship and tons of up-front cash, a podcast could grow from the ashes of tragedy to become a lucrative endeavor for everyone involved. So long as that tragedy was disturbing and morbid enough to draw an audience. The Westmont Prep Killings qualified.

Ryder wasn't going to allow the reality of Big Business to deter her. Quite the contrary. She'd worked too hard to give up now. She planned to piggyback on the success of the podcast. She wanted to pull Mack Carter in, to show him the cards she was holding. To gain his interest and make him take notice. Her YouTube channel provided a decent income from advertisers, and her gig at the paper paid the bills. But in her midthirties, Ryder Hillier wanted more from her career. She wanted to break out, and attaching her name to the most popular true-crime podcast in history would bring her to another level. And the truth was, Mack Carter needed her. She knew more than anyone about the Westmont Prep Killings, including the detectives who had investigated it. She just needed to figure out how to get Mack's attention.

Like hundreds of thousands of others, she had downloaded the latest episode of his podcast. She put the buds into her ears, tapped her phone, and took off down the running trail as Mack Carter's practiced voice rang in her ears:

Westmont Preparatory High is a well-respected boarding school nestled on the banks of Lake Michigan in the town of Peppermill, Indiana. It prepares teenagers not just for the rigors of college but for the challenges of life. Westmont Prep has been around for more than eighty years, and its rich history promises that the institution will be here long after those listening to this podcast are gone. But in addition to the honors and accolades, the school has a scar. An ugly, jagged blemish that will also be here for years to come.

This podcast is a retelling of the tragedy that occurred at this prestigious school during the summer of 2019, when the rules that normally define the school's conduct were loosened, just a bit, for those students who remained on campus through the hot summer months. It's the story of a dark and dangerous game gone wrong, of two students brutally murdered, and of a teacher accused. But at its core, this story is also about survivors. A story about the students who are desperately trying to move on but who have been mysteriously pulled back to a night they can't forget.

During this podcast we will explore the details of that fateful night. We will learn about the victims and about the reckless game that took place in the woods on the edge of campus. We will go inside the abandoned boarding house where the murders took place. We will meet those who survived the attack and take a closer look at life inside the walls of this elite boarding school. We will review police reports, witness interviews, social workers' notes, and psychological evaluations of the students involved. We'll go in depth with the lead detective who ran the investigation. Finally, we'll creep into the mind of Charles Gorman, the Westmont Prep teacher responsible for the killings. Along this journey I hope to stumble over something new. Something no one else has discovered, perhaps a piece of evidence that will shine light on the secret many of us believe is still hidden behind the walls of Westmont Prep. A secret that will explain why students continue to return to that abandoned boarding house to kill themselves.

I'm Mack Carter. Welcome . . . to The Suicide House.

Ryder shook her head as she jogged. Even the god-damn intro had her hooked.

I'm Mack Carter, and on episode three of The Suicide House *we're going to meet one of the sur-vivors of the Westmont Prep Killings, a student named Theo Compton who was present at the abandoned boarding house the night of June twenty-first. Theo has never before given an inter-view to the media but agreed to talk to me exclu-sively about what happened the night two of his classmates were killed. He reached out to me through the message board on* The Suicide House *web page. Per his request, I met him at the McDonald's in Peppermill.*

We sat at a back booth, where he whispered through most of our discussion. It took a bit of time to get him talking, so I've edited our conversation down to the last third. Here is a recording of the interview, with my comments added in voice-over throughout.

"So you were there the night your classmates were killed?"

Theo nods and scratches at stubble on his cheek.

"Yeah, I was there."

"Tell me about the abandoned house. What was the draw?"

"What was the draw? We're a bunch of teenagers trapped at a boarding school with strict

*rules and a dress code. The house in the woods
was an escape."*

"An escape from what?"

*"From the rules. From the teachers. From the
doctors and the counselors and the therapy
sessions. It was freedom. We went there to get
away from school, to screw off and try to enjoy
summer."*

*"You are about to start your senior year at
Westmont Prep, correct?"*

"Yeah."

*"But this current summer, you and your friends
don't go out to that house anymore."*

"No one goes out there anymore."

*"Last summer, on the night of the killings, you
and your friends got caught up in something. A
dark and secretive game. Tell me about it."*

*Theo's eyes go mad as his gaze jets to me, then
away as he looks out the window and into the
parking lot. His reaction gives me the sense that
Theo thinks I know more than I do. It's been just
over a year since Westmont Prep became infamous
for the killings inside its walls, and the students
who survived that night are about to start their senior year. The police have refused to answer questions about their investigation, and the silence has
fueled the flames of rumor. One of them is that the
students were playing a dangerous game the night
two of them were killed.*

*"Tell me about that night. What were you doing
at the house?"*

*Theo pulls his gaze from the parking lot and
looks at me.*

"We weren't at the house. We were in the woods."

"The woods that surround the house."

Theo nods.

"You were playing a game."

"No."

He says this suddenly, as if I've insulted him.

"This isn't about the game."

I wait but he offers no more, so I push.

"Many have suggested that you and your classmates were participating in a game called the Man in the Mirror. And that it was the commitments and demands of this game that might have brought the horrific events of that night."

Theo shakes his head and looks out the window again.

"We screwed up, okay? It's time to put the truth out there."

I nod my head and try not to look desperate.

"The truth. Okay, tell me what you know."

He takes a deep breath. Several of them, in fact, until he is nearly hyperventilating.

"We didn't tell the police everything."

"About what?"

"About that night. About a lot of stuff."

"Like what?"

Theo takes a long pause here. I wait anxiously for him to say more. Finally, he does.

"Like the things we know about Mr. Gorman."

My breath catches in my throat, and for a moment I can't speak. Charles Gorman is the Westmont Prep teacher accused of murdering Theo Compton's classmates. Slaughtering them, in fact,

*and impaling one of them on a wrought iron fence.
The case against him is profound, and there has
never been another suspect. But despite the
evidence against Gorman, many believe that there
is more to the Westmont Prep Killings than what
the public currently knows. Theo Compton appears
ready to produce the missing pieces of a very complicated puzzle.*

"What about him?"

I sound desperate, and Theo recognizes it.

"Shit. I can't do this."

Theo shifts his weight and starts to slide out of
the booth.

"Wait! Tell me about Charles Gorman. Do you
know why he did it?"

Theo suddenly stares straight into my eyes.

"He didn't."

I fixate, unblinkingly, on the young man in front
of me. I shake my head.

"Why do you say that?"

Theo stands up suddenly.

"I've gotta go. If the group knew I was talking
with you, they'd freak out."

"What group?"

He turns away from the table and is gone in an
instant, walking away through the doors of the
McDonald's, leaving me alone in the back booth.

I sit for a while, asking myself the same question over and over.

"What group?"

CHAPTER 2

Ryder had made it through half of the episode during her run. She was anxious to finish it but had an article due the next day. She wrote a weekly true-crime column for the Sunday edition of the *Indianapolis Star*. It was one of the paper's most popular columns, always generating long comment threads for the online edition, and popular news websites commonly linked to it.

After a shower, she pulled on jeans and a tank top and sat at her kitchen table, where she opened her laptop. She wrote for an hour, until 10:40 P.M., putting the final touches on an article about a missing South Bend man. There had been some recent developments in the case having to do with the timing of the man's life insurance policy, which brought his wife under suspicion. Ryder was trying her hardest to finish the article, but the writing came slowly, and she was frustrated with her lack of concentration. Mack Carter's deep and practiced voice rattled in her head, and all she wanted to do was get back to the podcast. Finally, she succumbed to her temptation, pushed her laptop aside, and tapped her phone to resume the episode.

So my interview with Theo Compton was what the kids would call an epic fail. *Epic, but not complete. Our short conversation was curious. The Westmont Prep Killings happened on June twenty-first. Charles Gorman came under suspicion after detectives found a manifesto in his home describing in explicit detail how he planned to carry out the murders. In neat cursive writing he explained the exact method in which he intended to kill the students, details about slashed jugulars and the particulars of using the tines of the wrought iron gate for impalement. After chronicling his plans in his journal, Gorman did exactly what his words promised.*

So, Theo Compton has my mind spinning. With so much evidence stacked against Charles Gorman, I'm curious to know if Theo, or any other student, possesses information that might refute this evidence. Of course, if listeners have any leads I encourage you to head to the message board on the website to share them with me, and the rest of the podcast community. For now let's focus on Gorman and get back to where we left off at the end of last week's episode. I told you that I was granted exclusive access to Westmont Prep's campus and, in particular, to Charles Gorman's home. Now we'll pick up with my tour, which was conducted by the dean of students, Dr. Gabriella Hanover. Here is a recording of the interview, with my comments added in voice-over throughout.

The Westmont Prep campus is both striking and ominous. The buildings are Gothic structures built

*from white sandstone and covered by ivy that
crawls to the eaves. It's noon on a summer
Saturday, and the place is quiet. Only a few
students stroll the grounds as Dr. Hanover steers
the golf cart over the winding campus paths.*

*"The house where the murders took place . . . is
it still off-limits?"*

*I can immediately tell Dr. Hanover does not like
the question. She shoots me a sideways glance that
connects with a split second of eye contact. It's as
if our fingers touched and sparked with static electricity. The look is just enough to tell me not to
press my luck. She and the school's attorneys explained during the negotiations that preceded this
guided tour that the portion of campus where the
murders occurred was not only off-limits to me and
the podcast but was inaccessible to the student
body as well. That area had been sectioned off by a
tall brick wall. I can see the partition in the
distance as Dr. Hanover drives me through campus. To curious minds like my own, the red brick
does not warn me to stay away; it does just the opposite. It begs me to discover what's beyond it. It
shouts to me that it's hiding something sinister. On
the other side of that wall are the woods, and in
those woods is a forgotten path that leads to the
infamous boarding house.*

*For years prior to the killings, the school's plan
had been to demolish the house and clear a portion of the forest to make room for a football field,
track course, baseball diamond, and soccer field.
In just the past few months, the school has secured*

the funding. Renovation is slated to begin as soon as the Peppermill Police determine that there is no more evidence left to gather from the crime scene.

Despite the case being so quickly solved, an executive order from the governor has held up the demolition of the house. Last year he was pressured by the district attorney's office, and they were pressured by the Peppermill Police Department, to delay the destruction of the boarding house. Someone inside the department is still convinced that there are unanswered questions about that night hiding in the walls of that house. And so, demolition has been held off. But the powers that be at Westmont Prep—the board of trustees and those with money tied to the school's success—long for the day the house will meet a wrecking ball. It's a nasty scar on the school's history, and the best way for it to fade is for the house to come down. For now, though, it stands. And I plan to find my way to it.

Today, however, I decide to leave my question unanswered rather than press Dr. Hanover on the issue and risk ending the tour. I knew I wouldn't be seeing the abandoned boarding house today, but Gorman's duplex had been promised. And now we are upon it. We approach the faculty housing—a long stretch of connected homes called Teacher's Row. It was here, in number fourteen, that Gorman lived during his eight-year tenure at Westmont Prep. An exemplary teacher of chemistry, he had only the highest marks of accomplishment and praise on his performance reviews. Reviews that, since the night of June twenty-first, have come under scrutiny.

We pull up to number fourteen. It's a small, efficient duplex made from burgundy brick and overflowing mortar. Narrow walkways cut between adjacent buildings and are lined by dogwoods and hydrangeas. Dual entrances are present out front, one for number fourteen, the other for fifteen. These are pleasant homes, comfortable faculty housing. It's hard to believe such a monster lived here.

The keys rattle as the dean unlocks the front door to number fourteen. We enter to an empty house but for bits of furniture that have sat unused for the past year. Dr. Hanover leads me through the front room, the kitchen, and a single bedroom. As we pass the small den, Dr. Hanover's phone rings. She excuses herself, stepping outside to take the call. Suddenly I'm alone in Charles Gorman's home. It's unnervingly quiet. There is something ominous about being here by myself, and I realize that there is a likely reason this unit has not been reassigned, and likely never will be. It has sat empty for more than a year because Gorman lived a secret life inside the walls of this home, and any faculty member who dared to take this place as their own would be walking in a killer's footsteps and dealing with the spirits of the students he killed. Spirits that surely roam this empty house looking for closure and answers.

I feel them now. I'm looking for the same things they are. But I shake the chill from my neck. I know

*I don't have much time. I also know better than to
do what I'm contemplating, but my instincts as an
investigative reporter are untamed. I walk quickly
into the small office. The room is empty.*

*Depression marks on the carpeting show me where
a desk once stood in the middle of the room. It is
likely the place where Gorman sat when he wrote
his manifesto. All that remains in the room now is
an empty bookshelf, a chair crooked from the loss
of a wheel, and a portrait of the periodic table
hanging on the wall. I know what's behind it.*

*I take a quick glance to make sure Dr. Hanover
is still outside. Then I remove the periodic table.
Behind it is a safe sunk into the plaster. It was here
that detectives discovered Gorman's manifesto.*

*I turn the handle on the safe and pull open the
door.*

"Close that right now."

*Dr. Hanover's voice is neither loud nor
panicked. It's just direct and firm. I turn from the
safe. She's standing in the doorway, and I know
I've been made.*

Eerie music chimed from her phone and pulled Ryder
back to the present, and away from Charles Gorman's
house, where Mack Carter had brought her with his allur-
ing voice and vivid descriptions. The music quieted, and
she heard Mack Carter's voice again.

On the next episode of The Suicide House, *more
on my discovery inside Charles Gorman's duplex.
You won't want to miss it. Until then . . . I'm Mack
Carter.*

CHAPTER 3

An advertisement blared from her phone, and Ryder tapped the screen in frustration to quiet it. She nearly threw the phone across the room. Mack Carter hadn't discovered a goddamn thing in that safe, and Ryder didn't need to wait for the next episode to hear him say it. It was a cheap bait and switch, an embarrassing self-promotion of his abilities as an investigative journalist. Anyone who knew anything at all about the Westmont Prep Killings knew that detectives had discovered Gorman's manifesto in the wall safe. There was nothing groundbreaking about Mack Carter's discovery, yet Ryder was sure that uninformed podcast listeners would be drooling with the idea that Mack had been caught red-handed just as he was about to break the case wide open with the contents of Gorman's safe. She knew *The Suicide House* website would be overrun with traffic as podcast listeners breathlessly scrolled through the pages to see the photos of the Westmont Prep campus and Charles Gorman's duplex and to view the cell phone pictures Mack Carter had snapped of the wall safe.

Ryder's blog and YouTube channel had much of this

information just after the killings. She had obtained the images from newspaper clippings and public records of campus and Teacher's Row. She had even managed to find a picture of the front of Gorman's home roped off by yellow crime scene tape the day after the killings, which had been posted to a student's social media account before being taken down. But Mack Carter's stunt, whispering as he pulled the wall hanging from its hook and hyperventilating as he described the safe behind it, was sure to bring huge numbers to the podcast. She was angry with herself for falling for it, for being as interested as everyone else. She cursed as she scrolled through Mack's website now, having taken the bait like so many others. The message board was already inundated with threads discussing Mack's findings—theories about Theo Compton's cryptic suggestion that Charles Gorman was innocent and about what Mack might have found inside Gorman's safe.

"It's friggin' empty, you know-nothings!" Ryder shouted at her computer. "Why would evidence still be present at a crime scene a year after the fact?"

After thirty minutes of reading the threads, Ryder could take no more. She was about to click over to her own blog to post some sort of update telling her followers that she was still the fearless, real crusader looking for the truth behind the Westmont Prep Killings and that her fans should not abandon her for such a transparent fraud of a podcast. But before she clicked off Mack Carter's site, she saw a video playing on a loop in the comments section. She recognized the footage immediately because she had shot it. It was from when she had snuck through the woods behind Westmont Prep a couple of weeks after the killings and captured shaky video of the boarding house. It had been difficult footage to obtain, since back then the area was still roped off with crime scene tape and the police were interested in keeping prying eyes away from the place. Under the video was a short cryptic comment:

> MC, 13:3:5 Tonight. I'll tell you the truth.
> Then, whatever happens, happens. I'm
> ready for the consequences.

Ryder saw that the comment, which was meant for Mack Carter, had been posted at 10:55 P.M. Thirty minutes ago.

She grabbed her car keys and dialed her phone as she ran out of the house.

CHAPTER 4

He slowed his car as he passed mile marker thirteen and then hit the reset button to bring his odometer to triple zero. He continued at a reduced speed as he watched the odometer click up from nothing. All the survivors knew the numbers: 13:3:5. It was how this whole thing had started. How different things would be had they never heard those numbers, had they never been lured to this place by the promise of adventure and acceptance. But the past could not be changed. He could control only the present in hopes of altering the future.

When the number three spun up on the odometer, indicating that he'd driven a third of a mile beyond mile marker thirteen, he pulled over, parked his car on the gravel shoulder, and turned off the headlights. The dark night swallowed the vehicle. He was invisible and wished he could stay that way. He wished he could don a cloak and hide from the world. From his thoughts. From his memories. From his sins and from his guilt. But he knew it wasn't that easy. If it were as simple as disappearing, he'd have long ago left this place and all its ghosts be-hind. How nice it would be to start over somewhere else, maybe at a different school, where he could return to being his old self and leave the past behind. But the demons had hold of him, and running would not cause them to release their grip. Had there been enough miles on this earth to outrun that night, the others would have run and run and run. Instead, they came here.

He opened his car door and stepped out from the driver's seat. Walking into the middle of the two-lane road, he looked up into the night sky. Heavy cloud cover had delivered a gray and dismal day, and the coming storm tainted the air with the pungent odor of humidity. The clouds erased the stars, reminding him that he was truly alone in this endeavor. Not even the heavens could look down on him tonight.

The quiet of night filled his ears, but he wished for the roar of an eighteen-wheeler, its tires screaming over the pavement as it approached. How much easier would it be to simply stare into the headlights? He could close his eyes and it would all be over. Not for the first time he wondered if the consequences that waited in the afterlife were less than those here on Earth.

Finally, he walked from the road and started his journey. Leaving the door wide open, he walked past the front of his car and into the woods. *Thirteen, three, five.* Mile thirteen, a third of a mile farther, and a half-mile hike through the woods. The path was easy to spot, but the trail through the woods was overgrown since his last trek on it. That had been the previous summer, on the night of the slaughter, and so much had happened since then that he barely recognized his life. He covered the half-mile stretch in ten minutes and came to the edge of the wooded path where a chain—rusted and corroded—drooped between two posts. A moss-covered placard read PRIVATE

PROPERTY and was a feeble last attempt to keep tres-
passers away.

He walked past the sign, and then the infamous boarding house was in front of him. Before that terrible night
had plagued their lives, he and his classmates had come
here often. Every weekend. Their use of the abandoned
building had kept it alive back then. But now, after a year
of absolute vacancy, the house was dying. Not like the
massacre that took place here, where mortality came
quickly and unexpectedly. No, the house was experienc-
ing a slower death. One day at a time. The bricks were
crumbling, and the cedar around the doors and windows
was warped. The eaves had rotted, and gutters poked like
hangnails from the roofline. The place looked ghostly in
the dark of night, with frayed yellow crime scene tape
still secured to the gate and flapping in the night breeze.
He hadn't been back since that night. When he and the
others had come to show the police what, exactly, had
transpired. As much as they were willing to tell, anyway.

He stepped into the clearing and walked toward the
house. Its wrought iron gate was like a moat surrounding
a castle. Rusted and decrepit, the hinges whined into the
night when he pushed the gate open, the bottom of the
tines clawing half circles into the mud. His mind flashed
back to what this gate had looked like the night of the
killings. He blinked his eyes, but the image stayed firm in
his vision.

His thoughts stuck on the images of that night—blood
and gore. He thought of the secrets they had kept, the
things they had hidden. His mind became dizzy with it all
until the rumble of the freight train pulled him back to the
present. He shook his head to gain his bearings, then hurried along the side of the house to where the path bent

and led to the tracks. The decisions they all had made that night brought him to this spot—the same spot where Mr. Gorman had come—and it was here that the rest of his existence would start. It was here that he would face down his demons and finally be free.

The train's whistle filled the night as the locomotive approached. Together with the thundering of the train cars on the rails, he could hear nothing else. As he waited next to the tracks, he sunk his hands into his pockets and grasped the item that was there. Like a child sucking on a pacifier, the feel of it between his fingertips provided a calming sensation. It always had.

As the train approached, with its headlamp like a beacon in the night, he didn't attempt to shield his ears from the thunderous roar. He wanted to hear the train. He wanted to feel it, and smell it, and taste it. He wanted the train to carry his demons away.

He closed his eyes. The thunder was deafening.

CHAPTER 5

Mack Carter sat in his rented house in Peppermill, Indiana; popped open a beer; and read through his notes one last time. He took a sip to wet his throat, adjusted his noise-cancelling headphones, pulled the microphone close to his lips, and spoke.

"The Westmont Prep Killings left the nation saddened and stunned that such a terrible tragedy could take place inside the protected sanctuary of a private boarding school. So far we've taken a look at some of the details of that fateful night. During the next episode, we will learn more about the two students who were killed, and we will take a deep dive into the dangerous game they were playing. To do this, we will take a closer look at what life was like inside this elite boarding school, and we will examine the teenagers that made up the student body. As always, I hope to stumble over something new along the way. Something no one else has discovered, a secret many of us believe is still hidden inside the walls of Westmont Prep. I'm Mack Carter, and *this* . . . is *The Suicide House*."

Mack tapped the laptop's touch screen to stop recording. He played the promo back as he finished his beer, tweaking segments of it and working on the timing of the delivery and the cadence of his voice. When he was satisfied, he e-mailed the intro to his producer. Already, his was the most downloaded podcast of the season. The Westmont Prep case was wildly popular within the true-crime community, and the story still had legs in the mainstream media. His network, where his popular nightly newsmagazine show ran five nights a week, was backing the production, and the huge sponsorship deals they had signed were a good predictor of success. *The Suicide House* was the next big thing.

He spent an hour in the small recording studio his network had built in the rental house in Peppermill. On the computer in front of him were all the recordings he had created over the past week. His producer had cleaned them up and trimmed them down, and now they waited for Mack's review and approval before his team would start organizing them into a coherent episode. Many of the sound bites were red-flagged, indicating additional voice-over work was needed from Mack.

He popped another beer and worked steadily until eleven-thirty P.M., when his phone rang. He didn't recognize the number, but he'd been getting many random calls since his arrival in Peppermill. Most of his interviews to this point had been conducted over his phone, which was fastened with a recording device that captured not only Mack's voice but the caller's as well. When played back on the podcast, the audio was surprisingly clear. He activated the recorder as he answered the call.

"Mack Carter."

"It's Ryder Hillier."

Mack closed his eyes. He almost stopped recording. Ryder Hillier was a true-crime journalist who ran a popular blog that hosted forums and chat rooms where other nuts shared conspiracy theories about all sorts of cases from around the country—from missing persons to homicides. The Westmont Prep Killings had been one of Ryder's most popular cases. She had researched and written about it extensively over the past year, and she'd been reaching out to Mack since word broke about him hosting the podcast.

"Listen, Ryder, I don't have time right now."

"Have you been reading the threads on your website?"

"I'm right in the middle of something, Ryder."

"Of course not. You probably have a slew of assistants who do that for you. I bet you've never even looked at the comments you ask your listeners to make. But there's one you should know about. Do the numbers thirteen-three-five mean anything to you?"

"Thirteen, three, what?"

"Shit," Ryder said in an annoyed voice saturated with condescension. "You really are clueless. And you're the one with the hottest podcast since *Serial*."

"Ryder, if you get ahold of my producer tomorrow, she can set up—"

"You better get out there. Like, right now. I'm on my way as we speak."

"Out where?"

"Thirteen-three-five."

"What the hell are you talking about?"

"Bring your recording equipment. Take Route 77 south. Once you see mile marker thirteen, go another third of a mile. That's the thirteen and the three. We'll handle the five when you get there. But I'm only waiting twenty minutes, then I'm heading in by myself."

"Heading *where*?"

"To the boarding house. Better hurry or you'll miss me."

The call ended abruptly, and Mack stared at his phone. Then he clipped his microphone to his collar, tapped it to confirm it was working, and ran out the door.

CHAPTER 6

Mack talked as he drove. His headlights brought Route 77 to life in the otherwise dark night. The country roads on the outskirts of Peppermill were pitch black, and listeners would detect urgency in Mack's voice when this segment of the podcast aired.

"I'm driving on Route 77," Mack said into the microphone on his collar. "It's almost midnight, and the road is dark and empty. A comment was left on the website message board about an hour ago asking me to come to a place called *Thirteen-three-five*, so that's where I'm headed."

The entrance to Westmont Prep High School was located on Champion Boulevard, and Mack knew from studying maps of the property that the campus expanded all the way back to Route 77. Maps had been posted on *The Suicide House* website to give fans an aerial view of the woods and the house where the murders took place. A half-mile-wide belt of forest separated the house from Route 77. Mack did his best to explain this as he drove, but his anxiety made him jumble his words. His producer would have to clean up his description, and he'd have some voice-over work to do if any portion of tonight's journey ended up on the podcast.

He watched the mile markers and announced each one that he passed.

"I see the green mile marker up ahead. It's pitch black out here, so I'm slowing down as I approach. I'm looking at mile marker thirteen. I was told to drive another third of a mile, so I'm watching my odometer as I do this."

A minute of silence followed as Mack ticked off the mileage. He noticed that, for the first time during the production of this podcast, he was nervous. He swallowed hard when the situation materialized in front of him and his headlights caught more and more of the scene.

"Okay," he said into his microphone. His mouth was parched from the sudden release of adrenaline. "Something's in the road up ahead. I'm just about a third of a mile past the marker, and there's a car parked on the shoulder. It looks like a sedan. The headlights are off, and the driver's-side door is open. I'm pulling behind the car now, and my headlights are brightening the interior. No one appears to be inside."

Mack put his car into park and looked around. He spotted Ryder Hillier off to the side of Route 77, in the shallow gulley between the shoulder and the woods. She was waving the flashlight of her cell phone for Mack to join her.

After climbing out of his car, Mack walked to the abandoned vehicle in front of him. He looked inside. "So, this car is located exactly one-third of a mile past mile marker thirteen. There's no sign of anyone inside the car. It looks abandoned."

Mack walked down the embankment and over to Ryder.

"What the hell are we doing out here?"

"You recording?"

Mack nodded.

"Good. So am I." She held up her phone. "Come on."

"Is that your car?"

"No."

"Whose is it?"

"Let's find out," Ryder said. She disappeared onto the path that led into the dark woods.

Before the flashlight from Ryder's cell phone was completely gone, Mack hustled after her.

"Ryder, tell me what's going on. Where are we going?"

"Half a mile farther on this path," Ryder said. "Thirteen, three, five. I can't believe you're doing a podcast about the Westmont Prep Killings and you don't know what those numbers mean."

After half a mile, they came to a chain-link fence that had been sheared by bolt cutters and curled out of the way to allow access to a dirt path. They both ducked through. Not far past the fence, the path ended at the edge of the forest. A rusty chain sagged between two posts and dangled a PRIVATE PROPERTY sign. When they made it that far, Mack Carter was staring at the shadowy structure where fourteen months earlier the Westmont Prep students had been slaughtered.

"So," Mack said into his microphone as he collected himself. His voice trembled. "I've walked about a half mile into the woods and now, as the trees end, a path leads to the wrought iron gate that surrounds the abandoned house on the edge of the Westmont Prep campus. This is the house—"

A thunderous rumble seemed to bubble up from the

earth as he spoke, shaking the ground beneath him. Then a deafening whistle.

"The train!" Ryder said as she took off toward the house.

Mack hesitated only a second before he chased her. They followed the path around to the back of the house and then cut to the right as the trail led through a brief thicket of woods and ended at train tracks. The train was already thundering past when they arrived. Ryder held her phone in front of her as she videoed the passing cars, some of which were decorated with graffiti but moving too fast to decipher. It took three minutes before the rattling finally ended as the last car passed, leaving the night assaulted but quiet.

Ryder pointed. "Holy shit."

Mack followed the direction of her finger across the tracks. There, on the other side, was a body lying in a heap. Ryder stepped onto the tracks and crossed. Mack took a quick glance in each direction and saw only the parallel rails as far as the night would allow. Then he stepped to the other side. When he approached the body, Mack followed the glow of Ryder Hillier's cell phone as she recorded the finding. Under the glow of the light, Mack saw limbs at grotesque angles and the head bent to the shoulder, surely broken and unfixable. One leg was trapped under the body, the other bent like a hockey stick at the knee. Both arms were tucked close to the torso with hands sunk in the pockets of his jacket. Mack's stomach roiled and he was tempted to look away, but something about the face drew Mack in. He slowly crouched down to get a better look. Through the blood and gore and the disfigured appendages, he recognized Theo Compton.

PART II

August 2020

CHAPTER 7

Dr. Lane Phillips sat in the back seat as the cab pulled down Michigan Avenue. He paged through his notes to bring himself up to date on the Westmont Prep Killings from the previous year. He had become lost in the pages and didn't hear the cabbie until the Plexiglas partition rattled with knocking.

"Here," the cabbie said.

Lane looked up from his notes. The cab driver stared at him in the rearview mirror and pointed out the passenger window. "We're here."

Lane noticed the lobby of NBC Tower on Chicago's Near North Side. He blinked his eyes a few times to come back from the pages that had set him in Peppermill, Indiana, and the gruesome killings that had taken place there.

"Sorry," he said as he closed his folder and handed his fare to the driver.

It was nine on a Tuesday morning, and Columbus Avenue was congested with foot traffic when he stood from the cab and looked up at NBC Tower. Lane Phillips was a forensic psychologist and criminal profiler. His best-selling true-crime book profiling the most notorious serial killers

of the past fifty years—many of whom Lane had person-
ally interviewed—had sold more than two million copies
in its first year of release. The total was closer to seven
million today, and the book showed little sign of slowing
down. It was the go-to manual for anyone interested in
the most heinous killers this world had to offer. Lane was
a consultant for numerous crime shows, and his frequent
television appearances, radio interviews, and op-eds kept
him in the public eye. He was good in front of a camera,
which made him a sought-after guest on both cable news
and the morning programs whenever high-profile cases
made it into the news cycle.

A few years back, a North Carolina girl name Megan
McDonald had gone missing for two weeks before mirac-
ulously escaping her abductor. In the aftermath, it was
Lane Phillips whom the networks called to explain what
the girl must have been going through as a survivor of abduction. A famed profiler, Lane was contacted by the FBI
when Megan's abduction was linked to the disappear-
ances of other women so that Lane would create a profile
of the man who might have taken them.

All of Dr. Phillips's talents, and the many opportunities they produced, required a talent agent to manage the
offers that came to him. As Lane walked from the cab,
Dwight Corey waited on the sidewalk outside of NBC
Tower. Lane spotted him immediately. Even on the
swarming streets of Chicago, which were populated by
every category of businessperson, Dwight stood out in a
crowd. He was a six-five black man who wore custom
Armani suits when Lane joined him for Saturday afternoon lunch meetings. *Casual* for Dwight Corey meant
that the crisply starched shirt he wore under his impeccably tailored jacket was without a tie. Today, though, for

this meeting, Dwight sported a sharp green tie with a beige Armani suit. The French cuff sleeves of his shirt protruded perfectly and were highlighted by gold cuff links. His shoes carried some sort of glow that caused Lane to squint.

Lane, on the other hand, gave off an entirely different aura. He wore dark jeans and a sport coat over an open-neck oxford shirt. His shoes were comfortable and scuffed, and his hair was a mess of wavy locks that he controlled with an open-palm swipe from front to back whenever the long strands fell into his face. He had carried this look when he was a poor PhD student hopping from one prison to another interviewing convicted killers, and despite a successful and prominent career, it had never varied.

Lane extended his hand as he approached.

"It's been too long," Lane said.

"Good to see you, friend."

Lane pointed at Dwight's shoes. "You have batteries in those things?"

Dwight smiled. "A little style might do you well. But don't worry, this new gig doesn't include anyone looking at your ugly mug, or your terribly out-of-date sport jacket. I'll only be subjecting the audience to your voice."

"This thing about the Westmont Prep Killings? It's not for television?"

"No. But it's the hottest thing going at the moment."

"I thought you said Mack Carter was involved."

"He is. And he wants you badly."

"How badly?"

Dwight slapped Lane on the back and looked at his watch. "Let's go find out."

CHAPTER 8

They sat across from each other at a coffee shop in the lobby of NBC headquarters. Lane poured a second sugar into his coffee.

"Sugar is one of our greatest carcinogens," Dwight said. "Probably as bad as the tar in cigarettes, yet we ingest it every day. No lawsuits. No legislation. Just a happy bunch of zombies sucking on Pixy Stix and dying of cancer."

Lane paused in mid-pour and looked up with mouth open and a confused expression on his face.

"No," Dwight said. "Don't stop now, you've already poisoned it. You can't undo it, and I'm not buying you another one."

"And you wonder why we don't have face-to-face meetings as often as we used to." After a brief pause, Lane finished emptying the sugar packet into his coffee. "The last time we went to dinner, you lectured me about my porterhouse."

"It wasn't a lecture, I just pointed out where the meat came from and how it was harvested. Most folks don't know."

"And I was very happy in my ignorance." Lane took a sip of his coffee. "Ah, now that's damn good."

"It's like drinking hemlock."

Lane ran his hand through his hair. "I hope I live long enough to hear this offer. Tell me about it."

"Do you listen to podcasts?"

"Podcasts? Yeah, I listened to one about bass fishing before I headed down to Florida last year. It didn't help."

"Well, they're big and popular at the moment. Radio, through the podcast medium, is making a comeback. It's a similar phenomenon to what's happening in television. Fewer people are watching broadcast television, but more people are streaming content. Radio is following the same path. No one listens to the radio anymore, but everyone is downloading podcasts. From politics to Zen parenting, there's something for everyone within the ether of podcasting. But one specific genre in particular is generating huge audiences—true-crime. Right up your alley. Most of these podcasts simply rehash old crimes, attempting to retell the stories in a unique way. A few of them attract big advertisers and make legitimate income. But the podcasts that make it big, well, they never die. They run again and again as new listeners discover them. Years later, listeners can download old episodes. The podcast resells their product to other advertisers, over and over again. If you're lucky enough to get a piece of the revenue, it could provide income for years."

Lane raised his eyebrows. "You want me to do a podcast?"

Dwight held up a finger. "Not *any* podcast. The biggest one out there. NBC is producing it, and it's already generated a massive audience after just four episodes."

Lane held up the folder he had been reading in the cab. "The Westmont Prep Killings?"

"Correct."

"Is this about the video of that kid who jumped in front of the train?"

"Theo Compton, yes."

"Isn't the guy who uploaded that video to YouTube being sued by the kid's parents?"

"It's not a guy, it's a woman. A journalist named Ryder Hillier. And yes, she's being sued by the family. YouTube banned the video, and now the footage is hard to find because it's so heavily restricted and scrubbed from the Internet. It's a perfect storm. An illicit video, a mysterious suicide, and a lawsuit. All tied to a huge, well-known murder case. Very bizarre, with a splash of gore and mystery. Everything true-crime fanatics salivate over. NBC has this podcast lined up to be the next big thing, including the investigator."

"Ah, this is where Mack Carter comes in."

"Correct. It's ingenious. Mack is on hiatus from his nightly television show, specifically for the podcast. His absence from television gives the podcast more urgency. When his eight million nightly viewers see that he's missing from the show and learn that he's preoccupied with an important assignment, they're naturally curious to know what the assignment is. People who have never listened to a podcast are starting to download it."

Mack Carter was the host of *Events*, the most popular newsmagazine show on television. Millions tuned in each night to watch Mack investigate everything from the Jon-Benét Ramsey case to the secrets of escaping from a submerged car. The tragic death of a family of four who drowned when their car veered into a retention pond prompted the live event when Mack drove a car into a swimming pool and then showed the world the best way to emerge alive. It was one of his most-watched episodes and put Mack Carter on the map.

"And now," Dwight said, "in addition to a big case and a big host, they've got a big mystery. That's where you come in. The YouTube video of that kid who jumped in front of the train? He was the third Westmont Prep student who survived the attack to go back to that house and kill himself on the tracks. Two girls, one guy. They all jumped in front of that freight train. The same train Charles Gorman—the teacher who was accused of killing the kids—jumped in front of as the police were getting ready to arrest him."

"Jesus Christ."

"The suicides have been a well-kept secret. Local law enforcement wanted to keep them quiet, but thanks to that video and Mack Carter's podcast, they're a secret no more. Mack is promising to get to the bottom of the mystery, and ratings are through the roof."

"And my role?"

"NBC wants you, as a forensic psychologist, to figure out why, one by one, every student who survived that night is going back to that house to kill themselves."

Lane leaned back in his chair, staring up at the ceiling of the café. His mind was already creating a profile of the type of person who would return to a place of such trauma to end their own life.

He finally looked back to Dwight. "From what I read about this case, Gorman jumped in front of that train but wasn't successful at ending his life."

"No, he wasn't," Dwight said. "The train threw him twenty yards into the woods. The guy's half a vegetable now, sitting in a secure psychiatric hospital wearing diapers and being spoon-fed. The three students who have actually succeeded at killing themselves have all used the exact spot Gorman attempted suicide. It's located right next to the abandoned boarding house. And that's where you come in. Mack Carter needs to tell his listeners why this is happening."

Lane shook his head, trying to take it all in.

"Podcasts are suddenly sounding pretty good to you, aren't they?"

Dwight's shiny gold watch beeped. He looked at it and then pointed to Lane's coffee cup.

"They're waiting upstairs. Bring your poison with. It's showtime."

CHAPTER 9

Rory Moore sat in the back of the courtroom. She hid behind thick-rimmed glasses and made sure her beanie hat was low on her forehead. Despite the summer temperatures, she wore a lightweight gray jacket buttoned to her neck. This was her battle gear, the outfit she wore in a number of various forms to protect her from the world. Her right knee bounced nervously, and the vibration in her foot reminded her that she was without a critical aspect of her gear. The rubber sole of her high-top canvas gym shoes had felt wrong ever since she started wearing them. Rory had been without her combat boots for six months now, but she hoped to remedy that situation today.

She sat in the last row while her eyes darted back and forth behind her glasses, taking everything in. The courtroom had filled steadily over the past thirty minutes. It wasn't packed to the rafters, but there was a constant flow into the room. First the bailiffs had unlocked the heavy courtroom doors for the early spectators to scurry in and claim the best seats. Most went straight to the front rows.

Rory opted for the back. Next came the beat reporters covering the story for the *Tribune* and the *Sun-Times*. Then came the families of both the victim and the man accused of killing her. Camille Byrd had been murdered more than two years ago, and her case had gone cold. Until, that is, Rory became involved. She reconstructed Camille's life, following the girl's footsteps up until the night her frozen body had been discovered in Grant Park. The reconstruction led to Camille's killer. Rory turned her findings over to Ron Davidson—her boss and the head of the Homicide Division inside the Chicago Police Department—who, in turn, delivered those findings to his best detectives. They confirmed all the dots Rory had connected and made an arrest less than a week later.

Since then, Rory had sat in on each of the court appearances, from the arrest and arraignment hearing to the grand jury. For a full week she hid in the back row during the trial, and she had spent an anxious weekend at home after closing arguments ended the previous Friday. Monday came and went, and now it was Tuesday morning and word was out that the jury was back and a verdict was in.

After twenty minutes, the courtroom was as full as it was going to get. Sadly, two years after her death, there were fewer people curious about Camille Byrd's murder than there had once been. Many who had originally been tasked with discovering what had happened to this beautiful young woman were now busy with other cases. And the public at large had been lured away by other topics and different headlines. But Rory would never forget Camille Byrd. Like all the cases Rory reconstructed, she had developed an intimate connection with the victim. There was something different, however, about Camille.

Somehow, the dead girl had allowed Rory to solve one of the greatest mysteries of her own life. How, exactly, that revelation came from a girl long dead Rory would never fully understand. But the otherworldly guidance that Camille Byrd had offered put Rory firmly in her debt. As repayment, she promised to bring closure to Camille's case. Her knee still tapped anxiously now that the courtroom was full because she hoped today would offer that closure.

Finally, the lawyers arrived and took their spots at the tables in the front of the courtroom. On cue, the defendant appeared, shackled and in jumpsuit orange. After a few suspended moments of courtroom silence and angst, the twelve members of the jury shuffled into their seats. The judge was the last to materialize. He brought the court to order and explained that the jury had come to their conclusion. He offered a ten-minute monologue on how things would proceed and addressed both families during the process. When there was nothing more to add, he turned to the jury.

"Mr. Foreman?" the judge said. "Have you come to a verdict?"

"Yes, Your Honor," the foreman said.

As he lifted the page to read their decision, Rory closed her eyes.

"On the count of first-degree homicide in the death of Camille Byrd, we the jury find the defendant . . . guilty."

Murmurs and cries filled the courtroom. The accused's mother openly wept and moaned. Camille Byrd's parents huddled together and also cried. Rory stood and headed for the exit. There were other counts and other crimes and more verdicts to be announced, but Rory had heard all she needed. As the foreman continued to read from his card, Rory opened the door to the hallway. Before she slipped out of the courtroom she caught a glance from Walter Byrd, Camille's father, whom Rory had gotten to know during her hunt for Camille's killer. He nodded at her from the front row and mouthed *Thank you*. Rory nodded back and then disappeared through the doors.

CHAPTER 10

An hour after she left the courtroom, Rory Moore walked into Romans shoe store on LaSalle. She strolled through the aisles until she found what she was looking for—Madden Girl Eloisee combat boots. They were tall and black, with laces that zigzagged up the front. The sight of them put a lump in her throat. She'd been wearing this style of boot for as long as she had existed on this planet. At least, as long as she could remember. She'd been without them, however, since her only pair had succumbed to an unfortunate incident involving a fireplace and lighter fluid. Rory had resisted the urge to immediately replace her boots after they burned to nothing. Instead, she decided to wait until after she'd provided closure to Camille Byrd's parents. Now, she pulled a pair of size 7 off the shelf and slipped her feet into them. She instantly felt better. A metronomic ticking inside her brain quieted for the first time in months, her body relaxed, and the inner balance of her mind normalized.

At the checkout counter, she handed the cashier the empty box.

"I'm wearing them home."

The woman behind the counter smiled. "That's not a problem," she said, scanning the barcode. "Eighty-five seventy-two."

Rory worried about any proof of her purchase, no matter how threadbare it might be. Even scanning the barcode set her radar on high alert, but she knew certain footprints were unavoidable. Rory handed the girl five twenty-dollar bills. Cash assured that no record of the transaction could be traced back to her. Inquiring minds who knew the details of the last half of the previous year might ask the whereabouts of her previous boots, and she wanted no one looking for them. Those old Madden Girls were nothing but a pile of ash. Some people, however, might consider them evidence, including her boss inside the Chicago Police Department. Other people, like talented forensic folks, could take that pile of ash and pull from it traces of the past. Rory wanted to keep the past, and all its secrets, dead and buried. So she paid cash and hoped for the best.

As she left, she dropped the canvas high-tops into the trash can. Wearing her new Madden Girls, she walked to her car with a moxie that she'd been without for the past six months.

CHAPTER 11

From the street out front, the house looked dark and empty. Inside, though, soft light seeped from the den and spilled across the cherrywood floorboards. Rory sat at her workbench in the dim room, the gooseneck lamp directed at the catalogue in front of her and her laptop emanating a blue glow. She was hard at work, and it had nothing to do with her job at the Chicago Police Department. Tonight was for research. Tonight was for tracing lineage. Tonight was for making sure her next purchase would be perfect. She sipped from a glass of Dark Lord stout as she worked.

The walls of her den were lined with built-in shelves that housed twenty-four restored antique porcelain dolls, each standing in perfect order—three per shelf, eight shelves in all. Exactly twenty-four dolls. Anything less set Rory's mind on a constant loop that obsessed over the vacancy. She had learned not to question this quirk, or the many other idiosyncrasies that defined her personality, but rather to embrace them. She enjoyed the company of the forty-eight unblinking eyes that stared down on her as she cross-referenced her research, moving between the catalogue filled with photos of antique dolls and various websites she had pulled up on her computer. She took copious notes in her journal until she finished her research, then picked up her glass of Dark Lord and took a long, slow sip. She'd found what she was looking for, her inquiries had confirmed its authenticity, and the photos she downloaded proved her selection was in dire need of her expertise.

Satisfied with her selection, she took a deep breath and pulled a folded piece of paper from her back pocket. She had printed the American Airlines boarding pass that morning in preparation for her flight the next day. Being trapped in a tube at thirty thousand feet with two hundred other passengers was nauseating. Just thinking about it brought a subtle layer of moisture to her forehead.

She heard the front door open and keys jingle as they were removed from the lock.

"Rory?"

"In here," she said, slipping the boarding pass back into her pocket.

She didn't bother to turn around. She sensed his presence in the doorway, then felt the vibration of his footsteps as he approached. Finally, she felt his lips on the side of her neck. She reached back and ran her fingers through his hair.

"Guilty on all counts," Lane Phillips said in her ear. "You said you weren't sure."

"I was cautiously optimistic."

"Well done. Did you talk to Walter Byrd?"

"Yeah," Rory said, remembering the nod Camille Byrd's father had given her on the way out of the courtroom. To Rory, it was a conversation.

"Now what?"

"Now I disappear for a couple of months," she said.

"How long until Ron shows up on the front porch?"

Rory shrugged. "He'll wait at least a couple of weeks. He knows to give me space."

Ron Davidson had a never-ending stack of homicide files he needed Rory's help with. Cases that had stumped his best detectives. A forensic reconstructionist specializing in cold-case homicides, Rory's expertise lay in her ability to piece together puzzles of crimes that had gone unsolved for years. Her brain worked differently than others, and her uncanny mind saw things others missed. No matter how hard she tried, she had never been able to explain how she noticed the missing pieces when she jumped into a cold case or walked into a crime scene from years before. She knew only that when presented with an unsolved mystery, something clicked inside her mind that prevented her from forgetting about it until she had the answers that had eluded everyone else. A parallel phenomenon occurred whenever she picked up an antique doll that was damaged and ruined. Her mind refused to settle itself until the doll was perfect.

The Camille Byrd case had brought two restless months of Rory retracing the girl's final days. She followed the footsteps of the girl's ghost until they led her to answers. It was a taxing routine that left her drained. Ron Davidson knew his star investigator well and recognized Rory's need for space after the conclusion of a case. Two weeks was the typical window he allowed; two months were what Rory usually took. The gaps were filled with Ron's frantic phone calls, incessant texts, threats of ending her employment with the Chicago Police Department, and the inevitable hunt when Ron tracked Rory down, one way or another, to corner her with an ultimatum.

Tonight, though, on the first day of her self-appointed sabbatical, none of that was present. It felt like the start of summer vacation when she was a kid.

"Two weeks will go fast," Lane said. "Then you'll need a place to hide. Ron's a detective, after all, and he knows where you live. It won't be hard to find you."

Rory turned with a smile to stare at Lane. "Something tells me you have a hiding place."

"I do. I've been asked to take part in a podcast for NBC."

"A podcast about what?"

"The Westmont Prep case from last year."

"When those kids were killed in Indiana?"

"Yeah. The podcast is already underway, with a lot of buzz, huge advertisers, and a big name attached—Mack Carter. It's being produced in Peppermill, Indiana. They need me for about a month, they're guessing. Maybe longer, depending on what Mack turns up."

"They need you for what?"

He took her hands and pulled her to her feet.

"There's a lot that doesn't make sense with the case, with the murders, with the teacher who was accused, and with the students who survived. There's a big psychology angle they want me to take on."

He pulled her closer.

"Come with me."

Rory raised her eyebrows. "Come with you?"

"Yeah."

"To *Indiana*?"

Lane nodded.

Rory rolled her eyes. "And here I thought you were going to jet me off to the Caribbean."

"No, it's not that glamorous. Come with me anyway," he said.

"To do research for you on some grisly case? I just finished a case."

Lane rested his forehead against hers. "I'll do the research. You keep me company and hide from Ron for a few weeks. He'll never find you in Peppermill."

"That's for sure."

"They set me up in a little cottage. They showed me pictures. It's cute."

Rory cocked her head. "Who exactly am I talking to right now? You've never used the word *cute* in your life. And you rarely leave the city unless you're on an airplane to New York."

"I'm trying to sway you into saying yes."

"*Cute* isn't doing it." Rory backed away and shook her head. "No, Lane. I'm not in the mood for that. You'd be working, and I'd be doing *what* exactly? Sightseeing in northwest Indiana? I want to be *here*. In my own house, close to my own stuff, and doing my own thing for a while. I need the downtime."

Lane nodded. "I thought I'd give it a try."

Her father's death the year before had left only one man on this planet who understood her. To the extent that Rory Moore *could* be understood.

"Sorry. I just . . ." Rory pointed at her workbench and the open catalogue of dolls glowing under the gooseneck lamp. "I need some time by myself. To unwind and get my mind straight."

Lane nodded again. "I get it."

Rory ran her hand over his cheek and kissed him. "I'm a pain in the ass, I know."

"I still love you. Even if you make me go to a cottage in Indiana by myself."

"I thought it was cute?"

Lane smiled. "That was the wrong play."

"So very wrong," Rory said. She turned around, closed the catalogue, and picked up her Dark Lord. "Wasn't the Westmont Prep case solved? Open and shut, no? One of the teachers killed those boys."

"It's a long story."

"I've got all night."

Lane pointed at Rory's beer. "I'm going to need one of those."

CHAPTER 12

Rory flipped switches as they walked, first the recessed lighting of the hallway and then the overheads in the kitchen. They were all set to dimmers that thwarted their full wattage, and the house awoke in a groggy amber glow. A night owl since childhood—ever since she wandered out the back door of her great-aunt's farmhouse when she was ten years old and made a grand discovery—Rory preferred the stalking shadows of a barely lit house to the infirmary fluorescence she witnessed spilling from the windows of the bungalows up and down her block. She opened the beer cellar, a glass-front cooler built into the wall next to the refrigerator. The top shelf held her supply of Dark Lord—twelve 22-ounce bottles of Russian-style imperial stout perfectly arranged in three straight, tight rows with labels forward. The only incongruence visible was the wax seal that dripped from the top of each bottle, the result of having been dipped at the brewery. Rory could live with this imperfection.

She knew Lane could no more stomach a Dark Lord than she could handle the light beer he preferred. They were opposites in that regard. She grabbed a Corona Light from the bottom drawer, kept hidden because the sight of a clear glass bottle filled with light yellow beer insulted the harmony of her cellar.

She popped the top and handed it to Lane.

"So, Westmont Prep. What's the draw?"

Lane took a sip of beer. "Two students were killed last summer at an abandoned house on campus. Three days after the murders, police had their man—a chemistry teacher named Charles Gorman. I'm going to take a look at the psychological aspect of the story. Dive into Gorman's mind-set."

"You've gotten permission to interview him?"

"I wish. He tried to kill himself a couple of days after the murders as police closed in on him. Jumped in front of a train that runs next to the old boarding house."

"Tried?"

"Yeah, came pretty close from what I've been told. Brain-damaged himself to the point that he drools the days away in a secure psychiatric hospital for the criminally insane. Hasn't talked since he came out of his coma, and EEG shows nothing going on upstairs."

"Sounds like a guilty man wanting to escape his demons, and a prison sentence."

"Maybe, but I think there's more to it than that. I'll put together a profile of the killer and make sure Gorman matches that profile."

"What makes you think there's more to the story?"

"Because over the past year, three Westmont Prep students who survived that night have gone back to the boarding house to jump in front of the same train as Gorman."

Rory stopped her glass just before her lips.

Lane raised his eyebrows. "Told you it was interesting." He took a sip of beer. "Something was going on with those kids last year, and it's carried over to today. Something they haven't told anyone about. The story that's out there now is too clean. Teacher snapped, teacher confessed in a handwritten letter, teacher tried to kill himself. I'm not buying it, and neither is Mack Carter. So together we're going to look into it." Lane paused a moment. "Sure you don't want to come with me?"

Rory offered a small laugh to buy some time. She thought of the earmarked catalogue in her den that displayed the hundreds of antique porcelain dolls she had researched. She remembered the feeling of balance that perusing the pages had brought to her mind, which had been running too hard for too long. She also remembered the boarding pass in her pocket for the flight that departed in roughly twelve hours.

"I'm sure," Rory finally said.

But she wasn't. Hearing the story of Westmont Prep had set loose a soft whisper that echoed in her mind. Within the reverberations was the suspicion that those victims who had gone back to kill themselves had a story to tell.

She took another sip of Dark Lord but couldn't stop thinking about the words Lane had just spoken.

Something was going on with those kids last year, and it's carried over to today.

Westmont Prep
Summer 2019

Session 2
Journal Entry: THE KEYHOLE

There was a keyhole in my bedroom door. It was a portal through which I spied on a world I hated. The things I saw through that keyhole were never discussed. I was supposed to believe they never happened. But they did. Even if my mother and I never discussed them, those things existed. I saw them, and I'm certain my mother knew I watched through that hole. I always wondered if the things that took place within the tunneled view of my bedroom door took place in that exact location for a reason. Was she asking for my help?

I looked up from the journal. My voice had cracked while I read the last sentence, and it took me a moment to gather myself.

"I'm sorry."

The woman sat in the chair across from me and waited. I inhaled deeply, looked back to the leather-bound journal, and began reading again.

The things I saw through that keyhole changed my life. It was the terrible things that happened in that narrow *scope of my vision that made me who I am. I wish I could say that I charged through that door and stopped my father. If I had—if I had at least* tried—*maybe things would be different. Maybe I'd be dead, because to confront my father during his moments of rage was to confront a wild animal. But I never opened that door to protect her. I cowered in my room like the weak and feeble child I was, and left that protected sanctuary only after the carnage was over. I would bring my mother a bag of ice for her eye, or a towel for her broken lip. Sometimes I even helped her apply makeup to hide her bruises. But I never left my room to protect her. Leaving my room during the onslaught would have been deadly, but dying would have been preferred to what actually happened.*

I heard my mother's scream, and I was up and out of my bed immediately. On my knees, I stuck my face to my bedroom door and peered through the keyhole. A short hallway lead to the dining room, where I saw my mother run to the far side of the table, trying to put an obstacle between her and my father. But there was nothing that would stop him. Certainly not a dining table. His shape entered the tiny world of my keyhole. He stood with his back to my bedroom door, facing my mother. His body obscured my vision so that I could no longer see my mother. I was relieved to no longer see her panicked face. As if not seeing her terror somehow made it go away.

"Stop," my mother said. "I'll fix it."

My father's jaw was clenched; I heard it in his voice. "Who. Broke. It?"

I knew immediately what they were talking about. The lamppost out front. It had shattered earlier in the day when I was playing catch with a kid from the neighborhood. I had made an errant throw that collided squarely with the glass panel, shattering it and sprinkling glass all over the driveway. My mother hid the damage as best she could, sweeping up the glass and hoping that the missing pane would go unnoticed until she could replace it. It had been our plan. It was obvious now that the plan had failed.

"I don't know who broke it, Raymond. But I will fix it tomorrow."

"You'll fix it?"

"I'll call someone to fix it."

"And who's going to pay for that?"

My father swiped his arm across the dining room table, sending everything that was on its surface to the floor. To my deranged father, wreaking havoc inside the house and racking up hundreds of dollars of damage was a proper response to the financial hardship of having to replace a broken pane of glass.

I should have opened my bedroom door then. I should have walked into the hallway and taken responsibility for what I'd done. But I didn't. I stayed on my knees and stared through the keyhole as my father reached across the table, grabbed my mother by the hair, and dragged her over the top of it. He beat her that night. I watched him through the keyhole. I watched the man I hated beat the woman I loved.

The next day, my father was dead.

I pulled the tassel up and laid it carefully in the crease of the journal before closing it. My hands shook slightly. When I finally looked up at the woman across from me, I recognized sympathy in her eyes. At least, that's what I took her stare to mean. My hands settled and my shoulders relaxed. The therapy sessions always brought me peace, even though I bared my soul and revealed my innermost secrets during them. Or, perhaps, because of it.

"I've been reluctant to talk about him. I know you're curious. Can I tell you about my father now?"

The woman blinked her eyes a few times. Was it not sympathy after all but pity I saw in them? Or was it something closer to terror. Either way, these were the rules. I would come to confess my innermost secrets and exorcise my demons. She would be bound by confidentiality, forever kept silent by my sins. If this scared her, it was an unfortunate side effect of our relationship. Because I couldn't stop confessing to her now, even if I wanted to. And I didn't.

"I want to tell you how he died. The police declared his death a suicide, but it wasn't. Can I tell you about it? Would that be too much to discuss during a session?"

"Not at all," the woman said.

I nodded. "Perfect. I'll see you next week."

I stood with my journal and headed back to campus.

CHAPTER 13

Tucked quietly into the northwest corner of Indiana, on the banks of Lake Michigan in the sleepy town of Peppermill, Westmont Preparatory High School was an elite boarding school with a reputation of preparing its students for the rigors of college. Its practices were strict, its expectations high, and its track record impeccable. One hundred percent of students who enrolled at Westmont Prep went on to graduate from a four-year university. No small feat considering the kids who made up the student body. In addition to the snobby rich kids, the gifted academics, and the overachievers, the strict disciplines found inside the walls of Westmont Prep also drew troubled and rebellious teens who had found themselves at life's crossroads. There were the teens whose parents had recognized the trajectory early on and had been sent to Westmont Prep to straighten out before it was too late. There were also those kids whose parents had realized too late the seriousness of their child's predicament and had found Westmont Prep only after some series of events had landed them in the sort of trouble that required planning and bargaining and concessions in order to prevent lifelong consequences. Those burned-out parents shipped their kids off to Westmont Prep because they feared if it wasn't a boarding school they were losing their kids to, it might be prison. Still, despite this mixed bag of students, the practices and principles of Westmont Prep brought them all into line. Isolate and educate, a tried-and-true practice of boarding schools across the country.

The campus architecture mimicked the elite prep schools of the East Coast, with buildings made from Bedford limestone and covered in ivy that wrapped around the windows and climbed up to the eaves, where cornices stood like sentries keeping watch over campus. The pediment of the library—the first building visible when one walked through the front gates—was a massive triangular gable supported by thick, sturdy columns. Stenciled into the stone was the school's logo: *Veniam solum, relinquatis et.* Arrive alone, leave together.

Gavin Harms and Gwen Montgomery walked past the building now. The night was thick with humidity, and even though it was approaching ten o'clock, the long summer day still offered the last efforts of the sun—a soft burn on the horizon that streaked the sky with brushstrokes of salmon. Their friends, Theo and Danielle, walked next to them. The four had been close since Gate Day, the ceremonious moment when students reported to campus at the start of each school year. As soon as students arrived at the front gates, whether they were incoming freshman or seasoned upperclassmen, they were on their own. Parents were not allowed on campus during Gate Day. Once a student walked through the wrought iron doors, they were responsible for themselves. Independence was a theme at Westmont Prep. Students were expected to find their way and develop a new support system inside the walls of the school. Arrive alone, leave together.

Many kids landed at Westmont Prep as defiant teenagers longing to be free from the reins of their parents. But for a few, the ceremonial closing of the entryway on Gate Day brought reality clearly into focus. As the students stood on one side of the wrought iron, their parents on the other, an array of reactions followed. Some cried. Others clung to the iron bars like felons in their cells and begged to come home. A few laughed at the dramatic symbolism before heading to their dorm rooms. The smart ones made friends and stuck together. Gavin Harms, Gwen Montgomery, Theo Compton, and Danielle Landry had been together since the beginning, and now they were entering the summer before junior year.

As they approached Margery Hall, they cut to the right to avoid the front entrance, where the house mom would certainly question where they had been that caused them to arrive back to the dorm so close to curfew. From there, the conversation would turn to Gavin's backpack, which was thick and swollen with cans of Budweiser. So instead, they walked to the rear entrance. Before they could reach for the door, it burst open and startled them all. Tanner Landing was standing in the doorway.

"Got my beer, bitches?"

Westmont Prep produced an interesting dichotomy of friendships. Some were organic, built from common interests and natural affection. Others were forced, created by the confines of campus and dorm assignments. Tanner Landing had been part of this group since just after freshman year, when most students went home for summer except for a handful of kids whose parents forced them to stay for the summer session. During the school year, Tanner could be avoided. In summer, Gavin and his friends were stuck with him.

"You scared the hell out of me," Gwen said as she pushed past Tanner and into the back hallway of the dorm.

Tanner's girlfriend, Bridget, apologized for his stupidity. "He's a Neanderthal," she said.

Gavin and Theo shared a dorm room, and they filed inside and locked the door. They pulled the window shades closed. Gavin unzipped his backpack and passed the beers around.

"I'll read it," Tanner said. He took three quick swallows of beer and belched. He pulled up his phone and read the text.

The Man in the Mirror requests your presence
13:3:5
Saturday night at 10:00PM

"That's the old boarding house, right?" Gwen asked.

"Yeah," Gavin said. "It's the back way. Off Route 77. We'll have to cut through the woods and then around campus. Who else got invited?"

"Just the six of us," Tanner said.

Gwen looked around. "Are we really doing this?"

"We're juniors," Tanner said before he chugged the rest of his beer and belched again. "Goddamn right we are! It's a rite of passage."

CHAPTER 14

Marc McEvoy walked into his basement. The air-conditioning kept the first and second floors forcibly cool, but during the summer months Marc preferred the basement. The cold earth radiated through the walls of the home's foundation and kept the basement a few degrees cooler than the rest of the house. He loved the basement for more than just the temperature, though. It was where he hid his secret.

They had constructed a small bar the previous year when they finished the basement. It was where he and his wife liked to entertain friends on weekends. He and his friends had bellied up to the slab of epoxy-glazed oak many times over the past winter to watch Colts games. He walked to the cabinet behind the bar now and opened the doors. Inside was his baseball card collection. He'd had it since he was a kid, adding to it each year. His collection spanned from the 1970s and '80s, featuring Johnny Bench and the Big Red Machine, to the '90s and early 2000s, when steroids had taken over the game, to the current generation of players defined by statistics that never existed before a few years ago. The collection was legitimate—old Topps cards that came with brittle chewing gum, as well as Goudy Gum Company and Sporting News cards. They were worth something today if he ever dared bring his precious cards to an auction. But Marc had no plans to sell his collection. Tonight, as he pulled the first box off the shelf, he was interested in something other than his cards. It was his other obsession, something on which he had been fixated since his high school days at Westmont Prep, that he was interested in tonight.

He laid the binder on the bar, unlocked the cover, and opened the two hatches to gain access to his collection. Inside, the baseball cards were organized in tight rows. On top were several sheets of plastic laminate with slots for the cards he kept in mint condition. On top of those protected pages were his notes and research. He had always kept his research hidden there. His wife had no interest in his card collection, and Marc was sure the secret he kept stashed there was safe. The first article he pulled was from the *Peppermill Gazette*, a local paper that had a small readership back when he was at Westmont Prep but that had since gone bankrupt. He found the article at the library when he was a freshman. It had originally been published in 1982. He read it now.

Inside Westmont Prep's Secret Society

If you ask the headmaster of Westmont Preparatory High School, or any faculty member for that matter, if there is truth to the rumor that a secret society exists inside Westmont Prep, you'll hear a resounding and forceful "No." But if you ask the students, they'll tell you that such a society not only exists but is thriving. Ask for details, however, and you'll get very few. Mostly, you'll hear conjecture and rumors about the misadventures of this secret club that hazes its new initiates and pulls raucous pranks on unsuspecting students and faculty. Concrete facts or first-person experiences are impossible to come by since there are no students who admit to active membership. The headmaster explains this lack of first-hand knowledge of the club by stating that the idea of such a society exists only in the minds of the students and stays alive through folklore and rumor. It is, the headmaster notes, a figment of the student body's imagination. Or, it could be argued, the reason you'll hear so little about the group is because its members are sworn to secrecy.

Marc put the article to the side and turned to a more recent piece published in the *Indianapolis Star*. Written by a true-crime journalist named Ryder Hillier, the lengthy article chronicled the history of secret societies in American high schools, touched briefly on the most famous collegiate societies of East Coast ivy league schools, and then settled down to examine the organization inside the walls of Indiana's most prestigious boarding school.

Westmont Prep was known for its strict discipline and rigid academics. The school was frequently ranked among the top preparatory schools and boasted a 100 percent conversion rate to a four-year university. Ryder Hillier had made more headway into the secret group that existed inside the walls of Westmont Prep than any other journalist Marc had come across. She had even, some-how, unearthed its name—the Man in the Mirror—and the location of the meetings, a cryptic spot marked only by three numbers. 13:3:5. Numbers that Marc knew to be the location of the entrance to the forest off Route 77 that led to the old boarding house.

From there, though, Ryder Hillier's facts ran dry. The article ended with a quote she managed to obtain from the current dean, Dr. Gabriella Hanover, who denied the existence of such a society, claiming that Westmont Prep did not permit exclusive clubs that promote elitism and secrecy, nor would the school allow a student association to run itself outside the supervision of the faculty.

But Marc had attended Westmont Prep, and as an alumnus he knew damn well that the club existed. He had waited through his freshman and sophomore years to get his chance to become part of the society, knowing that it was made up of only upperclassmen. But when his junior year came, he was passed over. The rejection had sent him into a fit of depression. A few of his close friends had been tapped, and after they had made it through initiation, they left him behind. He spent his junior year alone and isolated, and when he eventually became the target of the group's pranks, Marc McEvoy decided that he'd had enough of Westmont Prep. He transferred to a public school for his senior year. It had been a miserable end to his high school experience, and his senior year was blackened with thoughts of suicide. Only after finding a new support system during college had he snapped out of his depression. He met his wife, he graduated, he launched his career, and he started a family. But he never forgot about the secret society at Westmont Prep. The one he wanted so badly to be part of. The one that had rejected him. Marc McEvoy had not only been unable to forget about the Man in the Mirror, he had become obsessed with it. He had worked over the years to find out everything he could about the group and its rituals.

Tonight, with his family sleeping upstairs, he retrieved the articles he kept hidden with his baseball card collection and laid them across the bar. Then he opened his laptop and typed *The Man in the Mirror* into the search engine. It was June. He knew that initiation of new members took place on the summer solstice. He scrolled through the web pages. He'd read most of them a hundred times, but every now and then he'd come across something new.

He was no longer a teenager. Things like this should not interest him, and rejection from so long ago should no longer hurt. But his mind still dripped with curiosity, and his ego still ached from having been denied. A strange question came to him, like it did at the start of every summer: *What was stopping him from going to the abandoned house in the woods?*

Back when he was a student at Westmont Prep, easily influenced and intimidated, his fear kept him away. But there was no fear inside of him tonight. Now he was merely curious to learn everything he could about the myth. But as he paged through his research and scrolled through the websites that described the legend of the Man in the Mirror, he realized that in addition to his curiosity there was something else fueling his hunger. On a warm summer night, in the cool chill of his basement, he was finally able to define the emotion.

It was anger.

PART III

August 2020

CHAPTER 15

Claustrophobia, social anxiety, and the nagging need to forever be in control of her environment made air travel something Rory Moore avoided whenever possible, and something she did badly when it was mandatory. She had tried a little bit of everything over the years. From meditation (which drew the attention of other passengers instead of the opposite, desired, result) to pharmaceuticals (Benadryl and Advil PM had caused a violent vomiting fit that made one flight, in particular, more unpleasant than any other) to cold-turkey-suck-it-up-sit-in-the-middle-seat-and-deal-with-it (once, only once, and never, ever again).

Coach seating—three across, packed in like limp sardines and crawling over one another to use a tiny bathroom shared by two hundred other passengers—had for years been out of the question. Once, when Rory and Lane were needed in New York for a case related to the Murder Accountability Project, a wealthy client had agreed to charter a flight for them after Lane explained that it was the only way to get them to the East Coast. Lane, of course, could have gone alone. He could have booked a commercial flight and read a book for two hours like everyone else. But he didn't. He insisted on a private charter, and he got it. Rory loved him for more than just his good looks and his fierce mind. The man accepted her despite all of her suffocating peculiarities. He loved her just the way she was built and had never tried to rebuild her, as so many others in her life had attempted—from shrinks to teachers to law school roommates and professors.

When a terribly expensive private plane was not an option, however, first class was the next best thing. She chose the window seat, and by the time her seatmate joined her, Rory had barricaded herself with two pillows and a blanket. She had Lane's dissertation from his PhD days on her lap, and the prominent display of its title—*Some Choose Darkness*—was like a homeowner hanging a plastic owl on the side of their house to scare off woodpeckers. For good measure, Rory wore a surgical mask. A quick glance at the lady in 2A gave the image of a serial killer reading a how-to manual who either was trying to keep at bay the germs floating through the recirculated air so she could live long enough to make her next kill or was herself sick with the plague.

Rory knew she was no treat to sit next to on an airplane, but her efforts paid off. The gentleman in 2B sat down without a word, and for the entire three-hour flight to Miami, he never attempted conversation.

CHAPTER 16

Lane's invitation for Rory to join him on his assignment in Indiana was charming, and the more she
thought of it as she drove north from Miami International
Airport, the more his words ignited emotions that Rory
preferred dormant. She had no immediate family left to
spend time with, so the clinical and analytical portion of
her brain told her it was a waste of energy to feel guilty
for missed opportunities with them. But the emotional
segment of her mind told her not to repeat the mistakes of
her past by neglecting the single relationship that remained in her life. Rory wondered, after the events of the
previous year, if her life needed some serious tending to.
Perhaps some readjustment of priorities and some self-
reflection on the things that mattered to her.

Come with me.

Lane's words echoed in her mind, and she was helpless to quiet them. She attempted to channel her feelings
into a corner of her brain where she could cover them and
store them and keep them at bay the way she did with
other troubling thoughts that constantly bombarded her
and threatened to derail her life. Every day brought a fun-

neling twister of emotions. It was how her brain waves fired. If she wasn't worrying, she was obsessing. And if she wasn't obsessing, she was planning. Her mind never really settled down. There was always a low hum of activity going on in her head. Over the years she had learned to manage this affliction by compartmentalizing her thoughts. The obsessive compulsion that begged for her to perform mundane and redundant tasks, such as checking her speedometer now and making sure her headlights were on, were packed away into a part of her brain that allowed her not so much to ignore the urges but to stow them on layaway. She stored those desires in a place in her mind that prevented them from interfering with daily life. Then, later, she pulled off the dustcover when she had a place to deposit the yearnings in a neat and orderly fashion. A place where those thoughts could run free until they fizzled out without further affecting her life. This process bought Rory time. It allowed her to live her life free from the superfluous demands of her mind.

One outlet Rory used for this purpose was studying case files as a forensic reconstructionist. The repetition of reading and rereading interview transcripts, reviewing autopsy summaries until she had each page stored as an image in her mind, poring over detective's notes and evidence logs, and studying crime scene photos until she could see them with her eyes closed was a perfect exercise for a mind that never turned off. In the environment of forensic reconstruction, her affliction worked as an asset.

Away from work, there was another outlet for her obsessive compulsion. She discovered it when she was a young girl, before she understood that her mind worked in ways that others would consider unusual. Before she understood that the images and knowledge that ran like a never-ending scroll through her thoughts was the forming of her photographic memory. Before she knew that her intelligence was on a scale high above most everyone else's. Before she recognized that being so advanced in one area of life caused other areas to be neglected—like personal relationships and social interactions. Before the diagnosis of autism was in the mainstream of medicine, another technique had been used to rein in her condition. She learned the skill when she was a young girl spending time at her aunt's farmhouse. Tonight, as she snaked through the streets of Miami, she planned to hunt down the item that would permit her to use the talent she had learned as a child. It would allow her to live the next two months without worry that her quirks and idiosyncrasies would sidetrack her.

But she was struggling to compartmentalize the feelings Lane's invitation produced. The closer she came to her destination, the more her skin itched with anxiety and the more she wondered if, perhaps, feelings about the man she loved were not meant to be stored away and bundled with the nagging thoughts brought on by her obsessive-compulsive disorder.

Still, she tried. It was how Rory Moore existed.

CHAPTER 17

It was close to midnight when she paid forty-five dollars to park in a three-story garage in downtown Miami. The structure was lighted by bleached fluorescent that Rory would have hated had she been in her bungalow, but here in an unfamiliar city, she appreciated it. Her heart beat at an alarming pace, and her underarms and back were sticky with perspiration. She walked out of the parking garage and for ten minutes strode along the downtown streets. She had memorized the route the day before. Her watch sounded. It was ten to midnight and she picked up her pace. The Miami streets were populated with a steady chorus of couples and stragglers, but when she walked off the main thoroughfare and turned onto a side street, she was alone. The street lighting was minimal, and her combat boots echoed off the brick buildings. She saw the glow of a marquee up ahead and knew she'd make it. It was as sketchy as she imagined. The website had no photos, just an address and the estimated time for the auction.

The lighted canopy, which was cheap and ratty, promoted the place in red lettering as THE DOLL HOUSE. Entrance into the establishment required Rory to take four steps down from the sidewalk. She took a deep breath before descending the stairs and then pushed through the front door. A man with a thick neck and boring gaze lifted his chin at her when she entered.

"I'm here for the auction," she said.

The man grunted his response. "Through the back door. They're a little behind schedule."

The cavernous tavern was dark and dreary but well populated. The smell of charred burgers was heavy in the air, and the boisterous laughter of multiple conversations constricted Rory's chest. She willed herself to breathe as she scanned the room and saw the door in the back. She headed to the bar first. The row of taps offered a disappointing display—all watered-down light beer options.

"What can I get you?" the bartender asked.

"Got any beers by Three Floyds?"

"Three *who*?"

Rory shook her head and scanned the beer bottles lining the shelf over the bar. "Lagunitas PILS."

The bartender reached into the cooler and twisted off the cap, setting the bottle in front of Rory. She dropped money on the bar and took her beer to the back room. It was just past midnight. Another man waited outside and Rory flashed her printed ticket, which the man took as her admittance. As she walked into this back room, The Doll House became more impressive. The lighting was brighter here, a stiff contrast to the tavern. The walls were lined with glass cabinets that held an array of collectible porcelain dolls. Other collectors, who had no doubt been here for hours, filled the room. They were all scanning the options and researching their histories. Rory had already done her homework, and it took less than two minutes to find the doll she was looking for—an Armand Marseille Kiddiejoy German baby doll in terrible condition. She stared at it now through the glass.

Before Rory could inspect the doll, she had to chart her ID number into the log. She scribbled her number onto the log sheet and counted twelve entries above her, which meant she'd have bidding competition tonight. With no backup plan, this Armand Marseille was her only option. She had investigated the doll back to its origins and had come fifteen hundred miles to purchase it. She planned to do just that.

She got the attention of one of the auctioneers, who unlocked the glass case. Rory lifted the doll from its resting place. Her mind fired like lightning now. It wasn't quite an out-of-body experience, but in that moment Rory was not simply holding the doll, she was *part* of it. Her vision did not stop at the surface of the porcelain, but penetrated it. The porcelain face was covered in a lattice of cracks, and a large piece was missing from the left cheek and ear. There was a bald patch on the back right side of the doll's head, where a lesser restorer had attempted to repair a different crack with devastating results. The effort was so amateurish that Rory wondered how someone of such little skill had obtained a classic doll like this. But even this egregious insult put a thrill in Rory's chest. Her vision penetrated the doll and saw it from the inside out. Her mind was blind to the damage and only imagined the possibilities. The doll's potential mesmerized her.

"You good?" the auctioneer asked, pulling Rory from her trance.

She nodded and handed the doll over. Ten minutes later she sat in the back of the auction hall, sipped her Lagunitas, and waited. Four auctions had been scheduled that day. This was the last. The pristine dolls sold first to collectors who wanted to take them home and display them on shelves with other perfect figurines. Rory had no interest in the unblemished dolls. They held no histories. They kept no secrets. Their stories had already been told. She was after dolls that had travelled the world and had the scars to prove it. She was after imperfect dolls that had lost their connection to their previous owners and were badly in need of affection and attention.

She finished her beer and ordered another while the unblemished dolls sold, one after the other. With each successful auction, the small subterranean room thinned. By the time the ragged and dilapidated dolls came to the floor, there were just twenty or so collectors still present. It was almost one in the morning.

"Up next," the auctioneer said. "Is an Armand Marseille. Some damage to the face and ear, but in its heyday—"

"Three thousand," Rory said.

The man looked up from the doll. "The opening ask is seven fifty."

Rory stood from the back row and walked toward the podium, her new combat boots rattling with each step. "Three thousand should take it then?"

The auctioneer looked at the collectors remaining in the room. "Going once? Going twice? Sold, for three thousand dollars to the lady in gray."

CHAPTER 18

Lane had spent two days delving into the Westmont Prep Killings and learning everything he could about the case. NBC had provided a file folder of research, but Lane had his own sources, too, and had dug as deeply as possible in just a short couple of days. Now, his car was packed as he drove south from the city. Two hours after leaving Chicago, just before noon, he pulled past the WELCOME TO PEPPERMILL, INDIANA sign. It took a few minutes for the GPS to show him the way to Winston Lane, where his cottage was located. The small home sat in a cul-de-sac at the end of the long road that butted up against a lake. He pulled into the driveway and shut off his engine. The front door had a lockbox hanging from the door handle. Lane spun the numbers, and the box popped open to reveal a key. He carried his duffel bag into the house, which was exactly as advertised—small, comfortable, and out of sight. It would be perfect for everything he had planned.

A kitchen, sitting room with a fireplace, and an office made up the first floor. Upstairs was a single bedroom and a loft with a desk. He dropped his duffel bag onto the bed and headed back out to his car. From the trunk, he retrieved the box he had managed to pick up on the way down after some heavy negotiating and way too much money. But for his plan to work, the purchase was essential. He carried the box into the kitchen, opened the refrigerator, and lined the top shelf with the bottles it held, making sure they were in perfect order with labels out.

When he finished, he wheeled a second suitcase through the kitchen and into the three-season room attached to the back of the house. Floor-to-ceiling windows overlooked the small lake in the distance, and Lane knew it was perfect. On a desk in the corner he emptied the contents of the suitcase, again lining everything up in perfect rows. Then he removed a wrapped package and placed it in the center of the desk. Finally, he retrieved the large corkboard he had managed to cram into the back seat. He set it on a tripod and pinned photos to it.

Thirty minutes after he arrived in Peppermill, the house was prepped and ready.

CHAPTER 19

Rory sat in the first-class cabin of American Airlines Flight 2182 headed for Chicago. She wore her surgical mask, read her how-to manual, and had her new porcelain doll stowed safely under her seat. Her right leg vibrated and caused the buckles on her combat boot to jingle. The gyration would typically stem from anxiety, but this morning it was something else. Between the closure of her latest cold case, the long-overdue purchase of her new boots, and the acquisition of the Kiddiejoy porcelain doll, Rory Moore felt balanced and calm in a way she hadn't for months. Not since before she ventured out to a cabin in Starved Rock, Illinois, to look for closure for herself and so many others.

She closed her eyes and bided her time.

It was seven P.M. when Rory finally sat at her workbench. The shades were drawn, and the evening sun fought but failed to find a way around the edges. The den was comfortably dim, with the gooseneck lamp illuminating her workspace. Rory felt the twenty-four sets of eyes look down on her as she unwrapped her new purchase, as if the restored dolls on the shelves were as interested in Rory's acquisition as she was. Carefully lying the Armand Marseille Kiddiejoy German doll onto the workbench, she started the inspection process the same way a medical examiner would look over a body about to be dissected. But Rory had no plans to take this doll apart. She was going to put it back together, one painstaking piece at a time. It would keep her occupied for weeks and allow the grating and demanding calls from her mind to be liberated. She had boxed those burdens up and stowed them over the past few weeks for this exact reason. Antique doll restoration had the potential to provide joy and bliss, and Rory had certainly experienced those things. But the pastime provided something else as well. A portal to a world free from worry, where her foibles turned to strengths and where she could use the eccentricities that threatened to spoil her everyday life.

In her workplace she did not have to resist the irrational requests of her mind. She did not fight against the gnawing need to repeat things, over and over, until she achieved perfection. In this protected place, those tendencies were not only permitted but required. The repetitious activities involved in repairing antique porcelain dolls were an outlet for the obsessive-compulsive disorder that had once ruled her life. As long as Rory could exorcise her demons during the controlled practices that took place in the tranquility of her den, then the debilitating calls from her mind were quieted during most other parts of life. It was how she existed. Her dolls were her survival.

Tonight's inspection was for information gathering only. No restoration would take place. Rory needed first to understand the doll and the damage it held and to map out a path for restoring it. She ran her hand over the doll's face, feeling the lattice of cracks that spiderwebbed through the porcelain. Rubbing alcohol, which was many restorers' chosen solvent, was too harsh. The pastels were never absorbed as well into porcelain that had been stripped with alcohol, and this explained the washed-out look of other restorers' dolls presented at auctions. Rory's great-aunt had created her own formula from dish soap and vodka, a solution that Rory had been using since she was a kid and that would be perfect for this new restoration.

She took photos and notes for more than an hour before she admitted something was wrong. Before she accepted that something was preventing her from fully concentrating on the doll in front of her.

"Damn it," she said to herself.

To just about everyone who came across her, Rory Moore was a mystery. To the doctors who had tried to treat her through childhood and adolescence, to her boss inside the Chicago Police Department, and to the detectives who watched with some combination of confusion, awe, and aversion as Rory solved the cases that had baffled them. With the deaths of her father and great-aunt the previous year, only one person remained in Rory's life who understood the nuts and bolts of her existence. She remembered Lane's words again.

Come with me.

Standing from her workbench, she lifted her Armand Marseille and laid it back in the travel box. Upstairs, she packed a suitcase. On the way out of the house, she stopped in the kitchen and pulled the yellow sticky note Lane had left on the front of the fridge. It held the address of the cottage in Peppermill.

CHAPTER 20

A light beer rested on the coaster in front of him, and a
file folder lay next to it with pages spilling onto the
mahogany bar. Peppermill was a small town filled with
corner taverns. Lane's first meeting with Mack Carter
had been arranged for seven p.m. at an establishment
named Tokens, which was made up of a long bar with a
line of stools in front of it and a row of chest-high cock-
tail tables separating the bar from the booths that studded
the opposite wall. The beer was cold, the food was
greasy, and it was dark enough for no one to recognize
Mack Carter.

Lane was halfway through his beer when Mack walked
into the bar. He wore a T-shirt and a Notre Dame hat, and
he looked nothing like his television persona. When he
approached, the two shook hands. Lane guessed Mack
was in his early thirties, with a huge smile that, again,
looked different in person than when Lane watched him
on television.

"Lane Phillips."

"Mack Carter. Great to meet you. I was thrilled to hear
the network landed you. Your name will go a long way

toward lending credibility to the podcast, and I have to tell you"—Mack looked around the bar as if someone might be listening—"I'm going to need a shrink by the time I'm done with this story."

"I heard you had an interesting couple of weeks."

"Interesting is one way to describe it. Batshit crazy is another. Sorry, I probably shouldn't say that to a shrink."

"I'm not your typical shrink."

"So I've heard." Mack pointed at Lane's beer and called over to the bartender to order his own. "Let's talk."

They sat on adjacent stools. Mack's beer was delivered in a pub glass with foam slipping down one side, beer commercial style.

"There's so much going on psychologically with this story, you're going to be busy. The plan will be to introduce you in episode five. We'll do a formal interview to give listeners your credentials. Then we'll do an overview of the case with you offering your expertise on the psychology of both the killer and the survivors—what they went through during the night of the slaughter and what they've been going through since. We can do that all from the studio at my rental house."

Lane pointed to the file in front of him. "I did some homework and started a profile on the killer."

"A profile on Charles Gorman?"

"Well, possibly, but that's not how profiling works. You don't start with a suspect and work backward. That would defeat the purpose. I start with the crime—the victims, the methods used to kill them, the scene—and create a list of characteristics the killer would likely possess in order to commit such a crime. In this particular case, I've started to map out the mind-set needed to produce this level of violence. What I've done so far is just a start.

I'll add to it as I learn more about the crime. I've also started a second, *separate* profile of Charles Gorman. Once I'm finished with each profile, we'll see where they overlap, if they do at all, or if they are exact duplicates."

"Fascinating," Mack said. "What do you have so far?"

"Some early notes on Gorman, just from public records, tells me that he was a chemistry teacher at Westmont Prep. A bit of a loner. Socially reserved and awkward. Brilliant mind as far as chemistry is concerned but lacking in social graces. He was straight as an arrow for eight years at the school."

"What made him snap?" Mack asked.

"There's a lot more I'll have to uncover to answer that question, if it can be answered at all. We'll need to speak with the students and faculty who knew him. His friends and family. His parents, specifically, to see what sort of home life he had growing up. From what I've learned so far, he had a normal childhood. But digging into his past will help me see what was going on in his life from childhood, through his adult life, and leading up to the night of the killings. Unfortunately, speaking with Gorman directly is out of the question, from what I've heard."

"I heard the same thing," Mack said. "He doesn't know what day of the week it is, let alone what happened in those woods a year ago. I guess if you jump in front of a train, you better make sure you finish the job."

"I've got some connections at Grantville, the psychiatric hospital where Gorman's at. I'll put in a few calls and see if I can get more details about his condition." Lane took a sip of beer. "Tell me about the suicides."

Mack drained his beer and ordered another. "This is where a strange story gets stranger. The night of the murders, two kids were killed. The rest of the students ran from the house and escaped through the woods, but not before many of them saw the carnage of one of their classmates impaled on the wrought iron gate. So I'm sure it was quite traumatic. A couple of months after the killing, just as school was starting in the fall, one of the kids went back to the woods and jumped in front of the freight train that runs next to the boarding house. She was the first. A couple of months later, it happened again."

"Another suicide?"

"Yeah," Mack said. "Same way. Man versus train. Well, *girl* versus train, to be specific. It was another female student. And just a couple of weeks ago, as I'm sure you've seen if you're one of the twenty-some million people to have viewed the video, Theo Compton was the latest."

"It's bizarre. We'll have to find a way to talk with the students and try to understand what's pulling so many of them back to that house. Talk with their parents and siblings. Talk with the teachers and faculty."

"The school has been quite receptive to my inquiries. I can't tell if they are being openly transparent or trying to appease me because they think it's the path of least resistance. At any rate, they allowed me a tour of the campus, and I've interviewed the dean of students, Dr. Gabriella Hanover."

"There was something Theo Compton said to you about Charles Gorman. That he believed Gorman didn't kill his classmates. Any progress on that front?"

"No, I'm still working on that," Mack said. "And still confused by it. Theo decided to end his life before I had the chance to speak with him again."

"It appears that the young man was quite tortured by whatever it was he was keeping quiet about. I'd like to hear the full audio from your meeting with him. And also from the night you went out to the boarding house and found him. Maybe I can pick up on something he said."

Mack nodded. "What played on the podcast was heavily edited because it took a while to get him talking. The unedited conversation is on my laptop back at the house. But to listen to it all again, I'm going to need something stronger than beer."

"I'll pick up a bottle on the way over. Bourbon?" Lane asked.

"Perfect," Mack said as he dropped money next to their half-empty beers.

CHAPTER 21

Rory turned off I-94 and took the Peppermill exit. She pulled through town as night fell and lampposts blinked to life. Her GPS led her onto Champion Boulevard until she came to twin brick pillars joined by a tall wrought iron gate. WESTMONT PREPARATORY HIGH SCHOOL was chiseled into the concrete that arced above the gate and joined the two brick pillars. Beyond the gate, a tree-lined path led to campus, where the school's buildings were shadowed against the darkening night sky. To Rory, the majesty of the campus and the school, the historic buildings and the locked gate, it was all a mockery. It was all meant to demonstrate protection and sanctity. Inside such a fortress, the kids would be sheltered from the dangers of the outside world. Parents had sent their children here believing that myth. They sent their children here to straighten them out, or to teach them discipline, or truly believing that this institution was the best place to prepare their children for the challenges of life. What a sham. Had Rory not fallen under her great-aunt Greta's watchful eye, she might have ended up at a similar place.

Rory lifted the sticky note she had pulled off the refrigerator and read the address for Lane's cottage. She pulled away from Westmont Prep and headed to the north side of town. It took ten minutes for Rory to find the bank of rental cottages. They were spaced far apart and ran to the end of a long road that twisted into a cul-de-sac. The cottages were spread around a small lake. She slowed her car as she moved from house to house and read each address. When she found Lane's cottage, she pulled into the driveway but noticed the windows were dark.

She stood from the car and looked around the small community of homes. For the ride down from Chicago, Rory wore cutoff denim shorts and a tank top. Her new Madden Girl combat boots felt perfect, and she adjusted her thick-rimmed plastic glasses as she surveyed the row of cottages. Surprises and dramatic demonstrations of affection were not her strong suit, and as she stood in front of Lane's empty cottage she suddenly wished she had called ahead.

Rory left the engine running and the driver's-side door open as she approached the cottage and knocked on the front door. When there was no answer, she pulled her phone from her pocket and called Lane. The surprise was over. The jig was up. She'd just driven two hours and was ready for a beer. When the call went to Lane's voice mail, Rory dropped the phone into the back pocket of her shorts and stared out at the neighborhood.

Where the hell are you, Lane?

CHAPTER 22

It was close to nine p.m. when Lane pulled up to Mack Carter's rental house. It was on the opposite side of Peppermill as his cottage. The sun was at the end of its run on a long summer day, with just enough power left to push shadows of the maple trees across the front yard. Cicadas buzzed from the foliage in a constant hum that blended into the humid night.

Mack keyed the front door, and Lane followed him inside.

"They've set me up nicely," Mack said as he walked through the house and into the kitchen. "The studio is top notch, and we do all our recordings and voice-over work in here."

Off the kitchen, French doors led to the recording studio. Lane saw a bank of computers on the table with microphones and headphones in front of them.

"Everything I record out in the field is reworked in here. I also have a tech team back in New York that handles anything we can't. Because I'm doing the podcast in real time, the New York people jump in when we're behind on a deadline."

Mack pulled glasses from the cabinet and poured two fingers in each from the Maker's Mark that Lane had purchased on the way over. They headed into Mack's studio and placed headphones over their ears as they sat at the table. Mack cued up the soundtrack. A few seconds later, Lane was sipping bourbon and listening, enthralled, to Mack Carter's conversation with Theo Compton. Then the audio switched to Mack's quavering voice as he narrated his journey along Route 77, past mile marker thirteen, his discovery of the car that sat abandoned on the shoulder, his half-mile trek through the woods to the abandoned boarding house, and finally his discovery of Theo Compton's body next to the train tracks.

Lane made notes as he listened to the raw uncut footage. On the kitchen table outside the studio, the front display of Lane's phone lit up with Rory's face when it rang. The volume was set to high, and the ringtone chimed through the kitchen. Despite the studio doors being open, neither Lane nor Mack heard the phone. Their noise-cancelling headphones prevented them from hearing anything but Mack's voice as the audio played. The headphones were so effective that Lane's first indication that something was wrong came from his other senses. The odor of gas was first to take his attention from the audio he was listening to. Then it was the vibration of the explosion. He never heard a thing.

CHAPTER 23

Rory tried Lane again as she sat in her car, which was still parked in the driveway of the empty cottage. After several rings, the call went to voice mail. Finally, she swiped the screen of her phone until she came to the app that she and Lane shared. It allowed them to locate their phones when misplaced. She scrolled through the screen and tapped Lane's name. A map appeared with a blinking icon that represented his location. He was in Peppermill, about three miles away on the opposite side of town. She tapped the blinking icon and pulled out of the driveway while the GPS led her to the coordinates.

All the problems with her plan began to dawn on her as she drove. First, showing up unannounced was never a good idea. Suddenly, the idea that she would surprise Lane with a romantic gesture had her palms slipping off the steering wheel as her mind processed the situation she put herself in. Second, she considered herself skilled at many things, but stalking was not one of them. She realized that the tracking app didn't offer an exact address, only a location, and Rory wasn't about to go door-to-door through a residential neighborhood looking for Lane. Finally, the most chest-tightening thought was what she would do if she did manage to track him down. Open her arms wide and say *"Found you!"*

Rory wiped each palm on her cutoff shorts as she drove, her gaze alternating back and forth between her phone and the road, watching her progress on the screen. She turned down a long road and drove slowly until the two blinking icons—hers and Lane's—grew closer together. But something else caught her attention and pulled her attention away from the map on her phone.

Up ahead she saw a lone house at the end of the cul-de-sac. Smoke billowed from the roof, and flames spat from the windows as they reached up the side of the house and lit up the dark sky.

CHAPTER 24

Rory skidded to a stop at the curb. There were two cars in the driveway, and one was Lane's. She kicked open the driver's-side door and ran up the driveway, her combat boots jangling with her steps. The front door was locked. She cupped her hands against the side window and squinted inside. She saw smoke and flames toward the back of the house. She attempted a half-hearted kick to the front door, but it didn't budge, and at 110 pounds she wasn't delusional enough to believe another attempt would end differently. She ran around to the back of the house.

Thick black smoke tinged with yellow billowed from the windows on the first floor, rolling up the side of the house and drifting into the dark night. Rory reached the back door and tried the handle. As it opened, a giant plume of smoke nearly swallowed her. She crouched below the curl of ash as it spun over her like a creature slithering to the outside. She stared into the house. The door led into the kitchen.

"Lane!"

She waited for a response, but all she heard were the

strange sounds of fire—crackling and hissing and groaning. Turning her head toward the fresh air behind her, she took a deep breath and then ran into the burning house. Once past the initial cloud of smoke that filled the doorway, Rory realized that most of the flames and smoke were at ceiling level and she had decent visibility if she stayed low to the ground. The stinging in her throat and lungs told her she could spend only a minute inside the house. She took a quick trip through the first floor, past the kitchen and into the front foyer before she turned around. The open back door and the freedom it promised was a life raft from which she didn't want to stray too far.

On her way back toward the kitchen, she saw the French doors off to her right. Through the smoke and haze, she imagined a shape on the floor. Her lungs burned and her eyes streamed tears. She lifted her shirt and placed the fabric over her mouth. The smoke grew thicker, and she fell onto her hands and knees to continue her approach. She recognized Lane immediately as he lay unconscious on the floor. She checked his neck for a pulse, but her own heart was racing and it prevented her from registering the subtle feelings from her fingertips. She reached down and grabbed him under the armpits, dragging him across the hardwood floor as she backed out of the room and through the kitchen. She pulled him across the threshold of the back doorway and out into the hot summer night, moving as if the curl of smoke had spat her out of the house. Despite August's heat and humidity, the air outside was cool. Rory sucked in the fresh air as if gulping from a water fountain.

She continued her backward trek, her legs fatigued and her quads burning by the time she had Lane in the grass of the backyard and at a safe distance from the house. She knelt by his side and touched his face, feeling the sticky tack of coagulating blood. The flames from the burning house offered enough light to see that the source of the blood was a wound somewhere in his hairline.

She finally confirmed that he was breathing. Then she looked back to the house. Someone else was inside, and she thought briefly of attempting to enter again, but the flames had grown stronger now. The back door was like the mouth of a dragon breathing flame and smoke into the night.

CHAPTER 25

It was just before sunrise when Rory stood from the chair and stretched the stiffness from her muscles. She looked down at Lane. A mask engulfed his nose and mouth and forced oxygen into his lungs. A few minutes longer, the doctors had told her, and he'd have succumbed to smoke inhalation. As it was now, the time in the burning house had simply smeared his lungs with soot and inflamed his trachea—rather minor concerns when compared with his head injury. Whatever piece of shrapnel the explosion shot through the house had resulted in a hairline fracture of the skull and a brain hemorrhage that required close monitoring. The doctors were watching to make sure the swelling subsided and the blood resorbed before they would consider him out of the woods. A couple of days, likely. A week at most, depending on how he responded to the steroids and diuretics.

Rory dwelled all night on what might have happened had she not come down from Chicago. A gritty wave of selfishness washed over her, leaving her itchy and uncomfortable as she sat through the lonesome hours of night contemplating how Lane's death would have left her truly alone in this world. A soft knock on the door took her from her emotions. She looked up to see a woman in the doorway.

"Hi," the woman said. "I don't mean to bother you."

Rory reached for her glasses but realized she had removed them during the night while she sat at Lane's side. Instead, she ran a hand through her hair, wishing she had her beanie cap to shield her.

"I'm Ryder Hillier," the woman said. "I knew Mack Carter."

After Lane had arrived in the ER and his condition had been declared as critical but stable, a uniformed police officer had questioned Rory about the events of the night. The officer was young and inexperienced and had checked all the boxes of a formal, first-tier line of questioning. Precise, by the book, and totally useless in regards to gathering pertinent information. But in the process, Rory had learned that the other car in the driveway of the burning house belonged to Mack Carter and that it was his body Rory had seen in the house along with Lane. Mack had been pronounced dead at the scene. Rory recounted her decision not to reenter the house because of the heat of the fire and the smoke billowing from the back door. The officer assured her she'd done the right thing, although Rory took little solace in the condolence.

"I'm sorry about Mr. Carter," Rory said.

"I was just an acquaintance. We didn't know each other well. We worked together in a roundabout way on his podcast. I'm a reporter."

Ryder Hillier.

Rory suddenly remembered the name. This was the true-crime journalist who had posted video of the dead

Westmont Prep student to the Internet just hours after he'd thrown himself in front of a train.

Rory noticed the woman's eyes move to Lane. "Is he going to be okay?"

Rory nodded. "So they tell me."

"I heard Dr. Phillips had signed on to the podcast to offer his expertise into the criminal mind."

Rory focused her gaze somewhere over Ryder's head. She didn't answer.

"I'm not sure how much you know about the podcast Mack Carter was working on," Ryder finally said. "But this explosion . . . his death . . . it's all very suspicious."

Behind Ryder Hillier, two men appeared. Rory knew by their suits and their expressions that they were detectives.

"Excuse us," one of them said. "We're here to speak with Dr. Phillips."

"I'll let you go," Ryder said. She seemed to know they were cops, too, and Rory recognized in the woman's eyes a sudden urge to escape the room. She handed Rory a business card, like an ambulance-chasing attorney. "Tell Dr. Phillips to call me if he wants to talk."

Rory held the card in her hand as Ryder disappeared past the detectives. Rory reached into her rucksack, slipped the business card into a slot in the front pouch, and pulled out her glasses, pushing them up the bridge of her nose and feeling slightly more invisible.

"I'm Detective Ott," the older gentleman said. "This is my partner, Detective Morris."

Rory sized them up instantly, her mind firing through the possibilities until she settled on the one she knew was most accurate. Ott was about sixty. The skin under his eyes drooped with a combination of years and experience, and likely too much alcohol. He was close to retirement and maybe had another couple good years in him. Morris was younger, maybe thirty. His face was nearly wrinkle-free, and his scowl told Rory he was the protégé who was a bit too eager to prove himself.

"Rory Moore," she said.

"How's Dr. Phillips?"

"Stable," Rory said. "Some smoke inhalation and a nasty head wound."

"Has he been able to talk?" the younger detective asked with little emotion.

"Not yet. He's sedated. They're making sure the swelling in his head comes down and the hemorrhage starts to clear before they get too excited about letting him wake up."

"Well, he's in good hands. Docs here are great," Detective Ott said.

Rory nodded her thanks. She wasn't sure how good the health care was here, and she was reluctant to compare Lane's current level of care to what he might receive in Chicago. But the doctors had pronounced him stable and had told Rory they were being cautious during the first forty-eight hours. They assured her that they had the ability to transfer him, by helicopter if needed, to a higher-level trauma unit if he didn't progress as expected.

Detective Ott, too, pulled a card from his pocket. "Would you mind giving us a call when Dr. Phillips is up for a chat?"

"I'll pass along the request."

Detective Ott next pulled a notepad from his breast pocket.

"Do you have a minute to run through what happened?"

Rory knew it was a rhetorical question, so she didn't answer.

"You were first to the scene. Can you tell us about your night?"

"Sure," Rory said, briefing the detectives on her impromptu trip down from Chicago and how she tracked Lane to Mack Carter's rented house. About entering the house through the rear door and finding Lane on the ground in the room off the kitchen.

"Can you tell us what you and Dr. Phillips are doing in Peppermill?"

"Lane was working on Mack Carter's podcast about Westmont Prep. I was joining him to keep him company."

There was a moment of silence as the detective jotted on his notepad.

"The fire marshal said the explosion was the result of a gas leak. Considering the damage to the house, he's damn lucky to be alive," Ott said. "We're looking into how the leak started. We'll know more soon."

"We'll be requesting fingerprint samples from you," Morris said in a tone meant to assert competence and authority but only made Rory think he was compensating for a lack of it.

"That can be arranged at your convenience," Ott said. He looked down at his notepad. "When you arrived at the house, did you see any cars in the area? Or anyone else around?"

"No," Rory said. "I saw flames and I ran inside. Front door was locked. I tried to kick it open before I ran around to the back." She looked at Morris. "You'll probably find my footprint on the door. Size seven Madden Girl Eloisee combat boots. No need to call in the CSI guys for that one."

Her comment caused Ott's lips to curl.

They spent ten minutes asking Rory questions. Despite telling the truth, an itch materialized on each of her deltoids, just below the shoulder, that begged Rory to scratch and claw. She refused. She had nothing to hide, but her mind didn't work that way. She was suspicious by nature, and when she was the one being questioned, she worried that the detectives would misinterpret her body language and avoidance of eye contact as deception.

"Where will you be staying, Ms. Moore?" Ott asked as they finished their questions.

It was a good question and she hadn't thought about it until just now. "I guess I'll be at Lane's rental."

She gave them the address and shared her cell number. After the detectives left, she stood next to the hospital bed. Besides some fitful sleep in the bedside chair, she had been awake for nearly twenty-four hours, ever since she woke in Miami after the auction. Despite the early hour now, she was in desperate need of a Dark Lord and maybe a shower. She took Lane's hand in hers and squeezed before she left. He didn't move.

CHAPTER 26

The groggy glow of early morning shaded the streets of Peppermill as she drove past the shops and restaurants, through the main boulevard, and eventually onto Winston Lane, the shadowed road where her night began almost twelve hours earlier. Cottages lined each side of the street as she drove into the cul-de-sac. She had fished the keys from Lane's pocket after the nurses gave her a bag filled with his clothes. She parked in the driveway and walked to the front door, where she keyed the lock and entered.

Rory kept the cottage in shadows, only lighting the small lamp on the end table in the front room. She took a moment to study the small house, walking into the kitchen. Hunger growled in her stomach, and she pulled open the refrigerator door. It was empty of food, but filling the top shelf were six bottles of Dark Lord stout lined in perfect rows with the labels forward, as if Rory herself had arranged them. A smile found her face. He had known she would come.

She pulled a Dark Lord off the shelf and grabbed a glass from the cabinet. The beer formed a thick head as she poured it, and Rory allowed the stout to settle as she carried the glass with her and explored the rest of the house. When she reached the three-season room at the back of the cottage, she stopped and stared at the desk. Arranged on its surface was an array of pastels she used to color the dolls she restored. Next to them were brushes and swabs. The presentation represented just a fraction of the tools she used during a restoration, but Rory appreciated Lane's efforts. The rest of her equipment was packed in her car, along with her new Kiddiejoy doll. The makeshift studio here, isolated from the neighbors and with the tall windows looking out over the pond that held the subtle glow of early morning, was nearly as inviting as her workshop at home.

When she walked into the room she noticed a present wrapped and waiting on the desk. She spun the package around and saw her name scrawled on the tag in Lane's cursive. Peeling off the paper, she found a pine box the size of a hardcover novel. She lifted the top to reveal a set of Foldger-Gruden paintbrushes. The collection had been discontinued years ago, and Rory's current set had belonged to her great-aunt. Those brushes were worth more in sentimentality than practicality, as many were unusable after so many years of restorations. This sight of the pristine set prickled her chest with possibility and produced the urge to go to her car, retrieve her new doll, and put the brushes to use. Rory lifted one of the brushes from the foam casing that secured it. The handle, like the box, was made from pine. On one end were fine bristles made from sable hair. She stroked the back of her hand to feel the softness. The other end of the handle was beveled to a needlelike point, which was meant for sculpting. Rory took a moment to admire the collection of brushes, which ranged from fine to broad and would be perfect for restoring her new Kiddiejoy doll.

As drawn as she was to the workbench Lane had arranged for her, something else in the room called for her attention. Against the far wall she saw a large corkboard propped on an easel. It looked eerily similar to the one in Rory's office. That infamous corkboard in her Chicago bungalow was pocked with hundreds of holes from years of sticking pins through photos of victims from the cold cases she had solved. Once she tacked a photo to the corkboard, Rory embedded the victim's image in her mind in a way that prevented her from forgetting their face until she had found answers to what had happened to them. During this process, a relationship began—an intimate bond between Rory and the deceased that she had never been able to explain to another living soul. It was how her mind worked. It was the way she unraveled cases no one else could solve. She grew closer to the victims whose murders she investigated than she did to nearly anyone else in her life.

Rory carried her glass of Dark Lord through the room and stared at the corkboard. Pinned to it was a photo of Theo Compton, the most recent Westmont Prep student to go back to that boarding house and kill himself. Other photos were pinned below Theo's. As Rory moved closer to the board, she recognized the five faces that stared back at her. She'd done her research. After Lane had first told her about the case, Rory spent the night scanning the Internet and learning everything she could about the Westmont Prep Killings. It had been a distraction from the angst of preparing to board an airplane the next morning.

Two of the faces belonged to the students who had

been killed during the slaughter. The other three were the survivors who had gone back to that house over the last few months to kill themselves. Rory stood in front of the board and scanned each photo, hypnotized by the eyes that stared back. Finally, she looked at the table next to the corkboard. A glossy five-by-seven photo lay on the surface. It contained another face with eyes that were equally hypnotic. She lifted the photo from the desk, stared at it for a moment, and then pinned it to the top of the board, above the others. This photo was of Charles Gorman, the chemistry teacher who killed the first two students and hung one of them on a fence.

Rory took a step back to take in the entire board. The room was starting to brighten with the rising sun. It was approaching six in the morning when she sat in a chair in front of the corkboard and stared at the faces that held the mystery of Westmont Prep. She raised her glass and took a sip of Dark Lord. Something sinister lay hidden and buried out at that boarding house. Whatever it was, Mack Carter had started digging in the right spot to find it. And if it wasn't the exact spot, he had been close enough to spook whoever wanted it to stay buried.

Rory's expertise was reconstructing crimes to find the truth hidden within them—not just how they happened, but why. As she sat in the small cottage in Peppermill, Indiana, she was hard-pressed to come up with a case better suited to her talents than the Westmont Prep Killings. She settled into the chair and studied the faces in front of her. They were the students who once walked the campus but now were ghosts of the forest. And the teacher who turned on them.

She took another sip of Dark Lord and wondered what happened at that school that had caused so much death.

Westmont Prep
Summer 2019

Session 3

Journal Entry: A RELUCTANT ACCOMPLICE

I looked through the keyhole. After my father finished his purging, there was a long stretch of silence when the house was calm and quiet. The view through my keyhole offered nothing but an empty dining room and the blank table where my father had swiped everything to the ground. I thought about leaving my room. I wanted to run to my mother and make sure she was safe. Get her ice for her broken lip. I'd done it before, and she always told me how much she loved me for it. But tonight's beating was different. My father was possessed in a way I hadn't seen before. The broken lamppost was simply a catalyst for a much greater issue that he wanted to get out of his system.

I was scared to leave my room. Not so much because I feared he would hurt me but because I worried my mother would step in and try to prevent it. She'd done it before, and my father had emptied the rest of his wrath on her. As hard as it was to watch through the keyhole, another level of inadequacy always came over me when I watched him beat her in person. Through the keyhole I was anonymous. Out there I was not. Out there my *mother's eyes would occasionally meet mine in the middle of it. When I stood helplessly in the shadows during those moments, I felt less than human. It was better to stay behind the closed door of my bedroom, watch through my portal, and wait.*

Finally, after an hour of peering through my keyhole, I saw my father walk into the dining room. He seemed in a hurry as he picked the items off the floor and rearranged them on the table. There was something about his mannerisms that I couldn't place. Something about him I didn't recognize. After he finished cleaning the mess, he paced back and forth. As he did, it finally struck me. I understood what seemed so strange. He was nervous. The same look I had seen so many times on my mother's face as she anticipated his arrival home from work was now on my father's.

Before I could work out this strange role reversal, I heard sirens. Soon, flashing red and blue lights were painting my bedroom walls. Then I heard doors slamming and voices talking, and I suddenly knew why my father was nervous. Why the nastiness was gone from his face and the arrogance absent from his posture. He had hurt my mother tonight in a way he'd never done before, and he had called an ambulance for help.

I jumped to my feet and ripped open my bedroom door. I sprinted down the hallway and into the dining room, arriving just as my father pulled open the front door. There, on the landing, were two paramedics with a gurney between them.

"In here," my father said. "She's at the bottom of the stairs. She must have fallen."

The paramedics calmly entered my house and assessed the scene. I walked slowly toward the stairs, dif-

ferent from the way I had sprinted from my room. I took one hesitant step at a time. One after the other, until the dining room wall gave way and I had a clear view into the foyer. My mother was in a heap at the bottom of the stairs, her eyes closed as if sleeping but the rest of her body at strange angles. One arm was draped over her face and the other tucked impossibly under her body. One leg was straight, but the other was bent at the knee as if she were sliding into second base.

"It's okay," my father said to me.

I couldn't remember the last time he'd spoken to me.

"Your mother had an accident. I came home to find her like this. Did you see her fall?"

I stared at my father with a blank look. I didn't answer. The paramedics were tending to my mother when one of them looked up at me. "Did you hear anything? Did you hear her fall?" he asked.

Inexplicably, I nodded my head. "Yes," I said. "I didn't know what the noise was. I was in my room doing my homework."

"It's okay," my father said. "The paramedics are here. They'll take care of her."

The men went back to helping my mother. They loaded her motionless body onto the stretcher and wheeled her out to the ambulance. I saw a few neighbors on the front yard in the red glow of the ambulance light. They were staring at my mother as she was placed into the ambulance. I hadn't seen her move once, and her eyes never opened.

Then I noticed another set of eyes. My father's. He was staring at me. Although he never said a word, his glare told me everything he wanted me to know. Finally, he walked out of the house to ride with my mother to the hos-

pital. Mrs. Peterson from next door talked with my father in the front yard and then walked toward my open front door. She would stay with me overnight.

Before the front door closed, my father nodded at me. Like we were coconspirators. Like I planned to keep his secret. Like only he and I would ever know the truth about how I lost my mother. He believed he was nodding at the weak and feeble child who stared through a keyhole, too scared to leave the bedroom. But he was wrong. That child was gone. That child died when my mother was loaded into an ambulance never to return.

My father was right about one thing, though. I never told a soul about what he did. I killed him the next day, so there was no real reason to tell anyone.

I pulled the tassel into the crease of the spine and closed the journal. I looked up from the pages, and our eyes met. She said nothing. Usually, I sought insight when I finished reading from my journal. But after today's session, nothing needed to be said. Our relationship was unorthodox, some might even say inappropriate. But it worked for us. It worked for me, at least. I couldn't survive without her.

We stared at each other, our eyes holding for a long moment. For today, that was enough.

CHAPTER 27

Saturday afternoon, the day after the six of them had met to choke down warm Budweiser and discuss the mysterious invitation they had all received, Gwen sat in Gavin's dorm room. She paged through a stack of envelopes and stopped in the middle.

"Here's one from your mom."

Gavin rolled his eyes. "She's not my mom."

"Sorry, I forgot."

Although they'd been dating since freshman year, Gwen had never gotten the full story behind Gavin's home life, or why his aunt and uncle had taken full custody of him. She knew that his brother had died in an accident a couple of years before and that his family had never fully healed. That's all she'd been able to get out of Gavin. She had tried a few times to dig deeper into his life outside of Westmont Prep, but Gavin Harms never talked about his dead brother, or his family. He never talked about his aunt and uncle. That was the way he operated. Take it or leave it.

Gwen's inability to break through Gavin's walls was what she usually journaled about, and was the most common topic of discussion during her sessions with Dr. Casper.

"She refuses to communicate with me any other way," Gavin said. "Written letters sent through the post office, that's it."

"Snail mail is fun. I never get any. Can I read it?"

"I don't care. I know what it says. It's the same thing she wrote last summer, which is why I haven't opened it this year."

Gwen tore open the envelope and removed the single page that was folded in thirds. She cleared her throat and began talking in the overly genteel voice of a mother breaking bad news to her child.

"Dear Gavin, I hope this letter finds you well." Gwen looked over the top of the letter, her eyes emoji wide. "Oh my God."

"She's a robot. It's how she starts every letter to me."

Gwen went back to the page.

"I hope this letter finds you well. And busy. Your latest grade report was outstanding. I am very proud of you, which is why I am writing to inform you that arrangements have been made for you to spend the summer at Westmont in their advanced studies program. This was a very hard decision for us, but we believe it gives you the best chance for achieving your goals. The program comes at a tremendous cost, both financial and emotional. You know what a challenge this is for us, but we believe it will be money well spent. Although we would love to spend the summer with you, this opportunity will give more to your future than we could provide at home. Good luck to you this summer. I'm sure we will talk soon and often. With love."

Gwen looked up again. She shrugged. "I mean, besides the Shawshanky opening, it was sort of nice."

"Whatever."

"Oh, save your pouting for Dr. Hanover. You know you didn't want to go home this summer."

There was a pause; Gwen was nervous to ask the next question.

"How is she? Dr. Hanover?"

Gavin shrugged. "Fine."

Gwen was used to getting little out of Gavin about his therapy sessions as well. She decided not to push. Instead, she climbed onto the bed and snuggled into Gavin's side. She kissed his neck. "It's not all bad. You'll be here all summer with me. Isn't that a good thing?"

"Yeah," he said in a distracted tone. "It's good."

She rolled onto her back and pulled her phone in front of her face as she laid her head on Gavin's arm.

"What's the plan for tonight?" she asked.

"Wait 'til dark, and then head out."

"Have you ever been out to the abandoned boarding house?"

Gavin shook his head. "Never."

"Are you scared?"

"Are you?"

Gwen turned and looked at him. "Yes."

CHAPTER 28

"If anybody touches me," Gavin said as they walked through the dark campus, "or tries to paddle me, I'm fighting back."

They passed the Gothic structure of the library building, the gaudy display of the school's logo, and the spot where they stood each year on Gate Day.

"Come on," Gwen said. "No one's going to paddle us. There are, like, laws against that stuff."

"It's Andrew Gross and his group of goons. There's no telling what's waiting for us."

"Ignore him," Gwen said to Theo and Danielle. "He's been in a bad mood ever since he started seeing Dr. *Hangover*, who's known—"

"To give you a raging headache," Danielle said, finishing Gwen's sentence. "Why did they switch you? We're not supposed to get assigned to Hanover until senior year."

"She requested he switch over to her early," Gwen said.

"Ha! She must think you're really screwed up."

"I'm gifted, I guess," Gavin said.

"I don't know what I'm going to do when they switch me," Gwen said. "Dr. Casper knows my entire life story. There's no way I'd tell Dr. Hanover half of what I tell Dr. Casper."

"You're not supposed to tell your *therapist* anything," Gavin said. "You're supposed to tell your *journal*."

They laughed at this. Journaling was a Westmont Prep staple, and every counseling session included a segment when students were expected to read a passage from their journal.

"Let's all agree not to include whatever it is we're about to do in any of our journals," Theo said, and then pointed at a spot on the trail up ahead of them. "There it is."

The four of them stopped when they reached the path that disappeared into the woods. They paused, glancing around the quiet campus and surveying the dark buildings that were empty and waiting for the summer session to begin on Monday. Ground-level spotlights ignited the buildings and captured the ivy-covered exteriors in expanding triangles of brightness, while dying sunlight silhouetted the cornices and made them look like thorns of a crown sitting on the rooftops. The constant buzz of locusts filled the night, and they all allowed the background noise to occupy the silence between them.

Finally, Theo spoke.

"Are we waiting for Tanner and Bridget?"

"Tanner said they were heading to Route 77 by themselves, so we'll hook up with them there," Gavin said.

They all nodded at one another with nothing else to say, each feeling some level of hesitation and hoping for one of them to pull the plug on this idea. But none said another word, and they finally slipped into the woods.

The path was wide and well trampled. The heavy ceiling of foliage blocked out the remnants of dusk, so they clicked on the flashlights of their cell phones to guide the way. Heading into their junior year, they were no longer underclassmen; they were now nearly at the top of the food chain. They had been invited to the abandoned boarding house. Although many students knew of the house's existence, few possessed any details about what took place there. And even though just about every student had heard about the Man in the Mirror—rumors were great and exaggerated, and the folklore was legendary—few held any specifics. That was because membership into this group was exclusive, the demands of its brotherhood great, and the oath to secrecy absolute.

As they made their way through the forest, their steps were fueled by a steady dose of trepidation and curiosity. They had only the seniors to deal with, the summer to get through, and initiation to conquer.

CHAPTER 29

They followed the dirt path until they came to a clear-ing that delivered them onto a two-lane highway they all knew was Route 77. They turned right and walked along the dark shoulder, the gravel crunching underfoot.

"There it is," Gwen said, pointing up ahead.

Mile marker thirteen stood in front of them, shadowed but visible as the 1 and 3 caught the moonlight.

"Thirteen, three, five," Theo said when they reached the marker. "It should be a third of a mile farther now."

"This is freaking me out," Danielle said.

Gavin waved them along. "Just hurry. There's nowhere to hide if a car comes along, and we're past curfew."

In a single-file line, they fast-walked along the narrow shoulder until, about one-third of a mile past the marker, they spotted an entryway back into the woods. The bushes separated and offered a black hole into the forest. They walked down the embankment and toward the opening.

"Boo!"

The voice was loud and obnoxious. They all startled in

retreat. The girls screamed. Then came laughter as Tanner Landing walked from the edge of the forest.

"Tanner, you're such a shithead," Gwen said.

Tanner was bent at the waist, just like the previous night, laughing and pointing at them. "You should have seen your faces. That would go viral if I had recorded it."

"Sorry," Bridget said, following Tanner out of the darkness of the forest. "He thought it would be funny if we waited for you here."

"So funny," Gavin said in an overly excited voice. "I'm so glad you waited for us. I'm actually *so* glad you're here tonight. I'm not sure what we'd have done without you."

Tanner stood upright and slowly stopped laughing. "How does your girlfriend deal with your moodiness?"

"How does yours deal with your asshole-ness?"

This brought snickers from the others.

"Sorry," Gavin said to Bridget.

"Don't be," she said. "He *is* an asshole. He just doesn't care."

They headed into the woods to complete the final half mile of their journey. Under thick foliage, they followed the dirt path, trying to calculate the distance they travelled. When they reached the edge of the forest, a chain grinned between two posts and held a PRIVATE PROPERTY sign. Beyond it, the mythical boarding house came into view. It was cloaked in shadow, but from inside the house an odd, darkened glow spilled through the windows and fell onto the ground outside. Studying the windows, they realized the interior lighting was blunted by black spray paint that covered the windows.

The building's exterior was in the same tradition as the main campus buildings—Bedford limestone covered by ivy. But here, things were unkempt. The ivy ran wild in heavy froths around the windows and fell over itself when it reached the gutters. Multiple seasons of fallen leaves accumulated at the edges of the building and around the trunks of the trees that flanked the house. A massive oak stood in the front yard with sturdy lower branches expanding horizontally like the arms of a crucifix.

"Now what?" Gwen asked.

Danielle pulled up her phone and scrolled through the text messages until she came to the invitation they had each received.

"The Man in the Mirror requests your presence at thirteen-three-five," Danielle said, reading from her phone. "Upon arrival, proceed to the front yard and wait for further instruction."

"I'm not sure I want to do this," Gwen said.

Tanner smiled. "Oh, we're doing this. Let's see what all the hype is about."

CHAPTER 30

They walked from the edge of the forest and into the clearing in front of the boarding house. Then, together, the group passed through the opening of the wrought iron gate that surrounded the house. As soon as they made it onto the front yard, figures materialized from the darkness and slowly closed in on them. Cloaked in black hooded capes, the ghosts morphed from the shadows of the ivy that climbed the walls, poured out of the front door, and emerged like warlocks from the forest that surrounded the house. They approached quickly, and Gwen's vision blackened when she felt a blindfold being wrapped around her face, the soft nylon tied in a knot at the back of her head.

"This abandoned boarding house . . ." someone said from behind her.

Gwen recognized Andrew Gross's voice. Andrew was a Westmont Prep senior they all believed had been behind the invitation. He had long been rumored to be involved in the Man in the Mirror challenges that so many classmates gossiped about.

"It's not for anyone who decides to come. It's for the

chosen. You've all been invited to join the Man in the Mirror, a small and exclusive group at Westmont Prep. Whether you accept that invitation is still to be decided."

Gwen felt a hand on her elbow, which guided her through the grass and onto a gravel path. After just a few moments without vision she was disoriented from her surroundings. She stumbled down an embankment, feeling the grip on her elbow tighten to keep her upright. Finally, the hand moved from her elbow to her shoulder and forced her downward into a hard, wooden chair.

"You've all heard about the Man in the Mirror and the challenges he puts forth. There will be a series of them this summer, and your first is tonight. It's simple. Just sit where you are. That's all. First one to get off their chair loses, and trust me, you don't want to be a loser."

Gwen heard footsteps crunching over the gravel and through leaves as Andrew and the other seniors retreated. Finally, the shuffling disappeared, and all that remained was the buzz of cicadas. Finally, Gwen spoke.

"Gavin?"

She wasn't sure why she was whispering, but they all followed along.

"I'm here," Gavin said. "I think I'm right next to you."

Gwen felt Gavin's outstretched hand touch her shoulder. It startled her, and then she grabbed it and squeezed his hand.

"This is seriously screwed up," Theo said. "We're supposed to sit here all night?"

"That's right," Tanner said. "I'll stay for a week if I have to. But you guys feel free to be the first to quit."

No one spoke.

"Hello?" Tanner said.

Since Gate Day freshman year, Tanner had been desperate to fit in, Gwen knew. He was a social climber, jumping from group to group, seeking acceptance and approval from anyone who offered it. That he had been included in this small group that was invited to join the much-rumored secret sect inside the Westmont Prep student body was his ticket to friendship and popularity. Gwen knew Tanner wasn't bluffing. He would actually sit here all night if it meant that the seniors include him in their social circle.

"Hello?" Tanner said again.

"Tanner, just shut up," Gavin said. "Do you think you're capable of that?"

Just as the words were out of Gavin's mouth, a noise came from far off. A muted horn that disrupted the vibration of the locusts.

"What was that?" Gwen asked. She squeezed Gavin's hand harder.

It came again. This time louder.

"Should we leave?" she asked.

"I don't know," Gavin said.

Another whistle, louder still. Then a rumble. The chairs pulsated under them. Finally, they heard the chugging of an approaching train. With the blindfolds on and nothing but blackness in their vision, the train came from nowhere.

"Gavin?" Gwen said.

"Screw this," Gavin said. "Let's go!"

Gwen pulled the blindfold off her face. She saw that the six of them were lined up next to train tracks, the backs of their chairs dangerously close to the rails. When she looked to her left, she saw the headlight of a train barreling toward them. She let out a scream that caused everyone in the row to pull their blindfolds down. They all stood in a mass exodus, running down the embankment as the train stormed past. Tanner clipped his heel on the chair as he ran, causing it to topple backward onto the tracks. As the train sped by, the chair splintered when the train crunched over the wood and shattered it into a thousand pieces.

They all stood in the shallow gulley as the train blurred past, breathing heavily from shock and adrenaline, ears filled by the thunder of metal on metal. A mangled piece of Tanner's chair ricocheted off the train and came to rest at their feet. They all stared at it.

It was June 8. Thirteen days later the slaughter would take place at the boarding house behind them.

CHAPTER 31

Marc McEvoy had a plan. He would go to Peppermill on June 21. He would follow Route 77. He would take the route so many of his classmates talked about— 13:3:5—and find the abandoned boarding house. He would do it this summer, the way he should have done it during his junior year at Westmont Prep. He should have done it back then out of defiance, to prove that the students who chose only a select few to join their clique had no more dominion over the school than did the kids they shunned. Had Marc possessed the same courage as a junior in high school that he had today, much of his anger and curiosity would have been dispelled. Instead, he was a twenty-five-year-old man still scarred by rejection and still chasing a dream of acceptance. Pursuing a need to be part of a group that had excluded him years before.

He needed to keep his trip to Peppermill a secret. His wife could know nothing about it. He'd play it off as a business trip. He'd be gone for just one night, he'd tell her. He'd drive to the airport and park in the extended commuter lot, making sure to get a receipt. From there, he'd take the South Shore Metra Line. It was only two stops from South Bend—Hudson Lake and Carroll Avenue—before the Metra reached the shores of Lake Michigan and the town of Peppermill. His wife paid their bills, so he would have to use cash to leave no credit trail behind. Once in Peppermill, he'd have a drink at the corner bar, wait until the proper hour, and then find Route 77 and start the journey he should have taken years before. He'd finally see what the rumors were all about. He'd stay in the shadows. No one would see him. He'd be invisible.

He was aware of the possibility of a letdown. He was aware that during his years at Westmont Prep, he had likely made the Man in the Mirror initiation a bigger event than it actually was. Now, nearly a decade later, it was possible that what he found at the abandoned house would not live up to expectations, to his embellished thoughts of what transpired out in the dark woods at midnight each summer solstice. The whole excursion might not fulfill his fantasies. But he could *make* those fantasies come true. He was no longer a scared teenager. Rules no longer bound him. He could do anything he chose once he made it out to that house.

It was June 8. He had thirteen days to perfect his plan.

PART IV

August 2020

CHAPTER 32

The bedside chair was like granite, so Rory had opted to sprawl in the sill of the bay window, which at least had a cushion. She sat with her back against the side, her legs straight out in front of her, and combat boots crossed right over left. Always right over left, never the reverse. Her mind would not allow it. The window was to her left, and the pond and fountain four stories below were visible but ignored as she read. In her lap was Lane's notebook that contained his initial research into the Westmont Prep Killings. Included in his notes were the preliminary profile of Charles Gorman and another profile that listed the likely characteristics of the person who had killed the students.

The profile of Gorman depicted a reserved science teacher who excelled at chemistry. An introverted man with tendencies to be shy in public situations outside the classroom, he had always complied with the rules and never earned a serious mark against him—neither at Westmont Prep nor the public school where he taught for more than a decade before landing in Peppermill. Gorman had come from a traditional family, which was still intact. His parents were married, both retired teachers living on pensions and residing in the same Ohio home where they raised their three children. Gorman was the middle child, and by all accounts—according to Lane's research—had had a normal childhood. No incidents of violence in grade school, high school, or college. No red flags indicating he was a man on the brink of snapping into a fit of rage or plotting a terrible massacre.

Charles Gorman was single, and Lane's research had uncovered only one curious area of Gorman's past that had piqued his interest. This was marked in the notes by three red stars and two slashes that underlined the heading *Relationships*. A former girlfriend at Gorman's previous place of employment had reported him to the school's HR department after they had ended their eight-month relationship. The report stated that the female colleague, a civics teacher, felt "uncomfortable" by Gorman's continued attention and insistence that they work things out. After a meeting with HR and a teachers union rep, the case was resolved and nothing more happened between the two parties.

Gorman left the school at the end of the term and started at Westmont Prep the following year. The woman's name was Adrian Fang. Lane had also underlined her name twice, which meant that he had intended to speak with her to further his profile of Charles Gorman. Lane had also listed the names of Gorman's two siblings and parents as sources to speak with.

At the bottom of the page, Lane had listed his contacts inside Grantville Psychiatric Hospital, where Gorman was currently being cared for. Rory dog-eared the page and then turned to the next.

THE BOARDING HOUSE SLAUGHTER was scrawled

at the top in all caps. The profile that followed included characteristics that Lane believed the killer of the two Westmont Prep students possessed. The sketch depicted an organized killer, based on the scant evidence that had been found at the scene. Besides the bodies, the killer had left no fingerprints, fibers, or footprints at the scene. A disorganized killer, on the other hand—someone who flew into a fit of rage and killed out of reaction rather than calculation—typically left a crime scene littered with evidence and oftentimes offered a poor attempt at sterilizing the scene. The bloodbath at the boarding house, Lane surmised, was preplanned and carefully carried out by a skillful predator.

The only sloppiness discovered within the staged crime scene was the trace amount of blood that belonged to neither of the two victims. DNA had been taken from all the students and faculty, including Charles Gorman. The unidentified blood at the scene belonged to none of them.

WHOSE BLOOD WAS AT THE SCENE? Lane had written in all caps.

Adding to the theory of an organized killer who had carefully plotted the murders was the manner in which each student had been killed—one by a single slash that severed the right jugular, and the other by a wound to the throat, severing the trachea and causing asphyxiation. The absence of defensive wounds on either victim's hands or arms suggested an element of surprise. The original attack had occurred inside one of the rooms of the house, and then one student had been dragged outside and impaled on the wrought iron fence. Lane surmised that this represented a symbolic act of revenge.

This person was likely, Rory read, someone with a

troubled past and an abusive childhood or broken family. The fact that no female students had been injured suggested that perhaps the killer had ill feelings toward men, perhaps his own father. That there was a female student present but uninjured at the scene made feasible the idea that the killer was close with his mother, or at least had a strong maternal influence in his life. Lane made two observations here: The killer either lived with his mother during adult life and had an unnaturally intimate relationship with her, and by default was unmarried, or had lost his mother at a young age or through a traumatic event that caused him to develop an unnatural and inflated memory of his mother as a deity that other women could not live up to.

Violence was likely part of this person's past, either toward him or someone he loved. The trauma of this violence had been internalized, and later projected toward others. The Westmont Prep students may not have been the killer's first victims. He may have killed before. The killer had to be physically strong, with enough bulk to lift a 160-pound teenager onto the fence. The likelihood that this person was male was overwhelming.

Rory turned the page and saw that Lane had drawn a Venn diagram that included all the characteristics from each profile—that of Charles Gorman and that of the killer. The circles overlapped in the middle, creating an oval where the two profiles matched. Few characteristics were listed there. The oval included that the offender had knowledge of the abandoned boarding house and knew the students would be there on the night of the killing. The offender was likely someone familiar to the victims, perhaps with low self-esteem but with above-average intelligence. The offender was strong enough to overwhelm two healthy teenage men.

Rory looked up from the notebook and gazed out the window. Her mind was churning with anxiousness, an uncontrolled urge to begin the redundant calculations needed to decipher the pieces of a crime. Charles Gorman matched Lane's profile of the killer about as well as any random Westmont Prep teacher. She knew there was more to the story. An uneasy energy flushed through her circulatory system.

Rory stood from the windowsill and walked over to the bed, placed a hand on Lane's forehead, and leaned over so that her lips were close to his ear.

"I need you, so you can wake up anytime now."

CHAPTER 33

It was a rare occasion that Ryder Hillier walked into the headquarters of the *Indianapolis Star*. She took most of her assignments by e-mail and submitted her articles the same way. Staff meetings demanded her presence twice a month, but otherwise she was a crime reporter who chased stories on her own and waited for the okay from her editor after she found one she liked. Usually her efforts were met with glowing praise. Her track record had granted her a long leash. Today, though, her editor was tugging on the other end. Her presence at headquarters was not the result of a staff meeting or an overdue deadline for which she needed to coax an extension. She was there because she was in a world of shit.

The decision to post the Theo Compton video had been misguided, at best, and Ryder would admit that her motives were clouded by the opportunity to beat Mack Carter to a scoop. Posting the video was her way of showing the world her victory. It had backfired in spectacular fashion. She'd invited Mack along that night because she figured if anything significant transpired out at the abandoned boarding house, Mack would have no choice but to include Ryder in his podcast. Of course, Ryder had no idea what waited for her there. She never thought she'd find the kid dead, but when she did she knew the mystery of Westmont Prep was deeper than anyone knew. The kids were killing themselves for a reason, and she was determined to figure out what it was.

Without considering the repercussions, she had posted the video to her YouTube channel at 2:25 A.M., just after she finished her statement to the police. She figured she'd get in front of Mack's podcast by beating him to the punch. For what it was worth, the stunt was quite effective. By six in the morning, the video had over a hundred thousand views. As her fan base shared it, the video garnered hundreds of thousands more, and eventually millions. Until it was taken down, along with her entire channel.

If Ryder had been as well protected as Mack Carter, she would be in a much better position today than she was currently. Mack Carter had powerful lawyers and a network to shelter him. The higher-ups likely told Mack to stay as far away from the Theo Compton video as possible. But they still expected him to attack the angle. And he did, to enormous success. His podcast never linked directly to the video of Theo's body but produced the hell out of Mack's journey to the abandoned house after an "unidentified tip" had come through. Of course, they edited out Ryder's phone call, instead spinning the story to suggest that it was Mack himself who had seen Theo's message and decided to go out to 13:3:5. That there happened to be another reporter present at the house that night—described in the podcast episode as an "amateur sleuth"—was pure chance. That this amateur had made the ill-fated decision to record what they'd found by the train tracks was a problem that fell squarely on Ryder

Hillier's shoulders. Mack walked away clean. Better than clean, he walked away more popular than ever before. The fourth episode of the podcast was downloaded millions of times. But the genius in what Mack Carter had accomplished was that in order to distance himself from the video, he had to mention that it existed. Which he did, over and over and over again.

Every time he had scolded the "amateur sleuth" for posting such a heinous video, Mack Carter knew he was inviting his podcast listeners to search for the footage. Even without direct links to Ryder's blog or YouTube channel, she saw the uptick in web traffic and knew that Mack's audience was searching her site for the video. Mack had received the benefit of the recording without any of the legal ramifications. It was, Ryder had to admit, a bit of marketing genius.

"Shut it down," her editor told her now as she sat in front of his desk.

"It's already down. YouTube prohibited the video and did their best to erase its existence. Took my entire channel down, and when they put it back up it will likely be demonetized."

"Not just the video," her editor continued. "Shut it all down. Everything. No more Westmont Prep coverage."

"I've never done anything related to Westmont Prep for the paper," Ryder said.

She hadn't. Her fascination with the Westmont Prep Killings was her own endeavor, and her blog and YouTube channel were separate projects that she chased on her own, never expensing a dime to the paper and never missing a deadline because of her work on the case.

"And you never will," her editor said. "That includes writing anything about Mack Carter's death."

"I'm the one who *should* write about Mack. I'm the one who was with him a few nights before he died. And his death has to be related to Westmont Prep."

"Stay away from it, Ryder. I've already assigned it to someone else. And if you want to continue to write for this paper, you'll shut the side stuff down. At the very least, you're grounded from side work until we learn the depth and weight of the legal ramifications from your latest stunt. And if you get formally charged and convicted of *any* wrongdoing, obviously your time here is over. For now, stay busy and stay invisible. No bylines until this other mess gets solved."

"No bylines? You're taking my column away?"

"Putting it on hiatus."

"Look," Ryder said, trying to tame the conversation. "Mack Carter arrives in Peppermill and starts poking around a year-old case. Before long he's dead. The circumstances around his death are terribly suspicious. I'm intimately familiar with the case he was looking into, and now you're telling me I can't touch it? I could do a piece for the paper that would be gangbusters. And if the *Star* doesn't trust me, someone else will. Since when do you choose to back off a story?"

"When I'm worried about the paper being the next entity to be sued. Our attorneys think the only reason we haven't been slapped with a lawsuit already is because there are no direct ties between us and the Westmont Prep story. You're hanging out in between, and the predators are waiting for a way to go after the paper. I'm not going to allow it to happen. You're officially on the sidelines, no more discussion about it."

He looked at his computer and scribbled onto a loose

piece of paper, which he dropped in front of her. The page held several names and addresses.

"Here are a bunch of leads. A missing girl from Evansville. A convenience store robbery in Carmel. A melee at a preseason football game at Indiana U. A rape accusation at Notre Dame." He looked back to the computer. "Oh, and a guy who was shot in the ass when he broke into an eighty-year-old lady's house. Talk to that lady. I want her on the front page of the metro section."

Ryder looked down at the list of leads. At the bottom was the name of the missing South Bend man who disappeared the year before. She tapped it with her finger. "I've already covered the guy in South Bend. Nobody knows what happened to him. The story's cold, and boring."

"Then heat it up." Her editor waved her off. "Get me something interesting on all those leads. It'll keep you busy for days."

"And then what? Chase these leads and do what with them? You said no bylines."

"Correct. You're not writing a thing for a while. Bring your notebook back here, filled with research, and hand it off to another reporter to write the story."

"Are you seriously doing this to me?"

"You did it to yourself, Ryder. You want to write stories for this paper again, then get to work in the trenches until your legal headaches go away. Consider yourself lucky to still have a job. No other paper would take you at the moment."

Ryder grabbed the leads, crumpling the page in her palm as she stood, turned on her heels, and left the office.

CHAPTER 34

Rory had long wondered about her fascination with porcelain doll restoration. She used the obsession as an outlet for the pent-up thoughts of the mundane and redundant that worked to unsettle her life. She had used it to manage her affliction through her childhood. During her adult life, she had leaned on the diversion as a way to stay connected to her great-aunt Greta, who had first introduced Rory to the pastime of China doll restoration. In the process, Greta had saved Rory from a life of self-destruction. Despite these legitimate and admitted uses, Rory wondered, too, if she took solace in restoring antique dolls because it allowed her to fix the broken parts of them that she could never fix in herself. It was oxymoronic that her own faults and deficiencies were the very tools she used to mend the flaws and imperfections in the dolls. If channeled correctly, Rory's shortcomings of obsessive compulsion and some spectrum of autism could be used to restore the dolls back to perfection. Despite that Rory had always been broken and could never be fully repaired, the dolls made her as whole as possible.

She sat in the three-season room of the cottage and mixed a batch of papier-mâché. The smell brought back memories from her childhood at Aunt Greta's farmhouse, where she spent the summers of her youth learning the old lady's furtive formulas and secret techniques that, when applied properly, could transform the wreckage of an antique German doll into a masterpiece. When the papier-mâché had the correct consistency, she took a small amount and went to work reconstructing the doll's ear, where most of the previous porcelain had cracked and fallen away to leave a gaping crater. After creating a sturdy base, she dried the papier-mâché with an electric heat gun. Then she pulled a batch of cold porcelain clay from an airtight bag, placed a large dollop in the middle of the papier-mâché area, and molded it roughly into the shape she desired. She used her tools to sculpt the porcelain into a new ear and cheek and then heated the porcelain to stiffen it. Opening her new set of Foldger-Gruden brushes from Lane, she removed one brush and touched its end to her finger. Each brush handle was made of pine, the tip of which doubled as a sculptor's wand. The handles varied in sharpness, from blunt to piercing. Rory chose a blunt-tipped wand for the coarse work that was required during her initial sculpting of the porcelain clay. Later, she would use the sharper, more needlelike tips for the fine casting of the subtle features of the ear, cheek, and lateral canthus of the doll's left eye.

She worked steadily for two hours, purging her stored anxieties, discharging pent-up thoughts of redundancy, and dispelling the constant urge to repeat activities she had recently completed. When finished, she placed the Kiddiejoy doll back in the travel case, careful not to disturb her progress. Then she locked up the cottage and headed to the hospital feeling lighter than she had hours earlier.

Lane's eyes were open when she walked into his hospital room. They were wet and bloodshot from the medicine that dripped from the IV bag.

"Hey," Rory said.

"This wasn't how I planned to get you down here."

Rory smiled and put her hand on his cheek. "You scared the hell out of me."

"What a shit show," Lane said before grimacing.

Rory saw a Styrofoam cup next to the bed and handed it to Lane, who sipped from the straw.

"Throat feels like gravel."

"What have the doctors told you?"

"Haven't seen them yet, but two detectives were here when I opened my eyes."

"Yeah, I've already talked to them."

"My throat wasn't cooperating, so I wasn't able to tell them much. I wasn't able to ask any questions either. Christ, Rory, what happened?"

"I guess waking up in a hospital bed leaves a lot of blank spots."

Rory took a seat next to the bed and filled Lane in on everything from her trip to the auction in Miami, to her decision to come down to Peppermill, to her tracking Lane to Mack Carter's rental house and the fire she found there. That Mack Carter had died in the explosion and subsequent fire and that Detectives Ott and Morris were suspicious about the circumstances, to say the least.

"I thought all night about how mad I would have been at you if you had died."

"There's the warm and fuzzy woman I love," Lane said, and then sucked ice water through the straw.

"How's your head?"

"It hurts."

"Can you use it?"

Lane nodded.

"Good. I read your profiles on the Westmont Prep killer. We need to talk."

CHAPTER 35

The day after Lane opened his eyes, on a sunny Sunday afternoon, he was discharged from the hospital. The subdural hemorrhage was clearing and his lungs were functioning at 80 percent efficiency. He had a list of restrictions, limited mostly by his concussion, that included driving a car, riding in one for more than a mile or two, computer use, and reading. He left the hospital with the suggestion of sequestration in a dark room with no stimuli until his headache passed. Lane agreed to everything and signed the discharge papers. He would have signed just about anything in order to get out of the hospital bed. Rory helped him now as he shuffled up the driveway at the cottage on Winston Lane. Lane glimpsed his reflection in the car window. His head was dressed in white gauze.

"Good Christ, I look like Phineas Gage."

Rory took him under the arm. "The bandages stay on until the staples come out. It's probably better that we're trapped in Peppermill. It'll be easier to control you."

They walked up the steps to the front door.

"What do you think of the place?" Lane asked. "I told you it was cute."

"I like the Dark Lord in the fridge. How'd you manage that?"

"I stopped in Munster and talked with Kip, told him what I needed it for and that I was willing to spend a fortune to procure a few bottles. My head is starting to pound. Maybe I'll have one to quiet the drumming."

"Not a chance," Rory said.

She helped him onto the couch. The Foldger-Gruden brush she had used earlier on the Kiddiejoy doll poked from the breast pocket of her shirt.

"I see you found the brushes," Lane said as he sank down.

"I did. I'm sure those cost you a fortune, too. These have been discontinued for two decades."

"You can find anything on the Internet. It just depends on how much you want to spend." Lane adjusted himself. "All of it was money well spent, with the deliberate and transparent purpose of bribing you to stay for a day or two."

"You've got me for more than a day or two, Dr. Phillips. We're stuck in Peppermill until you're cleared to drive a car. Or ride in one, for that matter. Doctors said at least two weeks."

Lane laid his head back on the couch cushion and closed his eyes. "If you were anxious to leave, you'd load me into your car and speed back to Chicago, potholes and all. We're playing by the rules and staying in this little town because you're caught on the Westmont Prep case."

Rory sat next to him. "The corkboard in the other room definitely has my attention."

"And while I was sleeping peacefully in the hospital,

you read through my profile of the Westmont Prep killer. What do you make of it so far?"

Rory shook her head. "Something about the case feels off."

Lane opened his eyes and lifted his head. "Keep going."

"My first thought is that Charles Gorman doesn't match your profile of the killer. Besides some overlaps in geography and basic knowledge about the students, which would apply to *any* faculty member, Gorman doesn't sound like he possesses many characteristics of the killer you described."

"Let's review what we know." Lane pointed to his bandaged head. "I'm cloudy."

"The crime scene," Rory said.

"Isolated. Dark. Something someone could easily control, especially if he were familiar with the house."

"No chance of anyone unexpectedly stumbling upon him," Rory said.

This was how Rory and Lane operated in their professional relationship—freely and fluently, working off each other's thoughts and oftentimes finishing each other's sentences.

"Other than the students who were in the woods, there was no chance that unwanted spectators would see anything," she said.

"Correct. And no chance anything would be caught on surveillance video. A very controlled environment," Lane added. "Somewhere he could lie in wait. No defensive wounds on the vics means he surprised them. He was at the house when the two kids arrived."

"Organized. Preplanned. He chose the location, he chose the method, he chose the weapon."

They both paused a moment.

"Tell me about the killer," Rory said. "Describe his mind-set and where this type of violence came from."

"Well," Lane said. "Let's start with what we know about the victims. Both students. Both male. One was entering his junior year, the other his senior year. No drugs were found in either of their systems. The perp wanted them dead for a reason. The killings were not random. They were planned. What type of person would want to kill two teenagers? Someone with a troubled past. Someone with resentment toward men. The girl at the scene was unharmed. Assuming she encountered the perp and was allowed to live, the killer was likely close to his mother."

"Your profile suggested a strong maternal bond," Rory said.

Lane nodded. "Strong, but perhaps fractured in some way. The bond with his mother is unnatural. Maybe rooted in love, but one that has morphed to something abnormal and unhealthy. And a nonexistent or toxic relationship with his father. Either the father figure in his life was absent, for which the perp felt scorned, or his relationship with his father was abusive, for which the perp felt offended and resentful. We need to know more about the victims. Were they good kids? Were they bullies? Did they impact the perp's life in such a way as to trigger his inner thoughts about his father?"

Another pause filled the room as each of them ran through scenarios.

"So," Lane said. "We know *what* happened—two kids were killed at an abandoned boarding house. We know *how* it happened—they were ambushed and their throats were slashed."

"But to figure out the *why* and the *who*," Rory said, "we're going to need to do a lot of digging."

Rory's gaze drifted to the three-season room, where the photos of the victims were tacked to the corkboard. The two students who were killed and the three who had killed themselves. She wanted to go to the board now and stare at the photos. She longed for that feeling of intimacy to the lost souls that she conjured every time she reconstructed a homicide.

"The kids who are killing themselves," Rory said. "Maybe they're doing it to escape their misery. Maybe guilt is pulling them back to the scene of the crime, and death feels like their only option."

"What are they feeling guilty about?"

Rory kept her gaze focused toward the three-season room.

"A secret?" she finally said. "Secrets have a way of eating people alive."

"The Compton kid certainly had something he wanted to get off his chest when he talked with Mack Carter."

"So, if we agree that the portrait of the killer doesn't resemble Charles Gorman, and we work off the assumption that there is a group of students who know more about that night than they told the police, then it's a logical conclusion that the students' guilt stems from what really happened at the abandoned boarding house that night. And that guilt is pulling them back to that house and the train tracks to end their lives."

CHAPTER 36

Gavin Harms walked along the boulevard that ran in front of the school's main entrance. Summer session was winding down, and his senior year would officially begin soon. The campus was empty. Those students who were left to spend their summer at Westmont Prep were holed up in their dorm rooms or in the library studying for finals. The campus was noticeably quieter than normal, even for summer. Enrollment had dropped after the murders at the boarding house, the first contraction in the school's history. Westmont Prep had always been comfortably full, and enrollment had always needed to be capped, the overflow being placed on a long and doubtful waiting list. But since the killings at the abandoned boarding house the summer before, many students had simply never returned for fall session. Those who did promptly exited campus when the year was over, leaving summer enrollment scarce. June had marked the one-year anniversary, and Gavin was among only a score of students who studied through the summer. God forbid, he thought, his aunt and uncle allow him to come home for summer.

The sturdy balusters of the Westmont Prep's prestigious library building rose up to support the pediment where the school's motto was displayed: Arrive alone, leave together. Gavin had never bought into the saying. Not when he was a wide-eyed freshman, and not today when he was just nine months from graduating. He felt more alone now than ever before. But much of that sentiment came from his decisions over the past year. Much of it came from the secret he was harboring. A secret he was worried would stay hidden for only a short time longer. He had done everything in his power to prevent it from coming to the surface. He had done things he regretted, and things he wished he could take back.

Arrive alone, leave together.

He wondered if he and Gwen would be able to leave this place together, or if each of them would walk off alone and in different directions. He cinched his backpack tighter as he walked past the library and to his dorm. Inside, he locked the door and pulled up his laptop, where he looked up Ryder Hillier's blog. Since Mack Carter's podcast had been placed on indefinite hiatus, Ryder's site was his only source for updates. He had heard that Ryder was in a world of trouble for posting the video of Theo's lifeless body lying by the tracks. Theo's parents were suing her, and with any luck her site would soon be shut down, too. Then Westmont Prep would be shielded from the world and, with any luck, everything in its past would fade from memory. The less attention the rest of the country paid to Peppermill, Indiana, the better. All Gavin needed was to ride out this latest storm, get through his senior year, and leave this place behind. Then things would be better.

As long as Ryder's blog was active, though, Gavin would use it for updates. Today, however, she had posted nothing new. The message board was filled with conspiracy theories about the boarding house, the train that ran alongside it, the Man in the Mirror, and why students kept killing themselves. The latest theory among the true-crime fanatics was that the two Westmont Prep kids had died in a homicide-suicide scenario, with one killing the other, hanging him on the gate, then returning to the abandoned boarding house to slice his own throat. The other students who had returned to the house to kill themselves were following some coded message that was left behind. This theory had been refuted by the medical examiner's report that determined that neither neck wound had been self-inflicted. Still, the true-crime nuts ran with it and shouted about a police cover-up.

All the eager and over-the-top theories about Westmont Prep were caused by the case being closed so quickly. When police found so much damning evidence against Mr. Gorman in the days after the slaughter, the public at large received few details about what was going on that night in the woods. The public learned only that a teacher had gone on a psychotic rampage and had killed two students after writing a manifesto about his sadistic fantasies. Then, as police closed in on their man, Mr. Gorman went back to the scene of the crime and tried to kill himself. Enough of the story had been left untold for the true-crime crowd to run wild.

Without Mack Carter's podcast, Gavin checked Ryder's blog every so often to see if anyone accidentally stumbled over a morsel of truth. To this point, no one had. Of course, Gavin knew next to nothing about the ongoing police investigation, or how much of the truth they had actually uncovered. For now, the authorities seemed content to stand behind their original conclusion about Mr. Gorman and his motives. But Theo's suicide had started them off again on a quest to discover what they had missed. Gavin was worried they might find it.

There was a knock on the door, and Gavin quickly shut down Ryder's site and closed his laptop. When he opened his door, he found Gwen in the hallway. Gavin still hadn't gotten used to her appearance. Over the last year, since the night of the murders, Gwen had lost fifteen pounds from a frame that had already been petite. The result was gaunt cheeks and cadaverous shoulder blades. A straight-A student since birth, Gwen saw her GPA nosedive during her junior year. More alarming than her appearance or her grades was her lack of concern. Gwen had not only lost her interest in academics but withdrawn from nearly everything in her life, including her relationship with Gavin. This was most dangerous of all. The further Gwen drifted from him, the less he knew about her actions. Now, more than ever, they had to stay together. They had to stay quiet. Just for one more year. Just until they graduated from Westmont and headed off to college. Then things would get better. The images from that night would fade. Their consciences would heal. They would forget. Their secret would be preserved, and their lives would return to normal.

For the first six months after the slaughter, Gavin had tried to save his relationship with Gwen. But he felt things slipping away. After Danielle's suicide, things hit rock bottom, and now Gavin and Gwen talked only when necessary. Those times mostly consisted of situations like tonight, when Gavin needed to talk her off the ledge and keep her quiet.

Gavin motioned her inside and then leaned his head into the hallway to make sure she was alone.

"How do you feel?" Gavin asked as he closed the door.

"Terrible."

"You need to eat something, Gwen. Seriously."

"Theo's mom texted me."

"What did she want?"

"She said she can't get ahold of you and that she wants to talk to us."

"Don't call her back," Gavin said quickly.

"Gavin, her son died. She wants answers, and she naturally thinks we might be able to provide them."

"What are we supposed to tell her? She'll want to know what was going on. Not just lately, but last year, too. If we start telling people what we know, sooner or later one of us will say something we're not supposed to. Is that what you want? Do you want the police to start asking us about that night again? Do you remember *every single detail* you told them? Because *they* do. And they'll want to know why you remember things differently now, a year later, than you did back then. And once we screw up our story, they'll start poking around again. Do you want the police to start looking at what happened that night?"

Gwen shook her head.

"Then don't talk to anyone, okay?"

"Fine," she said. "Did you check Ryder Hillier's stuff?"

"Yeah, nothing new."

Tears welled in Gwen's eyes. "I don't know how much longer I can do this."

Gavin ran a hand through his hair. He stared at Gwen and worried that she wouldn't make it through the year.

"Just calm down," he finally said. "I'll figure something out."

Westmont Prep
Summer 2019

Session 4
Journal Entry: ASSISTED SUICIDE

I stayed in my room after the ambulance took my mother away. Mrs. Peterson knocked a couple of times to check on me. I stayed silent, sitting on the floor with my back pressed against the door, until she finally gave up. I heard my father come home in the middle of the night, and I strained to listen to his brief conversation with Mrs. Peterson. I didn't catch much. After the front door closed and Mrs. Peterson was gone, I hustled under my covers, certain that my father would come to give me an update. But he didn't. He simply climbed the stairs and went to bed.

Eventually, I went back to my door and stared through the keyhole until I was sure he was asleep. Something brewed in my chest the night my father ignored me, not even bothering to tell me my mother's condition. My father's disregard ignited whatever was smoldering inside of me, and in the days to come, when I learned that the mother I loved was gone forever, those flames burned like a wildfire and have never gone out.

My bedroom door squeaked slightly when I opened it. I knew what I needed and exactly where to find it. I had *planned this out many times but had never managed the gumption to go through with it. Back then when I plotted, I did so with the promise that I'd proceed with my plan if my mother ever needed it. But it was just a fantasy. A blatant lie I repeated to fool myself. I had used this fictitious time in the future, when I would put an end to my father terrorizing my mother, as a way to ignore the cowardice that ruled my life. The con allowed me to deflect how weak and feeble I felt every time I stared through that keyhole and watched him beat her. It worked for a while. Too long, actually, because it had allowed him to abuse her for the last time.*

I finally left my bedroom, crept down the basement stairs, and headed to the back corner that harbored the tools I needed. I had originally thought I'd have to do this with my mother home. But with her gone, it would be much easier. Back upstairs I stopped in the hallway. To my left was my open bedroom door; to my right was the spot where my father had pulled my mother over the dining room table earlier in the evening. I walked past the table, to the bottom of the stairs where my mother's body had lain when the ambulance arrived. I took the stairs one at a time. They creaked softly under my fourteen-year-old frame, but I was suddenly unafraid. A sense of purpose filled me as I carried the thick rope in my gloved hands. I felt a resolve telling me that even if my father woke, I would be able to carry things out as planned. There was nothing that could stop me.

When I pushed open the bedroom door, the light from the hallway slanted across his sleeping body. He was snoring the way he always did after he'd been drinking. He was on his back, and I wasted no time. I carefully laid the rope across his neck. He swallowed when I did this, and his snoring momentarily stopped. I stood still until it started again, then I slithered under the bed. It was dark without the light from the hallway to guide me. I felt for the ends of the rope and pulled them down so they hung by my ears. Then I carefully wrapped each length around my hands. I was wearing garden gloves from the basement to prevent rope burns. I slid my knees upward so they were against my chest. It was a tight squeeze, and in order to gain the leverage I needed I had to lift the mattress slightly. When I did, it caused my father to stir. I feared he was about to wake. There was no time to position myself.

I pulled down on each end of the rope. At the same time, I leaned backward into the floorboards while my knees pressed firmly against the mattress above me. I closed my eyes when I heard him cough and felt him squirm. I wanted to cover my ears, but I needed to hear him die. I had to be sure. The mattress bucked wildly as he thrashed above me. I held on with all my strength. Five straight minutes. Until the muscles in my arms cramped, and my back burned. Until my legs went numb, and until my father finally stopped moving. I forced myself to hold the rope tightly for five minutes longer.

When I finally released my grip, my muscles refused to relax. They stayed taut and contracted, and a searing pain coursed through my knees when I straightened them. I waited a few more minutes, but the only noise I heard was my breathing. I slid from under the bed and looked briefly at my father. I knew he was dead. I didn't need to check. Instead, I tied the ends of the rope to the top of the headboard and pushed his lifeless body until it hung from the edge of the bed. I made sure there was nothing in the room that would give away my presence there that night. Then I headed back down to the basement and dropped the garden gloves in the corner where I found them, climbed the stairs to my room, and closed the door. I stared through the keyhole all night long, until the dark shadows were replaced by dawn. My father never appeared in the keyhole again. It was a new day.

I pulled the tassel and laid it between the pages as I shut my journal.

"I was too young at the time to understand the way I felt about myself, but our sessions have clarified things for me. The feeling was disgust. Since that day, I've realized that the weak have no place on this earth and that those who prey on them are equally worthy of extinction."

We stared at each other the way we usually did after I finished reading from my journal.

"Do you disagree?" I finally asked.

She shook her head. "Not at all."

"Good. Then I want to tell you about what I have planned here on campus. It will take care of both the pathetically fragile and the bullies who take advantage of them. You're the only one who would understand, and since you're not able to tell anyone what we discuss during our sessions, I know you'll keep my secret."

CHAPTER 37

In Westmont Prep's long history, no student had ever been expelled. Once Westmont accepted the individual, the institution accepted the challenge of guiding them, reshaping them, and turning their lives around. They did it with discipline, structure, and counseling. Lots and lots of counseling.

Christian Casper held a medical degree in psychiatry and had completed a fellowship in child and adolescent psychotherapy. Along with Gabriella Hanover, Dr. Casper was the codirector of counseling at Westmont Prep. Drs. Casper and Hanover oversaw the caseworkers who did their best to guide the teenagers who spent their formative years at the school. Most teenagers who passed through the gates of Westmont Prep left the institution better human beings and more able to face the challenges of life than before they arrived.

Like much of Westmont Prep faculty, Dr. Casper had a residence on campus. In addition to his role as a therapist, he taught an AP U.S. History course, a full-time position to which he had dedicated the past decade of his life. He lived in the number eighteen duplex on Teacher's Row, which doubled as his office. Gwen Montgomery sat across from him now, their session coming to an end.

"You haven't brought your journal to our sessions lately," Dr. Casper said. "Have you been journaling?"

"Not as much as usual."

Dr. Casper did not respond, which Gwen knew from years of sessions with him meant that he was not satisfied with her answer.

"I haven't really been thinking about that stuff lately. Like, *me* stuff. I've been distracted all week."

"By what?"

Gwen shrugged. "Just getting used to being a junior and everything that goes along with it."

"What's so different about junior year?" Dr. Casper asked.

"Upperclassman stuff."

"Let me guess, you started going out to the abandoned boarding house."

Gwen looked away, and Dr. Casper laughed.

"It's the worst-kept secret at Westmont Prep. The old house in the woods where upperclassmen drink beer and do other stupid things? It's been going on long before you arrived here and will go on long after. Or at least until they tear that wretched thing down. Next year, when you're a senior, you'll be doing the same thing to unsuspecting juniors."

"Doing what?" Gwen asked.

Dr. Casper pulled up his laptop. "Giving them a hard time. It's tradition for the seniors to razz the juniors."

Gwen wondered if Dr. Casper's definition of "razzing" included being blindfolded and lined up on train tracks. And even if Dr. Casper knew about the gathering at the abandoned boarding house, Gwen was sure he knew nothing about the details of what went on there. She was just learning them herself.

"Put it in your journal," Dr. Casper said. "Write down your experiences, and what it is about those experiences that bothers you. We'll talk about them next time. Deal?"

Gwen nodded.

Dr. Casper tapped his keyboard. "Do you need refills on your prescription?"

Gwen was silent.

Dr. Casper looked up at her. Gwen nodded.

"Yeah. I need more."

"I'll send it in now and you can pick it up at the nurse's office tomorrow."

Gwen was silent until Dr. Casper stopped tapping on his computer and looked back up at her.

"It's summertime," he said. "I expect you to break a few rules. I'd be worried if you didn't. Just don't get carried away."

CHAPTER 38

The first week of the summer session was underway, and after only a single day of classes it was proving to be as awful as predicted. The students stared through classroom windows daydreaming of being anywhere else, romanticizing the summer they were missing and imagining their liberated classmates soaking up the sun during beach parties on long summer days and laughing around bonfires at night. The only positive was that the curriculum was light, with each pupil required to take only two courses. Gavin and Gwen had strategically planned the same schedule—Mr. Gorman's Chemistry class and Dr. Casper's APUSH course.

Mr. Gorman's class came with the added burden of a three-hour lab on Tuesdays and Thursdays to go along with the Monday, Wednesday, and Friday classroom time. Getting it out of the way while dealing with only one other course was a begrudgingly legitimate excuse for being trapped at Westmont during the summer, as Gavin's aunt had mentioned in the letter Gwen had read.

Gwen and Gavin stood next to each other in the lab, safety goggles protecting their eyes and test tubes and beakers in front of them. Across from them were Theo and Danielle, and at the neighboring lab table were Tanner Landing and Bridget Matthews, who had been partnered with Andrew Gross and another senior. Mr. Gorman droned in the background about the chemical reaction that was about to take place.

"You guys interested in heading up to Chicago one weekend this summer to catch a Cubs game?" Andrew asked.

Tanner nearly salivated at the invitation. He nodded. "For sure!"

"Good," Andrew said, a smile forming on his face. "I hear there's a train that runs right up to Wrigley Field. I'll see if I can get you a seat on it."

The other seniors laughed from the table next to them.

"But this time I'll get you a seat that doesn't splinter so badly."

Tanner smiled because he didn't know what else to do. His cheeks reddened.

Mr. Gorman came over to Gwen's lab table. "Miss Montgomery will demonstrate for us the chemical reaction first and then you will repeat the process at your own stations. Gather around."

There were just twelve students in the lab, three groups of four, and they all converged around Gwen's table as she poured pink liquid from a beaker into a Florence flask, which Gavin held with a clamp secured around the neck and with the bottom over the flame of a Bunsen burner. Inside the flask, crystals starting gyrating as the liquid boiled from the heat. Gwen held a pipette over the flask. When she titrated a single drop into the pink boiling liquid, it created a loud popping noise before a thick white gaseous fog formed inside the flask, which grew in intensity until the gas spilled over the edge and streamed down the side of the beaker.

"Mr. Landing, can you explain why the vapor is moving down the exterior of the flask rather than floating into the air?"

"Because it's got that pink stuff in it?"

Mr. Gorman looked around the lab. "Miss Montgomery?"

"Because the iodine vapor has a higher density than air. Basically, it's heavy and so it sinks."

"Correct. Mr. Landing, let's try again. Tell me about the reaction that is taking place between the ammonia and the iodine. What is the snapping noise we are hearing?"

Tanner looked at the pink bubbling fluid as it fizzled and spit off more vapor.

"Um, it's explosive?"

"Very cute. Can you tell us what's happening with the chemistry?"

"Um, some sort of reaction that's pretty sweet."

"Miss Montgomery?"

"Nitrogen triiodide is unstable," Gwen said, "because the nitrogen and iodine atoms are different sizes. The bonds connecting the nuclei are breaking, which causes the popping noise. When the ionic bonds break, they release the fog or vapor."

"Excellent, Miss Montgomery. Maybe you could show Mr. Landing where that information is in the textbook he clearly hasn't yet opened. Now let's add the other substance to the smoking flask."

Gwen titrated a few drops from a second pipette into the flask Gavin was holding. As soon as the substance met the fluid inside the flask, the fog dissipated.

"Buzzkill," Tanner said, offering a stupid smile. "I wonder what would happen if you swallowed that stuff."

This got a few chuckles from the seniors.

"You'd lose more brain cells than you have left to offer, Mr. Landing."

Mr. Gorman's comeback caused the entire class to burst into laughter. Gavin laughed so hard he had to steady the flask with both hands to prevent spillage.

"Settle down," Mr. Gorman said. "Everyone break into your groups and run the experiment yourselves. Discard everything into the sinks under the hood. The write-up summary will be due at the end of the period."

Mr. Gorman went to the front of the lab and sat at his desk to riffle through papers.

"Tonight," Andrew said while he was standing around Gwen's lab table. "Thirteen-three-five. Eleven o'clock."

Gwen and Gavin looked at each other and then to the others.

"It's a weekday," Gwen said. "Curfew is nine."

Andrew smiled. "Then don't get caught."

CHAPTER 39

The drive to Peppermill from South Bend was just under an hour. Marc McEvoy made the trip after a busy morning at the office. He left under the ruse of a lunch meeting with a client. Really, though, today was for reconnaissance. He took Indiana Route 2 west out of South Bend. It was a straight shot to Peppermill, and after an hour he pulled into the parking lot of the Metra station. From his parked car, he waited five minutes for the train to arrive, then watched as commuters stepped onto the platform and dispersed.

Next, he drove to the Motel 6 on Grand Avenue, clocking the distance on his odometer at 0.6 miles from the train station. An easy walk. Then, he drove north until he reached Route 77. That was another mile, also easily tackled when necessary. Finally, he drove Route 77 until he saw mile marker thirteen, after which he slowed to twenty miles an hour as he studied the foliage off to the right. He located the spot in the forest where he would enter. From there, he knew it would be another half a mile to his destination.

All told, from the train station, he'd have to cover about two and a half miles on foot the night of the Man in the Mirror. No problem.

To make sure he knew the route without question, Marc pulled a U-turn and headed back to the Motel 6 to rehearse the route one more time. When the night came, he wanted no surprises.

CHAPTER 40

The group made it to the edge of the forest by ten o'clock on Tuesday night, having followed the same 13:3:5 route they had taken on Saturday. The PRIVATE PROPERTY sign hung from the drooping chain with the boarding house in front of them. Interior lights attempted to penetrate the painted windows and resulted in a blunted glow that evaporated into the ink-black night.

Andrew Gross walked out of the front door and stood on the landing.

"All six of you came back." He shrugged. "I'm shocked the train didn't even get one of you to quit. Don't worry. We've got the whole summer."

Andrew disappeared back through the front door. Gwen and her friends waited for a moment before they headed toward the house. Walking up the stairs felt mythical. They had heard of the place for so long that walking inside felt like a dream. Although live with electricity, the ceiling bulbs had long since burned out and were too high to safely replace. Their absence cast the staircase and tall foyer ceilings in darkness. Construction-style orange-boxed spotlights stood on a tripod and illuminated the large front room off the foyer. The corners of the room were heavy with empty beer bottles, discarded bottles of Tito's Vodka, and crushed cans of mixers.

Andrew stood in front of the group of seniors who waited in the front room. The two groups—seniors on one side, juniors on the other—faced each other.

"Within the walls of Westmont Prep, a private group exists. Many have heard about this group, but few know anything about it. The faculty denies that it exists, and outsiders have been trying to penetrate its secrets for years. You are now looking at the senior members. Freshmen and sophomores are not worthy enough to be included, and only select juniors are considered for initiation. The six of you are the only ones to earn an invitation.

"But acceptance into the elite ranks of our society requires that you pass a series of challenges. Failure to complete a challenge results in expulsion from the group. The challenges culminate on the night you surely have all heard about—the night new initiates face the Man in the Mirror. This happens on the longest day of the summer— June twenty-first. The summer solstice tradition reaches back to the inaugural year when Westmont opened its doors in 1937. The things that take place at this abandoned boarding house are for society members only and can't be discussed with any nonmembers. Secrecy is one of our greatest oaths.

"Each year, the society chooses a teacher for new initiates to target. Last summer, it was Mrs. Rasmussen. As juniors, *we* were tasked with certain challenges geared around her. You all remember the smoke bomb that went off during her commencement speech? The dead raccoon in her desk drawer? The day she got locked in the bathroom until the fire department rescued her? The day her residence on Teacher's Row was breached and lightly vandalized? Police were called and students were questioned." Andrew opened his arms to indicate the group of seniors behind him. "None of us were implicated in any of the incidents. That's because of our oath of secrecy.

"You will be required to complete similar challenges this summer. Your subject should never see the strike coming. He should never know who delivered it. We work in the shadows, and although much of the student body will know the society was behind a particular prank, no one should be able to identify any members of our group. If you *are* caught during one of the challenges, the secrecy of our organization demands that you shoulder the blame yourself."

Andrew took a couple of steps toward them.

"Are all of these rules understood?"

Gwen and her friends nodded, none fully comprehending what they were agreeing to, still confused by the reality of standing inside the infamous boarding house.

"Good. Your subject this summer is Mr. Gorman. In a nutshell, you'll make summer very unpleasant for him. Tanner, do you have enough brain cells left to understand this?"

A few of the seniors behind Andrew laughed.

"After you have successfully completed the challenges, you will have an opportunity to become full members. This opportunity will present itself on June twenty-first, when you all gather in the woods behind this house on the night of the Man in the Mirror. You've probably all heard rumors about what takes place on the summer solstice, but trust when I tell you that whatever you've heard pales in comparison to the real thing. Those who make it through initiation remain members for life."

Andrew looked each of the juniors in the eye.

"Are there any questions?"

If there were, they didn't have the chance to ask them. Just as Andrew finished speaking, the whistle of the train's horn echoed in the distance.

"The train!" one of the seniors said.

Andrew smiled. "Time to move."

A rumble shook the walls, then a roar followed as the train approached.

"Open the windows!" Andrew said, looking at the juniors. "Open everything!"

Quickly, the seniors went to work pulling the spray-painted windows of the front room open. Others ran through the house doing the same. The doors to every room were thrown wide. In the kitchen, cabinets and pantries were ripped open.

Gwen knew the folklore. The train that ran next to the abandoned boarding house carried the spirits of those who had been claimed by the Man in the Mirror. The spirits entered the house but could reside only in rooms with windows and doors that remained closed. Closets, dressers, armoires. The spirits could rest anywhere that was sealed.

Gwen took off. She couldn't tell if what she felt was a sense of dread or just silly excitement over being part of the myth she had heard so much about during her first two years at Westmont Prep. She raced up the stairs with Danielle. They went into the first bedroom and pulled open the windows. When they did, the growl of the passing freight train grew louder. They opened closet doors, bathroom cabinets, and an old trunk that sat in the corner. They ran from room to room and did the same until they were sure everything was open.

When they made it downstairs, the others were returning from different parts of the house. In the front room Andrew began pulling a tarp over the tall standing mirror that rested in the corner. Spirits were also able to reside in uncovered mirrors, Gwen knew. And until the train was gone, one should never look at their own reflection.

The train's whistle blew just as Andrew cloaked the mirror. Before he had it fully covered, Gwen glanced at the surface for a split second. She was at a sharp angle and could not see her own reflection but had a clear view of Tanner's. He was staring at the same spot on the mirror. Gwen closed her eyes and squeezed her lids tight.

It was June 11. Ten days later, Andrew Gross would lay dead in that room and Tanner Landing would be impaled on the wrought iron fence outside.

PART V

August 2020

CHAPTER 41

It was evening when the doorbell rang. Rory and Lane had batted ideas around all afternoon until Lane grew exhausted. He was on the couch with his head back against the cushions. Through the front window Rory saw an unmarked squad car pull into the driveway and park behind her own.

"Detectives are here," Rory said, instinctually securing her glasses. "Are you up for talking?"

"If they're here on a Sunday, I don't think we have a choice."

Rory stood and headed for the door. She pulled her beanie cap low on her forehead before opening the door.

"Ms. Moore," Detective Ott said.

"Detective. Come on in."

Rory stepped aside to allow the detective to enter the cottage. Lane stood on wobbly legs and shook hands with Ott.

"Dr. Phillips. Henry Ott."

"Nice to meet you, Detective."

"We actually met already at the hospital, but you were just coming out of it."

"That's right. I'm afraid my head is still ringing. You mind if I sit?"

"Of course. I'll be brief. Or we can do this another day when you're feeling better."

"Let's get it out of the way now," Lane said.

They sat around the front room table—Rory and Lane on the couch, the detective in the adjacent chair. Lane ran Detective Ott through his presence in Peppermill, the podcast, and his association with Mack Carter. He went step by step through his three days in Peppermill, finishing with the evening he had gone back to Mack's place to review the audio from the night Mack had discovered Theo Compton's body by the tracks near the abandoned boarding house.

Ott listened carefully, asking few questions along the way. He pitched Rory a couple of lazy follow-ups from their first meeting. She recounted her version of events again. Besides having nothing to hide, she also had a photographic memory, so the second time through her story was a verbatim statement of the first—something that either solidified her honesty or shrouded it in doubt.

"You're the only detective I've ever talked to who doesn't take notes," Lane said.

Ott shifted in his chair as if what he was about to say was uncomfortable.

"Yeah, I guess my visit is both professional and personal. I'd rather not record it, in case what I'm about to ask doesn't go over so well."

Lane nodded his head. "Ask away."

"Officially, the Westmont Prep Killings are closed and have been for a year. Charles Gorman was accused and, although not technically convicted through the court system, he's our guy. He understood what he did and tried to get out of it by jumping in front of that train. We placed him under arrest and formally charged him in his hospital bed the next day while he drifted in a coma. He'll likely never stand trial, but officially it's a done deal."

"Officially," Rory said.

Ott ran his palm over the stubble of his chin.

"Yeah. *On* the record, the case is closed. But *off* the record, something about it has never sat right with me. Ever since I showed up on Westmont Prep campus the night of the crime and drove in a golf cart through those woods to that horrific scene, things fell perfectly into place. *Too* perfectly. Don't get me wrong, I was happy to close the case, and almost every bit of evidence we gathered led us to Gorman. But every time another student kills themselves, I question everything I've ever known about the case."

"Like what?" Rory asked. Her posture had changed. She was no longer sunk into the couch hoping for the cushions to hide her. She was now straight-backed and alert. Her mind allowed her thoughts to move only toward that which made no sense. Most people avoided confusion and chaos. Rory was drawn to it. The mysterious and unexplained intrigued her, and she could no more ignore them than a moth could resist a light source.

"Well, the biggest question I ask myself is whether we got the right guy, or did something else go on that night? Is something *still* going on?"

"That's what Mack Carter was trying to figure out," Lane said.

"Yeah, well, that's pop culture." Ott waved his hand. "He was a television personality producing a podcast for sensationalism and for ratings and profit and celebrity. That's why I never had any comment when he asked for it. I prefer to work in the shadows. I don't need the public knowing every step I take on the case or every lead I come across. And I definitely don't need citizen detectives chasing those leads." Ott shook his head. "But now Mack is dead, and I've got a fire marshal thinking the gas leak at his house was manufactured."

Rory and Lane looked at each other. They hadn't yet verbalized their fears about what had happened at Mack Carter's house, but they both sensed the unasked questions that floated between them.

"Someone wanted to stop Mack Carter from looking into this case?" Rory asked.

"I guess that's the million-dollar question," Ott said.

"The latest kid to kill himself, the Compton kid," Lane said. "He talked with Mack. Part of the conversation was aired on the podcast. The kid made it sound like there was a group of students inside Westmont Prep who knew something about that night that they've kept to themselves. He said Gorman didn't kill his classmates. Not in so many words, but he hinted at the idea."

"If those students exist," Ott said, "they're not talking. I've interviewed every kid at the school. Many of them more than once. None of them have anything new to say, so if there's a group of kids who are hiding something, they're staying quiet."

"Or killing themselves," Rory said.

There was a short stretch of silence in the room before Ott finally looked at Rory. "I guess that's why I'm here tonight."

"Do you have a different theory about what happened?" Rory asked.

"No. If I look back through the case, which I do every

time another Westmont Prep kid commits suicide, just about everything still points to Charles Gorman."

"How did you get onto Gorman?" Lane asked. "From what I've learned so far, there was no physical evidence tying him to the crime scene."

"There wasn't, but there was plenty of circumstantial evidence to go after him."

"You said *just about* everything pointed to Gorman," Rory said. "What didn't fit?"

Detective Ott leaned forward to rest his elbows on his knees. "That's my biggest problem." He looked at Lane. "You have anything to drink?"

"Unfortunately, not much. I've only been here a few days."

"We've got beer," Rory said.

"Could I have one?"

"Sure thing," Rory said, doing her best to act calm.

But as she walked to the kitchen to pour a Dark Lord, her hands were trembling with impatience and her mind ravenous for information.

CHAPTER 42

"I arrived at the boarding house in the early morning hours," Detective Ott said as he held a pint of Dark Lord in his hand while he leaned back in the chair. "Three or four o'clock. I found two dead kids. One was impaled on the gate outside, the other was in a puddle of his own blood in one of the rooms inside. Only one student remained at the house, a girl named Gwen Montgomery. She was in shock and sitting on the ground next to the kid on the gate. She had blood on her, and at first I thought she was injured. But most of the blood was Tanner Landing's." Ott took a deep breath. "She said she tried to pull him down off the gate before realizing it was futile. He was impaled quite dramatically. So she sat down next to him, called nine-one-one, and then rocked back and forth until the first responders arrived. She was so out of it, the officers allowed her to sit on the ground until I showed up."

Ott sat up and bit his bottom lip before shaking his head and looking at Rory.

"This girl," he said, "she's the only thing that doesn't make sense." He took a long sip of stout. "The blood on her hands and chest? *Most* of it belonged to Tanner Landing, but some of it remains unidentified. We've never been able to place it, never figured out who that blood belongs to."

"What's the girl say?" Lane asked. He, too, was sitting up and leaning forward toward the detective.

"She said she ran through the woods to get to the house, where all the students planned to meet. When she arrived, she found Tanner on the gate and tried to lift him off, bloodying herself in the process. Says she never went inside. The unidentified blood was also found on Tanner Landing's body. Not much, just traces. And there was a lot of blood at the scene. It looked like a goddamn slaughter. The Landing kid was cut across the throat and impaled through the chin and face. Most of the blood was his."

"So this unidentified blood could belong to the killer?" Rory asked.

"It could, yeah," Detective Ott said.

"But the blood didn't match Charles Gorman?"

Ott took another long sip of beer.

"It didn't match anyone. Gorman, Gwen Montgomery, or any of the students. We tested the entire faculty, too. No match."

"You tested everyone?" Rory asked. "The entire staff, custodians, part-time employees?"

"Anyone and everyone who stepped foot on that campus was tested," Ott said. "All blanks."

"So how did you get on Gorman so fast?"

"After I surveyed the scene, I allowed the crime scene guys to do their work of documenting everything—photo and video. The house, the bodies, the woods, the train tracks. While they were working I went back to the main campus and started gathering information. The whole campus was awake by that time, maybe five or six o'clock, with whispers about what had happened out at the abandoned boarding house. I had the dean of students, Dr. Gabriella Hanover, by my side. She walked me through the dorms. I questioned every student that morning. Quickly, informally, just to get a feel for what had happened. Most had no idea about the boarding house. But a few said they were there. They had gone the back way through the woods, and when they arrived at the house they saw Tanner Landing on the gate, panicked, and ran back to campus to call for help. The timing of the calls adds up. The Montgomery girl called first, and then a series of calls followed. I've read all of the nine-one-one transcripts and listened to the recordings. They all sound like panic-stricken teenagers.

"None of the students' stories sounded suspicious, and they all matched closely enough for my liking. None were on my radar at the time. Gwen Montgomery was the only student I didn't question that night. The EMTs transported her by ambulance to the hospital, where she spent the day and following night before they discharged her. By then, I was a day into my investigation and already on Gorman's trail.

"I talked with the faculty that morning after I questioned the students. I spoke with the assistant headmaster, Dr. Christian Casper. I spoke with a couple of teachers. The faculty was thin because it was summer and most of the teachers were gone. Nothing was interesting me during these interviews until I knocked on duplex number fourteen."

"Gorman's place," Lane said.

"As soon as he opened the door, I knew something was up. He was very nervous and evasive with his answers. There were a lot of inconsistencies with where he was the previous night and who he was with. I put him high on my initial list and told my supervisor about my suspicions. It was later in the day, after we pulled Tanner Landing off the fence and got him to the morgue, that we gained access to the kid's phone. We discovered a video that appeared to be shot through a bedroom window. The video depicted Charles Gorman . . ."

Ott glanced quickly at Rory and then took another sip of beer.

"Uh . . . mid-coital and in a state of ecstasy."

"Screwing?" Lane asked.

"Yeah. The video was of Gorman having sex in his bedroom and was . . ." Detective Ott looked up at the ceiling as he again searched for words. "The video was a total breach of privacy and could be considered quite embarrassing. We later learned that the Landing boy had uploaded the video to a social media site. The time line shows that he did this a few hours before he was killed."

Rory and Lane looked at each other. Partners in business for fifteen years, and lovers for more than a decade, they needed only eye contact to know what the other was thinking. Lane's profile of the killer included the likelihood that Tanner Landing's death—a wrought iron tine through the head—had been an act of revenge. The news of this video made the small oval on Lane's Venn diagram, the one that included the overlapping characteristics of Gorman and the Westmont Prep killer, grow a bit larger.

"I managed a search warrant the following day. Gorman wasn't home when Drs. Hanover and Casper unlocked his front door for us. We searched the house and found his manifesto hidden in a wall safe in his den."

"Manifesto?" Rory asked.

"Three handwritten pages describing in exact detail what he planned to do to Tanner Landing and Andrew Gross. It was a verbatim description of the crime scene. He named his victims. He described the way he would kill each of them. I later learned that Gorman had been the target of some sort of hazing by these two students. The video was the last straw and seemed to set him off. After we found the manifesto, we had enough to bring him in. The only problem was that we couldn't find him. We thought he ran, so we started looking for him. Put out an all-points to track him down."

"When did you find him?"

"One of our uniforms was at the crime scene, out at the abandoned boarding house. We were still collecting evidence at that point. When he did a sweep of the area surrounding the house, he found Gorman out by the train tracks. He'd jumped in front of the train. My guy thought he was dead at first, but he wasn't. We got medics on the scene and they kept him alive. They stabilized him at the hospital, but he was comatose for weeks before he finally opened his eyes. But Charles Gorman never really came back to us. His mind was gone. Traumatic brain injury left him in a persistent vegetative state."

"Brain dead," Lane said.

Detective Ott nodded. "He was eventually transferred to Grantville Psychiatric Hospital for the Criminally Insane. In fourteen months, he's never spoken a word. The doctors say he never will. I go to see him every so often. I used to go to make sure he knew I got him. Lately, though, I go to see if he's capable of telling me I got it wrong. He barely blinks when I'm in the room. I chased a few leads after Gorman tried to kill himself, just to tie up loose ends. They never led anywhere. Gorman was our guy, and that was that."

Rory adjusted her glasses again. "It adds up to a pretty convincing circumstantial case," she said. "A man with motive for revenge and a manifesto that's practically a confession."

"And we think Gorman understood this, which is why he tried to end his life."

"The only thing that never made sense was the unidentified blood?"

Detective Ott cocked his head back and downed the rest of his Dark Lord. "And the kids who keep throwing themselves in front of trains."

CHAPTER 43

Rory took Detective Ott's empty glass into the kitchen and poured him another Dark Lord. She poured one for herself as well.

"Thanks," Ott said when Rory handed him the glass of dark stout expertly topped with a thick head of foam.

"I'm getting the sense you didn't come here tonight to question Lane."

"No, I came for something else," Ott said, staring at Rory. "And I came alone for a reason."

She wanted to look away, as she normally would when someone forced eye contact. But tonight she didn't. Tonight she held the detective's gaze because she knew what he had come for.

"Yeah," she said. "I noticed your little pit bull was absent."

"Morris is a good detective, but he's young and green and he goes strictly by the book."

"But you bend the rules?" Lane asked.

"When I need to." Ott continued to look at Rory. "Full disclosure. After I spoke with you at the hospital, I recognized the name and did some research. Then I called your boss back in Chicago. Ron Davidson and I have a little history together, and he was pretty convincing when he told me you're good at what you do. I know the state guys down here have worked with you and Dr. Phillips through the Murder Accountability Project."

MAP was the company Lane had created to identify serial killers. He had developed an algorithm that tracked specific characteristics of homicides from around the country and found commonalities between them. When enough markers showed up, a hot spot was created and further analysis was done to see if the tags the algorithm picked up on pointed to a single person committing the murders. To date, MAP was responsible for uncovering a score of serial killers, and the software was being developed and licensed to police departments throughout the United States.

"Your work in forensic reconstruction is legendary," Ott said. "And frankly, I could use some help. I need someone else to take a look at the Westmont Prep case and come at it from a fresh perspective. I need someone who's able to piece together unsolved cases and find what others have missed."

Ott straightened his shoulders and expanded his chest. "I'm a proud man and a good detective. I believe I did everything I could with the Westmont Prep case. But if another kid goes out to that house and jumps in front of a train, I'll crumble."

The nape of Rory's neck was wet with perspiration and her lungs caught for a moment until she commanded them to expand.

"I'd need access to everything," Rory said before she knew the words were in her thoughts. "If I'm going to help you, I'll need it all."

Ott nodded as though he'd already considered this.

"I'll need to see the crime scene firsthand. Walk through it in person."

Rory didn't mention that walking in the footsteps of the dead was her way of gaining access to the victims whose souls waited for the closure she might provide. She had her own methods and her own philosophies when it came to breaking down a homicide that she had never tried to explain to others. She knew only that her routine allowed her to look at what everyone else had seen, and think what no one else had thought.

Ott nodded. "I can make that happen."

"And I'll need the files on the case. Not just what you want to feed me," Rory said. "Not just what you'd give the public. If you want me to find something you might have missed, I'll need everything you have. On the school, on the kids, on Gorman. No holding back."

Ott ran his tongue along the inside of his cheek as he considered this.

"Officially, as far as the public is concerned, we have our man. If my investigation into Mack Carter's death tells me otherwise, so be it. But as of right now, the Westmont Prep case is closed. The Carter case is being treated as a suspicious death, and my department is looking into all available leads. That's how my chief wants it, and I see his reasoning. If we were to formally reopen an investigation into the Westmont Prep Killings, dominos would start falling. Besides public fear that a killer is among us, there would be legal repercussions. Lawsuits from the victims' families. Lawsuits from Gorman's family. Heads would roll, and mine would be one of them. But off the record? Something about this case stinks, and I need help figuring out what it is."

Rory looked at Lane to make sure he was on board, but even before their eyes met she knew he was. It was why he had come to Peppermill to begin with, and why he had originally tried to convince Rory to join him. It was why he had stocked the fridge with Dark Lord and had created a replica of her home office in the three-season room.

"The true-crime nuts who followed Mack's podcast are going to have their own theories about what happened," Lane said.

"Yeah, well, nowadays everyone with an interest in crime thinks they can do twice as good as the detectives with half the information. The amateurs can create all the theories they want. Two-thirds of what those fools think they know is flat-out wrong, and the other third is inaccurate."

"Still," Lane said, "Mack's podcast had a big audience. People are going to be talking, especially now. Other reporters may even show up to finish what Mack started."

"Which is why I'm here tonight," Ott said. "I'm trying to get in front of this thing. See if I can figure out what's going on before the B team shows up and blows this thing up. You two on board?"

Rory adjusted her glasses and noticed that her right leg was vibrating, causing the eyelets on her combat boot to rattle.

"When can you get me your files?" she asked.

CHAPTER 44

On a crappy Monday morning, Ryder pulled her car to the curb outside the South Bend house belonging to the wife of the man who had disappeared more than a year ago. It was one of the leads listed on the shit list her editor had handed her the Friday before. The story was not new to her. Ryder had done her research on the mysterious case of the father of two who left one day on a business trip and never returned home. Ryder had originally written about it on her blog the previous year— *Local Man Goes Missing Without a Trace*—it was exactly what her blog was about. The true-crime fans who followed her were eager to chime in on unsolved cases and chase leads that the police and detectives had given up on. Any nugget of evidence the citizen detectives turned up that might aid in solving the mystery was considered a success.

The interest in the missing South Bend man died, however, after news of the Westmont Prep Killings stole the cover of every Indiana newspaper. As gruesome details of the school crime scene trickled in, interest grew until the entire nation started following the case. In just two days, the twenty-four-hour cable news cycle was saturated with Westmont Prep stories. It was the lead on the network morning shows, and the queen of morning television herself—Dante Campbell—had even clicked her high heels through the once unknown town of Peppermill.

With the media overanalyzing every detail of the story, when the first break in the case came—the discovery of a teacher's wall safe manifesto that described the specifics of the slaughter that had occurred at the abandoned boarding house—the news spread like wildfire. When that teacher, Charles Gorman, had then attempted suicide, coverage of Westmont Prep and the killings in Peppermill, Indiana, was wire to wire. The missing father of two from South Bend was forgotten. Interest in his whereabouts up and vanished, just like the man.

Ryder was as much to blame as any other journalist. She had jumped on the Westmont Prep bandwagon along with all her colleagues. The only difference was that Ryder had not so easily accepted what the police offered on the Westmont Prep Killings. When Dante Campbell and the other lords of the news media moved on to fresh stories and new outrages, Ryder lingered in Peppermill. She, and her followers, thought there was more to the story, and Ryder had spent the better part of a year chasing leads and uncovering inconsistencies in the case. Her hard work led only to Mack Carter landing his own podcast and stealing her story. Now, not only was Mack and his podcast gone, Ryder's chance at discovering anything more about Westmont Prep was slipping away.

She had thought long and hard about the best way to respond to her demotion. Her first reaction was to quit. Had she still been able to count on the income from her

YouTube channel, she would have told her boss to piss
off. But YouTube had shut her down, and it was unlikely
she would see another dime from her channel. She
needed her gig at the paper to pay the bills, and she was
uncertain what sort of financial headaches waited for her
from the pending lawsuit Theo Compton's parents had
levied. No matter how she figured things, at the moment
Ryder Hillier was stuck doing the grunt work for other
writers. That work started at a small home in South Bend
and a missing man named Marc McEvoy.

CHAPTER 45

After Westmont Prep died down, Ryder had gotten back to her other stories. One of them had been Marc McEvoy. He was a twenty-five-year-old father of two who had left for a business trip one afternoon and had never returned. His car had been found at the South Bend International Airport, but he was never seen again. In addition to the blog posts she had done on the case, Ryder had also written articles for the Star that chronicled the mystery of Marc McEvoy. The articles had mostly been brief updates on the stalled case, and rehashing of old details, but never anything substantial or ground-breaking. Since the very beginning there had been little to go on. The man simply vanished.

With a lack of details, however, there is generally an abundance of rumors. They varied widely, from Marc McEvoy escaping a failing marriage, to his running off with his mistress, to his wife having killed him and disposed of the body. But Ryder knew women rarely killed for reasons other than passion, and to date there had been no evidence of her husband having an affair. It was also rare to find any suburbanite skilled enough at murder to pull one off so cleanly and precisely as to leave no evidence behind. The nut who had killed his wife and two kids a couple of summers before in Colorado was under arrest shortly after he agreed to a television interview, where he begged for his family to come home. His shifty eyes and stuttering sentences were tells even the worst poker players could pick up. After he had practically convicted himself on television, police searched his home. He left so much physical evidence behind that it took police no time to arrest him. Even a diabolical killer like Robert Durst had done a piss-poor job of disposing of his neighbor's body after he killed him. After dismembering the body, he attempted to sink the body parts in Galveston Bay but failed to realize the black plastic bags into which he had stuffed the limbs would soon fill with gas when the extremities began to decay. Not long after he sunk the evidence, the bloated bags floated to the surface and littered the shoreline. It didn't take long for an unsuspecting passerby to rip one open. Durst was arrested the next day. So the theory that Marc McEvoy's wife, an elementary school teacher and a member of the church choir, had pulled off such a flawless homicide and had hidden the body for the past year was terribly unlikely. Ryder was working on the assumption that Marc McEvoy was still alive and out there somewhere. If she could find him, there was a chance she could salvage her career.

The only real news—Ryder was reluctant to call the information a lead—was the discovery that Marc McEvoy's wife was attempting to collect on a million-dollar life insurance policy. It wasn't much, but it might be worth an inquiry. Ryder climbed the front steps and knocked on the door. A woman answered a moment later.

"Brianna McEvoy?"

"Yes?"

"My name's Ryder Hillier, I'm a reporter with the *Indianapolis Star*. I was wondering if I could ask you a few questions about your husband."

The woman crossed her arms. "What do you want to know?"

"I'm writing a follow-up article about your husband, and police released details about a life insurance policy."

Brianna McEvoy rolled her eyes. "I've got two little girls and I'm trying to figure out how to raise them alone. I've got no idea what to tell them when they ask where their daddy is. Do you really think I give a damn what people think about a life insurance policy? He took it out three years ago. It's not breaking news. I'm trying to collect on it because I can't make ends meet on a teacher's salary alone."

The woman took a step closer and stared Ryder in the eyes.

"Does it sound like a mother of two, who teaches in the community, would kill her husband, the father of her children, for a life insurance payout? My suggestion to the police and all you newspeople is to stop watching so much television and spend some time figuring out what happened to my husband."

Ryder felt a draft over her face as Marc McEvoy's wife slammed the front door. She remembered why she hated the grunt work of chasing leads. She stuck her business card into the crevice of the doorframe and walked back to her car. The crumpled page of leads rested on the passenger seat. Ryder closed her eyes and pinched the bridge of her nose. What a shit show. Just a few days before, she was happily writing about crime for one of Indiana's biggest newspapers. She had a popular true-crime blog and a YouTube channel that was nicely supplement-ing her income. Now her career had gone to hell. She was chasing dead-end stories and turning anything useful over to other reporters to write the story.

Her phone vibrated. She didn't recognize the number. "Ryder Hillier."

There was silence on the other end.

"Hello? You've reached Ryder Hillier."

A woman cleared her voice. "This is Paige Compton. Theo's mother."

Ryder raised her eyebrows and glanced around her car as if she'd just been caught doing something illegal.

"Hi."

"I need to talk with you."

"Mrs. Compton, I want to apologize for taking that footage of your son. It was irresponsible and *so* inappro-priate for me to put it up on social media. It showed a complete lack of judgment on my part."

There was a long stretch of silence, and Ryder thought the connection had died. She looked at her phone to make sure the call timer was still running.

"Also," Ryder finally continued, "I want you to know that my newspaper had nothing to do—"

"I don't care about the video," Mrs. Compton said, cutting her off. "The lawsuit wasn't my idea. My attorney was the one who suggested it. He said I should go after the newspaper because there was a good chance they would settle out of court. He told me I had to go after you first, but I'm not interested in any of that. No amount of money will bring Theo back. I'll even drop the suit if you agree to help me."

Ryder pushed the phone more firmly against her ear. "Help you with what?"

There was another long stretch of silence.

"Mrs. Compton? Help you with what?"

"Theo called me the night before he . . . died. He wanted to warn me."

Ryder leaned forward in her seat, her eyesight focusing on a spot on the dashboard. "Warn you about what?"

"He and his friends had gotten themselves into some sort of trouble."

"*What* sort of trouble?"

Mrs. Compton cleared her throat. "I don't want to do this over the phone. Can we talk in person?"

"When?" Ryder asked without hesitation.

"Now, or as soon as you can get here."

"Where is *here*, ma'am?"

"Cincinnati."

Cincinnati was a four-hour drive. Ryder ran through a mental list of deadlines she needed to meet in order to keep her job. Chasing the Theo Compton story and the Westmont Prep Killings were not on that list.

"I can come this weekend," Ryder said. "Friday."

Ryder scribbled the address onto the sticky note, scrawling over the other leads she had been tasked with chasing. She underlined the address, scratching straight through Marc McEvoy's name in the process.

CHAPTER 46

Gwen Montgomery's legs twitched as she dreamed. She was attempting to run through the dark forest but could take only one or two steps before her feet sank into the thick mud. With great effort she pulled her foot from the earth, creating a loud sucking noise in the process. Then she tried to run again. As soon as she transferred weight onto her foot, it plunged into the soft ground. Her progress was agonizingly slow until she finally reached the edge of the forest. There, she saw the boarding house. She felt the tackiness of blood on her hands and chest and longed to run inside and wash it off, to stick her hands under the rush of water from the kitchen faucet and let the blood stream from her hands and swirl down the drain. It would disappear then, and she'd never again have to think of its origin.

Suddenly, her feet were free from the mud, and she ran toward the house. Then she saw the wrought iron gate and the body impaled on it. The moonlight brightened the bloated and disfigured face of Tanner Landing, his eyes half open with the blank stare of death, the tine of the gate poking from the top of his head. She let out a guttural scream as she hurried to him and tried to lift him from the gate. His body was wet, and when she looked at her hands they were covered in more blood than when she had left the forest.

She called for Gavin. There was no answer. She called again and again until her efforts finally woke her. She sat up in bed and knew it was happening again. The flutter in her chest, the sweat around her neck and down her back, the inability to handle even the most routine stimuli. She startled when she heard two classmates laugh in the hallway as they passed her dorm room. Her breathing was shallow and labored as she rose from bed and stood in her room; a panic attack was imminent. She thought about talking with Gavin. He knew about the nightmares. Gavin knew everything. But his once-reassuring voice had lost its effect over the past few months. They were the only ones left, and they had travelled too far down this dark road. So far, in fact, that Gwen was unsure they'd ever find a way out. Or if the way out was what she truly wanted. To veer off this road now would not be joyous. It would lead to a different road that was far more dark and ominous than the current one. But this path they were on—the one they all had taken that night in the woods—was proving to not only be unhealthy but dangerous too.

She pulled her hair into a ponytail, slipped into a pair of jeans, and pulled a tank top over her head. She left Margery Hall and hurried across campus to Teacher's Row. She knocked on number four. A moment later, Dr. Hanover answered.

"Gwen, what's happening?"

Since the events of June 21 last year, when Tanner and Andrew had been killed, every student at Westmont Prep had been watched closely. After Bridget Matthews had stepped in front of the train, those in her immediate circle had come under close scrutiny. Gwen, with her nervous demeanor, bouts of depression, weight loss, and panic attacks, had been more closely monitored than any of them. In a sit-down meeting with her parents and Dr. Casper, Dr. Hanover had announced that she would be transferring Gwen to her counseling schedule. As the dean of students at Westmont Prep, Dr. Gabriella Hanover wanted no more tragedy behind the walls of the school. Despite Drs. Hanover and Casper's efforts, after Bridget's suicide, Danielle and Theo soon followed. Gwen's condition continued to worsen.

Gwen tapped her chest now as she stood outside Dr. Hanover's house. "I can't breathe. I can't think. I'm freaking out."

"Come in," Dr. Hanover said, moving to the side. "It'll be all right."

Inside the office, Gwen sat down in her usual spot in the chair across from Dr. Hanover.

"Take a deep breath and tell me what's going on," Dr. Hanover said in her soft voice.

"I had another dream. I'm having a panic attack and I'm out of Xanax."

"The Xanax was a crutch I agreed to only at the beginning. The plan was to get you to better manage your anxiety without medication. Tell me about the dream."

Gwen shook her head. It was here that she always needed to be careful. She'd not been comfortable talking with Dr. Hanover and could never be as open in these sessions as she was with Dr. Casper.

"I was in the woods. Back at the house. I saw Tanner on . . . the gate."

"It's natural to have strong flashbacks, especially when you sleep. It's part of the process. Your mind is expunging those thoughts. At first, you blocked them out. Now your mind is working to purge them. Have you been journaling?"

Gwen shook her head.

"Your journal is where you are allowed to worry," Dr. Hanover said. "Your journal is where you are allowed to stress. You should store all your anxiety and anger and fear in those pages so that when you close the journal, all those things stay there and will be unable to interfere with your everyday life."

But they would, Gwen knew. Purging her worries onto the pages of her journal would make them real. It would bring the things she had done to life, where currently she could pretend they did not exist. Only times like this, when the reality of what they had done haunted her so deeply, did she risk exposure. She had spent an entire year fighting the buoyancy of her secret, working every day to keep it hidden beneath the surface.

"Okay," she finally said, her voice flat and unconvincing. "I'll try."

"Good," Dr. Hanover said. "Write out your entire dream. Everything you can remember. I'll check on you tonight. We'll discuss it all."

Gwen nodded and headed toward the door.

"Gwen," Dr. Hanover said.

Gwen turned back before she reached the door.

"You'll be amazed at how useful journaling is. Every one of my students has benefitted from it."

Gwen nodded and then turned back toward the door. When she made it outside, she finally exhaled. She hurried down Teacher's Row and walked up the steps of the number eighteen duplex, where she rang the bell. A moment later, Dr. Casper answered the door.

"Gwen," Dr. Casper said. "To what do I owe the pleasure? I haven't seen you for a while."

"I need to talk."

Dr. Casper's eyes squinted with concern. "Of course. What's on your mind?"

Gwen bit her lower lip as she contemplated what she was about to say. "Last summer, and everything that happened."

Dr. Casper's eyebrows rose a fraction of an inch. "Haven't you been talking with Dr. Hanover about that? We all decided it was best for you to see Dr. Hanover after everything that's happened."

"We *all* didn't decide. Dr. Hanover and my parents decided. You went along with it, and I had no say in it."

Dr. Casper's expression softened as he looked at his former patient. "Still, Gwen. A decision was made, and I think it's best if we stick with it. Speak with Dr. Hanover, she's a very skilled physician."

"I can't tell her everything."

Dr. Casper squinted his eyes. "Like what?"

A bloated moment of silence filled the space between them.

"We didn't tell the police everything about that night."

"*Who* didn't tell the police?"

"My friends and I." Gwen ran her hand across the top of her head and then down the length of her ponytail. "Can I come in?" she finally asked.

After a moment of hesitation, Dr. Casper nodded and Gwen walked past him into the house.

Westmont Prep
Summer 2019

Session 5
Journal Entry: GUIDANCE

I answered all their questions about my father. I was young and in shock. My mother was gone, and now my father had taken his own life. What a terrible tragedy. They all looked upon me with pity and sadness. They believed I had no chance in a life that had dealt me such a tragic hand at such a young age. I accepted their pity and absorbed their sadness, but I recognized it for what it really was—weakness. The police and the social workers and the court-appointed special advocate all looked on me—the suddenly parentless child—with such weakness that it made me sick.

They disguised their affliction and tried to pawn it off as sympathy. But I knew that under their sad smiles and behind their mournful eyes was fear. Working with me was like working with a leper. As if they got too close they'd catch whatever curse had touched my life. I felt their weakness and recognized it immediately. It was something that had once plagued me. I had made the decision to never allow that feeling to dominate me again. I would never again be the coward who stared through a keyhole. I vowed to rise above it all so that I could take *my new perspective out to the world and begin the hard work of correcting things.*

What had touched my life was not a curse, but enlightenment. It took a bit of time for me to fully realize this. Once I did, I got my life in order and came to Westmont Prep. Then I found you.

I pulled the tassel and closed my journal. The woman stared as if she wanted more from me today.

"My mother was gone. I had killed my father. I was alone in the world, until I found you. Since then, you've guided my life. You've guided my decisions. Every one of them."

I stared at her for a long time. I didn't need to say more; she understood my words. She understood how she had shaped my life.

"Are you ashamed of me?" I asked.

There was a long moment where she held my gaze. Then, finally, she blinked.

"Not at all."

CHAPTER 47

They all stood around their stations in Mr. Gorman's lab checking text messages and playing on their phones. Summer session was different than the regular school year, when phones were never allowed in a classroom. Phones were barely allowed outside of the dormitory. But in summer, things were more relaxed. They waited for Mr. Gorman's arrival to start their lab project.

Andrew Gross walked up to Gwen's table.

"Here," Andrew said as he threw a paper bag into the center of the station. Gwen and her friends stared at it.

"Better hurry before Gorman shows up," Andrew said.

Gwen pulled the bag over and peaked inside, then she dumped the contents onto the countertop. A cheap wooden mousetrap and a roll of duct tape rolled out.

Andrew pointed at them. "One of you has to set the trap and then tape it to the wall next to the light switch in the bathroom. When Gorman leaves to take a leak, which he does at some point during every lab, we'll hear about it."

Gwen shook her head. "Tape it to the wall?"

Andrew nodded.

"No way," she said.

"Not a chance." This came from Gavin, who was also shaking his head.

Theo and Danielle backed away from the counter with smiles on their faces. Theo shook his head. "Nope."

"I'll do it," Tanner said, reaching for the trap.

"Don't." Bridget grabbed his wrist. "You'll get in a lot of trouble."

Andrew smiled as he walked away. "You guys work it out, but remember what happens if you don't complete a challenge."

Andrew joined the other seniors who watched them.

"I'm doing it," Tanner said.

Gwen shook her head. "It'll break his finger."

"It's a cheap little mousetrap, it's not breaking anyone's finger. You should be thanking me, not trying to talk me out of it." Tanner looked each of them in the eye. "Without me, none of you would have a chance of making it. I'm the only one with the cojones to do any of this."

Tanner grabbed the mousetrap and the tape, looked around the lab, and then walked into the hallway. A minute later, the toilet flushed, and Tanner walked back into the lab with a stupid grin on his face. He made it back to his station just as Mr. Gorman entered the lab.

"Get to your stations," Mr. Gorman called out.

The students abruptly quieted down, stifling their laughter with quizzical smiles on their faces. Gwen shook her head when Gavin looked at her.

"This is a bad idea," she said.

Mr. Gorman unpacked his things onto his desk at the front of the room. He wore an ill-fitting short-sleeved button-down. His thin hairy arms hung from the sleeves, and the dark circles of his nipples showed through the thin fabric on either side of his crooked tie.

"Today we will be mixing the compounds to demonstrate the Briggs-Rauscher reaction. As always," Mr. Gorman said, placing his large safety goggles onto his face, "eye protection should be in place at all times and the ventilation hoods set to high."

Mr. Gorman took fifteen minutes to scribble instructions onto the chalkboard and another ten making sure each station had the correct ingredients. One of the chemicals needed to be heated to a boil, and once each group had their flasks set over the Bunsen burners, Mr. Gorman put everyone on a ten-minute watch, where they would monitor the boiling point by tracking the thermometer's progress. With the students occupied and a lull in the experiment, Gwen watched as Mr. Gorman slipped into the hallway.

Tanner bit his bottom lip before he smiled.

"Holy shit," he whispered.

Nervous energy filled the room. They heard the squeak of the bathroom door hinges and then, a second later, a loud snap.

"Goddammit!"

Mr. Gorman's voice echoed through the empty hallways. The students tried to muffle their laughter, Tanner being the least successful. When Mr. Gorman came back into the lab, his right hand was tucked under his armpit and he was holding the mousetrap in his left.

"Who the *hell* did this?" he screamed when he entered the room.

By then, every student but Tanner had managed to control themselves. Gwen was frightened, and everyone else carried expressions of shock. Tanner had his lips pressed tightly together to suppress a smile.

"Who did this?" Mr. Gorman yelled again.

Gwen walked forward. "What happened?"

"Someone taped this onto the light switch."

"Let me see," Gwen said.

Mr. Gorman stared at her.

"It wasn't any of us," she said as she stared him in the eye. "We all walked in the lab just before you." Gwen nodded. "Let me see."

Mr. Gorman held out his hand. His index and ring fingers were red and swollen with a clear demarcation line across the knuckles.

Gwen lightly touched his fingers. "Do you think they're broken?"

Mr. Gorman slowly pulled his hand away and flexed his fingers. "Go back to your station."

Gwen nodded and walked back to her spot next to Gavin.

Mr. Gorman swallowed hard and looked out at the group of students. "If your flask is boiling, move to step two," he said before walking back to his desk and tossing the mousetrap into the garbage.

Tanner cleared his voice. It was a piss-poor job of hiding his laughter.

It was June 13.

CHAPTER 48

The following day, Charles Gorman entered the faculty lounge. He grabbed a tray and walked to the buffet station, where he carefully chose his lunch items—roasted chicken and vegetables, a cup of chocolate pudding, and a fountain drink. He carried his tray over to a table where Gabriella Hanover and Christian Casper sat.

"What happened to you?" Gabriella asked.

Charles had gone to the pharmacy after his lab period and purchased a splint for his aching fingers. Now his index and ring fingers were immobilized by a sponge-lined piece of metal wrapped in white surgical tape.

Charles placed his tray onto the table and sat down.

"Summer pranks have started again."

"Who?" Gabriella asked.

"Probably Tanner Landing. Egged on, I'm sure, by Andrew Gross."

"I spoke to Andrew last year when Jean Rasmussen was being pranked. The dead raccoon and the undergarments hanging from the library. I warned him then and had a long discussion with his parents."

Charles shrugged. "I guess he didn't get the message."

"What happened?" Christian Casper asked. "We'll have to take serious action if any assault occurred."

Charles shook his head. "They'll never admit to it, and the smug little bastards know I won't be able to prove a thing."

"How did it happen?" Christian asked again.

"They taped a mousetrap to the bathroom light switch."

"Those little shits," Gabriella said.

"I don't think it was all of them. Just one or two."

"Still," Gabriella said. "We can't stand for it. I'll call a meeting of the student body to stop this before we get too far into summer."

PART VI

August 2020

CHAPTER 49

Detective Ott parked his car and turned off the engine. Eventually, his headlights faded and only the halogen of the lamppost lighted the parking lot. The precinct offices of the Peppermill Police Department were dark; only a few souls would be working the overnight shift, including the beat officers who would be out and about in their squad cars this far past shift change, the sergeant in charge who would be in his office, and the dispatchers who wouldn't bat an eye at a detective entering the offices at one o'clock in the morning.

He could tell no one the real purpose of his presence at the precinct this morning, and he had a cover story for anyone he ran into. He weighed the odds and decided that performing this heist during regular business hours would be impossible. There were too many people in the office during the day, and his young protégé followed him like a shadow when they were on duty. The dark overnight hours afforded him the best chance to stay invisible.

He pushed open the car door and stepped into the middle-of-the-night humidity. Then he reached into the back seat, pulled his suit coat from the hook, and slipped his arms through the sleeves before walking toward the front door. He swiped his ID card to gain access to the lobby and walked past the reception desk, where the night guard gave a groggy smile and a wave.

"Detective."

"How you doing, Donny?"

"Living the dream."

"You and me both, pal. You and me both."

Detective Ott walked into the pit, where he and twelve other detectives made up the team of investigators for the Peppermill Police Force. He poured a cup of coffee and stirred sugar into the Styrofoam cup while he surveyed things. Only one other detective was present—Gene Norton—who was hunting and pecking on his keyboard with such concentration, Ott knew he must be working on a report deadline. Norton hated computers more than any detective on the force, and it took him twice as long as anyone else to type his reports.

Ott sat at his cubicle, pulled up the active cases he was working, and logged into a file so that he had a cover for being in the office so late. He had saved some work from earlier in the day and went about typing up a report. He was more efficient than his colleague, and after ten minutes he had things completed. He left the case open and stood from his desk. Norton was still pecking away, swearing as he usually did that the keys were not in the same place they were the day before—a permanent fear ever since the guys had rearranged the letters of his keyboard.

From his cubicle, Ott walked to the evidence room. He again used his ID card to gain entry and then grabbed the box containing all the evidence from the case he had pulled up on his computer. He grabbed another box, too, and carried both to his desk. He sat and waited for a minute, listening to Norton peck and swear. Finally, he grabbed the second box and walked to the copy machine. Methodically, he slipped each section into the automatic document feeder. On the outside he waited patiently as the machine did the work at an alarmingly loud but efficient clip. Once one section was finished, he placed the copied pages into a fresh box, returned the original to its proper place, and started the process over with the next section. It took a painstaking twenty-two minutes to copy the entire contents of the box, and Ott noticed Gene Norton's head pop over the top of his cubicle somewhere in the middle of it, to which Ott raised his chin in Norton's direction.

"Frickin' deadline," Norton said. "And my keyboard is screwed up again. You know anything about it?"

"Wasn't me," Ott said.

Norton disappeared into his cubicle, and Ott slipped the last section of the file into the feeder. Five minutes later he had the original box back together and carried it, along with the box containing the copies, to his desk. He put the copied box to the side and carried the other two back to Evidence, swiped his keycard again, and replaced them in their proper spot.

He didn't bother to say good-bye to Norton but nodded to Donny on his way out. He placed the box in the back seat of his car and pulled out of the parking lot. The files represented the case that had woken him up at three in the morning the previous summer. He hadn't gotten a good night's sleep since.

He wondered if things would change soon.

CHAPTER 50

Rory sat in the three-season room of the cottage. The Kiddiejoy doll lay on the desk in front of her with the gooseneck lamp pulled close to illuminate the doll's face. The repaired area of the ear and cheek—which Rory had expertly reconstructed with papier-mâché and cold porcelain clay—had now set and was ready for sculpting. She went to work with her Foldger-Gruden brushes, using the tipped handles to carve tiny grooves that would become the detail of the ear cartilage. For this, she worked without a reference photo. All she needed had been stored in her mind when she researched the doll, as if the image of what she hoped to achieve was sitting on an easel in front of her and doused in spotlight.

Rory methodically progressed through the brushes, moving from dull to sharp and ending with the needlelike pine tip that easily carved through the clay. Her concentration was so intense that her vision tunneled and she barely remembered to blink. Each fine groove she created required the repetitious precision of an artist and the focus of a surgeon. The callings of her mind to repeat and perfect, which she stowed during the hours of her life not spent restoring dolls, were purged at her workstation. Here, those disruptive thoughts were useful and needed.

When she completed sculpting the ear, she moved to the edge of the mouth and whittled a perfect seam at the corner of the doll's lips. She finished by reconstructing the outer canthus of the left eye. It was detailed work that took hours. After carving the last notch, she slipped the brush into her breast pocket, blew away the residue, and finally sat back in her chair. Like theater lights slowly brightening at the conclusion of a film, Rory's vision widened. The doll was structurally back together. The texture and color were off, so the next step would be sanding smooth the areas she repaired and then glazing the porcelain with an epoxy coating to erase the lattice of cracks. Finally, she would polish and paint the surface, which would bring the doll back to its original beauty. There was still much to be done, but after only three sessions she had made great progress.

The slamming of a car door broke her concentration. When the doorbell rang, she checked her watch. It was one P.M. She'd been working uninterrupted for three hours and had lost track of time. Pulling the gooseneck lamp to the side, she laid the Kiddiejoy doll back into the travel box. She found her glasses and fumbled them into place, then pulled on her gray windbreaker to match her jeans. She buttoned it up to the top clasp near her neck and pulled on her beanie cap. Her combat boots covered her feet and completed her battle gear. On the way to the front door, she grabbed her rucksack and threw it over her shoulder. Lane was napping upstairs, and Rory decided not to interrupt his sleep, which the doctors had warned would come in long spells while his brain healed from the concussion. She opened the door, and Detective Ott was waiting on the porch.

"You ready?" he asked.

Rory nodded. Today she would walk through the crime scene—the abandoned boarding house tucked into the forest at the edge of the Westmont Prep campus, where two students had been killed one short year before. She knew what was coming. She knew what waited there. It was the same thing that waited at every crime scene she analyzed— the souls of those who had lost their lives. Rory's goal was to feel them and connect with them so that eventually she could communicate with them in her own subtle way. Her connection with the victims was not a physical one, and her communication was not verbal. To those lost souls Rory made one simple promise—to lead them to a proper place of rest where peace and calm would be found.

This far into her career as a forensic reconstructionist, Rory Moore had never broken a promise.

CHAPTER 51

She sat in the passenger seat as Detective Ott drove through the streets of Peppermill. Rory had never been comfortable in the presence of strangers, cops or otherwise. Airplanes and cars, in particular, were places of unrest. Perhaps a touch of claustrophobia added to her unease, but mostly it was her lifelong displeasure with another's company in such close quarters. Years ago, Lane had quickly broken through her walls to become the only man other than her father she allowed to physically touch her. So now, as they drove, Rory felt a familiar tremor in her chest. It was a signal that the proverbial IV line that offered a constant slow-drip of anxiety directly into her circulatory system had been opened a notch wider.

"We had two choices," Ott said. "We could take the back way—the lesser-known entrance that is accessible from Route 77. This was the route the kids took the night of June twenty-first. Or we could be more transparent and go through the front gates of Westmont Prep. Since I'm trying my hardest not to lose my job, we're taking the transparent route. I told the dean of students that I needed access to the house and tracks that run alongside as a follow-up to my investigation into Theo Compton's suicide. She agreed to escort us."

Rory nodded. "Probably the best way to do it."

They turned onto Champion Boulevard and pulled up to the two brick pillars connected by the tall wrought iron gate over which arched a concrete placard that announced Westmont Preparatory High School.

Detective Ott stopped at the speaker, pressed the button, and held his badge out the window to be scanned.

"Welcome to Westmont Prep," a female voice sounded through the speaker.

"Detective Ott to see Dr. Hanover."

A moment later, the iron gates opened inward, like two arms welcoming them in an embrace. Ott pulled into a visitor's parking spot. Rory opened her door, adjusted her glasses and beanie hat, and then followed Detective Ott toward the main building with its four Gothic columns standing sturdy in the afternoon sun. A man and a woman waited on the steps. Rory assumed they were Christian Casper and Gabriella Hanover, the co-deans of students. They stood next to a golf cart.

"Dr. Hanover," Ott said. "Good to see you."

"You, too, Detective."

They shook hands.

"Dr. Casper," Ott said, shaking hands again. "This is Rory Moore. She's working as a consultant and will be assisting me today."

Dr. Hanover held out her hand, which Rory didn't take. *Couldn't*, really. She'd never been able to shake hands with strangers, or anyone else for that matter. Her brain was not wired to do so. She was not a germophobe and had no aversion to disease. Her reluctance to shake another's hand stemmed from the same affliction that poured sweat down her back as soon as she closed the car door of Henry Ott's car—her general displeasure with human interaction. The affliction could neither be explained by Rory nor be understood by others. It was simply how she had lived for forty years, and changing now was not possible. To change, Rory needed motive and means. She had neither. She preferred the awkwardness of rejecting a handshake to the convoluted thoughts and discomfort that came from accepting one. Instead, she adjusted her glasses, offered Dr. Hanover a brief moment of eye contact, and then nodded. Dr. Hanover finally pulled her hand away. Dr. Casper knew enough not to offer his.

"Right this way," Dr. Hanover finally said, pointing at the golf cart. "It's a long walk otherwise."

Detective Ott and Rory climbed into the second row. Dr. Hanover drove, and Dr. Casper sat next to her. They wound through campus, passed the ivy-covered buildings, and eventually came to a tall red brick wall that ran a hundred yards in either direction before giving way to wrought iron that finished the job of cordoning off the woods on the other side from the campus.

Dr. Casper stood from the cart and used a set of keys to free the padlock and open the passageway in the brick wall. Dr. Hanover accelerated through the opening before Dr. Casper closed the door behind them. Rory felt a quiver of foreboding when the door closed behind her, as if the safety of the campus was gone and the dangers of the ominous forest waited.

Dr. Casper climbed back into the cart, and soon they were bouncing along a trail that cut through the forest. They emerged a few minutes later, and Rory saw the house in front of them. The limestone exterior was visible only in small patches where the ivy had failed to grow. So overgrown were the vines that they looked more like camouflage than decoration.

"We'll wait here, if that's okay," Dr. Hanover said.

"Of course," Detective Ott said as he and Rory climbed from the cart.

Rory didn't wait for Detective Ott to take the lead. She walked toward the house, her gaze drifting back and forth, taking in the entire setting as if her eyes were recording everything that entered her pupils. Of course, her mind was doing exactly that. The full understanding of her subconscious processing might take longer, but the cataloguing was immediate. She approached the wrought iron gate where Tanner Landing had been impaled. The tip of the prong was six feet above the ground. She walked through the opening of the gate, into the front yard, and then turned around to look from the other side and get a different perspective.

Detective Ott pulled a photo from the manila file he was carrying and handed it to Rory. Depicted on the eight-by-ten was Tanner Landing's lifeless body skewered by one of the pickets of the gate. Rory analyzed the grisly photo, then looked back at the gate and the top of the iron spikes. At six feet, the gate rose nearly one foot over Rory's head. To drop a 160-pound teenager onto the gate took strength and height. But also time. The killer knew he had time. It was someone who knew the house and knew the area around it. Someone who knew what the students were up to that night.

"When I arrived at the scene," Detective Ott said, "it was obvious the Landing boy's body had been dragged from inside the house. There was a trail of blood down the front steps, and blood was found within the dirt grooves that led from the bottom of the steps to this spot."

"So he was definitely first attacked inside," Rory said.

"Yes. In the front room just off the foyer."

Detective Ott handed Rory another crime scene photo. It showed smeared blood streaked across the hardwood floor of the foyer and doorway.

"No footprints found in any of the blood or in the dirt?" Rory asked.

"None. We found some fibers that made us believe the killer might have worn shoe coverings, like you'd see a service worker don before entering a house or walking on carpeting. But no definitive prints to pull."

"Organized," Rory whispered as she stared at the photo.

She looked back up to the spears of the gate.

"Give me a time line. How quickly did this go down?"

Ott handed her another picture, this time of Tanner Landing's naked body lying on the metal autopsy table.

"The medical examiner's report stated that the wound from the gate penetrated just below the victim's chin," Ott said. "And continued through the bones of the face, anterior aspect of the brain, through the frontal lobe, and out the forehead. These wounds were determined to have been made antemortem."

Rory continued to stare at the autopsy photo. "The Landing boy was dying quickly from the wound across his neck but still alive when he was hung on the gate."

"Correct."

"Then it happened quickly," Rory said. "Our guy didn't wait long after the initial attack to perform the ritualistic hanging. Lane suggested that it was ceremonial—done specifically for revenge. Killing him wasn't enough. He had to punish him."

"Pretty much lobotomized him."

"So far," Rory said, handing the photo back to Detective Ott, "at six foot three, Charles Gorman had the height, strength, and motive to pull this off."

Rory turned away from the gate and looked at the abandoned and unkempt boarding house, with red ivy bearding the windows.

"What were they doing out here? The kids. Why were they here that night?"

"The best I've been able to piece together, the kids were participating in a game called the Man in the Mirror. From my research, it's a ritualistic, cultish game played around the world. Mostly by teenagers, but the game has a big following of adults, too. Mostly overseas."

"What's it about?"

"Spirits. Curses. And an entity that resides in uncovered mirrors, whose power can be tapped twice a year, on the summer solstice and winter solstice."

"And the killings took place last June."

"Correct," Ott said. "On June twenty-first. The longest day of the year."

"How does it work?"

"Players find their way through a forest to an empty house. The first to arrive finds the designated mirror, uncovers it, and whispers *Man in the Mirror* to their reflections. Doing so allows you to live the year in peace and in good standing with the spirits of the Man in the Mirror. Failing to find the keys and complete the loop of whispering into the mirror before midnight brings a year of curse."

"Christ. It sounds terrifying."

"I've done a lot of research," Ott said. "The game is not new. There are many different versions, but it seems like the Westmont Prep kids took it to another level. This was definitely not the Ghosts in the Graveyard that I grew up with."

Rory continued to look at the house.

"Can you show me the room where it happened?"

"Yeah," Ott said, grabbing keys from his utility belt. "Follow me."

CHAPTER 52

R ory walked through the front door of the abandoned boarding house. The ceilings were tall, and the entrance foyer reached to the second story. A staircase with missing and broken spindles spiraled up to the second floor.

"Back in the day," Ott said, his voice echoing through the empty house, "this used to be where the resident faculty lived. There are eight rooms that were converted to private bedrooms with baths. The house was off the beaten path and offered privacy for the faculty."

He pointed to the large room to their right.

"This was the community dining area, a large kitchen toward the back of the house, and here"—he pointed to the left, where a short hallway led to a closed door—"is where the library had once been located. That's where Andrew Gross's body was discovered."

Rory followed Ott down the hallway and into the room. Ott retrieved another photo from his file folder and handed it to her. A blood-speckled mirror stood in the center of the room, a painter's tarp bunched on the floor next to it, and Andrew Gross's body was in a heap in front of the mirror, a perfect circle of dark congealed blood around it.

"The blood around Andrew Gross's body is undisturbed, so he bled out here uninterrupted," she said. "The Landing boy was dragged quickly outside and to the gate. He knew others were coming. He knew he had to hurry."

"Why skewer only the Landing boy?" Ott asked. "Why not both?"

Rory continued to stare at the photo. "Not enough time. Or maybe he just wanted revenge on Tanner Landing. Again, there's certainly a strong argument for Charles Gorman being our perp."

Rory continued to look at the photo.

"What's with the painter's tarp?" she asked.

"It's part of the game they were playing. Mirrors need to be covered until the Man in the Mirror is summoned."

Rory shook her head and walked to the window, which was doused in spray paint dark enough to prevent a view to where Tanner Landing had been impaled.

"No one else had been in the house that night?" she asked.

"Not that we're aware of. The other students were in the woods, and when they got to the house, they saw the massacre out front and ran back to campus."

"No foreign DNA found in this room?"

"No. The only blood we found in this room belonged to Andrew Gross and Tanner Landing."

"The unidentified blood. It was found only by the gate?"

"Correct," Ott said.

"It was on the girl's hands and chest, and also on Tanner Landing's body?"

"Correct. Gwen Montgomery had both Tanner's blood

on her, which was explained by her frantic attempt to re-move his body from the gate when she found him, as well as a small amount of blood that we haven't identified."

Rory turned from the window. "How did you get past the unidentified blood?"

"I haven't."

CHAPTER 53

A Dark Lord sat on the desk of the dim three-season room at the back of the cottage. Only the desk lamp lighted the room. It was enough to allow Rory to read the box of files Detective Ott had given her after they finished the walk-through of the boarding house and an inspection of the area on the train tracks where Charles Gorman had attempted to end his life. This was the same location where three students had since succeeded. Rory was still processing the whirlwind day, her subconscious organizing and cataloguing all she had seen and learned. She had reinforced her discoveries by recapping her excursion to Lane when she arrived home. Now the cottage was dark and quiet. It was past midnight—Rory's most productive hours were in front of her.

She took a sip of stout. She had already been at it for an hour, having first read through Gorman's folder to see everything Detective Ott and his police force had discovered about the forty-five-year-old chemistry teacher. She read about his life before Westmont Prep and about his eight years at the school. She read about the evidence Ott had used to secure his search warrant. Within Gorman's folder was the manifesto he had written, which Ott had discovered in the wall safe of Gorman's duplex on Teacher's Row—three pages of cursive writing in which Gorman had described in vivid detail what he planned to do to Tanner Landing and Andrew Gross. It was a disturbing piece of work that shook Rory to the core. She had seen the crime scene photos—both earlier in the day when Ott had handed her select choices, and more tonight as she paged through the photos that accompanied the manifesto. It was chilling for Rory to lay out the photographs, one by one, of exactly what Gorman described in his manifesto. A handwriting analyst's report confirmed that the cursive scribble of the manifesto matched samples of Charles Gorman's writing.

Finally, Rory read about the scene out at the train tracks when the officer had discovered a near-lifeless Charles Gorman after he had tried to end his life. A troubling question kept bouncing around her mind: If Gorman was innocent, why had he tried to kill himself? She was beginning to wonder if, perhaps, Henry Ott had arrested the right man. She was starting to doubt that the box next to her held any secrets at all, or if everything that needed to be found had already been uncovered.

A couple of red flags convinced her, though, that something had been missed. The first was the unidentified blood. The second were the students who had killed themselves. She took a sip of Dark Lord, returned the Gorman folder to the box, and pulled out the file of Bridget Matthews—the first Westmont Prep student to follow Gorman's footsteps onto the train tracks alongside the abandoned boarding house.

Rory was sure the mystery of the Westmont Prep Killings lay with these suicide victims.

CHAPTER 54

Rory read Detective Ott's notes on Bridget Matthews. They included his initial interview with the girl the day Tanner Landing had been found impaled on the fence and the detective's discussions with Bridget's parents in the wake of her suicide. Together, the transcripts painted Bridget as a typical teenager. She came from a wealthy family, and her relationship with her parents sounded no more strained than most kids her age who were sent to a boarding school for ten months out of the year.

Bridget's version of events on the night of the crime was a spot-on match when Rory compared it against the other students' statements, which meant they were all telling the truth or a well-rehearsed lie. The story went like this: They all met at a preplanned location off Route 77 on the south end of campus. This was the typical route the students took to reach the boarding house—a little-known back route that was off the beaten path and avoided the need to cross the main campus. On the night of June 21, the students gathered on Route 77 to partici-pate in the initiation of a game called the Man in the Mir-ror. Their task that night was to venture alone into the woods surrounding the boarding house and search for keys that had been hidden by the seniors. The keys would open the "safe room" inside the boarding house. They were required to complete this challenge by midnight.

The group consisted of five juniors—Bridget Matthews, Gwen Montgomery, Gavin Harms, Theo Compton, and Danielle Landry. Tanner Landing, who was Bridget's boyfriend, had gone to the woods earlier than the others. Each student offered the identical explanation for Tanner's isolation that night. They said Tanner was more enthusiastic about the night than the rest of the group and was determined to be the first to arrive at the boarding house and complete the challenge. The benefit of such a feat was becoming the leader of the initiates and the head of the group the following year when they took things over as seniors—a position that had been held by Andrew Gross.

After reaching the designated location on Route 77, they each set out into the woods. After an hour of searching, they had all found their keys and raced back to the house at different times. As they emerged from the woods, the first thing they saw was Tanner Landing impaled on the gate. Panicked, they all ran back to campus. All but one. Gwen Montgomery stayed behind and tried to lift Tanner off the gate before finally settling on the ground next to him and waiting for help.

Rory took a sip of Dark Lord and imagined teenagers stalking through a dark forest. Few of these details had made it to the public's attention. Ott had told Rory that after they caught the scent of Gorman's trail, they purposely kept the details of the cultish game to themselves for fear that a repeat of the '80s paranoia about satanic cults would plague their investigation.

Next, Rory pulled Bridget Matthews's medical records in front of her, including the transcripts of the girl's therapy sessions with Dr. Christian Casper. Rory read through them. Bridget's sessions prior to the summer of 2019 were benign and included the worries of most teenage girls— boyfriends, best friends, the stress of schoolwork, and the worries of finding the right college. But after the killings, the transcripts painted a girl beset with sorrow and grief over Tanner's death. Rory read a letter penned by Dr. Casper to Bridget's parents that described his concern over Bridget's mental state. Dr. Casper's letter described suicidal tendencies and the characteristic warning signs that accompanied them. Bridget displayed them all, and Dr. Casper suggested both medical treatment and psychotherapy. But it was too late. On September 28, 2019, three months after that night in the woods, Bridget Matthews stepped in front of the Canadian National freight train at roughly ten-thirty P.M.

Rory pulled Bridget's autopsy report from the file. She took a sip of Dark Lord to steady herself, then turned the cover and opened the report. Attached to the top left side of the inside flap was a small photo of Bridget Matthews. A beautiful girl, young and innocent and with so many unlived years in front of her. Rory felt an immediate draw to the girl. Bridget, like all the victims whose deaths Rory reconstructed, seemed to throw a grappling hook across the chasm between life and death that stuck to Rory's soul. It would stay there, Rory knew, creating a connection and generating a constant tug that would not relent until Rory could provide answers and closure. Rory was unsure how she felt about this vulnerability—the inability to forget about the dead until she was certain their spirits were at peace. It was the reason she was so particular about the cases she took on. The connections she formed with the victims were taxing and came with great responsibility.

Rory had not chosen the Westmont Prep case. Uncontrolled circumstances pulled her into it. Rory's uncertainty was rooted not only in fear that there was nothing new to discover about this case but also in the fact that multiple victims were involved. Five students had died— two were savagely killed, and three had taken their own lives. Building relationships with so many victims at once carried the potential to overwhelm her senses and take the edge off her ability to see what others had missed. But she knew she had no choice. The whispers had started, and only answers would mute them.

Rory spent an hour—and half a Dark Lord—reading Bridget Matthews's autopsy report, paging carefully through every finding and each line. Suicide by train was a grisly scene, and Rory read the ME's findings stating that devastating head and torso injuries led to death. Rory glanced over the autopsy photos but did not dwell on them. There were no drugs or alcohol in the girl's system. The report ended with the cause of death: Multiple blunt traumatic injuries. The manner of death: Suicide.

Rory read the final page and closed the file. She was about to push it to the side to start the review of the next student when something stopped her and called to her. She reopened the autopsy report and turned back to the last page. Quickly skimming the information, she ran her finger down the page. She had nearly missed it, and was sure others had. But Rory Moore saw everything. If a critical detail wasn't immediately obvious, her mind stored the information on a rolling and endless scroll and then sent out a beacon until her conscious mind noticed. That signal was bright now and pulled all her curiosity toward it. There was something in Bridget Matthews's autopsy report. It was not a physical finding but instead more benignly listed by the medical examiner along with the items included on Bridget's body at the time the postmortem exam was conducted.

In the pocket of Bridget's jeans were three items: a tube of ChapStick, an ATM card, and a penny. She might have skimmed right over the description of the penny, but she hadn't. She stopped and read the ME's notes that described the penny as "flattened and oblong."

Rory's mind fired. Like a short circuit, something flared until her memory spun the scroll to the exact location she needed. She pushed her chair away from the desk and fell to her knees as she rifled through the evidence box. There she found the notes from Charles Gorman's attempted suicide. She took the file and placed it on the desk, covering Bridget's autopsy findings—something she would never normally do, since the unorganized concept of having one open file touch another would typically have her out of sorts. But so fragile was the thread she was looking for that she had no time to organize things now into tight piles.

She opened Gorman's file, licked her index finger, and paged through the contents until she found the list of items discovered at the scene of his attempted suicide. Item seventy-two, imaged in the crime scene photo next to an inverted yellow marker, was a flattened and oblong penny found just three feet from where Gorman's near lifeless body lay. A clear and distinguishable fingerprint lifted from the penny had been matched to Charles Gorman, suggesting that he had been holding the penny at the time he was struck by the train. Analysis of this coin suggested that its unusual shape had been caused by placing it on the rails and allowing a train to pass over it.

CHAPTER 55

Her discovery was worthy of a middle-of-the-night discussion. After learning that an oddly shaped penny was both in Bridget Matthews's pocket at the time she killed herself and at the scene of Charles Gorman's attempted suicide, Rory had skimmed through the autopsy findings of the other students who had taken their lives. Catalogued in the personal items of both Danielle Landry and Theo Compton were flattened and oblong pennies. It was a common link that tied them together and was too unusual to be considered coincidence.

Lane sat at the kitchen table across from Rory. It was three-thirty in the morning.

"What does it mean?" Lane asked.

"I'm not sure," Rory said. "Other than it's an oddity that links them all."

"A lot of things link them," Lane said. "But this is certainly interesting. Kids put pennies on train tracks for the trains to run them over and flatten them. It could be as simple as that. They had all thrown pennies on the track since they spent so much time at the abandoned house and the rail lines."

"Except that a penny was found with Gorman, too."

Rory spun the glass of Dark Lord in front of her as she thought. Finally, she looked up at Lane.

"Let's run it through the MAP database. See if the algorithm picks up any hits."

Lane nodded his head at the suggestion. The Murder Accountability Project algorithm had certainly found stranger links than flattened coins.

"What's the marker?" Lane asked. "Pennies?"

"Pennies, flattened pennies, train tracks."

"We'll get a lot of hits with 'train tracks.' But I'll plug it in and see what the algorithm comes up with. It'll take a day or two to root through all the information and refine the search."

Rory took her last sip of Dark Lord and emptied her glass.

"I wonder if showing these pennies to Gorman would trigger anything."

Lane raised his eyebrows at the thought. He ran a hand down the back of his still-bandaged head. Rory's mind never rested. She burned through the midnight hours with no difficulty at all. Lane needed eight hours of sleep and then a pot of coffee before his neurons fired. And his neurons were groggy from both the early morning hour and the concussion.

"Ott said Gorman hasn't spoken since he's come out of his coma," Lane said. "The neurologists believe his mind is gone. An EEG says there's nothing there. But the brain is a mysterious thing. You never know what might stimulate it. I still know a few folks at Grantville Psychiatric Hospital from when I was writing my dissertation. I'll make a call to see what I can do."

CHAPTER 56

The nurse walked into Room 41 and saw her patient standing by the sink, toothbrush in hand, and staring into the mirror. It was a common scene. Her patient had had the wherewithal to begin a task but became stuck somewhere in the middle, having forgotten the end goal. The nurse tended to many patients but found the resident of Room 41 in these situations often. Sometimes standing next to the bathroom door forgetting that sitting on the toilet was the original intention of walking to that location, or sitting at the table with fork in hand but forgetting to eat. Today, it was standing in front of the mirror, confused by the toothpaste in hand.

The nurse walked over. Everyone deserved compassion and dignity, no matter how far gone they were. Human touch, the nurse had learned during her thirty-year career, was a way to bring patients with traumatic brain injury back to the present. A gentle stroke on a shoulder, a careful hand to the forearm—any small interaction went a long way. She always did this slowly and delicately, so as not to startle her patient. Then she achieved eye contact, as she did now.

"You were going to brush your teeth, do you remember?"

After several seconds, the nurse finally saw a nod. Facial expressions never changed—there was only a stoic look of detachment. But a nod of the head was a good sign. The nurse had broken through this morning. With a patient this far gone, it was all she could hope for. It was how things had always been, and how, the nurse believed, they would be forever. There was only one time when this particular patient showed any acknowledgment of life around the hospital, and that was when the visitor came. Once a week, like clockwork.

Slowly, the nurse watched the toothbrush rise. The aim was off, so she guided the brush to her patient's mouth and assisted as the bristles moved up and down.

CHAPTER 57

It was late afternoon on Thursday, the day after Rory had stumbled across the pennies that linked each of the Westmont Prep students who had killed themselves. That Charles Gorman also possessed one of these coins was another piece to the puzzle. Lane started the search through the MAP database by setting the markers—*pennies, flattened pennies, trains, train tracks*—and looking for matches to other homicides. He knew his search would be broad and that the algorithm would take time to sort through the findings. While he and Rory waited for the preliminary results, they turned their attention to Lane's laptop, which was open in front of them in the front room of the cottage. A thumb drive protruded from the USB port, and the computer screen played the video the crime scene investigators had shot when they arrived at the boarding house the night Andrew Gross and Tanner Landing had been killed.

A properly handled crime scene, especially a homicide, included a strict pecking order. After first responders determined that a homicide had occurred, they called their superiors to develop a chain of command. Detectives were dispatched, the crime scene investigation unit was summoned, and a log was started to document everyone who entered the crime scene. The initial group to set foot on the crime scene, after first responders, were the CSI folks. Their job was to document everything with still photos and video. This was done before others could disrupt the scene footprints and fingerprints and random dribbling of DNA. In the evidence box Henry Ott had delivered to Rory was a thumb drive that contained the crime scene photos and video recording. Rory and Lane watched now as the abandoned boarding house materialized on the laptop. The date appeared across the bottom of the screen: Saturday, June 22, 2019—12:55 A.M.

Spotlights offered a bubble of illumination within the black forest. The point-of-view video shot by one of the crime scene investigators bounced as the camera moved from the area behind the house and through the opening of the doorframe. The interior of the house, too, was lighted by bright spotlights that overexposed the camera as the technician first entered the house.

When the camera adjusted to the contrast, Rory and Lane saw a narrow hallway that led to the kitchen. Lane paused the video and pointed at the monitor.

"Why is every cabinet door open?"

"Ott told me about a game called the Man in the Mirror. The students were playing some version of it that night. The spirits that come with this mythical character find safe harbor in anything that is closed. Cabinets, drawers, closets, rooms. Opening everything in sight prevents spirits from staying behind to curse you."

"Lovely," Lane said. "Whatever happened to Spin the Bottle?"

"Oh," Rory said, resuming the video. "These kids were way past Spin the Bottle."

On the screen, the camera moved over the entire kitchen and through the first floor, where every door to every room was open. Then the camera shook its way to the front room library. Rory had walked through the room two days before with Detective Ott. A row of candles sat in front of a standing mirror. Matches were scattered on the floor next to the candles, and in front of it all Andrew Gross's body lay in a heap. Rigor mortis had yet to set in, and his body appeared to have deflated, as if his once-full limbs had depressurized to leave him in a mound on the floor. A clear-edged pool of blood surrounded his body, dark and syrupy. The mirror reflected the image of the crime scene technician as she swept the camera across the room, producing a strange collision of the living and dead. The surface of the mirror was speckled with blood, as was the wall behind it. The room was otherwise empty but for the red ivy that drifted through the open window, the cherry petals fluttering as the night air whisked it in from outside. The camera moved away from the window and pointed at the door to the room. On the floor of the doorway were spears of blood from where Tanner Landing's body had been dragged.

The scene cut from the front room, and the next image Rory and Lane saw was filmed outside. Spotlights that shot down from overhead brightly lit the area. The hum of a generator could be heard powering the police lights. As the camera moved across the front lawn, it documented the trail of blood and the gouges in the ground produced from Tanner Landing's body dragged across the earth. Slowly, the camera moved from the ground to the wrought iron gate. Rory unconsciously leaned backward, away from the computer, as Tanner Landing's body came into view. She remembered Henry Ott describing the scene as a slaughter, and as Rory took in the image of the tine piercing the boy's chin and protruding through the top of his forehead, she could think of no better word for it.

She paused the video and kept her eyes on the screen as she spoke to Lane.

"No signs of a struggle inside that room," she said. "A lack of defensive wounds on either of the victims. Our thinking has been that the killer snuck up on them, but maybe that's not right. Maybe the killer was *one of them.* Maybe the killer was with them."

"Another student?"

"Possibly. In that scenario, these two would have been caught off guard, not because someone snuck up on them but because they had no reason to think whoever was with them had any intention of harming them."

Lane reached forward and rewound the video until they were back inside the house.

"Look at the mirror," he said. "It's spattered in blood. That means the killer attacked from behind, allowing the blood spatter to protrude forward. Both kids were sliced across the throat. In order for blood to cause this kind of spatter pattern across the glass, both of them were facing the mirror and the attacker was behind them."

Rory nodded her head. "From what Detective Ott told me, and from what I have found in a quick Internet search, this game requires the kids to stare into a mirror and whisper 'Man in the Mirror' multiple times. Maybe they were doing this when they were killed."

Lane also nodded and scooted forward on the couch. "So the killer is either lying in wait or with them when they reach this room and stand in front of the mirror. He slices their throats, leaves one on the floor to bleed out, and drags the other outside to hoist him onto the gate. The assailant was either showing his dominance or exacting revenge. But to drag a 160-pound teenager outside and place him on the gate would have taken time. At least five minutes after the attack. That suggests that the assailant was both familiar with the area and in no rush. He was calm. Definitely organized. Definitely premeditated. This did not happen out of the blue. Once you get past the blood and the gore, what I'm seeing in this crime scene does not fit the idea that Charles Gorman snapped. This is too calculating and complicated to believe that he simply lost control."

Lane reached his hand to the back of his bandaged head and squeezed as he thought.

"Losing control might cause someone to kill unexpectedly," he said. "But the ritualistic hanging of this kid on the gate is something different. It wasn't reactionary. It was planned and it was intentional. No matter how much these kids bullied Gorman, his profile doesn't match someone who would lose control. It doesn't match someone who would kill like this, or at all."

"But Gorman described the scene exactly as it is shown here in the video," Rory said. "He wrote out the details of slashed throats and the impalement on the gate. That supports your profile of premeditation. That he carefully planned it out ahead of time."

Rory stared at the monitor a bit longer, and then finally turned to Lane.

"The students at Westmont Prep were required to meet with their counselors once a week. I read through Bridget Matthews's and Danielle Landry's medical records and noticed that their therapy sessions encouraged them to journal their thoughts. Their fears and their anxieties, and some of their most private inner reflections."

"It's a common tool in psychotherapy."

"Maybe Gorman's manifesto was simply that—his innermost contemplations put onto the page as a therapeutic way to dispel them."

Lane cocked his head to the side. "But that would mean . . ."

"Someone else could have read Gorman's journal and set up the scene exactly as he described."

Lane sat upright, interested in Rory's hypothesis. "Patient-doctor confidentiality dictates that only one other person would have had access to his journal."

"Correct."

"Does his file indicate that he was in therapy?"

"It does," Rory said.

"Does it mention his doctor's name?"

Rory nodded. "Gabriella Hanover."

Westmont Prep
Summer 2019

CHAPTER 58

They waited until midnight and met under the Gothic pediment of the library building. The upward-shining spotlights shadowed the etching of the school's logo: *Veniam solum, relinquatis et*. They were certainly together tonight, if only reluctantly. The latest challenge put forth by Andrew Gross required them to sneak into Mr. Gorman's house and steal a personal item. During their most recent trip to the abandoned boarding house, they had all drank Miller Lite beer while Andrew boasted about this phase of the challenges from the previous year when he was a new initiate and his group of juniors had stolen an entire drawer of Mrs. Rasmussen's bras. Word had spread of the theft, and rumors were whispered through campus that those involved in the Man in the Mirror challenges were responsible. A few days later, Mrs. Rasmussen's brassieres showed up hanging in a neat line from the eaves of the library building just below the school logo. This incoming class of initiates had little chance of topping Andrew's legacy of debauchery, and none of them were willing to go near Mr. Gorman's underwear drawer. But Tanner was adamant that they could pull something off that would draw the seniors' attention and respect.

The key Andrew had given them was supposedly a master to the back doors of all the houses on Teacher's Row. Whether it worked was to be determined. Gwen had mentioned that after Mrs. Rasmussen's bras had gone missing the previous year, perhaps the locks to all the duplexes on Teacher's Row had been changed. Gwen had also mentioned that since the mousetrap incident, another prank would not go over well. They were under close scrutiny, and both Tanner and Andrew had been called in to speak with Drs. Hanover and Casper, who warned that they would not tolerate the same level of disrespect that had taken place the previous summer. They were all reminded of the code of conduct Westmont Prep demanded. Breaking and entering was not part of it.

Still, here they were, hidden under cover of darkness and slithering their way to Teacher's Row. They each had their own reasons for tonight. Tanner was desperate to fit in and be accepted, and he would do nearly anything to one-up those he was trying to impress. Gwen and the others wanted, on some level, to be part of the exclusive group inside the walls of Westmont Prep. None would argue that point. But something else was driving them, too. Fear. Since arriving at Westmont Prep as wide-eyed freshmen, they had chased the myth of the Man in the Mirror. Nearly every student had. The folklore was so prevalent on campus that only a handful of students were able to escape the lure of the legend. Now, somehow, this group of six had been given the opportunity to participate in that fable. Not some cheap replica of it that a few other students had tried to create. June 21 was the real deal. But to get there, to receive the privileges that came from completing the Man in the Mirror challenge, they had to go through the initiation challenges. They believed in the myth just enough to follow Tanner tonight through the shadows of campus.

None knew how much their lives were about to change.

CHAPTER 59

The plan was for Tanner to enter the back door of Mr. Gorman's duplex and grab the first thing he saw from the kitchen. It didn't matter what it was, it only mattered that it belonged to Charles Gorman. Then they would quietly lock the door and disappear into the night having completed the final challenge before the summer solstice event.

They stayed in the shadows and made it to Teacher's Row, where only a few porch lights were ablaze. The rest of the houses were dark and silent. They approached number fourteen and went around back, their individual footsteps soft, but the collection of them together sounded like an army brigade. When they made it around the building, they noticed that one of Mr. Gorman's windows was bright with yellow light.

"Shit," Tanner said. "He's awake?"

"Let's just call this off," Gwen said.

"No way. We can't fail a challenge."

"If we get caught, we'll get kicked out of school. Hanover and Casper are already watching us this summer."

"You can leave then," Tanner said. "But Bridget and I are doing this."

Tanner looked at the rest of them.

"In or out?"

"Just go see what's going on," Gavin said. "If he's awake, it'll be impossible to sneak in. We'll have to come another night."

Tanner turned from the group and crouched down as he approached the back window. His silhouette crept along the edge of the house until he was just to the side of the lighted window; then he leaned over and peeked inside. There was a moment of stillness as the others watched him. Each of them held their breath. They were on a trip switch, ready to bolt into the night if the back door opened or the curtains moved. But instead, they saw Tanner's dark silhouette frantically waving them over to the window.

"Get over here!" he said in a desperate whisper. "Now!"

Gwen and Gavin looked at each other, and they all moved in a slow group toward the window. Tanner was laughing in a wheezing cackle, holding his chest as if he might have a heart attack. He pointed to the window.

"Mr. G's going at it."

Gwen and Gavin leaned past the window frame until the inside of the house was visible. Theo, Danielle, and Bridget did the same, each of their faces catching the soft yellow light that spilled through the window. Inside, the light came from a bedside lamp, the glow of which shadowed Charles Gorman's naked body as he thrust his hips in a rhythmic cadence. Slender legs were wrapped around his waist, and they all got a voyeuristic look at their chemistry teacher's rear end as he clenched and unclenched his butt cheeks.

"Holy shit," Gavin said as he quickly pulled away from the window. They all did the same and muffled their laughter.

"Let's get out of here," Gwen said. "We're not doing this tonight."

"This is too good to miss," Tanner said, pulling out his phone.

He clicked on his camera, swiped it to video, and began recording the action through the window. At one point, Mr. Gorman positioned himself as if performing a push-up, turned his head to the side, and offered a priceless expression of ecstasy before thrusting his buttocks forward one last time as his body shuddered. Tanner tried to hold the camera steady, but his laughter shook the frame back and forth.

The others, too, had turned their gaze back to the window, finding it impossible not to watch. They were like gawkers staring at a car wreck. When Mr. Gorman turned his head so that his face was visible, they all ducked below the window frame. Tanner held his phone above the sill for another few seconds.

"Let's go," Gwen said.

"Almost," Tanner said, pulling his phone down and slipping it into his pocket.

From the same pocket he retrieved an air horn. Then he crawled from beneath the window and hurried to the back door. The others watched, still giddy from what they had just witnessed and not fully aware of Tanner's intentions. Until, that was, they heard the soft squeak of Mr. Gorman's back door opening. Tanner disappeared inside for a moment and then reappeared with a leather-bound journal in his hand.

"First thing I could find," he said, out of breath from the surge of adrenaline.

"You are so crazy," Gavin said. He grabbed Gwen's hand. "Let's get out of here."

They all turned from the still-open door and began their silent escape. That's when the air horn sounded. Three long bursts that shattered the silence of the night with an earsplitting squeal.

"Better run, losers!" Tanner said as he streaked past them. Mr. Gorman's door was still wide open.

With hearts thumping, they all took off into the night.

CHAPTER 60

Charles Gorman was breathing heavily when he collapsed onto the woman under him. He felt her fingernails run the length of his back.

"Stay tonight," he whispered into her ear.

"You know I can't," she said.

He never pushed, only asked. They were both quiet, only their breathing audible as they lay tangled together. Then an ear-piercing screech tore through the house. Then another, and another. Three loud screeches that startled them both.

"What the hell!" Charles yelled as he rolled off the bed and crashed to the floor as if the burst of noise had physically lifted him and thrown him down.

The woman pulled the sheets over her naked body. Charles heard laughter and stampeding footsteps. He pulled on his underwear and bolted out of the bedroom, down the hall, and into the kitchen. The back door was wide open. He turned on the lights and looked around. The house was empty. He hurried outside and looked up and down the path that ran behind the duplexes. The pounding of feet was off to his left and quickly fading into the night. He took a few steps in their direction and listened again, but all he heard was the hum of locusts. Another moment passed, and he was tempted to run into the darkness and follow the footsteps. He was sure he could catch them. He figured they were headed for the dorms. But he was wearing only his white underwear. He turned and walked back into his house. When he made it back to the bedroom, Gabriella Hanover was already dressed. She was visibly shaken.

"Goddamn kids," Charles said. "They think they run this place in the summer."

Gabriella's hand was shaking as she ran her palm across her mouth and over her cheek. "Who was it?"

"I didn't see them, but it had to be Andrew Gross or Tanner Landing."

"Charles, do you think they saw us?"

"How could they have seen us?"

"They were in the house, Charles! Do you think they saw us?"

"No. It's just a stupid dare. Open the door and blow an air horn, or whatever the hell that was. They wouldn't have the balls to come into my house, the little shit-heads."

"We could get in a lot of trouble if anyone found out about us. There are rules against what we have been doing."

"No one's going to find out, Gabriella. No one saw anything. It's stupid kids on a stupid dare."

"I'm your superior, Charles. This shows a complete lack of judgment on my part. If anyone found out about this, the school board would release me immediately. Not to mention that I'm sleeping with one of my patients. I could lose my license, Charles!"

He came over to her and tried to comfort her, but she pushed him away.

"I have to go," she said. "We'll talk tomorrow."

Gabriella Hanover hurried out the back door. Gorman stood in his kitchen and watched her leave. He walked over to the door and slammed it shut.

PART VII

August 2020

CHAPTER 61

Rory woke Friday morning as the matte copper of predawn filled the window frames. She heard Lane's still-labored breathing, the slight gurgle when he exhaled—a lingering symptom of the smoke inhalation. She checked the bedside clock and saw that it was 5:12 A.M. A light sleeper for life, Rory woke from the softest of noises. And once taken from sleep, finding it again was difficult. Opening her eyes was like firing up a computer. Her mind churned and processed, ready to be put to work. This was especially true when she was in the middle of a case.

She slipped from bed and walked into the hallway in her tank top and shorts. She pulled a button-down flannel shirt over her shoulders. Inky shadows crept across the lower level of the cottage. Rory padded down the stairs, snatched a Diet Coke from the fridge, and headed to the three-season room. Sitting at her desk, she clicked on the lamp. The Armand Marseille Kiddiejoy lay in the travel box. She lifted it now to examine the work she had done restoring the ear and cheek. She had glazed the porcelain and epoxy, which had erased the lattice of cracks. She went to work this morning stripping the mismatched colors with Aunt Greta's secret mixture of vodka and dish soap. When Rory finished, she took on the challenge of sanding smooth the porcelain. It was meticulous and tedious work, requiring redundant rounds of sanding with consecutively finer grade paper—the last of which was 600 grit, so fine she could barely feel it on her fingertips—until the texture of the repaired side was an exact match to the other. After two hours, Rory closed her eyes and ran the pads of her fingers over the doll's face, feeling for imperfections her eyes might have missed. She found none. Next she started the process of staining the porcelain to bring it back to its original color. Rory consulted lineage photos she had obtained at the auction, as well as pictures she pulled from the Internet. The German doll catalogue was open and resting on an easel in front of the desk, the current page earmarked to display an Armand Marseille Kiddiejoy doll in its natural form with cheeks the color of rosé wine over pale white skin.

She started with the broadest Foldger-Gruden brush, the bristles of which were just under an inch wide. She used this broad brush to apply the first layer of foundation primer, which colored the surface of the doll's face almond yellow. After the first coat, she applied the heat gun before running the blue ultraviolet light over the porcelain. A second coat of primer followed. As she moved between coloring and drying, Rory slipped the brushes into and out of the breast pocket of her flannel in swift motions, barely thinking as she conquered the scrupulous demands of her craft.

It was another two hours before she realized that her back was aching. She stood and stretched the stiffness from her muscles before placing the doll to the side. She was nearly finished. All that remained was adding the details of the eyelashes, the blushing of the cheeks, the shadowing around the nostrils, and the coloring around the edges of the lips. In a flash, Rory's mind ran through each meticulous brushstroke that would be required— thousands and thousands of them, one after the other. She itched to get started on those final details. It was, perhaps, her favorite element of restoration. But she needed the porcelain to dry before it would properly accept the fine pastels she would add.

She grabbed another Diet Coke from the fridge and heard the chair in the upstairs loft skid across the floor. She knew Lane was back at his computer, plugging more markers into the MAP database and looking for any connection he could find that dealt with suicides and pennies flattened on train tracks. Lane had spent most of the previous afternoon working on Rory's penny discovery— cataloguing each hit the database spit out and trying to make sense of it all. Late last night he said he had come across a promising lead. She was anxious to hear what he'd found, but just like Rory, Lane had his own quirks. One of them was the need for isolation while he was in the middle of a project. She'd give him space until he was ready to share what he had learned.

She sat back down at the desk in the three-season room. It was nearly ten o'clock when she moved her attention to the evidence box. Across from her was the corkboard that held the faces of the Westmont Prep students and the man accused of killing them. She pulled Theo Compton's file in front of her. Rory had read through it once before, on the first night after Detective Ott had delivered the box of files. She read it again now. Her mind had recorded everything during her initial reading, but a distant thought kept bubbling to the surface of her mind—

a subconscious inkling she could not immediately identify or recognize. Rory only knew that this underground thought needed excavating. If Rory ignored this notion, if she failed to dig and find its significance, some part of her mind would be forever preoccupied with what she had missed. Soon, that preoccupation would turn into an obsession. The obsession, if not quelled, a compulsion. In her everyday life, Rory fought against this affliction. In her day-to-day routine, this type of thinking was an illness powerful enough to ruin her life. In her work, however, Rory harnessed that illness and all its idiosyncrasies to find what everyone else had missed.

She pulled photos from Theo's file and laid them on the desk. They were large eight-by-ten prints of the train tracks, Theo Compton's body, shoe prints, and the surrounding area. During Rory's first time through the file, she had been focused on the flattened and oblong penny found in Theo's pocket at the time of his suicide. But there was something else. Something her subconscious mind had noticed. She worked now to figure out what it was.

The photos had been taken by medical legal investigators from the LaPorte County coroner's office and were shot after Mack Carter had called 911 and after EMTs had arrived on the scene to attempt to revive the victim. In the process, they had repositioned Theo Compton's body before pronouncing him dead. The folks from the coroner's office arrived next to document the scene. Despite the photos Rory studied now, she remembered a different image of Theo Compton. This snapshot that blinked in and out of her memory was taken before the medical legal investigators or coroner or EMTs had arrived on the scene. It was from when Mack Carter had found Theo's body. There was a recording of that moment, and Rory had seen it. The shaky video Ryder Hillier had taken was a grainy, poor-quality cell phone recording with only the phone's flashlight attempting to break through the ink-black night. Despite the amateurish quality of the video, Rory remembered something about the recording now. Whatever it was had been stored in her mind, where it sat dormant and untouched. But tonight as she stared at the crime scene photos of Theo Compton's body, that other image came to life. Something about it was clawing at her brain and causing the synapses of her mind to fire. Rory tried to conjure the image and figure out what was bothering her, but the notion was just out of reach.

She opened her laptop and pulled up Ryder Hillier's blog, hoping to view the video. But the footage had been restricted. Rory checked the journalist's YouTube channel next, only to find the same result. She searched the Internet, but every site that promised the forbidden recording was a dead end. *This video is no longer available* was listed on each link Rory clicked. The recording was gone.

Rory sat back in her chair. There was something about the video that didn't match the photos she was looking at now. She closed her eyes and attempted to spin the scroll of information in her mind back to the moment when she had viewed the video. No matter how hard she tried, though, she could not raise the image she knew was there. She knew only that the stored image had her questioning an assumption everyone had made to this point.

What if the Westmont Prep students hadn't been committing suicide? What if they had been killed?

Rory stood from the desk and grabbed her rucksack, then unzipped the front compartment and pulled out the business card Ryder Hillier had given her the night they met at the hospital. She clicked her phone to life and dialed.

CHAPTER 62

Ryder Hillier sat across from Theo Compton's mother at the kitchen table. She had made the four-hour drive to Cincinnati early Friday morning, and now, at just past ten, Ryder accepted Mrs. Compton's offer of coffee. The steam spiraled up from the mug when Paige Compton placed it in front of her.

"Thanks for coming all this way," Mrs. Compton said.

"Of course," Ryder said. "Thank you for inviting me. I'm anxious to hear your story, but I want to mention again how very sorry I am for posting that video of your son. Please believe me when I say I'm filled with regret and remorse."

"Thank you for saying that. But whether you posted that video or not, my son would still be gone. Tell me," Mrs. Compton said as she sat down at the kitchen table, "how did you know Theo would be at the boarding house that night?"

Ryder put her hands around the hot mug to keep them occupied. She was still hesitant to be sitting in the Comptons' kitchen—first because of the lawsuit Paige Compton had levied against her, and second, because if her editor found out she was chasing this story, he'd fire her on the spot.

"Theo left a message on Mack Carter's podcast website," Ryder said. "The message indicated that he'd be out at the house that night."

"Doing what?"

"At the time I read the message, I had no idea."

"What did the message say?"

"Haven't the police gone through this with you?"

"No. They've barely talked to me. They informed me that Theo killed himself but haven't given me or my husband a second thought since. And because we're so far away, all we can do is leave messages and hope for a call back."

"Would you like to see the message Theo wrote?" Ryder asked. "I could pull it up on my phone."

Mrs. Compton's eyes grew wet with tears. She nodded.

On her phone, Ryder pulled up the *Suicide House* web page. It had been two weeks since the last episode aired, and despite the death of Mack Carter she knew his massive audience was hoping for further installments. She scrolled through the message board until she found Theo's cryptic comment. "Here. It said, 'MC, thirteen, three, five. Tonight. I'll tell you the truth. Then, whatever happens, happens. I'm ready for the consequences.'"

Mrs. Compton took the phone when Ryder offered it.

"What do the numbers mean?" Mrs. Compton asked as she stared at the message.

"They're coordinates of sorts. Directions on how to get to the abandoned boarding house through a back route."

"How did you know what they meant?"

"I've done quite a bit of research on Westmont Prep since the killings last summer, and I have written about it on my blog. During my research, I stumbled across the coded message. An alumnus I interviewed clued me in on the meaning. It sounded as if most of the student body knew what the numbers stood for. There's some folklore around the code, and a lot of rumor and speculation about what goes on at the boarding house."

"Does it have to do with that game they were playing?"

Ryder shrugged and shook her head. "I'm not sure exactly. I only knew that Theo was asking Mack Carter to meet him out at the boarding house. That's why I went. I was chasing a scoop. Trying to break a story and be the first to report on it."

"What sort of breaking news did you think you'd find?"

"I wasn't sure. I knew that Theo had started to reveal some details when talking with Mack Carter before he decided against it at the last minute. Your son was featured on one of the podcast episodes. I've always believed there's more to the Westmont Prep story than what's out there, and I suppose I figured your son knew something about it. But please believe me when I tell you that I had no idea I'd find Theo the way I did."

Mrs. Compton sat in silence until she looked up from the phone and stared Ryder in the eye.

"Why would my son ask an investigative reporter, who was doing a podcast about the murders at his school, to meet him at the very place where the murders took place, only to kill himself before that reporter arrived?"

The question was so blunt and direct that it caused Ryder to blink several times as she considered it.

"I . . . don't know," Ryder finally said.

"Theo never talked to me much about what happened the night he and his friends went to that house in the woods. He never talked about the boys who were killed last summer. He said it was too hard to discuss and that the doctors at school were helping him and the students get past the tragedy. I never pushed. I thought he was going through enough without his mother nagging him. But then Theo called me. It was the night before he died. He said he was worried."

"Worried about what?" Ryder asked

"About what he was thinking of doing."

Ryder leaned forward. The steam from her coffee rose up into her chin. "What was he thinking of doing?"

"He said he was going to talk to a reporter about what happened that night in the woods, and about some things that were going on since that night."

"What things?"

"Theo had a group of friends he was close with at Westmont. Kids he had known since freshman year. He said they had something they wanted to tell the police about that night. Theo said he was ready to get it off his chest."

"What was it?"

Mrs. Compton shook her head. "He never told me. He was only calling to warn me that it was going to get him in some trouble. He said he couldn't hide it anymore. He knew something about his chemistry teacher. The one who killed those boys."

"Mr. Gorman? What did Theo know?"

"Again, he never told me. But he wanted to tell *someone* and had decided that someone should be Mack Carter. But before he did . . ."

Mrs. Compton began to cry.

"But before he did . . ." Ryder said with a measured tone. "Theo killed himself?"

Mrs. Compton shook her head. "Not my Theo. He would never do that."

Ryder allowed the implication to settle. But she needed to be sure she was on the same page.

"So, if Theo didn't kill himself . . ."

Mrs. Compton looked up, tears rolling down her cheeks. "Someone killed him. Someone who didn't want Theo to talk about whatever happened with his friends that night."

Ryder scooted her chair forward a bit. "Have you spoken to the police about any of this?"

"I've tried," Mrs. Compton said. "I've tried to convince them that Theo would never end his own life. He would never do that to his family. But they won't listen to me. They think I'm just a grieving mother unable to come to terms with her son's suicide. That's why I called you. The police are not going to give my son's death a second thought. But I know you will. I need your help. I need you to figure out what Theo wanted to get off his chest. What he was going to tell Mack Carter."

So many things ran through Ryder's mind. The Westmont Prep case was not dead. She was suddenly looking at it from a new perspective, coming at it from a different angle, armed with a conclusion no one else had made. She knew cold cases were solved when new eyes looked at old evidence.

"Okay," Ryder finally said, collecting her thoughts. "I'm going to look into this for you. See what I can find. I'll do what I can, but no promises that I'll make any progress. I think I'll start with Theo's friends."

"That's the problem," Mrs. Compton said. "There are only two of them left. And for all I know, they were the ones Theo was scared of."

Before Ryder could ask another question, her phone rang.

CHAPTER 63

Gwen Montgomery climbed the stairs of the library building until she reached the top floor. Six sturdy wooden desks were positioned in precise order between shelves that held old periodicals and encyclopedias. Students came here for quiet. Students came here to *really* study, not to chat and laugh like what happened on the main floor of the library. During summer session, with only a scant number of students on campus, the upper level of the library was always vacant. It had become the spot for her meetings with Gavin. The dorm had been deemed too dangerous for their discussions.

She walked to the row of windows that overlooked the front entrance of campus—the giant brick pillars that were connected by the tall wrought iron gate that ceremoniously closed each year on Gate Day, trapping the students inside. Although not visible from her perspective inside the library building, Gwen knew the windows she looked through now were positioned just below the etched letters on the building's pediment that reminded students that they came to Westmont Prep alone but left together. She wondered now if she'd ever leave at all.

"Hey," Gavin said in a whispered voice behind her.

She startled and turned away from the windows.

"What's wrong?"

His question, all by itself, bothered her. Gavin knew goddamn well what was wrong, and his nonchalance about the situation had always disturbed her, but never more so than over the last few weeks. Their actions had affected so many lives.

"I feel like we have no idea what's going on," she said. "We have no idea what anyone knows. Ever since the podcast ended, and Ryder Hillier's site was scrubbed, we've been in the dark."

"That's a good thing," Gavin said. He walked closer to her. "Remember how worried you were when we heard about the podcast in the first place? The less people poke around, the better for us."

"But at least we had information to go on. At least we knew what the pulse of the investigation was. Now, we know nothing."

"We know no one's asking to talk to us. That's all we should care about at the moment. You want people poking around? You want to see what would have happened if Theo had spilled his guts?"

"Jesus, Gavin! You talk like it's a good thing that Theo killed himself."

"It's a goddamn tragic thing! But it might have been worse had he told Mack Carter about that night. Shit, Gwen. I'm the only one thinking clearly here. And for that, I'm crucified. Where would we be right now if I weren't holding things together?"

She didn't answer.

"Listen," Gavin said, his tone softer. "I know this is hard. But we don't have a choice anymore. We did at one point, and we made our decision. Now we have to ride this out. We have to stick together. We're the only ones left, Gwen. It's just me and you."

Gwen nodded and shook her head. She wrapped her arms around her bony shoulders and hugged herself.

"I just wish we had a way of knowing about the investigation. I wish we had a way of knowing what *they* know."

"Don't you see? A lack of information is a *good* thing. It means they don't know anything. And as long as you and I stick together, it will stay that way."

He came over and took her in his arms. But Gavin's touch had lost its comfort. He was no longer endeared to her. He had changed so much since last year that Gwen barely recognized him.

CHAPTER 64

Gwen wiped the tears from her eyes as she walked from the library. The pressure was starting to crush her. It was actually far past starting. It was killing her. It was as if she had been carrying a massive boulder on her shoulders for the past year, struggling with quivering thighs to move through life. Finally, after fourteen months, it was too much to bear. Gavin's words no longer comforted her. His reassurances that time would heal her wounds and take away her guilt were no longer believable. He was part of it all. He was, perhaps, the cause of it all. It had been his idea.

Without Gavin, Gwen needed someone to guide her. She couldn't turn to her parents. Not now. Not after so much time had passed. Dr. Hanover's efforts, too, had been ineffective. Only one person had ever eased her pain. Only one person had quelled her guilt for that night. She trusted him with her life, and with no one else to turn to, she finally decided to tell him everything.

She walked through campus until she reached Teacher's Row. She didn't look at number fourteen when she passed it. Doing so reminded her of the night she and her friends had wreaked so much havoc. The night her life changed forever. How different things would be had they not gone to Mr. Gorman's duplex that night. How different her life would look today had they not taken that video or followed Tanner Landing like a herd of sheep. Gwen pushed the memories and what-if thoughts from her mind. She'd driven herself mad over the last year with dreams of going back in time. Of fantasies that the clock could be turned back for her, that she could change the decisions she made that night.

When she reached Dr. Casper's duplex, she walked up the stairs and knocked. The front door opened. She didn't give him the chance this time to protest her presence. She didn't give him the opportunity to refuse her pleas for help.

"I have to talk with you," she said, and then walked past him and into the front room that acted as his office. She took a seat in the high-backed plush chair where she had always sat during her sessions with him, until she had been reassigned to Dr. Hanover after the killings.

It took a while before Dr. Casper appeared in the doorway. Gwen could sense his apprehension, as if he knew her words were about to change her life. As if he knew she was fragile and on the brink. She saw him morph into the person he had always been to her. The doctor who had always known how to help her. Someone who would never turn her away, no matter how terrible a thing she had done.

"What's on your mind?" Dr. Casper finally asked in a slow, calculated tone.

Gwen rubbed her fist across her mouth, bit on her knuckle as she thought.

"I want to tell you about the night Tanner and Andrew were killed."

Dr. Casper stood rock-solid still in the doorframe. He raised his eyebrows. "Haven't you already told the police about everything you know?"

"No. Something happened that night with my friends and me. We haven't told anyone."

She looked down into her lap, collecting her thoughts, and then finally back to Dr. Casper.

"It's about Mr. Gorman. We know he didn't kill Tanner and Andrew."

Dr. Casper took a couple of steps into the room.

"Gwen, I'm not sure I'm the person you should tell this to."

"You're the *only* person I can tell."

Westmont Prep
Summer 2019

CHAPTER 65

By nine A.M. on Tuesday—just a couple of days removed from their Saturday-night trek through the shadows of Westmont Prep and to the back of duplex number fourteen—word of the video had circulated to each corner of campus. Nearly every student was clamoring to see the footage. Because Tanner had taken the video, and it currently resided solely on his phone, he used it as a magnet to attract the attention he was so thirsty for. In the chemistry lab, students huddled around him, watching and rewatching the semipornographic but mostly comical video of a naked Charles Gorman thrusting his hips, bunny-like, until he turned his head to the side and offered the camera a frenetic expression of ecstasy. Gwen didn't need to watch the video to gauge which part the others were viewing. When the group burst into laughter she knew Tanner had paused the video on Mr. Gorman's face. She felt sad for Mr. Gorman. Such a private part of his life had been stolen and was now being dished out to everyone with a voyeuristic need, by someone who craved acceptance from his peers more than he respected the basic tenets of privacy.

Tanner had created memes from what he considered the best parts of the video. There was one titled *The Jackhammer*, which included Mr. Gorman's naked buttocks bouncing furiously up and down in a fast-forward loop. Another was labeled *Mr. G's Money Shot* and included a zooming close-up of Gorman's grainy and darkened face when he turned his head to the side.

"He's an idiot," Gavin said to Gwen. They stood at their lab station with Theo and Danielle. "He's going to send that video to someone, and before long it's going to show up on social media. Then we're all screwed."

"Tell him," Gwen said.

"I did. Last night when I saw the memes he was creating. I told him we'd get in a lot of trouble if that video leaked. He doesn't care. He thinks it's his ticket into the good graces of Andrew Gross, and he's sure it will be considered a clear trump of Mrs. Rasmussen's underwear hanging from the library."

"Good morning," Mr. Gorman said as he entered the lab. "Quiet down and break into your lab groups." He looked at the group huddled in the back corner of the lab. "Mr. Landing, what's so amusing over there?"

"Nothing," Tanner said, slipping his phone into his back pocket. Smiles and snickers plagued the entire class. "I was just preparing for the experiment we're doing today."

"Excellent," Mr. Gorman said. "Surely, then, you'll be able to explain it to the class?"

"Uh, yeah," Tanner said, barely able to control his laughter. He looked at Andrew Gross, who was standing across from him. "Today's experiment will create a slow buildup to a sudden eruption."

At once, the classroom broke into laughter. Mr. Gorman waited for silence.

"There is a short video we'll watch about today's experiment," he said as he dimmed the lights and pulled the projector screen down. He started up the projector and a blue square of light fell onto the screen. As soon as it did, Gwen's stomach dropped.

"Oh, God," she whispered to Gavin. "Please tell me he didn't."

Mr. Gorman started the video. The blue color vanished, and a second later the meme titled *The Jackhammer* appeared. The classroom was silent as Mr. Gorman's naked body popped up on the screen. It took a moment for Charles Gorman to understand what he was seeing, because the video played for several seconds before he shut the projector down and quickly left the room.

It was June 18.

CHAPTER 66

Charles Gorman was in a panic. Somehow they had recorded him. He guessed that the video had been taken through his bedroom window, but he had only gotten a short glimpse of it before shutting the projector off and hurrying from the lab. Now his mind played tricks on him, and his memory was spotty as the recurrent loop of the video ran through his mind. It got worse and worse every time he thought of it. Combined with his other discovery, it was enough to have him at the edge of rational behavior.

He had searched every corner of his duplex for it. Now he was on a fast walk to Gabriella's office. He knocked on her door harder than intended. She opened it a moment later.

"Charles," she said, glancing over his shoulder to see who might be witnessing them together.

"I need to talk."

"I'm in the middle of a meeting at the moment—"

"It's about the other night."

Gabriella lowered her voice. "Charles, this is not a

good time. And nothing has changed. We need to keep to ourselves for a while."

"That's not possible anymore," Charles said as he brushed past her and into the house. When he walked into the front room, he found Christian Casper sitting in the chair.

"Charles. Good to see you," Christian said.

"Charles just stopped by," Gabriella said from the doorway, "to discuss—"

"My journal is missing," Charles said.

"Pardon me?" Gabriella said.

"My journal. I can't find it. It has everything you and I have ever discussed during a session in it."

"I think I'll leave you two alone," Christian said as he stood.

"No," Charles said. "You'll need to know about this, too."

"Charles," Gabriella said, "I can tell you're upset. Let's discuss this privately."

"I told you it was too late for that. They recorded us."

Christian Casper swallowed awkwardly. "I'm going to excuse myself."

"They did *what*?" Gabriella said.

Charles took a deep breath. "The other night." He glanced quickly at Christian and then back to Gabriella. "When we were . . . together. They recorded us through the window."

Gabriella placed her palm over her mouth. Her jaw unknowingly hung open.

"Who, exactly, are we talking about? And what did they record?" Christian asked.

Charles closed his eyes. "Gabriella and I are in a relationship. She was at my duplex on Saturday night when students opened the back door and blew an air horn through the house. I thought it was just a stupid prank, until today. I started my projector and instead of a chemistry lesson, a video of the two of us started playing."

"Good God," Gabriella said, sitting in a chair.

He looked at her. "Please tell me I left my journal here after our last session."

Gabriella shook her head. "No, it's not here."

Charles ran his hand through his hair, swallowed hard. He, too, sat down. "They took it. The little bastards took it."

"What was in it?" Christian asked.

"Everything," Charles said. He looked at Gabriella. "Everything about my past." His teeth clenched again, as if he had no control over his jaw. "And all my ramblings about what I wanted to do to Tanner Landing and Andrew Gross."

Gabriella placed her hand on her forehead, as if a feverous spell had come over her. "What did you write, Charles?"

"Everything I told you about! Everything you encouraged me to document as a way to get it out of my system."

"Stop, please," Gabriella said. She looked at Christian. "Will you please excuse us?"

"He knows what I wrote, Gabriella. I told him about it, so let's get past the idea that we can keep any of this private any longer. If those kids read my journal, I'm screwed. And I'm not talking about losing my job over a consensual relationship. I'm talking about legal consequences. For Christ's sake, grade school kids have their lives ruined by doodling pictures of guns. What I wrote about was . . . awful. And gruesome. And detailed."

"I'll call them in," Gabriella said. "We'll have a meeting with the students."

"Yes," Christian said. "This has gone too far."

"Do you honestly believe they would admit to taking my journal? Or to the video?"

Gabriella finally looked up at him. "What are our other options?"

"I think we should cancel classes for the rest of this week," Christian said. "Until we get a handle on this situation."

Gabriella nodded her head. "I agree."

Charles Gorman's eyes were glazed over, wet with worry as he stared off into the distance. His face was stoic and detached.

PART VIII

August 2020

CHAPTER 67

The algorithm had produced thousands of hits from the initial set of criteria Lane had entered—train, train tracks, railroad, rail system, suicides, and all versions of irregularly shaped pennies. Apparently, he learned, rail yards are dangerous places. With a list ten pages long, he would need an army of help to follow up on all the leads. Had he been back in Chicago he could employ a few of his graduate students to dig through the findings, but here in Peppermill it was just him and his aching head. He had no choice but to narrow his search until the algorithm spit out a manageable list of leads. He had spent all of Thursday doing just that. Of the ones that remained, the most interesting was one he was chasing from New York. He had worked the phone the previous afternoon and into the evening, and then this morning until now, at noon on Friday, he finally connected with someone useful inside the NYPD.

"The guy you're looking for is retired down in Florida."

"Do you have a number for him?" Lane asked.

"Sure. But don't be offended if you don't get a return

call. He had some . . . issues," the voice on the other end of the line said. "He's been MIA for a while. Not even the guys up here have had any luck reaching him."

"I'll take the number just the same," Lane said. "If you don't mind."

"Yep. Here it is. Good luck."

Lane scribbled the number, offered his thanks, and prayed it wasn't a dead end.

CHAPTER 68

Retired detective Gus Morelli carried his La Rubia, a blond ale from Wynwood Brewing, out of his condo and hobbled down the steps to the beach on Friday evening. He typically watched the sunset from the screened-in lanai of his third-story condo, but tonight he needed to clear his head. The rented condominium was fifty steps from the beach—he'd counted, a habit he'd taken up since cancer had claimed his right leg three years ago. He gauged just about everything nowadays by how many steps it would take to get there.

He'd all but mastered his gait on even ground, but sand was still a son of a bitch. He took his time when he stepped onto the beach. None of the other retired folks around the condominium complex knew that he walked on a titanium prosthesis. Despite the Florida heat and humidity, he wore long pants and kept to a reasonable enough pace on the sand to fool most people. For those who did notice something unusual about his gait, they'd suspect many other scenarios before concluding that he'd lost a leg. Maybe he was recovering from surgery. Since arriving down south, he had learned that nearly every old person in Florida had been under the knife in the last year. It was like a sport for them, trying to one-up each other by comparing surgical procedures. Or perhaps he was recovering from a fall, another common hobby among the population he had found himself part of. Old people stumbled around like drunks, and nearly every one of them sported a boot or brace at some point during the year.

He paused a moment to take a pull from his La Rubia, hoping to drown out his cynicism. Despite the serenity of Sanibel Island, Detective Morelli still had work to do to curb his contempt for old folks. They brought back dark memories from his time at the rehabilitation hospital, where he spent several weeks after he lost his leg. There, he was lumped in with the helpless and forlorn. For a few weeks he was a member of the feeble elderly class who depended on nurses and aides to do everything from eat dinner to take a leak. Gus was determined to never again be grouped into that demographic. The years were out of his control; how he handled them was completely up to him.

Maybe, he considered, anyone who spotted him walking gingerly across the beach might believe he was simply taking his time, enjoying the sand and surf during retirement. That would be a hard sell, though, because he didn't believe it himself. Now a case from his past was waking from a long slumber and jostling Gus along with it. He headed to the beach tonight attempting to figure out if he was angry about being taken from hibernation or if it made him feel alive again.

Swallowing his beer he moved gingerly across the sand and down to the surf, where the ground was smoother. He sipped his beer and looked out across the ocean. He watched for the moment when the top crest of the sun dipped below the horizon. According to an old man he'd met on his first day on Sanibel, a green flash appeared the instant the sun sank below the horizon. After three months of sunsets, Gus was starting to think the old man was full of shit. Still, he squinted his eyes at the horizon and waited for the sun to sink into the ocean. All he was really thinking about, though, was the phone call he had received earlier in the day from the forensic psychologist out of Chicago who was interested in an old case Gus had been involved with. The setting sun and its reflection glistening across the ocean disappeared as his thoughts drifted back to an autumn day in New York when a teen-aged boy was killed on the train tracks.

The Bronx, New York

Oak Point Yard was home to freight trains that passed through New York on their way west. The cargo included lumber from Canada, produce, fuel, and imported goods that had made the trek across the Atlantic. The trash train ran through this rail yard, too, as did two Amtrak lines that used the electrified tracks and ran at high speed. It was dark when Gus arrived at the scene. The local police had roped the place off, and he ducked under the tape as he headed toward the tracks. The terrain was rocky, with stones giving way under his weight as he walked. The medical examiner met him.

"What's it look like?" Gus asked.

"A total mess," the ME said, a short woman in a windbreaker and black jeans. "High-velocity train meets pedestrian. It's never pretty. I estimate the train was moving about fifty miles per hour. The victim was struck by the lead car, carried a couple hundred yards down the tracks—two hundred twelve yards total—before finally being pulled under. The freight train was a mile long and the conductor never saw the kid, so he never stopped."

"What's left of him?"

"Not much."

"How was it called in?" Gus asked.

"The vic's brother was with him. Said they were play-ing on the tracks when it happened. The brother ran home, parents called nine-one-one."

"Are they here?"

The ME nodded and pointed toward a group of people. "Over there. Do you want to see the body before we wrap it up and take it in?"

Gus shook his head. "Nah. I'll take a look at the pho-tos when you're all done."

The medical examiner turned to head back to her team.

"Hey, Doc?" Gus asked.

She turned back.

"You said the train dragged the kid two hundred twelve yards. How did you get such an exact number?"

"Two ways," she said. "First, we found blood and skull fragments on the gravel where we suspect the kid was initially struck. Between there and the location of the body, we found bits and pieces of him, along with a dis-cernable trail of blood."

Gus nodded. "But two twelve is pretty specific. How do you know you aren't off by a yard or two?"

"Because of the second way we narrowed down the exact spot he was hit," the ME said. "The train knocked him out of his shoes. One of them, anyway. It was still on the track where the first bits of skull and blood were lo-cated. Figured that was the exact spot. We measured from there."

"Christ," Gus said. He took a deep breath and headed toward the dead kid's parents. They were speaking with an officer when Gus walked up.

"I'm Detective Morelli. I'm so sorry about your son."

The parents nodded. "Thank you," the woman said, barely holding back tears. Her face was flushed and her eyes red-rimmed.

"I understand your other son was present at the time William was struck by the train?"

The woman nodded. "He's our foster child, but yes, he was with William."

"Can I speak with him?"

The woman nodded. "He's with one of the officers."

Gus followed the woman to a group of officers. Sitting on the ground was a teenaged boy. "This is Detective Morelli," the woman said. "He wants to talk with you about what happened to William."

The boy looked up. Gus noticed that his eyes were clear, not red-rimmed like his mother's. Foster mother, Gus reminded himself.

"Hey," Gus said.

"Hey," the kid said back.

"Sorry about your brother."

"Thanks."

"Let's take a walk. You okay with that?"

The kid shrugged and stood up. Gus put his hand on the kid's shoulder, and they walked through the group of uniformed officers and away from the kid's foster parents.

"Can you tell me what happened?" Gus asked as they headed south, with the tracks to their right and the commotion of everything that had transpired behind them. Gus led the kid out of the train yard and into the parking lot, where his unmarked squad car was located.

"We were playing on the tracks like we always did."

"Like you always did?"

"Yeah. We came here all the time."

"To do what?"

The kid shrugged again. "Watch the trains go by. See how close we can get to them. If you get close enough you can feel the wind move you."

"Sounds dangerous."

There was a short pause.

"I don't know. I guess."

"Is that what happened to William? He got too close to the tracks?"

"Kinda," the kid said. "We were flattening pennies."

Gus raised his eyebrows. "Doing what?"

The kid reached into his pocket and pulled out a penny. Gus saw that it was thin and flat and oblong. "We put pennies on the tracks and let the trains run them over. They look like this when we're done."

Gus took the penny from the kid. It was stretched thin and reminded Gus of a piece of Play-Doh but still sturdy and stiff. Lincoln's face was recognizable in the copper, but there were no longer grooves or edges to his image. He ran his thumb over the surface. Smooth as a freshly sanded piece of wood.

"You said you come to the tracks a lot?"

The kid nodded.

Now Gus shrugged. "So you probably have other pennies?"

"Yeah," the kid said without hesitation. "I have a bunch."

"Yeah? Where?"

"My bedroom."

Gus looked at the penny one last time and then handed it back to the kid.

"So what happened tonight? With William?"

"I don't really know. He got too close, I guess. We both

put our pennies on the track, and then the train came. I sort of backed away, but William stayed close and the train just . . . I don't really know. He was just gone."

"Can you show me where it happened? The spot where you and William were standing and where you placed the pennies?"

The kid shrugged one last time. "Sure."

In the gritty glow of the rail yard lighting, with the dark night beyond, Gus followed the kid back to the tracks.

CHAPTER 69

L ane removed the bandages from his head and checked the damage in the mirror. A large swath of hair had been shaved along the upper right side of his head, and the staples looked as if they were holding together a package of pork tenderloin. He briefly considered removing them himself, but he knew there would be hell to pay for such a stunt. He was already having trouble convincing Rory to go along with his plan. Ripping staples from his own head a week before they were due to come out would not help matters. He left them alone and took his first shower in nearly a week. It felt heavenly, despite the sting on his scalp.

He shaved and dressed in a button-down oxford and sport coat. His shaggy hair was long enough to hide the ribbon of baldness where the staples were located, but he opted for a ball cap to make sure he didn't turn anyone's stomach. He walked down the stairs and into the three-season room where Rory was working.

"What do you think?" he asked.

Rory looked up from the file she was reading.

"Ah, back to human," she said. "The hat's a nice touch.

It clashes nicely with the sports jacket. How do you feel?"

"Like a hundred bucks."

"Cute. Maybe you should rest for a couple more days before you do this."

Lane shook his head. "Not a chance. This detective was anxious to talk, but also anxious in general. I got the impression it was now or never with this guy."

"Then talk over the phone. What if you go all the way down to Florida for a dead end?"

"I've got a feeling the old-timer has something substantial for us. He said he wants to talk in person, wouldn't do it over the phone. He's one of those old-school dicks. He's not about to give up information to a stranger over the phone."

"Are you sure you're up for this?"

"I'm sure."

"The doctors said no driving for at least two weeks."

"And I agree. I won't be doing a lick of driving."

The doorbell rang just as the words were out of his mouth.

"See? There's my escort."

Rory stood from her desk, putting her glasses on in the process. "I feel terrible that he came all the way down here for this."

"Don't," Lane said. "I've made him a wealthy man over the years. Plus, he got me involved in this thing to begin with. He owes me."

Lane walked out of the three-season room and to the front door. Dwight Corey, his agent, stood on the front porch. Dwight was dressed in gray tailored pants that fit him perfectly, bright almond shoes, and a button-down shirt that was without a hint of wrinkle.

"Now how the hell did you manage to drive down from Chicago without wrinkling your shirt?" Lane asked.

Dwight pinched his eyebrows together as he looked at Lane. "You look like crap. I'm not allowing you to wear a baseball hat with that jacket."

"You should have seen him with his head bandaged," Rory said.

Dwight leaned to get a look at Rory over Lane's shoulder.

"Good to see you, Rory."

"You, too, Dwight. Sorry to make you come all the way down here."

"Not at all. I needed to check up on my star client, anyway."

"Come on in," Lane said.

Rory and Lane sat on the couch, Dwight in the adjacent armchair.

"All kidding aside, how you feeling, pal?" Dwight asked.

"Been better, but getting better, too," Lane said.

"Good to hear it. Listen, I'm happy to help out, but there's another reason I came, too. It has to do with both of you, actually."

Lane looked at his watch. "We've got thirty minutes before we have to leave."

"I'll get right to the point. NBC has been in touch since . . . Mack Carter passed. They're in a tough situation with the podcast. It's very popular, with a huge following. They've put it on indefinite hiatus, but behind the scenes they're looking for someone to continue the series. They floated the idea of you and Rory committing to eight episodes over the course of two months. One episode a week. Basically, they're asking you to see what you can find, and report on it."

Lane shook his head. "We're not entertainers, Dwight. We'd do the podcast a disservice. And currently we don't have anything to go on. We're still chasing leads."

"I thought you told me on the phone that you had an in with someone at the Peppermill Police Department."

"We do. The detective in the Westmont Prep case has given us a peek into the files. But he did it off the record."

"No one's asking you to give up your sources. The network wants the podcast to continue, and they want you two to host it. They've made a lucrative offer."

Lane glanced quickly at Rory. She didn't need words to tell Lane what she was thinking. He stood up. "Let's go to Florida. Podcasts aren't our thing, Dwight. I was happy to offer my opinion, but I'm afraid hosting is not for me."

"I had to ask," Dwight said.

Lane strapped his bag over his shoulder and kissed Rory good-bye. "I'll call you tomorrow after I hear what this detective has to tell me."

"He can't drive," Rory said to Dwight.

"I'm on it," Dwight said.

"And he's supposed to get eight hours of sleep."

"I'll tuck him in tonight."

"No alcohol, either," Rory said.

Dwight winked at her. "I'll watch him like a hawk."

"A fifty-year-old man with babysitters," Lane said as he walked outside. He climbed into the passenger seat of Dwight's Land Rover and they headed for the airport to catch a seven P.M. flight out of Indianapolis.

Rory's keen eye had discovered a promising thread that ran through the Westmont Prep mystery. That thread led to a retired detective in Florida and a case he had worked years before. Lane hadn't swallowed a pain pill for forty-eight hours. Besides a dull headache, his mind was clear and his thoughts were ordered. He was itching to get back to work. With only a light carry-on, he and Dwight made it through security without incident. By seven-thirty, the plane reached its cruising altitude. Lane reclined his first-class seat, pulled his ball cap down over his eyes, and fell asleep. He would land in Fort Myers, Florida, at 10:52 P.M. Eastern time.

CHAPTER 70

Rory was in full battle gear, the August heat be damned. She wore her thick-rimmed nonprescription glasses on her face, her beanie hat low on her head, and her gray windbreaker buttoned up to her neck. She had her rucksack over her shoulder and, as always, her Madden Girl Eloisee combat boots on her feet.

Rory typically worked her cases solo. Besides her collaboration with Lane, her investigation into a cold case involved her, a box of files, and whatever clues waited to be discovered. Occasionally, though, the leads required interaction with other humans—Rory's least-favorite part of the job. She had already walked the crime scene with Henry Ott and had to endure the awkwardness of meeting Gabriella Hanover. Now the clues she had found in Theo Compton's case file had led her to this coffee shop on a Friday night to meet with the reporter named Ryder Hillier. Nights like this were the hazards of her occupation—perils no workmen's compensation package would cover.

She parked a block down from the corner coffee shop and was surprised by the crowd when she pulled the café door open. Young people fueled by caffeine tapped away on laptops and occupied every table in the place. She recognized Ryder Hillier from their meeting at the hospital, spotting her at a table near the back corner. She adjusted her glasses one last time, took a deep breath, and walked over.

"Hi," Ryder said. "I was starting to think I had the time wrong."

"Sorry," Rory said. "I was in the middle of something and couldn't get away."

"It's no problem," Ryder said. "Want a coffee?"

Rory shook her head. "No thanks." She sat down. "Sorry to call you out of the blue like I did, but I have a . . . favor to ask."

Rory knew favors from journalists were never free.

Ryder nodded. "I'm listening."

Rory saw the apprehension on Ryder's face.

"I need to see the video you shot of Theo Compton the night he died. I've tried to find it on the Internet, but it's gone."

"Lawsuits seem to do that. It's been scrubbed as if it never existed. Probably a good thing. I never should have posted it."

"Do you still have the original, though? On your phone?"

Ryder nodded again.

"I need to see it."

"Why?"

"Because of a thread I'm chasing."

"So you *are* working the Westmont Prep case."

Rory paused and looked around the café.

"Not officially," she said. "But I'm quietly taking a look at the case."

"What's in it for me?" Ryder asked.

"Not much," Rory said. "But if I find what I think is in

the video, I'll tell you my theory. I'd only ask that you not write about it for your paper. At least, not yet."

"I don't really have a paper at the moment. My editor and I are not seeing eye-to-eye about my current legal problems."

Ryder took a sip of coffee.

"I'll let you see the video if you not only clue me in on what you're looking for but also bring me up to date on your other theories about the case. I won't put any of it in the *Star*, but I'll cover it on my true-crime blog."

"How do you know I have any theories at all?"

"You're a bit of a legend inside the true-crime world. There's no way you've been in Peppermill for a week without coming to any theories."

Rory reached for her beanie hat and adjusted it lower on her forehead. As usual, she was never as anonymous as she believed.

Rory nodded. "I'll tell you what I have so far if you promise to give me a week before you write anything."

"Deal."

Ryder reached across the table to seal their agreement with a handshake. Rory shook her head.

"Honor system. Just two women agreeing to help each other."

Ryder nodded and withdrew her hand.

"Let's have a look at the video," Rory said.

Ryder pulled out her phone and swiped the screen a few times, then scooted her chair so she was next to Rory. The video began to play. The footage was as bad as Rory remembered, with the screen mostly filled by black night with the occasional shaky image of foliage from the forest coming into view. Then the abandoned boarding house as Ryder ran past it. The audio was turned to high, and Rory heard a rumble from the phone's speakers that was barely audible over the noise in the café. Then the train filled the screen, the blur of cars passing from right to left. It seemed to go on forever. Then, suddenly, the train was gone and the screen filled with black again until the wobbly image of Theo Compton's body materialized.

"There," Rory said. "Stop the video."

Ryder touched the screen to pause the footage.

"Go back," Rory said. "Just a few frames. Just after the train passes."

Ryder slid her finger across the screen, pulling the speeding train backward into the shot and then moving forward in slow motion until the last car slid out of the frame. Then the grainy image of Theo Compton's body materialized on the other side of the tracks.

"Go a little further," Rory said.

Ryder let the video play for another second or two and then stopped when Rory asked.

"Look," Rory said, pointing at the screen.

She had seen the video just once before, but in that single viewing she had remembered the exact position of Theo Compton's body. Now, as she stared at Ryder Hillier's phone, she knew for sure.

"Look at his hands," Rory said.

Ryder pinched the still frame on the screen and then expanded her fingers to enlarge the image.

"What am I looking at?" Ryder asked.

"Both his hands are in his pockets."

Ryder noticed that they were. "What does it mean?"

"People kill themselves by stepping in front of trains all the time," Rory said. "According to the statistics, it's one of the leading methods of suicide. I just wonder how many of those suicide victims are so calm about ending their lives that they keep both hands in their pockets as the train bears down on them."

Ryder took a closer look. Theo Compton's body lay faceup on the ground, both hands sunk into his pant pockets.

"The photos taken by the medical examiner show a different scene," Rory said. "In those photos, Theo's hands are out of his pockets."

"We moved him," Ryder said. "Mack and I. We didn't know he was dead, so we moved him and tried to resuscitate him. Then, when the EMTs arrived, they did the same until they officially pronounced him dead and called the coroner. During all the jostling, his hands must have come out of his pockets."

Ryder took her gaze from the phone and looked at Rory.

"I spoke with Theo's mother earlier today. She was adamant that Theo would never kill himself. I wasn't sure what to make of her argument, because it's the same thing almost every parent would say. But maybe she was right. She said Theo called her the night before he died to warn her."

"About what?"

"That he was going to tell Mack Carter something about the night of the Westmont Prep Killings that he and his friends hadn't told the police."

Rory kept her gaze focused on the image of Theo Compton's body, his hands secured in the pockets of his jeans. "Maybe someone pushed him," Rory said.

"And if someone pushed Theo, maybe they pushed the others."

"Maybe," Rory said, "someone pushed Charles Gorman, too."

The Bronx, New York

The day after the train had knocked William Pederson out of his shoes and dragged him for two football fields, Gus pulled to the curb outside the family's two-story home. He slipped his arms into his suit jacket, walked up the stairs, and knocked on the front door. Mrs. Pederson answered. Gus noticed the same ruddy rings around her eyes and nostrils that he'd seen the night before. It had been a delirious night for her, Gus was certain. He'd seen other mothers who had lost their kids. It was a hazard of the job that he'd never fully learn to deal with.

"Mrs. Pederson," Gus said. "Is now a good time to talk with your son?"

The woman nodded and opened the screen door. Gus walked into the home and followed her to the kid's bedroom. She waited in the doorway while Gus stepped into the room. The kid was lying on his bed, one arm behind his head and with his legs crossed. A MAD magazine on his chest.

"Hey, buddy," Gus said.

The kid looked up but didn't speak.

Gus lifted his chin. "I used to read those when I was your age."

"William had a bunch. He let me read them."

Mrs. Pederson walked into the room and snapped the magazine from his hand. "I asked you not to touch these. William had them in chronological order and didn't like you going through them."

The kid put up no protest or resistance. He didn't move, in fact, as his foster mother yanked the magazine away from him.

"He said I could look at them," he said. "I wouldn't have taken it if I thought he didn't want me to have it."

Gus looked at Mrs. Pederson and then back to the kid.

"If you don't mind, I want to ask you some more questions about yesterday."

The kid shrugged like he did the previous night. "You already asked a bunch."

"I did. But I have a few more."

The kid was silent.

"You and William? Were you guys close?"

"I don't know. Sometimes, yeah."

"You said that you and William went to the tracks all the time. Is that right?"

Another shrug. "Yeah. We went a lot."

"Did your parents know you went to the tracks?"

"Earlier in the summer," Mrs. Pederson said from the doorway, "they were caught out on the tracks by a police officer, who brought them home."

Gus had already found the incident report.

"So you were caught on the tracks before, you and William? And you were told not to go back, right?"

"Yes," Mrs. Pederson said, the anger audible in her

voice. "I told him not to take William to the tracks again."

Gus turned and looked at Mrs. Pederson. "I'm going to let him tell me in his own words."

She nodded.

"Your parents and the police told you to stay away from the tracks, is that right?"

The kid nodded.

"But you went out there anyway."

Another nod.

"What was so interesting about the tracks?"

The kid shrugged. "I don't know. We just liked to go out there and flatten our pennies. William was always asking to go."

"William had never gone to those tracks," Mrs. Pederson said. "Only in the last six months had this been an issue."

Six months, Gus thought. That's how long the Pedersons had been fostering this young man.

"Can I see your collection?" Gus asked. "You said you collected the pennies you flattened."

"My penny collection?"

"Yeah. You said you and William had gone to the tracks a bunch of other times to flatten pennies. You mentioned last night that you kept them all."

"I did."

The kid stood from his bed and walked over to the desk. He picked up a bowl and handed it to Gus. It was filled with flattened pennies. Gus stuck his fingers into the bowl, copper jingling against porcelain, and grabbed one. It looked identical to the one the kid had shown him the day before. Thin and flat and smooth.

"*This is a lot of pennies. What would you say? Thirty?*"

"*Twenty-eight,*" the kid said.

"*Every time you went to the tracks, how many pennies would you flatten?*"

"*I don't know. Sometimes two, sometimes three.*"

"*Tell me how it worked. You laid the pennies on the tracks and then watched the train run them over? Then, once the train was gone, you retrieved them?*"

"*Yeah.*"

"*So what happened yesterday?*"

"*I don't know. William just got too close.*"

Gus held up the bowl of pennies. "*But you'd done it so many times before. What did William do differently yesterday evening that he hadn't done all the other times?*"

The kid locked eyes with Gus. "*He got killed.*"

Gus Morelli sat on his lanai and listened to the surf as it rolled up onto the beach. It was late now, past ten P.M. The cloudless night offered a half moon, its reflection gamboling along the surface of the ocean until it spilled onto shore to shadow the beach with ashen hues of gray. The sun had set hours ago and here he was, still thinking about the old case that had been stirred awake by a random phone call. He sipped his La Rubia but had an itch for the brown stuff. If there were a bottle in the condo he might have poured himself a couple of fingers, but he'd sworn off it ever since he'd lost his leg. Before cancer tried to kill him, the hard stuff had come close. Now he limited his intake to two beers a day. It wasn't textbook sobriety, but was as close as Gus Morelli was going to come to it.

He thought back to that day in the kid's bedroom. He still remembered the jingle his fingers made when he reached into the bowl of the flattened pennies. The sound echoed in his ears now and muted the surf three stories below. He reached for his beer and took a sip. It wasn't the first time a case from his past awoke from a long slumber. This time, though, he was prepared for it.

He carried his beer back into the condo. He had work to do before tomorrow.

CHAPTER 71

Things were out of control. I felt it in my gut. I had felt something similar the day my foster brother died. I thought then that I might have miscalculated. Every time he bullied me, every time he ripped one of his *MAD* magazines from my hands, my anger grew. In those moments, my foster brother reminded me of my father. And when I lay docile on my bed as he stood over me intimidatingly, holding the magazine as if he were about to strike me with it, it reminded me of that feeble child who stared through the keyhole of his bedroom door and allowed his mother to be beaten. That frail and pathetic soul no longer existed. He was long gone, and only I remained—someone who no longer tolerated bullies or the weak souls they preyed on.

My planning had helped me weather the storm. My meticulous preparation had helped deflect the pressure the detective put on me. I came through unscathed then, but this time I've been less careful. I've allowed my emotions to override my reason. I've been reckless and impulsive. When I witnessed the things that took place at Westmont Prep, I had no choice but to act. I executed my original plan flawlessly. To perfection, really. It went off without a hitch. But some people refused to accept the reality I set forth. Some continued to dig for answers. Some who dug too deeply were now gone. But there were others still, and it was unrealistic to think I could avoid each of their shovel thrusts. Gwen was my biggest problem. Her unwillingness to stay silent, and her desire to share with others what she knew about that night, was enough to show me the end was near. But the end of my journey was tied to someone else's. It always had been.

I went through the usual routine when I entered the hospital, and soon I found myself in the east wing. Doctors rarely entered this ward. It was for the downtrodden and those too far gone to be positively affected by anything medicine could offer. Palliative care was all that remained for those here. Doctors signed off on copious doses of drugs to sedate the patients who might harm themselves or others. An abundance of narcotics were rationalized by the claim that they prevented the detached and ambivalent patients from wandering any further into the abyss. Really, though, they were meant to keep them there.

The patient I came to see tonight was the same one I'd sat with once a week since I was allowed visitation privileges. There has never been hope of improvement, and perhaps that was why I came so often. It certainly explained why I came tonight. Things were falling apart, and the patient in the east wing of this hospital would be inextricably part of my downfall.

The bed was calm when I walked into the room. The patient lay wide awake under the covers, eyes wondering but blind, as if sensing I would come tonight. This was normal, and not for the first time I imagined what life was like in such a state, staring out at the world while being trapped in an inescapable bubble. Tonight, though, escape *was* possible. Freedom was tangible. I could never leave this world without taking this person with me.

I closed the hospital room door. It took effort and time, but I eventually secured the patient in the wheelchair. A moment later, I pushed the chair past the nurses' station and received only smiles and nods. I paused in the sitting area, where the television was on but muted and where other patients stared, openmouthed, at the contraption. We joined them for a moment, just long enough to blend in. I looked back to the nurses' station. They were all staring at their computers and preparing for the long haul of the night shift. None were interested in the subdued patients watching the soundless television.

I stood up and drifted casually to the elevators, where I depressed the down button. I heard the cables engage as the elevator car rose from the ground floor. I strolled back to the wheelchair and slowly pulled it, and its occupant, toward the elevators. When the doors opened, I backed inside, pressed the button for the ground floor, and waited patiently for the doors to close. They finally did, and we were alone.

"I'm taking you out of here tonight," I said.

I bent around the chair and looked into those wide, wondering eyes that have never changed since I started visiting. They didn't change then, even when freedom was so close. The elevator bell rang and announced our arrival on the ground floor. When the doors opened, I showed no hesitation. I simply wheeled the chair past reception and to the sliding glass doors of the entrance. They opened like curtains welcoming us onto a grand stage. We passed through the threshold and into the night.

CHAPTER 72

The following morning, the nurse started her shift at seven o'clock. She spent thirty minutes in the exchange—the overlap between the night shift ending and the morning shift starting, when nurses who were going off the clock brought the arriving nurses up to date on the events of the previous night. It had been a quiet night with no emergencies and no 911 calls. It had been two weeks since a resident had died—a long streak at this hospital.

It was seven-thirty when the nurse started her rounds. She went room to room, waking the residents and taking breakfast orders, seeing who needed assistance out of bed, organizing the morning dosing of medications, and checking off items on a laundry list of activities that would keep her busy until noon. When she entered Room 41 she expected to find her patient in bed. Instead, though, the bed was empty. Worse than empty—it looked undisturbed, as if no one had slept in it. She checked the bathroom as a light flutter of fright tingled her sternum. Sometimes she found her patient standing in front of the mirror, confused and disoriented. Last time, her patient held a toothbrush with no cognitive understanding on how to use it. Before that, she had found her patient standing in front of the toilet with soiled pants, having forgotten the purpose of entering the bathroom. But when she slowly pushed the bathroom door open on this Saturday morning, it, too, was empty.

She hurried down the hallway to check the dining area, then to the community area where residents gathered to watch television. Finally, she ran to the nurses' station and picked up the phone.

"I have a code yellow," the nurse said in a hurried tone. "Missing resident. Room forty-one."

CHAPTER 73

Dr. Gabriella Hanover's life had been in upheaval since the events of last summer. She would never survive if the truth came out about her relationship with Charles. The board of trustees would never keep her as dean of students if it were known that she had been in a relationship with one of her patients, and her career in medicine would be gone as well. She had convinced herself that it was best to keep quiet about the things she knew. Specifically, that the manifesto the police had used to convict Charles was her idea. That it had not been a declaration of intent, but rather a psychotherapy tool used to expel anger. Admitting those things now would change little.

Gabriella found a spot in visitor parking on Saturday morning and walked into Grantville Psychiatric Hospital for the Criminally Insane. She had gone through the process so many times over the last year—every week, in fact—that it had become routine. The nurses had told Gabriella the remarkable difference they saw in him after each of her visits, and so she tried never to miss one.

Grantville was not like other hospitals. Admission was

a process. It required photo registration, the creation of a visitor's badge, and the company of an armed guard as she made her way through one locked door after another until she found the fourth floor. But the reward was worth it, because when the rigmarole was over, she got to see him. He was nothing like he used to be. Still, though, the sight of him calmed some part of her. She was skilled at analyzing and understanding others' emotions but was lost when she tried to decipher her own. How she felt about the last year was still a subject she had refused to examine.

Her stomach stirred with excitement now as she approached his hospital room; it always did. She closed her eyes for a moment as she held the handle of the door, took a deep breath, and then pushed the door open and walked inside.

He was in his wheelchair when she entered. His expression remained stoic when she stood in front of him. It didn't change when she lowered herself to make eye contact; it never did.

"Hi, Charles," she said. "How have you been?"

She didn't expect an answer. He had never once spoken during Gabriella's visits. But today, his silence affected her more than ever before.

"Oh, Charles. I never wanted any of this to happen."

She placed her hand on his cheek and watched his eyes blink but register nothing. Gabriella took a deep breath and sat in the chair across from him.

Westmont Prep
Summer 2019

CHAPTER 74

Marc McEvoy kissed his wife earlier in the morning before loading a small suitcase into his car and driving to the airport. He had told her that a business meeting in Houston required him to be gone overnight. He parked his car at the airport, made sure to get a receipt, and then boarded the Metra. An hour later, he was rolling his suitcase behind him as he made his way from the train station, found Grand Avenue, and walked into the lobby of the Motel 6.

"Last name?" the young woman behind the reception desk asked.

"Jones. Marc Jones."

"Yep. Here it is. Just one night?"

"That's all."

"I'll need a credit card for the security deposit."

Marc smiled. "I'm having a bit of a credit issue currently. Someone stole my identity, so my credit cards have all been cancelled. Can I pay cash?"

"Sorry to hear that. Um . . ." The woman tapped on the keyboard. "Sure. Cash will work. We require a two-hundred-dollar deposit against damage. When you check out tomorrow, we'll refund the difference after you pay for the room."

"Perfect," Marc said, pulling his wallet from his pocket and peeling off two $100 bills. "Sorry for the inconvenience."

"It's no problem."

The woman tucked a keycard into a Motel 6 envelope and scribbled *201* across the front.

"There you go. Second floor, just to the right of the elevators."

"Thanks," Marc said, grabbing the envelope. A couple of minutes later he was in Room 201, lying on the bed. It was four P.M. on Friday, June 21. He had just a few hours to kill.

CHAPTER 75

The night of the Man in the Mirror initiation had finally arrived, although it came with more fear and uncertainty than it should have. They were supposed to be scared of what waited for them in the dark woods on the edge of campus. Finding the keys and making it to the safe room was meant to stir anticipation and angst inside them, as were the imaginings of what they would find when they opened that door and whispered into the mirror. The initiation rules were created to separate them and force them into the woods alone while they searched for their keys, each racing to be the first to the house.

Although none of them openly admitted it, they each wanted to be the first to arrive. They each wanted to emerge from the woods and find Andrew Gross waiting by the front door. Andrew had explained weeks before that being first to the safe room was meaningful. It was the winner of the Man in the Mirror who moved to the top of the food chain the following year when they all became seniors and sent out invitations to unsuspecting juniors. The winner of the night was also tapped to lead the Man in the Mirror festivities for new initiates, as Andrew would do tonight. Andrew was the only senior who would be at the abandoned boarding house. He would assist all those who successfully found their key and made it through the woods. At midnight, the other seniors would leave campus and head to the house to see which initiates had made it. There would be an epic ceremony for those who had.

But the events of the past week had soured their anticipation of the night. Since Tanner had loaded the video of Mr. Gorman into the projector and allowed the footage to play during lab on Tuesday, classes had been cancelled for the rest of the week. The faculty had been silent about their reasons for shutting classes down, but it didn't take long for rumors to spread through campus. By the end of the week, everyone had heard about Tanner's prank. Repercussions were rumored to be coming the following Monday.

Tonight, as Gwen and her friends prepared for the initiation, they each had self-preservation on their mind. All of them except Tanner, which was fine with the rest of them. Having him out of the picture was the only way to accomplish what they hoped to pull off tonight, which was to secretly return Mr. Gorman's journal before heading to the abandoned boarding house. They didn't tell Tanner about their plan, instead agreeing that they were each on their own tonight. Finding their own way to 13:3:5 and venturing into the woods alone—survival-of-the-fittest style.

Gwen, Gavin, Theo, Danielle, and Bridget were all in a circle in Gwen's dorm room now. Tanner, they were sure, was already on his way to the boarding house. Or had even started stalking through the woods by now in search of the key. They conceded the win to him. They would soon join him but had to secure their futures first, and put out the fire that Tanner had set blazing.

Bridget reached into her purse.

"Here," she said, producing Mr. Gorman's leather-bound journal that she had taken from Tanner's dorm room earlier in the night.

She placed it on the floor in the middle of them all.

"And," Bridget said again, pulling a Ziploc bag from her purse, "while I was stealing things from his dorm, I took this, too."

Inside the plastic bag was a single joint.

"Good idea," Gwen said. "I'm freaking out right now."

Bridget removed the joint, clicked her lighter, and touched the flame to the tip. Gavin opened the window, and they each took tokes before blowing smoke out into the night. Before long, their heads were spinning and they laughed as they stared at Mr. Gorman's journal.

"I couldn't believe the son of a bitch blew that air horn," Gavin said.

They all laughed again.

"When that video popped up in Gorman's lab," Theo said.

"I nearly crapped myself," Gavin said.

They continued to laugh as they took hits from the joint.

"It's ten-thirty," Danielle said. "We need to get going if we want to make it before midnight. Who knows how long it will take to find the keys."

Gwen's eyes opened widely. "I have an idea. And I think it might be brilliant."

The others stared at her with glassy eyes.

"Tanner has thirty minutes on us," she said. "Let's get rid of Gorman's journal as planned. But instead of hiking it all that way out to the house, I'll drive! We'll get there in a quarter of the time. We might even catch him!"

During the school year, students were not permitted to have cars on campus. But during the summer session, the rules were lightened and vehicles were permitted.

"Let's do it," Gavin said with a smile.

Gwen grabbed her keys and Mr. Gorman's journal, and they all snuck out the back of Margery Hall and into the night. They stayed in the shadows, like they had the last time they had snuck to Teacher's Row. This time, though, the effects of the marijuana had them relaxed and confident.

They made it to the path that ran behind the duplexes and found their way to number fourteen. It brought back memories from the other night. They crept to the back wall.

"We should leave it on the front steps," Gwen said.

Gavin nodded. "Give it here. I'll do it."

Gwen handed him the journal. Gavin pointed at the kitchen window, where light spilled out into the night.

"Take a look," Gavin said. "Tell me when it's all clear."

Gavin snuck to the edge of the duplex and waited for the signal. The others slowly raised their heads above the windowsill. They saw Mr. Gorman. His back was to them, and he was stirring a pot on the stove. They all ducked down quickly, too high to notice that they were close to being spotted. Gwen waved at Gavin, who took off around the building, dropped the journal on the front stairs, and rang the doorbell.

By the time Gorman answered the door, Gwen and her friends were halfway to the student parking lot where her car waited.

* * *

Charles Gorman stirred the pasta as it boiled on the stove. He shook salt into the pot just as the doorbell rang. He checked his watch and wondered if it was Gabriella, wanting to tell him what she had planned to do on Monday when an assembly had been set up for students and faculty. He knew she was nervous.

He put the spoon down and headed to the front door. When he opened it, his front porch was empty. He walked outside and looked up and down Teacher's Row. The front porch lights of other duplexes glowed in the summer night, but the sidewalk was empty. When he looked down at the stairs, he noticed it. His journal lay on the second step. He quickly picked it up and riffled through the pages. It was all there. He looked again up and down the path before heading back inside.

He took the pasta off the stove as he sat at the kitchen table and read through his journal for ten minutes. Then, when he was satisfied nothing was missing, he stood and walked into his office. He removed the periodic table wall hanging and spun the dial of the wall safe. He placed his journal inside, closed the safe, and replaced the wall hanging. Then he reached for his phone to call Gabriella.

CHAPTER 76

They stayed in the shadows until they reached the student parking lot. Gavin climbed into the passenger seat, and the others crowded into the back. Gwen jammed the key into the ignition, made sure to keep her headlights off, and then tore out of the lot. Once they were past the entrance of the school, she clicked on the headlights to bring Champion Boulevard to life and then pressed her foot to the accelerator. If they hurried, they could catch Tanner.

Five minutes later, she pulled a hard right onto Route 77. It was inky black, so she turned on her high beams. They concentrated on the green mile markers as Gwen raced along the empty road. The first was eleven. It flew past in a blur but brightly reflected the car's headlamps. A minute later they saw mile marker twelve as they bore down on it. Then they waited as the dark night filled the windows, looking—hoping—to see mile marker thirteen. They knew they were close.

They were so concentrated on looking for the next marker that none of them saw a thing, but they all heard the thud. It sounded like a baseball bat smacking a plastic garbage can filled with water.

Thump.

Gwen slammed on the brakes, screeching the wheels as the car fishtailed to a stop. No one moved for several seconds. No one breathed. Then, finally, they slowly turned and looked through the rear window. A heap of something lay near the shoulder of the road, barely visible through the dark night. The mound didn't move as they stared and waited.

"What was it?" Gwen asked, her voice shaky and her hands tightly grasping the steering wheel. She was still facing forward, the only one who refused to look at whatever lay behind the car.

Gavin took a deep breath. "Probably a possum."

"That's way too big to be a possum," Theo said. "Maybe a deer?"

Gwen finally turned her gaze from the windshield and looked at Gavin through the dark space between them. Then she twisted the steering wheel and made a three-point turn. The car rolled slowly toward the heap, all five of them hoping to see a deer. Hoping to see any sort of animal. But the closer they got, the better the headlights illuminated the pile on the shoulder.

PART IX

August 2020

CHAPTER 77

Brianna McEvoy had lost her husband a year ago. She refused to believe Marc was dead; it was a thought she could not consider. But this far along, the thought was hounding her more than ever before. In the first days after Marc had gone missing, she met with detectives regularly to receive updates. They'd located his car at the South Bend airport, where Marc had parked for his business trip to Texas. But detectives quickly learned that Marc's company had no itinerary that sent him to Texas, or anywhere else, the week he disappeared. In fact, Marc had requested two personal days that week. Brianna had been stunned to learn of her husband's deceit.

The detectives were receptive for the first few weeks, but once they had ruled out foul play, trying to figure out what had happened to her husband and where he was became less vital.

When Brianna called at the beginning of the investigation, the detectives answered. Twelve months later, they responded only after she filled their voice mail with a string of messages. When they did call, it was to take swings at why her husband had disappeared. The detectives had uncovered some embarrassing debt that led to the theory that Marc had ducked out of town to hide from bill collectors. Brianna knew this was ridiculous. And the theory that Marc might have run off with a mistress was equally preposterous. He rarely went anywhere besides home and work—a small consulting firm with five other employees—three of whom were male, and the other two were women in their sixties.

The latest development had been the addition of Marc's name to the National Missing and Unidentified Persons System, or NamUs—a nationwide information clearing-house that listed the tens of thousands of Americans who go missing each year. The detectives had added all of Marc's information to the website, including the DNA sample Brianna had provided. They didn't have to tell her the purpose of this. She understood. If an unidentified body turned up somewhere, a coroner or medical exam-iner could run the DNA through the NamUs database for a match.

Brianna knew the detectives were simply running through their checklist of the usual suspects and situa-tions. She also knew that had she been completely forth-coming with the things she had discovered about her husband, the detectives might have made more progress on finding him. At this point, though, honesty was not an option, and the police were not the ones who would help her.

She descended the basement stairs and opened the cabinet where Marc kept his baseball card collection. She removed the three cases and laid them on the bar. She un-snapped the button on the first case, unfolding the wings of the binder to reveal four columns of neatly lined base-ball cards. On top of the cards were the loose papers she had stumbled across the previous fall, three months after Marc had disappeared. Across the top of the page was written *The Man in the Mirror*. Several articles were included in the stack of papers, all having to do with the strange ritual that took place twice a year at Westmont Preparatory High School—once in the winter during the shortest day of the year and again in summer during the longest. The previous year, it had been June twenty-first. The same day Marc disappeared, when two students had been killed at the school.

Brianna had spent the last several months wondering if the two events were connected, too scared to mention her findings to the detectives for fear that Marc would somehow be linked to the Westmont Prep Killings. She decided the mystery had gone on too long. Although she was still not ready to tell the police, she was prepared to tell someone else.

She pulled the card from her pocket and stared at the reporter's name.

CHAPTER 78

As so often happened in her line of work, things had gone from quiet to chaotic in a moment's notice. Just a week before, Ryder had been demoted to the trenches of the newspaper business, her YouTube channel had been censored, and her blog was all but gone. Then Theo Compton's mother had called to ask for Ryder's help with a troubling secret she believed her son was carrying. Rory Moore's call had followed, solidifying the idea that Theo may have, in fact, been killed rather than having committed suicide.

Now, on Saturday morning, she hung up the phone with Marc McEvoy's wife and wondered how the hell a missing-persons case out of South Bend could possibly be related to the Westmont Prep Killings. The only thing she knew for sure: The Westmont Prep case was alive and kicking. New life had been breathed into it, and if Ryder played her cards right she would be part of finding the truth. She started her car and headed to South Bend.

CHAPTER 79

Dwight Corey drove the rental car out of the hotel parking lot on Saturday morning. Lane was in the passenger seat.

"I like this," Lane said. "You and I have never been on a road trip before."

"I was on your book tour a couple of years ago," Dwight said as he merged onto the Sanibel Island causeway.

"That wasn't the same. We didn't share a hotel room and you didn't chauffeur me around."

"I promised Rory I'd watch you closely because your current mental state is worse than normal. That's the only reason I shared a room with you. I know enough not to break a promise to her. You snore like a son of a bitch, by the way."

"It's my lungs. They're not clear yet. The coughing wakes me up."

"Really? You seemed to sleep right through it. I was up all night listening to it."

"Part of the job description, I guess."

"Maybe Rory was right to tell you to wait a few days.

I honestly didn't know how bad your condition was until I saw you."

"I'm good. And I owe her. I got her involved with this case for purely selfish reasons. There's really nothing in it for her. I just know how her mind works. If I got her down to Peppermill, the case and all its mysteries would do the rest. And maybe I'm having one of those life-is-too-short moments after my close call, but I feel shitty about doing that to her. But now that it's done, I can't undo it. Rory won't rest until she has answers. It's the way her mind works. And now that she might've found one of those answers, I owe it to her to track it down whether I feel like crap or not."

Dwight nodded. "Damn. How hard did you hit your head?"

"This is the new warm and fuzzy Lane Phillips."

"I think I like him. Is he going to give up steak and stop poisoning his coffee with sugar?"

"Not a chance."

"Just when I thought there was hope for you."

As late-morning sun glistened off the surface of the ocean, they sped across the long bridge that connected the mainland of Florida to Sanibel Island.

CHAPTER 80

Lane climbed out of the rental car and into the shade of the palm tree Dwight had parked under. He pulled on his baseball cap to hide the ghastly-looking laceration that streaked across the back of his head and then walked through the parking lot of Doc Ford's Rum Bar & Grille. It was just past eleven a.m. when Lane entered the restaurant and found retired detective Gus Morelli in a back booth. He was easy to spot with the place mostly empty. A sturdy-looking older man, Lane guessed he was in his late sixties. He had white hair, a silver goatee, and the chest of a man who lifted weights in his youth. If Merriam-Webster offered the definition of a retired New York detective, an image of Gus Morelli would be included next to it.

The man stood up when Lane approached.

"Gus Morelli."

"Lane Phillips." They shook hands. "Thanks for taking the time. I really appreciate it."

"I'm retired. All I've got is time. And this must be important for you to come all the way down to Florida on such short notice."

"It is. Or at least it might be."

Gus gestured to the booth, and Lane sat down. He noticed a file on the table. His name was printed on it.

"Homework?"

Gus smiled. "When I get a cold call from an ex-FBI profiler asking about an old case I worked, I tend to do some research on them."

Lane lifted his chin. "Find anything interesting about me?"

"Lots. About you, *and* your partner." Gus opened the folder. "I was a New York cop for more than thirty years, and I still have all my connections. I'm assuming you figured I'd look into you?"

"I expected it."

Gus opened the file and read from it. "Dr. Lane Phillips, professor of forensic psychology at University of Chicago and founder of the Murder Accountability Project. Ex-FBI profiler with the Behavioral Science Unit where you spent a decade tracking, studying, and writing procedure about serial killers. PhD accolades include the famous *Some Choose Darkness* dissertation, a handbook about the thought process and reasoning of serial killers that just about every homicide detective in the country has read. Best-selling author and talking head. Does that just about cover it?"

Lane nodded. "The highlights, yes."

"And," Gus said, turning the page, "partnered with a gal named Rory Moore, whom I'm told is one hell of a cold case specialist."

"She prefers *forensic reconstructionist*."

"Yeah, well, that's modern-day BS. Back in my time, it meant she figures shit out that we all miss."

Lane nodded. "Means the same thing today. And yes, she's pretty damn good at it."

"From what my contacts tell me, she's got a hell of a solve rate on some of the oldest and coldest cases. This angle with the pennies that you called me about? It came from her?"

Lane smiled. "I'm sorry to say that I'm not smart enough to have seen the connection myself. I'm just following up on it."

"Well, I have to admit . . . your phone call stirred a part of me I thought would sleep forever. I'd be fascinated to hear how this connection came about."

The waitress approached and took their orders. Two iced teas.

"My partner and I are working on a case up in Indiana. The Westmont Prep Killings from last summer?"

Gus pouted his lower lip and shook his head.

"You haven't heard about it? The case was widely covered last summer and has been in the news recently."

"I don't follow the news," Gus said. "I don't subscribe to cable, and I haven't watched the evening news in two decades."

"Ever read a newspaper?"

"Every morning, but only the sports section. The rest is liberal bullshit or conservative nonsense."

"Internet?"

"What's that?"

Lane smiled. Gus Morelli was *hard-core* old school. "Westmont Prep is a private boarding school in Peppermill, Indiana. Two kids were killed there last summer."

"Students?"

"Yeah."

"At the school?"

"On the edge of campus, out at an abandoned house where faculty used to live. The case was open and shut—one of the teachers snapped and killed the kids. At least, that's the working theory. But there's more to it than that. Over the last year, three students who survived that night have gone back to the house, specifically the train tracks that run past it, to kill themselves. Something isn't adding up, and the lead detective who ran the investigation has asked my partner and me to quietly look into the case. When Rory dug into the files, she came across the penny connection that linked all the suicide victims and the perp. I used the MAP algorithm to see if there were any similar cases. It led me to you."

The waitress delivered the iced teas. Lane took a sip.

"By the time I got ahold of you and headed down here, Rory had sniffed out another inconsistency. She's wondering if the Westmont Prep kids didn't actually kill themselves."

Gus slid the folder to the side and placed his elbows on the table. "Meaning?"

"She's still working that angle, but she thinks maybe the kids were killed. And somehow the flattened pennies found on each of them is a link."

"To the killer?"

Lane raised his eyebrows. "I guess that's what I'm here to fig-ure out."

Lane saw Detective Morelli's gaze shift off to the right. His eyes were focused on nothing in particular. Lane understood the detective's momentary detachment from conversation to be the man's mind working something out. Then Lane saw him pull a card from the file and scribble across the back of it.

"This is my address," Gus said. "I've gotta check a few things out. Stop by tonight. Seven?"

Lane pulled the card across the table. "You got something?"

"I might," Gus said. "Give me the day to find out?"

Lane nodded. "You got it. See you tonight."

CHAPTER 81

It was midafternoon by the time Ryder made it back to Peppermill. She'd spent exactly one hour with Brianna McEvoy before she jumped back in her car. Now she walked into the café where she and Rory had met the night before. Rory was sitting at the same table. She saw the woman adjust her thick-rimmed glasses, the tops of which touched the beanie hat she wore, as Ryder joined her at the table.

"What did you find?" Rory asked.

"I'm not sure. Maybe nothing, but . . . probably something."

Ryder reached into her purse and pulled out the *Indianapolis Star* articles she had written about Marc McEvoy, the South Bend man who had gone missing the previous summer. Only after Brianna McEvoy had pointed it out did Ryder realize that Marc had gone missing on June 21, 2019—the same night as the Westmont Prep Killings.

"I've been working this case, off and on, for the last year," Ryder said. "Marc McEvoy, twenty-five-year-old father of two from South Bend who disappeared last summer. Supposedly left on a business trip to Texas and never returned. His car was found at the South Bend airport, but no one's ever heard from him again. Come to learn that he had no business trip scheduled to Texas. Police found no foul play, guy had no enemies, and the best anyone can tell he wasn't sleeping around."

Rory nodded slowly. "What's it got to do with the Westmont Prep case?"

"McEvoy disappeared the same night as the killings. A couple of months after he up and vanished, his wife went into the basement and found a bunch of press clippings he had hidden away with his baseball card collection."

Ryder pulled more articles from her purse and added them to the others on the table.

"The guy's wife showed these to me today."

Ryder pushed them across the table.

"A few of these were written by you," Rory said, scanning the headlines and byline.

"Yeah, I've done a lot of research on the Westmont Prep case, and the school in general. Looks like Marc McEvoy was obsessed with a game the kids were playing called the Man in the Mirror."

Rory nodded as she scanned the articles. "Detective Ott." Rory looked up at Ryder. "He ran the investigation into the Westmont Prep Killings. He told me about this game. Said these kids took it to a whole new level."

"What I've discovered over the past year," Ryder said, "and what I've written extensively about on my blog, is that it takes a lot to get invited to play. Not many students know exactly what goes on because so few have firsthand knowledge. And those who do tend to keep the details to themselves. It's like a little clique inside the school."

"Like a secret society."

"Right. But instead of a skull and crossbones, it's mirrors and spirits. Brianna McEvoy knew all about it. Marc was a Westmont Prep alumnus, and he told her about the game. About how he never made it into the club. She said he shrugged it off when he mentioned it, but she could tell he was troubled by whatever happened when he was at Westmont."

"Kids can be assholes."

"No doubt. Brianna seemed to think McEvoy might have still been bothered by the rejection, but she had no idea he was so obsessed with it."

"Obsessed how?" Rory asked.

"Brianna McEvoy learned that Marc had put in for two personal days from work the week he disappeared. He wanted his wife to think he was on a business trip, and he wanted his work to think he was taking personal time off."

"To do what?"

"No one knows. But Brianna McEvoy is worried it had something to do with the Westmont Prep case."

Ryder saw something change in Rory's expression. She kept her eyes on the articles. The woman rarely made eye contact, but she did now, looking up suddenly from the newspaper articles.

"There was unidentified blood at the scene," Rory said.

Ryder blinked as she worked to register what Rory was talking about. "At the boarding house?"

Rory nodded. "The police kept it away from the media because it's the one piece that never made sense. Three DNA profiles were found at the crime scene. One that matched Tanner Landing. One that matched Andrew Gross. And one they've never been able to ID."

Ryder leaned over and stared at one of her headlines.

South Bend Man Goes Missing. No Clues in Sight.

"Marc McEvoy?" she asked in a drawn-out voice as she looked back at Rory.

"We need to get a sample of his DNA."

"We already have one," Ryder said. "His information was added to the NamUs database."

"The National Missing and Unidentified Persons System," Rory said.

"Correct. It includes his DNA profile."

"I have access to the DNA profile of the unidentified blood. We can run it through the NamUs website and look for a match."

"When?" Ryder asked.

"Right now. The information is at my rental house."

They both stood and hurried out of the café.

Westmont Prep
Summer 2019

CHAPTER 82

Gwen and her friends climbed from the car and stood in the beam of the headlights. Each of their shadows crept along the pavement and flanked the body that lay in the road—a heap of wilted limbs and broken bones that didn't respond to Gwen's soft voice when she called out to ask if the man was okay. Finally, Gavin walked over and crouched down next to the body. He listened for a breath and watched for the man's chest to rise and fall. After a minute he stood up and walked back to the group.

"I think he's dead," Gavin said.

Gwen, already a wreck, began to moan as she cried. The others took instinctual steps backward. Gavin ran his hand over his mouth and up his cheek, where he nervously scratched the area behind his ear.

"Okay," he said. "Let's, uh . . . let's think this through."

"We should call the police," Danielle said.

Gavin held out his hands, the index finger on each raised while he thought. "That's what we *should* do. But let's think about what happens if we do that. We're all stoned. Gwen's driving under the influence. We just . . . *killed* a guy. If we call the cops, we all go to prison."

"It was an accident," Danielle said. "She didn't mean to hit him."

"Correct," Gavin said. "She didn't mean to kill him, but he's still dead. That's called manslaughter. *Involuntary* manslaughter, if she's lucky. But she's stoned, so they'll argue that it wasn't so involuntary after all. You go to prison for that. If we call the cops, Gwen's life is over. And so is each of ours. You think you're going to college with something like this on your record?"

"Okay, okay," Theo said. "Let's not fight. Let's just figure out what to do."

"Look," Gavin said. "It was an accident, just like Danielle said. We didn't mean to do it. And what the hell was the guy doing out on a dark road dressed in black, anyway? If we were stone-cold sober, we still might have hit him. None of us deserve to have our lives ruined because of an accident."

"You're not talking to a jury, Gavin!" Theo said. "What's the friggin' plan if we don't call the cops?"

Gavin nodded as he thought. "Okay." He shrugged as if what he were about to propose was the easy solution. "We hide the body. Take him down to the ravine and sink him in Baker's Creek. It's deep, and there's a strong current. No one will find him. Then we all venture off to find the keys and get back to the house to meet Andrew. We go through with the initiation just like we planned."

"Are you insane?" Theo said.

"Listen to me. If we decide not to call the cops—and I think we're all on the same page about that decision— then we're all going to need alibis for tonight. Someday soon, people will start looking for this guy. We all have to have solid stories for what we were doing tonight."

"I'll do it," Gwen said, interrupting Gavin and Theo.

They all looked at her.

"I'll put him in the creek. I hit him. I'll hide him. You guys get going. Go to the house. Go through with initiation. I'll meet you there when I'm done."

"I'll help you," Gavin said.

"What about your car?" Danielle said.

"I'll drive it back to campus when we're done," Gavin said. "I'll come back on foot. Hoof it. I'll be late, but I'll get there. I'll just say I couldn't find my key."

They all looked at one another in the dark of night. Their heads were buzzing from marijuana, their minds racing with confusion, and their heart rates rapid from shock. Then, one by one, they nodded. A plan was created.

Theo, Danielle, and Bridget set off down the shoulder of Route 77 to find the entrance into the woods that would lead them to the abandoned boarding house. When their friends were out of sight, Gwen and Gavin looked down at the body. Gwen took a deep breath to numb herself. Then she reached down and grabbed the dead man under the arms, feeling the sticky tack of his blood on her hands.

PART X

August 2020

CHAPTER 83

It was seven o'clock on Saturday evening when Lane knocked on the door of Gus Morelli's condo—a stucco building splashed in the soft salmon and blue hues of Florida. He had taken the outdoor stairwell to the third floor and now stood on the gangplank. The door opened, and the retired detective stood in the frame.

"So," Lane said. "How'd you do?"

"Come on in and I'll tell you all about it," Gus said, waving Lane inside. "I've got beer or soda."

Lane reached for the back of his ball cap and felt the aching wound it was hiding. He'd love a beer right about now but thought better of it.

"I'll take a Diet Coke, if you've got one."

"Sure thing."

Lane walked into the kitchen, which bled into a dining area and then a living room with furniture positioned around a television that hung on the wall. Beyond the living room was a screened-in balcony, the doors of which were wide open to allow the warm ocean breeze to rush through the condo.

"We can talk on the lanai," Gus said as he reached into the fridge and grabbed a Coke and a beer.

The third floor offered a splendid view of the gulf with the beach running east and west. To the south, across the water, the buildings of Naples could be seen. The sun was angled off to the west, skipping its reflection along the water and stretching long shadows from those walking the beach.

Lane took a seat in one of the patio chairs. Gus sat across from him. The detective took a sip of beer.

"I worked the phone all day. My contacts came through and pointed me in the right direction. I took it from there. It made me feel like a cop again, and I think you'll find what I stumbled across pretty interesting."

"I'm all ears."

Gus stood up. "Follow me. To get the full picture, we should probably start at the beginning."

Lane put his Diet Coke down and walked from the balcony, watching as the retired detective limped for a few strides until he seemed to get his rhythm. They headed to a room off the living room. When Gus swung the door open, Lane saw a bedroom filled with boxes. The brown cardboard boxes lined the far wall and were stacked three high.

"What's all this?" Lane asked.

"I'm a retired detective. Boxes follow me everywhere I go. I used to keep these in a storage unit up in New York. When I decided to finally retire, they followed me down here."

Lane walked a little closer to the room, eyeing the scores of boxes. "What are they?"

"Cases from my career that never stopped whispering to me."

"Meaning you never solved them?"

"Some are cold. Others bothersome."

Gus pointed to a single box that rested at the foot of the bed. "This one is flat-out disturbing, and I was never able to let it go."

Gus walked into the room and grabbed the box by the handles.

"I called it the penny case."

CHAPTER 84

Rory and Ryder sat in front of the computer as the hourglass spun on the screen. They were in the three-season room of the cottage, and Rory didn't bother explaining the makeshift corkboard that stood on the easel and displayed the faces of every dead person connected to the Westmont Prep case. Nor did she explain the antique porcelain doll that sat next to them on the desk, the finishing touches of which Rory had completed this morning.

Rory caught her reflection on the computer screen and saw the outline of her glasses where they jetted from her temples. She adjusted them now as she waited for the results of the DNA search she and Ryder were conducting. Rory pulled her beanie hat lower on her forehead and was about to adjust the top button on her windbreaker when the computer went black for a moment, and then blinked back to life.

MATCH

Rory looked at Ryder.

"It was Marc McEvoy's blood at the scene," Rory said.

"Son of a bitch," Ryder said, barely moving her lips. She turned to Rory. "Now what?"

Rory remembered the description and the details of the report. Trace amounts of unidentified blood were found both on Tanner Landing's body and on the girl who was found at the scene.

"Now we talk to Gwen Montgomery," Rory said. "And find out what she knows about Marc McEvoy."

CHAPTER 85

Gwen Montgomery cried as she stared at the woman across from her. She looked around the room and took deep breaths. She had come here prepared to share her secret. Prepared to finally reveal the things she knew about the night Tanner and Andrew were killed. She had run through the events many times in her mind but had never spoken them aloud. Until now. She had come here to clear her conscience and dispel her demons. To finally reveal the truth about that night. To finally divulge what they had hidden from the police.

Gwen and her friends knew Mr. Gorman was innocent. They knew he hadn't killed Tanner and Andrew. They had seen him that night when they peeked through the kitchen window. He was cooking at his stove. Gavin had rung the doorbell a moment later, and they all ran into the night, to her car, to speed toward mile marker thirteen on Route 77. The time line of when Tanner and Andrew had been killed made it impossible for Mr. Gorman to have done it. They all knew this. As rumors spread through campus, and as details about Mr. Gorman's involvement in the killings trickled into the media's coverage of the killings, they knew those rumors and details were incorrect. But to reveal this to police would require Gwen and her friends to lay out their own time line of that night, and they were scared that doing so would reveal more than they wanted the police to know—specifically, that they had hit and killed a man while speeding along Route 77 on the way to the back entrance of the woods that led to the boarding house.

When they made it to the house that night, they found Tanner impaled on the fence and ran for their lives. All but Gwen. She had tried to take Tanner off the fence. In the process she had covered herself in his blood. Tanner's blood mixed with that of the man she killed, whose body she had rolled into Baker's Creek. In the days that followed, she learned his name—Marc McEvoy. Mr. Gorman soon came under suspicion, and they heatedly debated whether they should come forward with what they knew or stay silent. They argued long enough for Mr. Gorman to take his own life. Days turned to weeks, and weeks to months. Their guilt smoldered until it lured Bridget first, and then Danielle and Theo to do the same thing. At least, that was what Gwen believed. Until now. Until she sat in this room and stared at the woman across from her.

She had come here to cleanse her soul. She could not live with her secret any longer. Now she was staring at the woman across from her and nervously fidgeting with the flattened penny between her fingers. She cried again and wanted to scream. But she knew it was pointless.

CHAPTER 86

Back on the lanai, the cardboard box sat on the patio table. Detective Morelli fingered through the folders until he pulled one from the box and opened it to his notes. As Gus paged through a file, he spoke without looking at Lane. He turned one page after another, shuffling through the notes as if looking through a forgotten childhood diary.

"I was called out to Oak Point Yard, a rail yard in the Bronx. Teenage kid versus train, and I was the detective on call. When I got there, it was a mess. The ME was already on the scene. The vic was in pieces, not much left of him after the train dragged the life out of him. When I arrived I talked with the parents. They were distraught, as you can imagine. But then I learned the vic's brother was with him when it happened. So, of course, I wanted to talk with the brother. I wanted to get him alone so he couldn't rely on his parents. But I could sense right away a weird dynamic between the parents and this kid. Then I heard that the family was fostering this kid. They had taken him in six months earlier."

"How old was he?"

"The foster kid was fourteen. The kid who was hit by the train was sixteen."

Gus took a sip of beer and turned the page in the folder. Lane got the impression that Gus didn't need his notes. The retired detective seemed to remember the case as if he had worked it the day before.

"So, I managed to get the kid alone. He told me that he and his foster brother had been playing on the tracks and that they had done it a bunch of times before. Said they went out there to flatten pennies on the tracks."

Lane's forehead creased in concentration at the mention of the flattened pennies.

"The story went like this," Gus said. "They'd each put a new penny on the rails, then back away and watch the train run them over. The night the brother got killed, they were doing the same thing. Only this time, the brother got too close to the tracks and the train hit him."

Lane nodded and cocked his head. "That's a tragic story."

"Maybe, if it were true. But to me it sounded like a load of bullshit. First off, the kid said they'd done it many times before. So, you'd figure they get better at it with each time, not worse."

Lane shrugged and pouted his lower lip. "Yeah, I see your point. But kids are dumb. They're risk-takers. They think they're immortal. I can see a kid getting too confident the more he goes to the tracks, and then getting *over*-confident. Getting too close."

"Agreed," Gus said. "But there's a problem with that theory. The foster kid said William Pederson got too close to the tracks and the train hit him. But the ME said in her autopsy report that the train hadn't simply hit the kid, it obliterated him."

Gus pulled the autopsy report from the box, opened the file, and slid it across the table. Lane saw a photo of the kid's body. He could barely recognize the lump on the autopsy table as human. He closed the file.

"The train crushed his skull like a pancake and destroyed just about every organ in his body. Dragged him for two football fields before finally dumping his body on the tracks and leaving what was left of him behind."

"Looks awful," Lane said.

"It was awful. And that's why I thought the kid's story was bullshit. If William Pederson had simply gotten too close to the tracks, wouldn't you figure the train would have hit him and thrown him *away* from the tracks? For the train to have impacted his entire body and dragged him so far, he would have had to be standing *on* the tracks, not just leaning over them. And I think the little shit pushed him there."

Lane looked out at the ocean and remembered Rory's theory that the Westmont Prep kids hadn't committed suicide.

They're not killing themselves, he remembered Rory saying. *Someone's pushing them in front of those trains.*

Lane felt a tingle in his chest, just below his sternum, as he sensed a connection between the cases.

"Please tell me you tracked this kid down."

Gus took a sip of beer. "Of course I did. That's why I asked you to come to Florida."

CHAPTER 87

Rory had considered the best way to track down Gwen Montgomery, and she decided a stealth approach was her only option. If the girl knew anything about Marc McEvoy, and why the man's blood was on her hands the night of the Westmont Prep Killings, she certainly wasn't going to tell Rory about it over the phone. And if she'd been hiding this secret for a year, Rory was going to need some help getting the girl to talk. A combination of trusted allies—the faculty and staff at Westmont Prep who taught and counseled her—along with an authority figure Gwen would think twice about lying to. To assemble this team, Rory did the only thing she could think of. She called Henry Ott. Rory hated tipping her hand on a case before she had all the answers, but she was far from home on this one and needed to rely on others in ways she was not accustomed to. Not to mention that confronting Gwen Montgomery would require access to the Westmont Prep campus. Rory had visited the campus with Detective Ott earlier in the week. The gates had been locked and opened electronically only after Ott had displayed his detective's badge. If it had been a challenge for Henry Ott to gain access to this place, Rory had no chance of getting through the gates if she showed up unannounced.

She parked on Champion Boulevard just outside the entrance to Westmont Prep. During her conversation with Detective Ott, Rory had covered all the things she learned over the last few days—the mysterious pennies that connected all the students and Charles Gorman, her suspicion that the suicide house was something much more ominous, and her findings that identified the source of the mysterious blood. If she had a few more days and access to all her usual resources, Rory would have played things out on her own. But in Peppermill, Indiana, teamed with a reporter who was surely itching to write her story, Rory had no choice but to bring others into the fray.

When Rory headed to Westmont Prep, Ryder had gone off to work the Marc McEvoy angle and see if she could find any evidence that put him in Peppermill the night of the Westmont Prep Killings. Rory promised to call her later, when she knew more about Gwen Montgomery. Henry Ott had made a call to the school to speak with Gabriella Hanover and Christian Casper and bring them up to speed on this latest development. He told Rory that he'd meet her at the front gates. Together, and by the book, they would all track down Gwen Montgomery and find out what she knew about the missing man named Marc McEvoy. So, here she waited, sitting in her car, headlights on, and parked outside the gates of Westmont Prep. Her skin itched. Perspiration had the back of her neck sticky and damp. Her right leg vibrated, and the eyelets on her Madden Girls filled the car with a subtle jingle as she watched the dark road in front of her, waiting for Henry Ott's headlights to appear.

Instead, though, the gates to Westmont Prep rattled open. A figure stood in the darkness and waved Rory forward.

CHAPTER 88

Gus reached back into the box and pulled out another file. Inside were photos of the scene. He handed Lane an eight-by-ten that captured the tracks where William Pederson had been struck. A high-top basketball shoe sat isolated on the rails.

"The train knocked the kid out of his shoes," Gus said. "Ray Brower style."

Lane pulled the photo close to him. "Truth is stranger than fiction. Who knew that was possible?"

"The reason it's significant is because the train taking the kid clean out of his shoes confirms the idea that he was standing on the tracks when the train struck him."

"But the foster brother never denied this, did he? He never said he was just leaning over the tracks?"

"He only said that William got too close. That he was there one second and gone the next. He claimed that he didn't see exactly what happened."

"Maybe he blocked it. It's common with trauma. Could have been suffering from PTSD."

"No offense, Doc, but that's a bunch of psychobabble.

The kid knew goddamn well what happened. And he had everything he told me prepared well in advance."

"Like what?"

"Like the history. It was too perfect. He practically gloated when he told me that he and William had been to the tracks before. That they'd done the penny trick many times. That they'd been caught a few weeks earlier and written up by a patrol cop. That they'd been reprimanded by their parents. And he had that goddamn collection of pennies just ready to show me."

"Maybe he had the story prepared because it was the truth."

Gus shook his head. "No way. It was choreographed. But the little shit was so calculating that I could never prove it."

"What made you so sure he was lying about it all?"

Gus pointed to the picture Lane was holding. "See that?"

Lane looked back to the picture. "Yeah. It's the kid's shoe. We've already been over this."

"No. It's not what's *in* the photo that bothers me. It's what's *missing* from the photo."

Lane scanned the image. "What's missing?"

Gus leaned forward. "His fucking penny," he said, pointing at the photo. "There's only one in the photo. The kid said they laid *two* pennies on the tracks—one for each of them—just before William was struck. Then, after the train swept his foster brother away, the kid panicked and ran home to tell the Pedersons. But that's not what happened. The little shit waited for the train to pass, then picked up his own penny before he went home. He still had it in his pocket when I arrived that night at the rail yard."

CHAPTER 89

R ory squinted through her glasses and out into the darkness as she slowly pulled forward. When she was close enough she recognized Christian Casper. Just as Rory passed the gates, he stepped forward and approached her window. Rory adjusted her glasses and rolled the window down. Dr. Casper leaned down.

"Miss Moore," he said. "Good to see you again."

Rory remembered the awkward meeting from Wednesday when Drs. Casper and Hanover had driven her and Henry Ott out to the abandoned boarding house. The memory of her refusal to shake Dr. Hanover's hand reddened her face and sent butterflies floating in her gut. Dr. Casper clearly remembered the incident, Rory figured, because he didn't offer a hand tonight.

"I just received Detective Ott's phone call," Dr. Casper said. "He said he was on the way over. I thought you were him when I saw the headlights."

"He should be here any minute. I was waiting for him."

"He said you two were looking for Gwen Montgomery?" Dr. Casper said.

"Correct. We need to speak to her about . . . last year. Something's come up."

"Does this stem from something you found during your visit to the boarding house?"

"Partially, yes," Rory said.

"After I received Detective Ott's call, I checked with my staff. I'm sorry to inform you that Gwen went home yesterday. The summer session ended yesterday morning. She left in the afternoon. She won't be back until the fall semester begins in a couple of weeks. Is this an urgent matter?"

"Possibly," Rory said, not wanting to confess all she knew until Detective Ott was present. "Where is home for her?"

"Michigan. Ann Arbor."

"Would it be possible to get her contact information? Phone number and address?"

Dr. Casper paused and offered a tight smile. He was hesitant with his words. "I'd need to speak with Detective Ott before I could give out personal information about one of our students."

Rory nodded and adjusted her glasses again. "Of course." She checked her watch. "I'm expecting him any minute."

"Why don't you pull into guest parking? We can wait in my office. I've called Gabriella Hanover, and she's on her way over. I'll pull Gwen's file while we wait."

With the base of her neck wet with perspiration, Rory pulled past the wrought iron gate and into Westmont Prep.

CHAPTER 90

Lane continued to stare at the photo of the lone high-top gym shoe sitting on the tracks and the single penny that accompanied it. Finally, he put the picture down.

"Did you ever ask the kid about the pennies? Why they both weren't on the tracks that night?"

"No," Gus said. "I figured I'd save it for later, but later never came because I could never get anywhere with my suspicions."

"Did you tell the foster parents?"

"I never came right out and said it, but they were as suspicious as I was. They didn't verbalize it, either, but the way they looked at me every time I came to the house told me that they were begging for help."

"Whatever came of it all?"

"Just another box that wound up in a storage unit. I was up to my eyes in homicides. This case was considered suspicious at first but eventually labeled an accidental death by the ME and stamped clear of the NYPD's docket. There was nothing I could do."

Lane stared Gus in the eye. "Something tells me you didn't simply let this die."

"I didn't. Not for a while, anyway. I couldn't peg that kid for William Pederson's death, but something about him felt sinister. His eyes, maybe. His demeanor. I don't know. But something about him had me on edge. So I looked into him. Researched how and why he entered the foster system."

"What'd you find?"

"He was placed in state custody after his father hung himself from the bedpost in their home. The kid found him."

"Christ. Where was the mother?"

"The day before the kid's father killed himself, his mother suffered a mysterious fall down the stairs."

"The day before?"

Gus nodded. "I pulled the case file on the incident. Looks like the ER docs indicated that the woman's injuries were not consistent with a fall down the stairs. Someone had beaten the shit out of her."

Lane thought for a moment. "The husband?"

"Maybe. He would be the most likely suspect, but he killed himself that night. The kid found him the next morning, called nine-one-one."

"So the kid's father beats the mother to death, makes it look like she fell down the stairs, and then he kills himself. With no other family, the kid ends up in foster care?"

"No," Gus said. "The kid's mother didn't die. She was beaten to within an inch of her life, but she lived. She spent half a year in a coma. When she woke up she was an invalid. She was never able to take care of herself again. With his father dead, and his mother in a near-vegetative state, the kid became a ward of the state and went into the foster system. Six months after the Peder-sons took him in, William died on the tracks."

"What happened to the kid's mother?"

Gus reached into the box and pulled out another file. "Like I said. That's why I asked you down to Florida. I think our two cases might be linked."

CHAPTER 91

Rory turned off the engine after she pulled into the guest parking lot. She opened the door and climbed out into the night. Dr. Casper waited on the sidewalk. It was nine o'clock, the August night thick with humidity and ripe with mosquitos. Rory slapped one that landed on the back of her neck, drawn, she was sure, to the sweat that had collected there.

"Was Detective Ott going to be long?" Dr. Casper asked

Rory recognized the apprehension in his voice, as if he were talking to a child lost in the supermarket. *Did your father say he would be gone long, sweetheart?* Rory had heard this level of condescension her whole life. Of course, Christian Casper was a psychiatrist, and after their meeting on Wednesday, and the awkward encounter when Rory refused to shake Gabriella Hanover's hand, she was sure Dr. Casper had created a working diagnosis for her antisocial behavior. It likely included an underlying fear of germs that produced her social anxiety, to go along with a touch of agoraphobia. He had surely placed her on the spectrum, and had considered a long list of medications that would fix all of her problems.

A fat mosquito landed on her cheek, and Rory slapped it away, bringing her back to the present and taking her away from her distrustful thoughts.

"Not long," Rory finally said. "He told me he was heading right over."

"Let's head inside. It's much cooler and mosquito-free. Dr. Han-over will be joining us, and Security will notify us when Detective Ott arrives."

Rory followed Dr. Casper to Teacher's Row and up the steps to the number eighteen duplex.

CHAPTER 92

"I did some research on the kid's mother today," Gus said, opening the file he had pulled from the box. "The family had no money and no insurance. She spent six months in the hospital after her injuries, and when she came out of the coma and it was determined that she would need long-term care, she became a ward of the state. Her kid went into the foster care system; she went into a state-run adult care facility in upstate New York. Spent twenty-three years there."

"And then what?" Lane asked. "She died?"

"No. Two years ago she was transferred to a hospital in Indiana. About an hour outside of Indianapolis."

Lane's mind began to churn. There was a connection there waiting to be made, but he couldn't straighten it out.

"But here's the catch," Gus said. "I put a call in to the hospital today to see if I could find out anything about her condition, and apparently . . . she's missing."

"Who's missing?"

"The kid's mother."

"What do you mean *missing*?"

"They can't find her. I talked to the local police department," Gus said. "They're checking security footage right now, but it looks like someone dropped her in a wheelchair and pushed her through the front doors."

Lane blinked a few times. "When was this?"

"Last night."

Lane shook his head. "Who would abduct an elderly vegetative woman?"

"My guess? Her son."

"The Pederson kid?"

"Yeah, but his name's not Pederson. That was the foster family's name. He never used it. He kept his own name."

"Which was?"

Gus looked down at the file. "Casper. The kid's name was Christian Casper. He was fourteen in 1994 when his foster brother was killed. Best I can tell, he's now a faculty member at Westmont Prep. Co-director of student counseling, in fact."

"Holy shit." Lane reached for his phone.

CHAPTER 93

D r. Casper walked up the steps and keyed the front door of his duplex. Rory followed him inside, adjusting her glasses and reaching to make sure the top button of her windbreaker was clasped as she crossed the threshold of the doorframe.

"Can I get you something to drink?" Dr. Casper asked.

"No thanks," Rory said.

To the left of the entryway was Dr. Casper's office. Rory noticed an executive desk sitting proudly in the center of the room, cluttered with papers and folders. Next to the desk were two chairs that faced each other across a coffee table. Rory's skin burned with eczema-like irritation at the thought of sharing her deepest secrets while sitting in one of those chairs. She had pulled a dust cover over the secrets of the past year of her life, secured the corners with anvils, and planned never to speak of them again. The idea of sharing the most intimate parts of her life with someone she barely knew but for once-a-week appointments made no sense to her. She had been taught other means of handling the inner workings of her mind.

"So what is this all about?" Dr. Casper asked. "Detective Ott sounded anxious to speak with Gwen."

"We came across some new information and wanted her . . . feedback on it."

"Anything for us to be concerned about?"

"I . . . don't think so," Rory said, but the hesitation in her voice betrayed her.

"It's unfortunate timing, with the summer term just ending. Otherwise we could simply walk to her dorm room for a chat. And I apologize." Dr. Casper pointed into his office. "I'm afraid my office is a mess as we finish up summer report cards and prepare for the new school year. We've temporarily moved the student records to the lower level."

Dr. Casper glanced at his watch.

"Gabriella will be here any moment. Come down with me and I'll grab Gwen's file."

Lower level. The phrase stuck in Rory's mind. She wondered for an instant, just a fleeting second, why he would use that term. They weren't in the grand library building Rory had passed on the way through the front gates, where a basement could be considered a *lower level.* They were in a two-story duplex that doubled as Christian Casper's office. Any stairs downward led to a *basement.* Rory forced a smile and adjusted her glasses again. She pulled the beanie hat down on her head, trying to hide behind the brim. She didn't like basements, the one in her own Chicago bungalow or anyone else's.

Dr. Casper opened the door located on the other side of the staircase. Rory saw a dark landing and shadowed stairs.

"It'll take me just a minute to locate the file. Would you mind helping me?"

Rory smiled and, despite the misfiring in her brain, started off toward the cellar door.

CHAPTER 94

Lane held his phone to his ear and listened as Rory's voice mail picked up.

"Hey," he said. "It's me. I'm down here in Florida and I think I stumbled onto something. You've got to call me back. Right away. As soon as you get this."

Lane checked his watch. It was 9:15 P.M. Central time. He fired off a text with the same message and then set his phone on the table so he was sure to catch Rory's call back.

"No luck?" Gus asked.

"No." Lane checked his watch again and wondered why Rory wasn't answering her phone. A sense of urgency swelled in his chest, but fifteen hundred miles separated him from Rory, and Lane knew he was helpless until Rory called back. He finally looked up to Gus. "I'm sure you did some digging into Dr. Casper."

Gus nodded. "I did. He stayed in the foster system but was never picked up by another family. When he turned eighteen, he was free as a bird. I lost track of him back then, but after you called I tapped my contacts and we did a records search."

Gus turned the page in the folder in front of him.

"While he was in the foster system, he managed his way through high school. Then he applied for, and received, a grant to go to college. It's pretty rare for a foster kid who never found a home to make it past high school. But this kid did. He went to New York State College."

Gus looked up from the page he was reading.

"Guess what happened to his freshman-year roommate."

Lane shook his head.

"Casper lived in the dorms. In October of his freshman year, his roommate killed himself. Casper found him hanging from the rafters when he came back to the dorm room one night."

Lane remembered the profile he created of the Westmont Prep killer. The organized nature of the crime scene indicated that this was not the first time he had killed. Lane had also guessed that the killer came from a broken family and likely had developed an unnaturally intimate relationship with his mother. This maternal bond was in opposition to a troubled relationship with his father.

"It seems everyone around this guy dies," Gus said. "After college he went to medical school. Eventually went into psychiatry, specializing in adolescent and juvenile psychotherapy. My source tracked down an old patient of Casper's from when he practiced in New York. Casper's previous patient is almost thirty now and had only the nicest things to say about his old shrink. When asked if Dr. Casper had any unusual techniques or practices, the guy said that Casper had a unique way of calming his patients during therapy sessions."

Lane waited a second. "Which was?"

"He had them fidget with a flattened penny. Guy said that it worked so well that after a while it was like an infant sucking on a pacifier."

Lane's mind was firing, and the urgency in his chest grew to something closer to dread.

"When combined with everything that's happened at that prep school," Gus said, "it's either a very eerie coincidence that so many deaths surround this guy, or it's proof that we've stumbled onto the footprints of a lifelong serial killer."

Lane grabbed his phone and dialed again. "Pick up, Rory. Pick up the goddamn phone."

CHAPTER 95

As soon as the basement door closed behind her, Rory knew something was wrong. She took three steps downward before her intuition told her to turn around, run up the stairs, get herself aboveground and out of this house. As Dr. Casper disappeared around the corner of the landing, and she heard him descend the last of the stairs, Rory decided to do just that. Part of her—the paranoid part—worried about the embarrassment she would have to deal with after she was out of the stairwell and standing in the front yard of the house. Dr. Casper would surely reappear with Gwen Montgomery's file in his hand, wondering why a grown woman had run out of his office. But that same distrustful part of her mind was screaming for her to leave this setting. Adrenaline from her fight-or-flight system washed through her body, quickening her heart rate and increasing her blood pressure. Any awkwardness that came from running now would be easier to deal with than the impending panic attack she would experience from staying one minute longer in the confined space of the stairwell.

"I could use a hand down here," Dr. Casper yelled from the basement.

Upstairs and outside, she could wait for Detective Ott. He was on the way. Hadn't Dr. Casper also mentioned that Gabriella Hanover was on the way over? It was hard for Rory to believe how badly she longed to see perfect strangers. The sensation confirmed the danger she had walked into.

"I think I've found what you're looking for," she heard Dr. Casper call out. "And she . . ."

Rory turned and ran up the stairs, the thumping of her combat boots drowning out the last of Casper's sentence. She reached the closed door and twisted the knob. It was locked. The clicking noise she had heard when the door closed behind her was now obvious. The door had locked automatically from the other side. In the darkened stairwell she frantically ran her fingers over the doorknob, feeling the keyhole in the handle.

She heard shuffling on the stairs, scratching of shoes as Dr. Casper methodically climbed up the first few steps. He appeared on the landing below her, his face shadowed and his eyes hidden by darkness.

"I told you I found what you're looking for," he said. "Now come back down here."

Rory tried the door handle again.

"The door locks automatically when it closes. It's the safest way. Now, I'll tell you only one more time. Come down here."

CHAPTER 96

Henry Ott pulled his Chevy to the front gates of Westmont Prep. He checked his watch and then squinted through the windshield to stare up the dark road before him. He glanced at the rearview mirror and then back to his watch. He wondered how the hell he could have beaten her here. Rory had called forty minutes earlier to tell him about her findings. She asked him to meet her at the front entrance of the school so he could use his influence to track down Gwen Montgomery. Ott changed clothes quickly, had a quick bite to eat, and then came right over. He was as eager to speak with the Montgomery girl as Rory was, and to figure out how Mark McEvoy's blood had stained her hands the night of the Westmont Prep Killings.

He waited another minute before he swiped his phone and pressed the return call icon. After a series of rings, the call connected.

"This is Rory Moore. Leave a message."

Ott ended the call and checked his rearview for a second time. A cop for more than thirty years, he trusted his instincts whenever they were loud enough to be heard.

Right now, they were screaming that something was wrong. He reached over to the glove box, grabbed a small flashlight from inside, and then climbed out of his car into the humid summer night. He opened the rear door and pulled his suit coat off the hook, stuck his arms into the sleeves, and shrugged it onto his shoulders. It was hot as hell, but he preferred to keep his firearm concealed. He adjusted the holster now, positioning it so the butt of the gun rested just below his left armpit.

Then he clicked on the flashlight and walked toward the front gates of Westmont Preparatory High School.

CHAPTER 97

As Dr. Casper turned and shuffled down the stairs, Rory reached to the back pocket of her jeans, but her phone was missing. She checked her windbreaker, then her jeans again, as if a second pass would produce a different result. She had set her phone on the passenger seat of the car after she called Henry Ott and must have left it there. She fought with the door handle for another minute as her skin burned with itch and perspiration rolled down her spine. Finally, Rory turned and looked down the dark stairwell. Fight or flight. Her first choice was gone, so she pushed her glasses up her nose, took a deep breath, and started down the stairs. When she reached the landing, she turned to her right and saw the last few stairs leading to the doorway beyond. It was brighter here, light from the basement spilling onto the bottom steps.

She took the last few steps slowly. At the bottom, she saw file cabinets lining a wall and a desk cluttered with papers. For a fleeting instant, Rory thought that perhaps she had misread the situation. That the danger she felt was only in her mind. But then she saw Dr. Casper through the doorway to her left. He was sitting in a chair with his legs casually crossed. A leather-bound journal was in his lap as if he were reading a novel and enjoying an evening glass of wine. As Rory moved through the doorway, another image came into view. Sitting across from Dr. Casper, propped up in a wheelchair, was an emaciated woman with sunken eyes that were open but seemed blind to the world around her.

"Mother," Dr. Casper said. "This is Rory Moore. She's part of the reason you're here tonight. And, of course, you've already met Gwen."

Rory walked farther into the room, beyond the doorframe. When she did, she saw a girl bound to a chair. Her mouth was covered with a strip of gray duct tape. She had tears running down her cheeks, and she was feverishly fidgeting with something in her right hand. When the girl saw Rory, her eyes went wide and a moan came from her taped mouth.

Rory recognized the word. *Help.*

The girl suddenly dropped the item she had in her hand. Rory looked to the floor and saw that it was a flattened penny.

"Gwen," Dr. Casper said, uncrossing his legs and standing from the chair. "The penny is supposed to calm you down, not make you nervous. It's always worked for you in the past. Let's try it again."

He walked over, picked up the penny, and placed it back in her hand. Then he walked back to his chair and picked up a bowl from the side table, holding it out and offering it to Rory. It was filled with flattened pennies.

"I'd offer you one, too, Miss Moore. It might calm you for what's about to happen, but I assume your spectrum disorder has also plagued you with mysophobia?"

Rory stayed still and silent.

"I figured as much," Dr. Casper said, placing the bowl back onto the table. He sat down and opened his journal. He looked at Rory.

"My mother and I were just about to have a session when Detective Ott called. I've read nearly the entire journal to my mother. I'm almost at the end. You may as well listen in."

Rory stayed rigid still, not even blinking as she watched Christian Casper open the journal, move aside the tassel that held his place, and begin to read.

Session 6
Journal Entry: THE END IS NEAR

I arrived to the abandoned boarding house and waited in the place the students called the "safe" room. It was an ironic name, because that night it would be anything but safe. I had kept a set of keys to the old house from when it was operational. The door opened easily, and I took my place in the corner. I knew what was transpiring that night. It was the summer solstice, which meant the juniors were being initiated. Although believed by its members to be shrouded in secrecy, I knew just about everything about the game they called the Man in the Mirror. Many faculty members did, including Charles Gorman.

He had shared his journal with me the previous week, and I read what he fantasized about doing to the students who were tormenting him. My plan came clearly into focus then. I would go to the house and wait for the students to arrive, one by one. I had planned initially to kill them all that night, but the two Charles hated most arrived first, and when no one else immediately came from the woods, I hurried back to campus. I knew the police would eventually suspect Charles. He was weak and *feeble, and when he came to me after the tragedy in the woods to confess his worry that his darkest thoughts had somehow come to fruition, I convinced him that the only way he could dispel the demons that haunted him was to go out to the house and the tracks and face them down. We went together. It was there that he stumbled, like my foster brother had years before, onto the tracks. It was considered a suicide attempt. I wanted to rid the world of the weak and feeble—the type of person I had once been—but somehow Charles survived. It was better that way. Charles would be forever displayed to the world as the helpless and pathetic soul he was. He deserved to suffer for his weakness. His tormenters, though, they deserved to die. Just like my father.*

That night in the safe room, Andrew Gross died in a pool of his own blood. Tanner Landing, from a tine that speared his brain. I had to wait on the others. But slowly, one by one, they came to me during our therapy sessions and confessed their guilt for having driven Charles Gorman to murder and attempted suicide by hiding from the police the fact that they had seen him that night, alone in his home, and that the time line of events made it impossible for Charles to have gone out to the abandoned house.

But something else had occurred that night that also plagued their souls. They had accidentally killed a man. A man they then dropped in Baker's Creek. They each came to me, desperate for my help. Frantic to find a way past their guilt. I offered the perfect solution. The only way for them to clear their conscience, I told them, was for each of them to face their demons in the exact place that produced them.

Bridget was first. I convinced her to go to the aban-

doned boarding house. I offered to accompany her, to stand next to her as she faced her demons at the train tracks. At the exact location where they all believed Charles Gorman had attempted suicide. When we made it there, she closed her eyes and waited for the train to take away her demons. Just like with my foster brother years before, it was almost too easy.

Danielle and Theo followed. Everyone believed they were suicides. But then the reporter arrived and the podcast began. New interest formed around the suicides and, despite my best efforts to quell that curiosity and end the podcast, I knew it was only a matter of time before they came back to me. I'm at peace with it all, though. I knew this day was coming. Back when I peeked through the keyhole of my bedroom door and allowed that weak and helpless child to die—the one who watched his father beat his mother—I knew this day would eventually come.

When Gwen came to me yesterday, I knew the day had arrived. She had a grand plan to go to the police, but I knew I couldn't allow that to happen, Mother. Not before you and I shared this last moment together.

I closed the journal and looked at my mother. I felt the presence of the other two women in the room—Gwen, bound and staring at me, and Rory Moore, surely panicked beyond rational thought.

"Do you think what I've done is wrong, Mother?"

There was a long stretch of silence, but tonight eye contact alone was not enough.

"Mother! Do you think what I've done is wrong?"

"Not at all," she said.

I smiled at the reassuring words. They washed over me and calmed me. Of course, those were the only words my mother has been able to speak since she woke from her coma more than twenty-five years ago. Still, I enjoyed hearing her voice. I needed her reassurance that I have lived my life to her approval. I am who I am today, and I've done what I've done throughout my life, because of her. Because of the things she allowed me to witness through the keyhole in my bedroom door. Because of her weakness.

I placed the journal onto the table next to my chair. I stood, reached into my pocket, and removed the knife. I unfolded it and locked the blade into place. I took a step toward my mother, knowing this was necessary, despite how difficult it would be.

CHAPTER 98

Rory listened as Christian Casper read to the cadaverous woman who sat across from him. Had he called her *Mother*? She thought so, but the scene was so confusing that Rory wasn't processing things correctly or logically. She only knew that she felt that same sense of obligation now as she had the year before when she stood in a cabin tucked in the woods. A few minutes earlier, when she stood on the stairs, her main goal was self-preservation. But now, it was something else. The other women in the room needed her. Rory could no longer consider running.

She took a deep breath and listened as Dr. Casper confessed to killing Tanner Landing and Andrew Gross. She listened to how he had pushed Charles Gorman and the others in front of the train that ran next to the boarding house. Surely, this man was responsible for the explosion that claimed Mack Carter's life, and nearly ended Lane's as well. Sweat ran down the length of her back as her mind flashed to the corkboard in the three-season room of the cottage and to the faces that were pinned there.

Casper stopped reading, and the silence snapped Rory to attention. She watched as he stood from his chair. He reached into his pocket and removed something. The overhead lighting reflected off the metal, and the blade of a knife grinned ominously in his hand when he unfolded it. The frail woman did not so much as flinch as he approached her. She appeared to be detached from reality.

"You made me this way, Mother," Rory heard Casper say in a quiet voice. "And now that I'm ready to leave this life you've given me, I'm taking you with me."

Rory had no time to consider her options. She simply bolted toward him. Like a linebacker, she lowered her head and crashed into his waist. Her right shoulder connected squarely with his groin, and he released a howl as the air left his lungs and they both crashed to the ground. She immediately reached for his right hand to isolate the knife, but as she grabbed his wrist she saw that his hand was empty.

Casper turned onto his stomach, still groaning from the blow, and began to crawl for the knife that had landed a few feet away. Rory reached her right arm around his neck and secured a tight choke hold when her hands came together. She squeezed with all her strength. It slowed his progress but didn't stop it as he crawled, inch by inch, toward the knife. She squeezed harder, hoping the lack of blood and oxygen to his brain would eventually stop him. A muffled wheeze escaped from his constricted trachea, but he continued to drag Rory on his back, one elbow over the other, until he was within arm's reach of the knife.

Rory pressed her eyes tightly closed as she cranked her choke hold with everything she had left inside of her.

As Casper reached for the knife, fear overwhelmed her and Rory took a deep breath, reaching for her last bit of strength, and squeezed his neck with all her strength.

Still, his fingers managed to creep toward the knife's handle. A guttural scream came from Rory's throat when Casper's hand grasped the knife.

CHAPTER 99

Detective Ott splayed the flashlight beam over the gate at the entrance of Westmont Prep and along the cobblestone pavement beyond. The library was visible in the distance, with its four bold columns lighted by upward directed spotlights. Off to the right was the visitor parking lot, and he noticed a lone car parked there. He craned his neck to get a better view, but the brick wall that the wrought iron gates were connected to blocked his vision.

He took a minute to consider things and then headed down the sidewalk that ran parallel to the red brick wall. The barrier was eight feet tall, and he walked for a distance that he estimated put him in direct line of sight to the visitor lot. He dropped the flashlight into the breast pocket of his suit, reached up to the top of the wall, and pulled himself upward so his head peeked over the upper edge of the bricks.

He grunted as he exerted himself, and not for the first time he considered that he was getting too old for this shit. But old or not, his instincts never led him astray. He remembered Rory Moore's Toyota from when he had gone to Dr. Phillips's place to speak with them. He was staring at her car now and wondering why she had gone onto the campus without him. She told him she would wait outside the gates.

Ott pulled himself upward and lifted his right leg until his heel reached the top of the wall. He groaned and grunted until he was straddling the bricks. He swung his left leg over until both dangled on the campus side of the wall. An angry knee from college football would protest his next decision, so he didn't give himself time to change his mind. He placed his palms on the bricks, lifted his rear end up, and jumped. He crashed to the ground and was thankful to find grass instead of concrete. Still, his knee ached when he landed.

He headed off to the parking lot and shined his flashlight into Rory's car. He noticed her cell phone on the passenger seat. He took only a minute to look around before he walked onto the path he remembered was called Teacher's Row. It was from here that he had walked into Charles Gorman's duplex the previous year. He stood there now, looking down the quiet path that ran in front of the buildings. That's when he heard it. A muffled scream that came from the duplex to his right.

His eyes went wide as he reached for his gun. He heard another scream and ran toward it.

CHAPTER 100

The scream that came from Rory's mouth, as Casper's fingers found the knife's handle, startled her. It was foreign and animalistic, and Rory couldn't believe it belonged to her. But she knew what it meant. She was in a fight for her life, and the unfamiliar voice inside of her was screaming for her to do everything possible to win it.

When Casper grasped the handle, Rory released her choke hold and rolled off him. Like a vacuum unclogging, she heard Casper inhale a giant lungful of air. Rory had her back to him and was on a mad dash for the doorway. Her only hope was to get to the window well she had spotted on the way down to the basement and crash her way through it before he gained his bearings. She didn't come close. He was on her in an instant, hurtling himself into her from behind. She went face-first into the doorframe, the drywall caving in from the impact of their bodies. Rory screamed again as she managed to slither around so that her back was to the wall and they were face-to-face. Casper brought the knife up. Rory had just enough time to grab his wrist as he pushed the blade toward her neck. Surely, her mind reasoned in some strange tangent of thought, this was the same knife he had used to slash Andrew Gross's and Tanner Landing's throats.

Banging came from upstairs. Someone was pounding on the front door. She saw Casper's eyes go wide. His jowls vibrated with effort as he pushed the knife closer to her. Rory's left arm alone was not strong enough to stop the knife's progress, so she brought her right hand up for reinforcement. When she did, her hand brushed across her left breast and she felt the pinprick through her jacket. In a flash, she ripped down the zipper of her windbreaker, reached to the breast pocket of her shirt, and withdrew the Foldger-Gruden brush. It was the last one she had used on the Kiddiejoy doll earlier that morning, meant for fine sculpting and with a needlelike point on the handle.

As Casper pushed the blade of his knife toward her neck, Rory jabbed the pointed handle through his left eye socket. Like a ruptured balloon, he deflated in front of her and crumbled to the ground, his face flopping onto her Madden Girl Eloisee combat boots and coloring them red with the blood that poured from his eye.

CHAPTER 101

Christian Casper's autopsy revealed that the handle of the Foldger-Gruden brush had passed through his left eye socket—a clean puncture through the cornea, iris, crystalline lens, retina, and the soft orbital bone—to rupture the internal carotid artery. A massive brain bleed, formally termed *exsanguination from cranial hemorrhage*, was the cause of death. Justifiable homicide, the manner.

The emaciated woman was indeed his mother, Liane Casper. She was hospitalized for three nights following the ordeal in the basement of her son's duplex before returning to the long-term care facility near Indianapolis. Gwen Montgomery, too, spent time in the hospital. She had no physical injuries, but her mental state—already tenuous from the past year—was at a breaking point. A week after her release, she found some relief from finally sharing her secret with Detective Ott and the Peppermill Police Department. She and Gavin Harms were facing involuntary manslaughter charges for the death of Marc McEvoy, whose body had been fished from Baker's Creek. Gwen and Gavin faced a wide range of potential sentences, from probation to years in prison.

It was a week after the events in Christian Casper's basement that Rory walked into the den of her Chicago bungalow. She sipped Dark Lord stout as she sat down at her workstation. The Armand Marseille Kiddiejoy German baby doll lay on the workbench under the glow of the gooseneck lamp. It was, to both the casual observer and a seasoned collector, flawless. The face was without defects, the fissures erased to perfection. The reconstruction of the ear and cheek seamless and balanced.

Rory ran a brush through the doll's hair, straightened its clothing, and then walked to the row of built-in shelves. There was a single vacancy, created that morning when Rory took an older doll down and stowed it away. She placed the Kiddiejoy in the empty spot and backed away to admire her handiwork. Something inside her reset, and she felt balanced again as her latest restoration blended into the collection. The assortment of dolls that filled her den was not just her life's work, it was her salvation. A lifeline that guided her beyond the affliction that otherwise had the power to lure her thoughts and destroy her existence.

She returned to the desk, sat in the chair, and took a sip of Dark Lord. A large manila envelope had arrived in the mail that morning, and she saved it for now to open. After ripping the top away, she pulled the folded newspaper from within. It was yesterday's edition of the *Indianapolis Star*. The story was on the front page, above the fold.

Missing South Bend Man Unlocks Mystery of the Westmont Prep Killings

PART ONE OF A THREE-PART SERIES
by Ryder Hillier

Before Rory started in on the article, she pulled a yellow sticky note off the front of the newspaper.

> Rory—
> My meeting is tomorrow.
> Thank you one hundred times over!
> —Ryder

Rory took another sip of Dark Lord. It was her first and last of the night. She had to be sharp for the flight the next day, although this time she would have Lane as her seatmate, and the flight to Florida would surely be much more enjoyable than her last.

She picked up the newspaper and read Ryder's article.

CHAPTER 102

Ryder Hillier made the drive up to Chicago in just under two hours. She now rode the elevator to the thirty-fourth floor of the office building set squarely in the middle of the Loop. Butter-flies stirred in her stomach, and she worked hard to keep her emotions under control. The elevator opened, and she wheeled a small suitcase behind her as she pulled open the glass doors and headed to the reception desk.

A young man with a pleasant smile greeted her.

"Hi, how can I help you?"

"Ryder Hillier to see Dwight Corey."

"Yes," the young man said with enthusiasm. "He's expecting you."

He picked up the phone.

"Mr. Corey, your one o'clock is here. Ms. Hillier."

A moment later a tall man impeccably dressed in a tan Armani suit opened the door next to the reception desk. He, too, sported a broad smile.

"Ryder?" he said as he approached, extending a hand. "Dwight Corey. So nice to meet you."

Ryder shook his hand. "Thank you. I really appreciate the opportunity."

"It's more than an opportunity," Dwight said. "From what Rory and Lane have told me, this is what you're made for. Come on in. The NBC people will be here in thirty minutes, and I want to brief you on the offer."

Ryder swallowed hard and followed the agent into the office. She was about to make her pitch to NBC why she was the perfect host to continue Mack Carter's podcast. Her heart pounded as she wheeled her research behind her.

CHAPTER 103

Their flight was scheduled for one p.m. They left the house at ten, much too early for Rory's liking since such an early departure would put them at the airport at ten-thirty with hours to spare. Even with first-class tickets and the benefit of the Admirals Club, so much downtime at the world's busiest airport was unappealing. But Rory had a stop to make before they headed to O'Hare.

Lane drove so that they could forgo parking. They turned onto LaSalle Street, Lane clicked on his hazards for a quick double-park, and Rory jumped out of the car and headed into Romans shoe store. After nearly a decade in the same pair of Madden Girls, she was now purchasing her second pair in as many weeks—her last ones destroyed when Christian Casper's pierced eyeball had leaked blood over them.

She sunk her feet into a pair of size 7's and felt the same calm she had when she was here at the beginning of the month. She paid at the register and again wore the boots out of the store. The Florida heat be damned. She was never a flip-flop girl, anyway.

* * *

Their plane landed in Ft. Meyers at 4:05 P.M., and they were driving the rental car across the Sanibel Island causeway thirty minutes later. In her more than ten-year relationship with Lane, they had never taken a vacation together. There were many reasons for this. Rory preferred to spend her downtime between cases alone, or at least in the self-serving manner of restoring a new doll and fighting back the oppressive affliction that was constantly working to disrupt her life. Lane was simply not the vacationing type. Neither of their brains was capable of relenting enough to allow them to lie by a pool and sunbathe. Rory's aversion to sand, and all the crevices it had the potential to penetrate, was enough to keep her away from a beach for her entire life. Which was why this trip was a leap of faith. Lane had promised that there was method to the madness of renting a condominium on Sanibel Island. For the life of her, Rory couldn't see what it might be. But Lane's close call with death and her traumatic time in Christian Casper's basement were enough for them both to rethink their lives. Lane had promised Rory that he knew what she needed and would deliver it on this trip. The man had never once lied to her, and she believed him when he told her that going to Florida was the right thing for her.

Rory Moore was not the type of woman who could be swept off her feet, literally or figuratively, and romanced back to some state of bliss. Lane knew this. He understood how her mind worked and how her DNA was coded. Rory's mind needed constant stimulation, either from a cold case or at the workbench in her den repairing a damaged antique doll. The cases Rory solved were not just her occupation, they were her way of life. A delicate balance that helped her exist. She needed the mysteries of unsolved cases because without a puzzle to solve, her affliction would take over her life.

The causeway delivered them onto Sanibel Island, and Lane steered the rental through the only road that cut through the island. He turned onto a side street flanked and shadowed by long lines of palm trees until they finally came to the entrance of the condominium complex.

"I can see it on your face," Lane said. "You're starting to worry."

"No," Rory said. Then she forced a smile and made a show of looking up through the windshield. "This is beautiful. It's . . . just what I need."

"You still think I brought you down here to sit on the beach and drink piña coladas, don't you?"

"I'm not exactly sure what we're going to do while we're here, but I know for certain you don't believe I'd *ever* drink a piña colada or walk on a beach."

They found a parking spot, and Lane pulled their luggage from the trunk. They took the outdoor elevator to the third floor, where Lane keyed the door and held it open for Rory. Inside, they dumped their bags in the bedroom before Lane walked her to the lanai. The Gulf was on majestic display before them as the afternoon sun shimmered on the surface of the ocean.

Rory grimaced when she looked down at the beach.

"Seriously, Lane. Don't make me walk barefoot in the sand."

"Please," Lane said. "Don't you think I know you by now?" He put his arm around her and pulled her close, then checked his watch. "There's someone I want you to meet. He has something to show you."

"Do I have to wear flip-flops?"

"God, no, bite your tongue."

CHAPTER 104

They knocked on the door of the condo three doors down from theirs. Rory stood in gray jeans and a gray T-shirt, her new Madden Girls stiff but comfortable. When the door opened a moment later, Rory adjusted her glasses, but for some reason the desire to hide behind them felt less than usual. The older gentleman who answered the door had an aura that immediately put her at ease.

"Lane!" the man said with a grin and a handshake. "Good to see you."

"You too, Gus."

Lane turned to Rory. "Gus Morelli, this is my better half. Rory Moore."

"Rory," Gus said. "I've heard a lot about you. From this guy and others."

Rory smiled. "Nice to meet you."

She noticed that he didn't attempt to shake her hand.

"Come on in," Gus said. He pointed at Rory. "I've got something for you." He checked his watch. "Ah, it's five o'clock somewhere."

Inside, Rory stood close to Lane as the man opened the refrigerator and produced a bottle of Dark Lord stout.

"A real son of a bitch trying to get my hands on this stuff. But *Christ*, is it good."

He peeled the wax from the top and popped it open. "Doc, can I pour you one?"

"No," Lane said. "The dark stuff upsets my stomach. But I'll take a light beer, if you have one."

Gus pointed. "La Rubia is on the bottom shelf."

Gus handed Rory a glass. It had been perfectly poured with a thick gray head over the black stout below.

"Cheers," Gus said, holding his glass out.

Lane held up his bottle of beer. Rory looked at the two of them, who seemed like long-lost friends. She was still confused by what was transpiring.

"What are we toasting to?" she asked.

Gus cocked his head as if there were something for Rory to see behind him. Then he looked at Lane and smiled.

"You didn't tell her?"

"Not yet," Lane said.

Gus smiled at Rory. "Follow me."

Rory trailed Gus as he walked to the hallway off the living room. He reached for the handle of a closed door and pushed it open. It was as if the room emitted a magnetic current that pulled Rory toward it. Inside she saw stacks of boxes. She walked through the doorway.

"What is all this?"

"Every case from a thirty-year career that I've never been able to figure out or stop thinking about. Lane said you might be interested in helping me with them."

Rory slowly walked over to the boxes and ran her

hand across the tops of them. Her mind began to fire and flicker at the possibilities that this room possessed. Her heart fluttered at the mysteries that waited to be solved inside the boxes.

She sat on the bed, placed her Dark Lord on the side table, and pulled one of the boxes onto her lap. Slowly, she lifted the top.

AUTHOR'S NOTE

All of my novels are stand-alone thrillers. However, astute readers will find little nuggets of the previous book sprinkled within the pages of each subsequent one. Although this is the second book in the Rory Moore/Lane Phillips series, I was careful to write each story so fans could read the books in any order.

If *The Suicide House* was your first adventure with the incomparable Rory Moore and you would like to read more about her, check out *Some Choose Darkness*. It fills in some background on where her quirkiness comes from. It's also a hell of a thrill ride.

If *The Suicide House* offered your first dose of Gus Morelli, the crafty and wise detective, check out *Don't Believe It* to discover more about his history, his fight with life, his contempt for people his own age, and how he came to walk on a titanium prosthesis.

Then, if you read *Don't Believe It* and find yourself intrigued by the forensic pathologist named Livia Cutty, check out her original story in *The Girl Who Was Taken*.

Readers will also notice that the town of Summit Lake appears in *Don't Believe It*. If you're curious about the history (and secrets) of that town, you can read the novel named after it. *Summit Lake* is my first novel, and many readers' favorite.

Thanks for reading my books. I'm forever grateful.

Charlie Donlea

ACKNOWLEDGMENTS

My list of folks to thank for helping me bring this novel to life includes many of the usual suspects.

Amy—for helping me through a tough writing year with love and encouragement. During which you proved to be an amazing wife, an unstoppable mother, and a best friend. It's good to know that when I lose my grip on the reins of our life, I have a co-pilot to take over.

Mary—for being such a willing co-conspirator to this story. I find it hilarious that many of our early conversations ended with the utterance "Wait, I forget where I was going with all that." But we figured out just enough to get the story started, and it took off from there.

Jen Merlet—for donating your special gift of finding my mistakes after everyone else has looked for them.

Mrs. Desmet—for lending your first name to such an important character. Many thanks.

Retired Detective Ray Peters—for answering my questions about police procedure. And for sharing some amazing stories from your career.

Marlene Stringer—for your steadfast counsel regarding my career. And for continuing to remind me not only about where we are going, but about where we currently are.

And, as always, to my talented team at Kensington Publishing who continues to blow me away with all the effort and support that goes into my novels. Special nods to Vida Engstrand and Crystal McCoy for your creativity. And to my editor, John Scognamiglio, who is always calm and collected when I'm in panic mode.

In this gripping new thriller from #1 international bestselling author Charlie Donlea, a TV news host sets out to uncover the truth behind a brutal, decades-old murder . . .

Avery Mason, host of *American Events*, knows the subjects that grab a TV audience's attention. Her latest story—a murder mystery laced with kinky sex, tragedy, and betrayal—is guaranteed to be ratings gold. New DNA technology has allowed the New York medical examiner's office to make its first successful identification of a 9/11 victim in years. The twist: the victim, Victoria Ford, had been accused of the gruesome murder of her married lover. In a chilling last phone call to her sister, Victoria begged her to prove her innocence.

Emma Ford has waited twenty years to put her sister to rest, but closure won't be complete until she can clear Victoria's name. Alone, she's had no luck, but she's convinced that Avery's connections and fame will help. Avery, hoping to negotiate a more lucrative network contract, goes into investigative overdrive. Victoria had been having an affair with a successful novelist, found hanging from the balcony of his Catskills mansion. The rope, the bedroom, and the entire crime scene were covered in Victoria's DNA.

But the twisted puzzle of Victoria's private life belies a much darker mystery. And what Avery doesn't realize is that there are other players in the game who are interested in Avery's own secret past—one she has kept hidden from both the network executives and her television audience. A secret she thought was dead and buried . . .

Please turn the page for an exciting sneak peek of Charlie Donlea's newest thriller TWENTY YEARS LATER coming soon wherever print and e-books are sold!

Catskill Mountains
July 15, 2001
Two months before 9/11

D eath was in the air.
    He smelled it as soon as he ducked under the crime scene tape and stepped foot onto the lawn of the palatial estate. The Catskill Mountains rose above the roofline as the early-morning sun stretched shadows of trees across the yard. The breeze rolled down from the foothills and carried the smell of decay, causing his upper lip to involuntarily twitch when it reached his nostrils. He wasn't sure if it was because this was his first case as a newly minted homicide detective or if it was because of some perverse fetish he had never known he possessed, but the odor filled him with a sense of purpose.

A uniformed police officer led him across the lawn and around to the back of the property where he found the source of the foul odor. The victim was hanging from a second-story balcony, his feet suspended at eye level. The detective looked up to the terrace. A white rope stretched over the railing, tight and challenged by the man's weight. The twine disappeared through French doors that led, he presumed, into the bedroom. Walking closer to the victim, he noticed the man's pants sagged on his left hip, exposing part of the buttocks. That the man wore no underwear was his first observation. The thin bruise marks that started at the waistline and surely covered the man's right buttock was the second. The contusions flared a faint lilac against the liver mortis blue hue of the dead man's skin and looked to the detective a lot like whip marks.

A spiraled bundle of rope wrapped around the man's ankles. Rigor mortis had bent his bloated feet at ninety-degree angles to his shins. The detective reached into his breast pocket and removed a pair of latex gloves that he slipped his hands into. He walked around to the back of the body. The man's right arm was swollen and stiffened at his side, wanting but unable to extend further due to the rope that bound the man's wrists together. The left arm was bent behind the man's back with a bundle of rope wrapped multiple times around each wrist. The length of twine connecting the wrists was stretched tight as rigor mortis attempted to bloat the man's arms away from his sides. Cut this rope, the detective imagined, and the guy would look like a scarecrow.

He gestured for the crime scene photographer, who waited at the periphery of the lawn.

"Get close-ups of the wrists and ankles."

"Yes sir," the photographer said.

The crime scene unit had already been through the property, taking photos and video to log as the *before* evidence. This second time through would be during and after the detective had his first look. The photographer raised his camera and peered through the viewfinder.

"So what's the initial thought here?" the photographer asked as the camera's shutter clicked redundantly as he snapped a series of photos. "Someone tied this guy up and threw him over the balcony?"

The detective looked back up the second story. "Maybe. Or he tied himself up and jumped."

The photographer stopped shooting and slowly took his face away from the camera.

"Happens more than you'd think," the detective said. "That way, if they have second thoughts they can't save themselves." The detective pointed at the dead man's face. "Get some clicks of that gag in his mouth."

The photographer squinted as he walked to the front of the body and looked at the dead man's mouth. "Is that a ball gag? As in S&M bondage?"

"It would certainly go hand in hand with the whip marks on this guy's ass. I'm heading upstairs to see what's holding this guy in place."

Latex gloves covered the detective's hands and plastic wraps enclosed his shoes as he walked into the bedroom. The balcony doors opened inward and allowed the same breeze that had earlier filled his nostrils with the smell of death to gust through the bedroom. The pungent odor was less noticeable here, one story above where death hung in the morning air. He stood in the doorframe and moved his gaze around. This was clearly the master suite. A king-sized four-poster bed stood in the middle of the room with night tables on either side. A dresser sat against the far wall, its mirror reflecting his image back at him. Through the open balcony doors, the white rope curved up over the railing and ran at waist height across the room and into the closet.

He stepped into the room and followed the rope. The closet had no door, just an arched entryway. When he reached it, he saw a spacious walk-in filled with neatly organized clothes hanging from scores of identical hangers. Shoes filled the thick pine cubbyholes that covered the back wall. Against the far wall, amid the cubbies, was a black safe about five feet tall, likely weighing close to a ton. With an ornate knot, the end of the rope was tied to a handle on the side of the safe. The other end, the detective knew, was attached to the man's neck, and whether he jumped off the balcony or was pushed, the safe had done its job. It had not budged an inch—the four legs indented the carpeting with no adjacent depression marks to suggest the safe had moved from the weight of the man's body.

A large kitchen knife lay on the floor next to the safe. He pulled a flashlight from his pocket and shined it at the carpeting. Morning sunlight spilled through the balcony doors and trickled into the walk-in closet, painting his shadow across the floor and up the far wall. He was interested in the small fibers next to the knife. He crouched down and examined them in the bright glow of his flashlight. They appeared to be bits of frayed nylon from when the rope had been cut. Within the carpet fibers were three small drops of blood, and a fourth on the handle of the knife. He placed a triangle-shaped yellow evidence placard over the blood droppings and fibers, and another next to the knife.

He turned and walked out of the closet, noticing a nearly empty wineglass on the night table. He was careful not to disturb it as he placed another yellow evidence marker next to it, noting the lipstick that smeared the rim. High-stepping over the taut rope, he walked past the mirrored dresser and into the bathroom. He slowly looked around and saw nothing out of place. Soon, the forensics team would be in here with luminol and black lights looking for hidden blood evidence. At the moment, the detective was interested in his first impression of the place. The toilet lid was open but the seat was down. The toilet water held a yellow color, and the faint smell of urine registering now as his nose caught up with his eyes. Someone had used the toilet but failed to flush. The lid was up but the toilet seat was down, and dry. A lone segment of toilet paper floated in the bowl. Another evidence placard found the toilet.

He walked from the bathroom and into the main area, once again surveying the room. He slipped his suit coat off his shoulders and draped it over the chair next to the dresser, and then followed the rope out to the balcony. He looked down at the dead man hanging from the other end. In the distance, the Catskill Mountains were cloaked by early-morning fog. This was the house of a very wealthy man, and the detective had been tasked with figuring out what had happened to him. In just a few minutes he had identified blood evidence, DNA from the lipstick on the wineglass, and a urine sample that likely belonged to the killer.

He had no idea at the time that all of it would be matched to Victoria Ford. And the detective could have no idea that in two short months, just as he had all his evidence organized and a conviction all but certain, commercial airliners—American Airlines Flight 11 and United Airlines Flight 175—would fly into the Twin Towers of the World Trade Center. In a single sun-filled, blue sky morning, three thousand men and women would die, and the detective's case would go up in smoke.

Manhattan, New York
May 3, 2021
Twenty years after 9/11

The New York City Medical Examiner's office was located in a nondescript, six-story white brick building in Kips Bay on East 26th Street and First Avenue. If offices had occupied the top two floors, they would provide views of the East River and the north end of Brooklyn. But the upper floors were not meant for the scientists and doctors who roamed the building. They were instead reserved for water and air purification systems. The circulated air within the world's largest crime lab was clean, pure, and dry. Very, very dry since humidity was bad for DNA, and DNA extraction was one of the crime lab's fortes.

In the cold, damp basement was the bone-processing laboratory. A technician opened the airtight seal of the cryo tank, releasing liquid nitrogen fog into the air. A triple layer of latex gloves protected the technician's hands. His face was safe behind a plastic shield. He reached into the tank with a pair of forceps and lifted the test tube from the fog. It was filled with a white powder that had minutes earlier been a small bone fragment specimen. The liquid nitrogen had been used to freeze the bone, and then the frozen specimen was shaken violently in the bulletproof test tube. The result was total pulverization of the original bone sample into fine powder. The technique allowed scientists to access the innermost portion of the bone, which made the chance of extracting usable DNA more likely. The concept was remarkably simple and had been developed based on two of the basic concepts of physics—the law of motion, and thermodynamics. If an apple were thrown at a wall, it would break into many pieces. But if the same apple were frozen solid by liquid nitrogen and *then* hurled at the wall, it would shatter into millions of pieces. When it came to extracting DNA from bone, the more pieces the bone could be broken into, the better. The finer the powder, better still.

The tech placed the test tube into a rack with a dozen others containing pulverized bone. With the nitrogen fog still spiraling from the latest tube, he dipped a titrating syringe into a beaker of fluid, drew ten ccs into the chamber, and added the extraction products to the pulverized bone. The next day, instead of bone powder, a pink liquid would fill the tubes. It was from this liquid that a genetic code would be procured—a sequence of twenty-three numbers unique to every human on the planet.

In the room next to the bone-processing lab, a continuous bank of computers lined all four walls. It was here where scientists took the DNA profiles generated from the original bone fragments and attempted to match them to profiles stored in the Combined DNA Index System databank known as CODIS. But this was not the national databank the FBI utilized to match DNA profiles gathered from crime scenes to previously convicted criminals. The databank searched here was a standalone archive of DNA profiles provided by the families of 9/11 victims who were never identified after the towers fell.

Greg Norton had worked at the Office of the Chief Medical Examiner for three years. Most of those years were spent in the computer lab. Each morning he was met with a stack of DNA profiles recently sequenced from bone fragments that had been collected from the rubble of the twin towers. He entered each sequence into the CODIS databank and searched for matches. In three years of employment he had never made a single match. But this morning, just as he sat down with his second cup of coffee and pecked away at the keyboard, a green indicator light blinked at the bottom of the screen.

Green?

A red light meant no matches had been found on sequences entered, and Greg had become so accustomed to misses that the red light was all he ever expected. He'd never seen a green indicator light during his tenure at the OCME. He clicked on the icon, and two DNA profiles popped up onto the monitor—white numbers against a black background. They were identical.

"Hey, boss?" he said in a careful tone, keeping his eye on the set of twenty-three numbers in front of him to make sure they didn't change.

"What's up?" Dr. Trudeau asked as he worked his fingers over a keyboard on the other side of the room.

As the head of Forensic Biology, Arthur Trudeau was in charge of identifying the remains of mass casualties from across the sate of New York. For nearly twenty years it had been his mission to identify every specimen collected from those killed in the World Trade Center attack.

"We got a hit."

Trudeau's fingers stopped tapping the keyboard and he slowly glanced to the Greg Norton's station. "Say that again."

The tech nodded and smiled as he continued to stare at the numbers on his screen. "We got a hit. We got a fickin' hit!"

Dr. Trudeau stood form his desk and walked across the lab. "Patient?"

"One one four five zero."

Trudeau pulled the keyboard from a standing computer station toward him and typed the numbers.

"Who is it?" Greg asked.

Other technicians had heard the news of a confirmed identification and gathered around. Trudeau stared at the monitor and the small hourglass that spun as the computer searched. Finally, a name appeared on the screen.

"Victory Ford," he said.

"Next of kin?" Greg asked.

Trudeau shook his head. "Parents, but they're deceased."

"Any other contacts?"

"Yes," Trudeau said, scrolling down the page. "A sister. Address in New York State."

"Want me to make the call?"

"No. Let's run it one more time to be sure. Start to finish. If it hits a second time, I'll give her a call."

"First one in how long, boss?"

Dr. Trudeau looked over at the young technician. "Years. Now run it again."

Connect with

Us

Visit us online at
KensingtonBooks.com
to read more from your favorite authors, see books
by series, view reading group guides, and more.

for sneak peeks, chances to win books and prize packs,
and to share your thoughts with other readers.

facebook.com/kensingtonpublishing
twitter.com/kensingtonbooks

Tell us what you think!

To share your thoughts, submit a review,
or sign up for our eNewsletters, please visit:
KensingtonBooks.com/TellUs.